The
Married
Girls

DINEY COSTELOE is the author of
twenty-three novels, several short
stories, and many articles and poems.
She has three children and seven
grandchildren, so when she isn't
writing, she's busy with family. She
and her husband divide their time
between Somerset and West Cork.

Also by Diney Costeloe

DINEY COSTELOE

The Married Girls

First published in the UK in 2017 by Head of Zeus, Ltd.

This paperback edition first published in 2017
by Head of Zeus, Ltd.

9 7 5 3 1 2 4 6 8

A catalogue record for this book is available from
the British Library.

ISBN (PB): 9781784976149
ISBN (E): 9781784976118

Typeset by Adrian McLaughlin

Printed and bound in Great Britain by
CPI Group (UK) Ltd, Croydon CR0 4YY

Head of Zeus Ltd
First Floor East
5–8 Hardwick Street
London EC1R 4RG

WWW.HEADOFZEUS.COM

For George Papworth, Venetia Craggs and Colin Warman.
Thank you for patience with all my questions
and allowing me to pick your brains!

Part One
September 1949

The evening sun lay heavy on the fields as Billy Shepherd called goodbye to his parents and took the footpath back to the village and home. Home was no longer Charing Farm, where he'd been born and brought up, but Blackdown House on the edge of the village of Wynsdown. As always, his heart quickened at the thought of his beloved Charlotte waiting there for his return, she and his two children, three-year-old John, named for his grandfather and known as Johnny, and baby Edie, just three months. Every day he walked across the fields to his parents' farm, working with his father as he had ever since he'd left school, and every evening he retraced his steps to find them all waiting.

'I'm home!' he called as he paused in the back porch to take off his boots. The kitchen door opened and his son erupted into his arms.

'Daddy, Daddy, you're back. I done you a picsher. Come and see.' He tugged at his father's hand, trying to pull him to his feet.

'I'm coming, Johnny, I'm coming,' laughed Billy, 'just let me get my boots off. Mummy won't want muddy boots in the kitchen, will she?'

'Mummy's in with Edie. She's giving her some milk. She told me to stay in the kitchen and wait for you.'

'Well, here I am,' Billy said as he got to his feet. 'Now, show me your picture.'

They went together into the kitchen, always the warm centre of the house where the range burned, summer and winter. The kettle was singing softly at the back and Billy, opening up a hotplate, pulled it across, ready to make tea the moment it returned to boiling.

Johnny went to the table and picked up a piece of paper lying amid some crayons. 'Here it is, Daddy,' he said proudly, thrusting the paper into Billy's hand. 'It's Mummy and you in the garden.'

Billy perused the two stick figures standing by three huge daisy-like flowers under the rays of a large yellow sun. 'So it is!' he agreed warmly. 'It's a lovely picture, Johnny. We'll have to put it up on the wall.'

One wall of the kitchen was already covered in similar pictures, for Johnny was nothing if not prolific. Johnny looked up at it.

'There isn't room,' he said.

'We can always take down one of the others to make room,' Billy said.

'But I don't want to.'

'No, I can see that,' agreed Billy. 'We'll have to talk to Mummy about it, see what she thinks, yes?'

Johnny nodded.

'Good lad,' smiled Billy. He made the tea and leaving it to brew, said, 'Let's go and see how Mummy and Edie are getting on, shall we?' He took his son's hand and together they went upstairs to the nursery.

Charlotte was changing Edie when Billy tapped on the door, saying, 'Can we come in?'

'Course you can,' she cried. 'We're just finishing, aren't we,

4

darling?' She looked down into the sleepy face of her daughter. 'Here, have a cuddle before she falls asleep.' She got to her feet and passed Edie into Billy's arms.

'She's always asleep,' Johnny remarked. 'Why does she sleep all the time?'

Charlotte laughed. 'Because babies do, darling. They need lots of sleep.' She gathered Johnny into her arms and gave him a hug. 'Edie won't sleep so much when she's big, like you.'

She looked across at Billy, holding his daughter close against him, his face against the fluff of her hair, and her heart turned over with love for him. Her Billy, so strong and yet so gentle. She was glad that little Johnny looked so like him, his fair curly hair springing in an untidy halo about his head, his eyes a velvety blue. He'd had blue eyes when he was born, and Charlotte had been afraid that they might change as he grew from a baby to toddler. Over the first months they had altered, but remained blue, deepening to almost navy, just like Billy's.

'I went to see the vicar this afternoon,' she told Billy later as, with both children safely tucked up in bed, they sat down at the kitchen table to eat their supper. 'To sort out Edie's christening. He would like it to be part of a service and suggests a fortnight on Sunday – that's a service of Morning Prayer. That way anyone from the village who wants to can be there. I said it sounded fine to me, but that I'd ask you.'

Billy shrugged. He wanted his children christened, but he was not a great church-goer and was happy enough to leave the actual arrangements to Charlotte. 'Sounds all right to me, as long as it suits Mum and Dad.'

'I'll take the children over to see them tomorrow and ask, then I can confirm to the vicar. He wanted to know who her godparents were going to be.'

'And what did you say?'

'I said we were going to ask Clare and Caroline to stand as godmothers,' Charlotte said, 'but we hadn't chosen a godfather yet.' She smiled across at Billy. 'Who would you like as her godfather?'

'Don't know,' said Billy. 'Who do you think? What about your uncle Dan?'

Charlotte had thought of Uncle Dan too. He and his wife, Naomi, had taken Charlotte into their home when she arrived in London as a refugee from the Nazis, in 1939. They had looked after her and helped her adjust to her new life in an foreign country. They had lost touch with each other during the Blitz, when Charlotte had been evacuated to Wynsdown, but after the war they had been reunited and Dan had been proud, as her foster father, to give Charlotte away when she married Billy in Wynsdown village church.

'D'you think they'd come down?' she wondered. 'It'd be lovely to see them all.'

'Why don't you ring them and ask?'

Charlotte beamed at him. 'You're right! I'll phone as soon as we've finished supper. But,' she continued, 'that's not my only bit of news. After I'd seen the vicar, Mrs Vicar asked us to stay for a cup of tea.'

During the war, the evacuees from London, uncertain of how to address Avril Swanson, the vicar's wife, had called her Mrs Vicar. The nickname had stuck and now most of Wynsdown used it and despite the closeness that had grown up between them over the years, Charlotte never called her anything else.

'She was telling me all about Caroline's wedding,' she went on. 'Caroline's coming down to live at the vicarage for three weeks before her big day. Anyhow, we were sitting in the vicarage kitchen drinking our tea when Mrs Bellinger arrived. She'd come to see Mrs Vicar and was absolutely bursting with news.'

'So, what's up?'

'Her son, Felix, rang last night. He's got engaged and he's bringing his fiancée to meet his parents in a few weeks. She's called Daphne.'

'Are they pleased?' Billy asked.

'Difficult to say,' Charlotte said. 'Of course she'd come to tell Mrs Vicar. She wasn't expecting me to be there, so really all she said was that Felix had got engaged and would be coming down soon. I got the impression it was a total surprise, that she and the squire weren't sure what to think. They don't seem to have known anything about her. Anyway, I brought the children away, so's she could talk to Mrs Vicar properly.'

'It's probably a good thing,' Billy said now as he pushed his empty plate away. 'Squire's not getting any younger and Felix should be coming home to take over some of the responsibility for the estate. He's been away too long.'

'I don't think I've ever seen him,' Charlotte said. 'He's hardly come home since I've been in the village.'

'Well, you haven't missed much,' said Billy dismissively. Billy had only a distant interest in Felix Bellinger. Though they had grown up in the same village, the ten-year difference in their ages had meant that Billy was still a child when Felix had left his boarding school in Sherborne and gone up to Cambridge; and the only time their paths really crossed was just before the war when they rode to hounds with the local hunt.

During the war, Felix had been a fighter pilot in the RAF, scrambled night after night to take on the bombers coming in waves across the coast heading first for the RAF bases and later for London and other major cities. Miraculously, to the overwhelming relief of his parents, he had survived. So many others in his squadron had not and when peace broke out, he didn't want to return to Somerset to vegetate, as he put it. He knew he would miss the buzz, the excitement and the camaraderie of the RAF, so he'd signed on again and been posted to an air base in Germany. More recently he returned to work at the Air Ministry in London. He had been home on leave for a few days once or twice, but apart from when he was out riding with his father, he was seldom seen about the village.

'They'll be so pleased that he's coming home, even for a short visit,' Charlotte said. 'I wonder what this Daphne'll be like?'

Billy laughed. 'Charlotte Shepherd! You're getting as bad as everyone else in this village! Always wanting to know everyone else's business.'

'I am not,' Charlotte replied hotly. 'But if Johnny was bringing home a fiancée, I bet everyone would be watching to see what she was like.'

'Johnny's only three,' said Billy, still laughing. 'We'll worry about that when the time comes! Now,' he went on, 'I've got news for you. Jane phoned today and says she's got a few days off, so she's coming home for the weekend. Mum's asked us all over for Sunday dinner. I said yes, OK?'

'Of course,' said Charlotte. 'That'll be lovely.' She was fond of her in-laws, though she still didn't feel she knew Billy's sister, Jane, very well. She was a nurse and lived in Bristol. On occasional weekends she caught the bus home to visit, but her life was in the city now and they hadn't become close. In truth, Charlotte found her rather opinionated, always ready to give advice whether it was asked for or not. She had been pleased when they'd asked her to be Johnny's godmother but seemed to think it gave her the right to tell Charlotte how to look after him and Charlotte found her very wearing.

Still, she thought, Johnny'll be pleased to see her and it's only for half a day. I can bite my tongue for that long!

When Charlotte had left the vicarage, Marjorie Bellinger took the chance of having a heart-to-heart chat with Avril Swanson. Avril was the only person Marjorie felt she could confide in. As the wife of the squire she felt she had a position to maintain in the village, and couldn't open her heart to just anyone. Gossip was rife in such a small community and she didn't want her family to become the latest topic of conversation. Everyone would soon know about Felix's engagement, but they needn't know of his parents' doubts about his choice of bride. Avril, however, was different and Marjorie knew that anything she told her would go no further, or at least no further than David. The vicarage was never a source of gossip.

Marjorie's husband Peter was never one to speak of emotional things and it was a relief for her to unburden her worries to Avril.

'We've never met this Daphne,' she told her. 'We don't know who she is or who her people are. All we know is that Felix first met her during the war and then again when he was posted to the Air Ministry.'

'It sounds as if she moves in the right circles,' Avril said reassuringly. 'I mean, if he met her at the Air Ministry.' She smiled across at Marjorie who looked anything but reassured. 'Marjorie, if Felix loves her I'm sure you will, too, once you get to know her.'

'I certainly hope so,' sighed Marjorie. 'The thing is, we haven't seen Felix himself for nearly six months and that was in London last time he was on leave. He doesn't really talk to us these days.'

'When are they planning to get married?' asked Avril. 'And where? Wherever Daphne lives, I suppose.'

'That's the other thing. They're not having a church wedding at all, they're getting married in London at Chelsea Town Hall. Felix says Daphne isn't close to her family, so it'll only be a small wedding. Peter suggested that they got married down here, but Felix said no, that the wedding would be in the next month and it was easier to arrange it in London where they both live.' She looked across at Avril with a stricken face. 'You don't think… well, I mean… you don't think that they have to… You know, do you?'

'No,' cried Avril, shaking her head even as she'd been wondering that very thing. 'I doubt that very much.'

Marjorie nodded. 'You're right, of course. I expect it's to do with his leave.'

'Well, you're going to meet her very soon,' Avril reminded her, 'which'll set your mind at rest.'

'I don't think it will,' she said to David later as they sat over the remains of supper in the kitchen. 'Poor Marjorie! It's too bad of Felix to spring it on them like this, she's very upset.'

'So, she and Peter have got to go up to London for the wedding,' David said. 'I'd have thought they'd enjoy the trip.'

'Oh, I don't think it's the going up to London that worries them, that's easy enough on the train. No, it's the fact that they'd never heard of this girl before Felix announced that he was going to marry her. Poor Marjorie is afraid that she's in the family way, which would account for all the haste.'

'Well, if she is, she won't be the first to hurry up the aisle to stop the child from being a bastard,' David grinned ruefully, 'and she surely won't be the last. If it is the case,' he went on, 'at least Felix is doing the decent thing and standing by her.'

'I suppose so,' Avril agreed. 'But there isn't any aisle, it's a register office wedding, and that certainly isn't how the Bellingers thought their only son, well, their only child, would get married. They've hardly seen him since the end of the war, and all the time they've been waiting for him to leave the RAF and come home to help Peter run the estate, but he hasn't. Everything's different and naturally they're disappointed.'

'The war changed lots of things,' David pointed out. 'Duty has become an unfashionable word. People are viewing life differently. Look at the number of divorces there are now. With men being away during the war, some women have found solace elsewhere and when their husbands have come home, they've been less than welcome. And then there are the women who've been widowed and left on their own, struggling to bring up small children; people are morally less scrupulous than they were. They tend to seize the day and damn the consequences, and after what many of them have been through, who can blame them?'

'Don't you blame them?' asked his wife. 'Surely you must think it's wrong.'

'I do think it's wrong,' David agreed, 'of course it's wrong, but I try not to judge people. That's not my job and never has been.' He got to his feet. 'I need to spend an hour in my study before we go to bed,' he said. 'By the way, when's Caro coming down?'

'She'll be here on Friday evening,' Avril answered with a smile. 'I can't wait to see her and discuss all her plans.'

David laughed. 'Well,' he said, 'at least *you've* got a wedding here to look forward to.'

When he'd disappeared into his study, Avril cleared the table and washed up, but as she did so, her mind was far from the dishes in the sink. She was thinking about her sister, soon to marry the local doctor and coming to live in the village.

How lovely it'll be, she thought, to have Caroline so close. Goodness knows, they've taken long enough to get round to it.

It was clear that they'd fallen in love, but Avril had been beginning to despair of confirmed bachelor, Henry Masters, the village doctor, ever coming to the point. But at last he had, and Caroline had finally given in her notice at the London children's home where she'd worked for so long.

Charlotte had been pleased too, when she heard that Caroline was moving down to Wynsdown at last. Though she had only been thirteen when she first met Caroline, as Charlotte had grown up and they'd worked together at the Livingston Road children's home in the latter part of the war, they had become very fond of each other and the twelve years that separated them slipped away to nothing. They had cemented a lasting friendship and Charlotte had been sorely missed by Caroline when she'd moved back to Somerset to marry Billy.

Chapter 2

Next morning, Charlotte put Edie in the pram and with Johnny dancing along at her side, set off down the lane to the village shops. As soon as she walked into the post office she was greeted by an excited Nancy Bright. The postmistress, always the fount of information, was bursting with news.

'Oh, Charlotte, you'll never guess. Felix Bellinger's getting married. Isn't that exciting news? He's such a lovely young man, isn't he? And I hear he's bringing his bride-to-be down to meet Squire and Mrs Bellinger very soon. Such a handsome man!'

Charlotte smiled and said, 'Is he? I don't think I've ever seen him.'

Nancy clapped her hand to her mouth. 'Oh my dear, haven't you? But never mind, I know you'll like him when you do. He looks just like Clark Gable!'

'Does he now?' Charlotte smiled. 'Very handsome, then.'

When Charlotte had done her shopping she continued along the track leading out of the village and across the fields to Charing Farm, where Billy had grown up and his parents still lived. It was a beautiful September morning and her heart lifted as she pushed the pram along the well-worn path between hedgerows burgeoning with blackberries, rosehips and sloes. She had come to love the Mendip countryside, its wide open spaces where trees dressed in autumn colours stood against the clear blue sky; the sweep of the hills, the hidden hollows, its fields divided by age-old dry-stone walls, covered in moss and ivy. It was the place she'd been happiest in her life, the place where she could put the misery of the past behind her and look forward to a peaceful future. She had Billy, Johnny was running along beside the pram delighted to be going to see Gr'ma and Gramp, and baby Edie was blissfully asleep after her bath and a good feed. Who could ask for anything more?

They arrived in the farmyard and were greeted by the dogs, prancing round them, barking their delight. Johnny, who was always entirely unfazed by this excited welcome, ran between them to the kitchen door and his grandmother.

'Gr'ma,' he cried as he ran and clasped her round the knees. 'We comed to see you.'

'So I see, darling,' cried his grandmother as she swept him up into her arms and gave him a hug. 'Billy said he thought you'd be over.' She smiled across at her daughter-in-law. 'You'll stay for dinner?'

'We'd love to, if there's enough.'

Margaret Shepherd laughed. 'There's always enough! Come on in. You can leave Edie out there in her pram if she's asleep. She'll come to no harm, 'tis warm enough.' She bent over the pram and looked down fondly at her granddaughter, fast asleep, the fingers of one hand curled round the blanket that covered her. 'Come your ways in,' she said, taking Johnny by the hand, 'and we'll see what I can find in my pantry. Gramp will be in shortly for a cup of tea.'

'Can I go out with him?' demanded Johnny. 'I want to go out with Gramp and see the an'mals.'

They went into the big farm kitchen and Margaret pulled the kettle on to the range's hotplate, ready to make the tea.

Charlotte sat Johnny up at the table and Margaret found him a piece of cake to go with his drink of milk.

Almost immediately John Shepherd came in and Johnny was off his chair again, pulling at his hand and begging to be taken to see the an'mals.

'Let Gramp have his tea first,' laughed Charlotte, 'then he might take you.'

John was given enough time to gulp down his mid-morning tea before he and Johnny set off for their usual tour of the farmyard.

'I'm glad he's gone for a minute,' said Charlotte as she and Margaret sat at the table to drink their tea in peace. 'I wanted to talk to you about Edie's christening. The vicar's suggested two weeks on Sunday at the morning service. Would that suit you both?'

'Of course it would,' said Margaret. 'We'd be at church then anyway.'

'And Jane? D'you think she'll be able to come?'

'I don't know about Jane, depends if she's on duty, but I'm sure she'll do her best to be there. You can ask her on Sunday. I'm sure she'll want to be there for little Edie Martha's christening.'

Jane had been surprised at Charlotte and Billy's choice of names for their new daughter. 'They're both very old-fashioned names,' she remarked to her mother when she'd heard them.

'Well, Edie's for Miss Everard who was Charlotte's foster mother, here in Wynsdown, and Martha for her real mother; you know she died at the end of the war.'

'Yes, I know that, but they haven't even chosen Martha as the name they'll call her by. I'd have thought they'd have named her after you, rather than that funny old Miss Everard.'

'It's their choice, my dear,' Margaret pointed out. 'Miss Edie was very important to Charlotte at an extremely difficult time in her life. She took her in when she was evacuated here and over the years they became very close. When she died, Charlotte was devastated.' Margaret gave her daughter a smile. 'And let's face it, "Margaret Martha" would be an awful mouthful, wouldn't it?'

'I suppose,' Jane said, thinking that Edith Martha was as well. It was clear that she didn't approve. Margaret could only hope she didn't say so to Billy.

'Of course, we'll see her on Sunday,' Charlotte said. 'I thought we'd invite you and the godparents and the vicar and Mrs Vicar back to the house for something to eat afterwards. Jane, too, of course. Make a party of it.'

'Sounds a lovely idea, Charlotte, and we can all help with the food. Who are the godparents?'

'We're asking Clare and Caroline Morrison to be godmothers,' Charlotte said.

'And godfather?'

'I rang Uncle Dan last night, and asked him,' Charlotte replied. 'He said he'd be honoured and so he and Aunt Naomi and Nicky are coming down to stay.'

When she'd phoned Dan the previous evening as Billy had suggested, he hardly knew what to say.

'Oh, Lisa, are you sure, me duck? I mean, well you must have lots of friends what'd do a better job of godfathering than me.'

Charlotte had heard an emotion in his voice that matched her own. 'Uncle Dan,' she said, 'I can't think of anyone else who could possibly be a better choice. Billy and I would love you to be Edie's godfather, her special uncle... like you've been mine.'

'Then I'll be there, Lisa. Your aunt Naomi and Nicky and me.'

'The pips'll go in a minute,' Charlotte said. 'I'll write to you with all the details, but we'll expect you to stay with us for the weekend.'

The pips did go then and the call ended, but Charlotte, known to Naomi and Dan by her German name of Lisa, had realised during the three-minute call how much it meant to Dan to be asked and how much it meant to her that he'd accepted. Her London family would all be there.

'How lovely,' Margaret said. 'Will you be able to fit them all in?'

'With a squeeze,' Charlotte laughed. 'But I can't wait to see them.'

Since she'd been hustled out of Germany on a Kinder-transport train as a child of thirteen, Charlotte's life had been one of continual change. As the war had swirled her through the blitzed streets of London, into a hospital, out to a children's home, it had finally washed her up in the village of Wynsdown.

The lifelines to which she'd clung for her very survival in the turmoil of her life had been Naomi and Dan Federman, a boy named Harry Black, Miss Edie Everard and Billy. Miss Edie had died and Harry had vanished, but they, and the others who were still there, were woven into the very fabric of her life.

After the midday meal John took Johnny out to the paddock where Barney the Shetland pony was grazing peacefully.

'Can I ride Barney today?' Johnny asked, skipping along beside his grandfather. 'Can I, Gramp, can I?' Ever since his dad had put him up on Barney the first time, Johnny had been begging to ride him again.

'I should think so, old son. Shall we fetch him in, then?'

'Yes, yes,' Johnny cried, prancing round in delight.

The little boy was almost bursting with excitement as his grandfather collected Barney's tack from the stable and got him ready for Johnny to ride.

Together they spent a wonderful half-hour in the paddock, John leading Barney round with a triumphant Johnny sitting on top crowing with delight. However, after a while John looked at his watch and said, 'I'm afraid it's time to get off now, Johnny.'

'Oh, no, Gramp! I don't want to,' Johnny cried in dismay. 'I want to go on riding him. Barney likes it.'

'I'm sure he does,' John agreed with a smile, 'but it's time to feed the pigs. They'll be getting hungry.' He led the pony back into the yard and lifted Johnny down. 'You're coming for your dinner on Sunday, if you're good you can have another ride then. All right?'

Johnny nodded. 'When's Sunday?' he asked.

'Four more bedtimes and then it's Sunday.'

'Can I ride Barney with Daddy?'

'I'm sure you can. He'll want to see how well you ride.'

'Then can I go out riding with Daddy?' Johnny asked, brightening at the thought.

'When you're a bit bigger, old son,' replied his grandfather, 'but I'm sure Daddy will help you with Barney on Sunday. Now, come and see how big our piglets have got since you were here.' He picked up the bucket of swill and taking Johnny by the hand, led him towards the pigsty.

'Gramp says I can ride Barney again on Sunday,' Johnny announced when they came back into the kitchen. 'He's promised.'

'Then I expect you can,' Charlotte agreed.

'Just me and Daddy,' Johnny said firmly. 'You'll be looking

after Edie. And anyway,' he added as a truthful afterthought, 'Daddy's a better rider than you!'

Charlotte laughed at that. There was no denying that he was right. When they'd got married, Billy had tried to teach her to ride, but she was not a natural horsewoman and she was never comfortable in the saddle. These days she was happy enough to use Edie as her excuse to keep her feet firmly on the ground.

'You're right,' she said. 'You can go riding with Daddy, Edie and I'll stay here.'

At the end of the afternoon, Billy joined them in their walk back to the village. As they reached the village green, Charlotte said, 'Will you take them on home, Billy? I just want to go to the grave for a few minutes. Give it a tidy. I won't be long.'

The grave was Miss Edie's, and Charlotte occasionally went, ostensibly to keep it tidy, but actually to tell Miss Edie what was going on in her life. Billy had followed her once and heard her apparently talking to herself, but realised as he listened that she was speaking to her foster mother. Ashamed of himself for eavesdropping, he'd slipped away, unnoticed.

Since then he'd got used to Charlotte going to Miss Edie's grave and telling her things. At first he'd thought it a bit macabre to go and talk to a woman who'd been dead these seven years, but he'd seen how much it meant to Charlotte occasionally to have a few minutes alone at the graveside and he'd accepted that it was just something she needed to do. She had nowhere to mourn her real parents, and Miss Edie's grave supplied the need.

'Yes, fine,' he said, lifting Johnny down from his shoulders where he'd been riding. 'Come on then, Johnny, let's take Edie home. Mummy won't be long and you and I can find ourselves a biscuit and a drink.'

For a moment Charlotte watched them walk on up the lane towards Blackdown House, and then she turned in through the lych gate and went across to Miss Edie's grave. It lay in a quiet corner of the churchyard in the shade of an aged yew tree. It was marked with a simple granite headstone engraved with her name, Edith Everard, and her dates, Born 7th June 1892 Died 21st July 1942.

'Only fifty when you died,' said Charlotte softly. 'Far too soon, Miss Edie. I do miss you.'

She knelt on the grass beside the headstone and pulled up a couple of weeds that had seeded themselves since her last visit.

'We're naming our baby after you, Miss Edie,' she murmured as she tossed the weeds aside. 'I wish you could see her. You'd adore her. She's so pretty and she's very smiley now. The christening is in a couple of weeks' time, which is a good thing really because she's growing so fast that she'll soon be too big for the Shepherds' christening robe. Billy was christened in it and Johnny too, of course. Uncle Dan's going to be her godfather. You never met him, but I think you'd have liked him. He's very down to earth, but then, so were you. I wish you could be there too, singing in the choir. I still miss you very much, but living in the house, I know you're never far away.'

Reluctantly, Charlotte got to her feet, resting her hand on the headstone for a moment before turning away and walking slowly home to Blackdown House. She had lived there with Miss Edie for nearly two years and Miss Edie had left her the house in her will. If she were alone there, Charlotte could almost feel Miss Edie's presence. She'd never said as much to Billy, he would have thought her too fanciful, but she loved the feeling that Miss Edie was still there, watching over them all.

The Saturday before the christening, Charlotte waited impatiently for the Federmans to arrive. It was nearly three years since she'd seen them. They'd moved to Feneton in Suffolk during the Blitz when their house had been burned out in an air raid, and after the war, with no home to return to, they'd stayed there. Dan still worked at a local RAF base and Naomi was the cook and part-time barmaid at the Feneton Arms. It was quite an expedition for them to travel all the way to Somerset just for a weekend, but they'd been determined to come and as she waited for them to arrive, Charlotte found herself full of nervous anticipation. They were coming by train and Billy had borrowed his father's car to go and pick them up at the station. Johnny had gone with him, excited to see Uncle Dan and Aunt Naomi. They had visited once, when he was a baby, but of course he had no recollection of that. He had helped Charlotte make room for Nicky to sleep on a mattress in his bedroom and was thrilled at the thought of sharing his room with his big 'cousin', who was nearly nine.

At last Charlotte heard the car coming up the lane and she went out to the gate to meet them. As they all climbed out of the car, Johnny bounced round them excitedly, shouting, 'Mummy they've comed, they've comed. We went to the station and they comed on the train!'

'So they did,' laughed Charlotte, and found herself enveloped in Aunt Naomi's arms.

'Lisa, Lisa,' Naomi cried, 'it's so good to see you.'

'It's good to see you, too, Aunt Naomi,' replied Charlotte as, with tears welling in her eyes, she returned the hug.

Uncle Dan had never been a demonstrative man, but he too hugged Lisa, before turning back to Johnny and saying, 'Did you hear the guard blow his whistle, young'un?'

'I did,' squeaked Johnny, 'and he waved his flag to me, so I waved back.'

'Come on in,' said Charlotte. 'Billy'll just take his dad's car back and then we'll eat. Edie should be waking up any time now. I can't wait to show her to you.'

She led the way indoors and Naomi was soon cooing over Edie, asleep in her pram.

When she woke up Charlotte lifted her out of the pram and handed her to Dan. 'Here you are, Uncle Dan, meet your goddaughter.'

Dan sat down with the baby, holding her stiffly at first, but relaxing a little as he recalled the feel of his own son in his arms.

'She's beautiful, Lisa. Just like her mother!' Then he looked up and added, 'Sorry, we should call you Charlotte now. I will try, I promise you, but you'll always be Lisa to me.'

'And that's how I want to stay,' Charlotte said. 'You and Aunt Naomi are the only ones left to call me Lisa.'

Over the dinner table they caught up on all their news.

'We've found a cottage on the edge of the village,' Naomi told Charlotte. 'We're hoping to move in in a couple of weeks. Of course, it's been wonderful living at the Feneton Arms with Jenny and Jim, but trade's picking up again now and really they want the rooms back for overnight guests.' She smiled across at Charlotte. 'And to be honest we want our own home.'

'You aren't thinking of going back to London, are you?' Charlotte asked.

'No, we went back and had a look at Kemble Street, but our side of the road had been demolished and they was building blocks of flats. Dan finally got some compensation cos they requisitioned his taxi, so we decided to stay in Feneton.

We've both got work there and Nicky's happy at school, aren't you, love?'

Nicky looked up from his plate of cottage pie and shrugged. ''S all right.'

'What happened to that lad you knew? The one what used to look out for you at school?' asked Dan. 'You ever see him? What was his name?'

'Harry,' said Charlotte with a quick glance at Billy. 'Harry Black. No, he disappeared. He was planning to go to Australia at one time, so I s'pose he went. We haven't seen him since before we were married, have we, Billy?'

'No,' replied Billy shortly. 'No we haven't, and good riddance.'

As Harry Black clearly caused tension between them, Dan hurriedly changed the subject and asked Charlotte what he had to do at the christening service, and they were soon deep in discussion about the next day; what was going to happen at the church, and at Edie's party afterwards.

Chapter 3

Felix and Daphne travelled down from London by train. Daphne had wanted Felix to drive them in his open-topped car. She was proud of landing such an eligible fiancé and wanted to make a splash arriving in the village, but he'd been adamant.

'No can do, darling. Can't get the petrol for a trip like that.'

'You could get extra coupons from the office if you wanted to,' pouted Daphne. 'What's the point of working in a place like the Air Ministry if you can't get the odd bonus from time to time?'

'I'm sorry, dearest,' Felix replied, 'but no one's going to hand out petrol coupons for a visit to the country. The train's easy enough and we can get a taxi from the station. I'll get my father to arrange for Fred Jones to be waiting when we arrive.'

The journey was easy. They travelled first class, had lunch in the restaurant car and Felix ordered some wine with the meal.

'It's to celebrate our visit to meet my parents,' he said cheerfully as he filled her glass. He looked across at her rather pale face and said, 'You aren't worried about meeting them, are you, darling?'

Daphne took a sip of her wine. 'No, of course not,' she said. But she was. She knew that she wasn't going to be top-drawer enough for Felix's parents. If they knew where her family came from and where she'd been brought up, they'd be horrified. Felix knew and said he didn't care, but then even Felix didn't know the whole story.

They had first met during an air raid when Daphne had sprained her ankle in the rush to get underground as the sirens blared. Felix had come to her aid, and when the all-clear sounded and it was obvious that she couldn't put any weight on her ankle, he had hailed a taxi.

As the cab took them to her home, they chatted. Felix told her that he flew with Fighter Command and was on a forty-eight-hour leave. Daphne told him she worked in a factory making parts for aero engines.

'Just think,' she marvelled, 'you could be flying a plane I helped to make! That would be something, wouldn't it.'

'It certainly would,' Felix agreed, thinking privately that it would also be highly unlikely. It was awkward sitting in the taxi with her. She was even younger than she'd seemed at first sight, probably only about sixteen or seventeen. Her thick fair hair had escaped from its combs and tumbled about her face. She was pretty enough, he supposed, with a small pointed nose and a Cupid's bow of a mouth, scarlet with lipstick, but it was her eyes that were her most arresting feature: large, speedwell blue, fringed with almost impossibly long lashes; not more than a child really, an over-made-up child, and Felix couldn't wait to deliver her home and go back up to town.

Home was a tiny house up an alleyway behind a run-down backstreet garage in Hackney. She'd been ashamed of it then and she was even more ashamed of it now.

After Felix left that night, Daphne had sat down in the kitchen and while her mother Ethel bandaged her sprained ankle, she told her parents how the young flight lieutenant had come to her rescue.

'If he hadn't been there, Ma,' she said, 'I'd have been stuck in the street with the Jerry bombers over my head.'

'Well, you just watch yourself, my girl,' said her mother darkly. 'We don't want no more trouble caused by officers.'

'Leave it, Mother,' Daphne's dad, Norman, said. 'It was good of him to bring our girl home.'

'I didn't say it wasn't,' snapped his wife, 'but our sort don't mix with officers.'

No more was said, but Daphne thought about Felix all the time, building a romance around him, so that when the other girls at the factory were talking about their boyfriends, she would mention Felix by name as if he were hers. She could weave about him whatever stories she liked. Fantasies that soon became as real to her as the stories the other girls told.

It was safer that way. She hadn't had a boyfriend recently, not since the young officer who'd got her pregnant and disappeared. Her baby, Janet, was just over eighteen months now, being brought up by her mother as her own. Janet was Daphne's 'little sister'.

When Daphne turned eighteen, tired of the daily grind in the factory, she left and joined the WAAFs. She had long ago learned to drive and working alongside her father in his garage, she'd learned the inner workings of the combustion engine. At weekends she often helped him get an overworked car up and running again, and she could coax the most recalcitrant engine back into life. The WAAFs welcomed her with open arms.

Once she'd done her basic training she was employed as a driver and spent much of her time behind the wheel, taking officers to and from meetings, driving them to various air bases all over the country.

It was at RAF Northolt that she saw Felix again. His face imprinted on her memory, she recognised him at once as he emerged from a hangar with another officer and they paused outside to light their cigarettes. The other officer glanced across at her waiting by the parked car and made some comment to Felix, who looked up. The two men wandered across to where she stood.

'Hello there.' It was the other man who spoke. He held out his cigarette case. 'Want a smoke?'

'Thanks,' Daphne replied, 'don't mind if I do.' She took a cigarette and ducked her head to accept a light.

'Haven't seen you before, have we? My name's Toby, Toby Squires.'

'No, I just brought Group Captain Hayes up for some meeting.' She was answering Toby, but her eyes were on Felix. Would he recognise her now they were standing together?

Fixed by her blue eyes, Felix frowned thoughtfully, saying, 'Do I know you? Have we met somewhere before?' He was racking his brains. She did look vaguely familiar but where did he know her from? Perhaps one of the air base hops, or at a party? She was only a WAAF driver, but he might have come across her before.

'In an air raid,' Daphne told him. 'I sprained my ankle.'

'Good God,' exclaimed Felix, remembering. 'Was that you?'

Daphne nodded. 'Yes, you took me home in a taxi.'

'Did you, by George?' interrupted Toby. 'That was quick work, old boy.'

Felix ignored him and said, 'But you weren't a WAAF then, were you? You were making planes!'

Daphne laughed. 'Yeah, and pretty boring it was, too. Soon as I was old enough, I joined up.'

'Good for you,' said Felix. 'Where're you based?'

'In London, but I drive all over the country.'

At that moment Group Captain Hayes appeared from one of the buildings. He carried a briefcase and strode across to the waiting car. Daphne hastily threw her cigarette to the ground, stepping forward to open the rear door. Felix and Toby Squires moved away and walked back to the hangar. Hayes tossed his briefcase on to the back seat and then slid in beside it, saying as he did so, 'Back to the Air Ministry, Higgins, and don't hang about.'

Some of the officers she drove preferred to ride beside her in the front, sometimes chatting to her on the journey; others, like Group Captain Hayes, always chose to travel in the back and spoke not a word.

Daphne hurried round to the driver's side and started the car; the last she saw of Felix and his friend, Toby, was through the rear-view mirror, as they finished their cigarettes before going back inside.

On the way back to London, the engine began to splutter and cough. Daphne felt the car lose power and pulled over to the side of the road.

'What's the problem, Higgins?' snapped the group captain.

'Not sure, sir, I'll have a look.' Daphne got out of the car and lifted the bonnet. It was not the car she usually drove, the one that she kept serviced and running sweetly. That had been commandeered for the day by some top brass. She'd had to make do with a car from the pool and she saw at once that little maintenance had been carried out on this engine for some time.

She went round to the boot and pulled out the tool kit that always travelled with any of the staff cars, then returning to the engine, she set about removing and cleaning the plugs.

'Is this going to take long, Higgins?' demanded Hayes. 'I'm due at the Air Ministry this evening.' He sat fuming in the back of the car. All very well to employ women as drivers, he thought angrily, but when the car breaks down they're useless.

Higgins drove well enough, he'd had her before, but it was unlikely she'd be able to repair the car without a trained mechanic.

'I'll be as quick as I can, sir,' Daphne replied from under the bonnet.

Moments later he was glad that he had not expressed his thoughts aloud, for when she came back into the car and pressed the self-starter, the engine gave one further cough, one further splutter and then started purring as if it had never stopped.

'Should be all right now, sir,' Daphne said, and let in the clutch.

'So,' Hayes said, addressing her for the first time as if she were a person and not simply his driver, 'where did you learn to do that?'

Daphne laughed. 'My dad has a garage, he does motor repairs. I learned it off him.'

Back in London, Group Captain Hayes passed the message on. Aircraftswoman Higgins was wasted as a driver. She understood engines and should be retrained as an aircraft mechanic.

Someone listened to him and Daphne found herself posted to RAF Halton, where she was trained in aircraft maintenance, and for the rest of the war she checked and maintained the aircraft that finally defeated the Luftwaffe and inflicted retaliatory bombing on the cities of Germany.

She was a sergeant when the war ended and she could have left the air force and returned to Civvy Street with her head held high, having done her bit for England, but she was enjoying life. She had matured from being a very pretty girl into a beautiful woman, the sort that turned heads whenever she entered a room. She now moved in circles entirely different from those she had inhabited before the war. Officers took her dancing or out to dinner. Life was good and Daphne was determined that she would never go back to her pre-war life in Hackney. Janet didn't need her. She was six now and entirely Ethel's child. Her father's business was beginning to pick up again as people took their cars off blocks, dusted them down and despite petrol still being rationed, put them back on the road. No, Daphne decided, no one in Hackney needed her any more and she moved on with scarcely a backward glance. She had listened to how the officers and their lady friends spoke and with careful attention to accent and grammar she could now pass muster among his friends if an officer asked her out for an evening. She was seldom short of an escort, several of them keen to entice her into bed, but none of them mentioning anything that seemed to offer more than a quick roll in the hay before they were posted elsewhere, definitely *not* what Daphne had in mind. And then she met Felix again.

He flew into Biggin Hill, where she was overseeing a complete service and overhaul of an elderly Spitfire which, having seen valiant service during the war, was about to be sold off to a private buyer. Alerted by the tower that a plane was coming in, she went out on to the tarmac to greet the pilot, and there he was, Wing Commander Felix Bellinger. As before, she recognised him at once as he clambered out of the cockpit and took off his flying helmet. The same dark good looks, the usually smooth dark hair slightly ruffled by the helmet, the same dark eyes, the same neat moustache above a generous mouth; the same Felix about whom she'd fantasised as a young girl.

Felix, dropping lightly to the ground and removing his helmet, saw a WAAF sergeant coming towards him. She wore regulation overalls, her hair turban-tied out of the way for work. There was a smudge of oil on her face, and she was regarding him with huge, speedwell-blue eyes. It was the eyes that captured him; wide, with laughter lurking in their depths. He'd seen them before, but surely belonging to some girl, not this beautiful woman, standing smiling at him. But where?

She stepped forward and saluted. 'Welcome to Biggin Hill, sir,' she said. 'We'll get you checked over and refuelled directly.' All efficiency, Daphne made no allusion to either of their previous meetings.

Felix nodded and said, 'No hurry, Sergeant, I'm not leaving until tomorrow.' But even as he spoke he was racking his brain to remember where he'd seen those blue eyes before.

'Squadron Leader Peterson is expecting you, sir. He's in the mess.'

It wasn't until he and his old mate, Gerry Harper, wandered down to the local village pub that evening for a change of scene, that memory came back to him.

Daphne was in the lounge bar, sitting with a young flight lieutenant, whose eyes seemed to devour her. Felix wasn't surprised at the young man's admiration. The woman sitting at the table with him was stunning, her hair, no longer confined to her working turban, was smooth and shining, coiled into luxuriant rolls about her ears and neck. Her mouth, a neat Cupid's bow, was lightly touched with red. Wearing a bright blue dress that drew out the colour of her eyes, its wide skirt cinched with a broad black belt at her narrow waist, her perfect figure, previously concealed by her overalls, was displayed for general admiration, for her escort and for Felix.

'Who's the girl in the blue dress?' Felix asked Gerry as they waited at the bar for their beer to be drawn.

Harper glanced over his shoulder and gave a grin. 'That's Daphne Higgins... and it's no good looking at her, Felix, because you'll have to join the queue.'

Felix hadn't joined the queue, he had given Gerry a grin and picking up his pint, had crossed to where the couple were sitting.

'Daphne!' he said. 'How lovely to see you again. How've you been keeping? Can I get you a drink?' He glanced at the young officer and added, 'You don't mind, do you? Daphne and I go back a long way.'

'N-no, of course not, sir,' stammered the young man.

'Good,' beamed Felix, and knowing he was shamelessly pulling rank to interpose himself into another man's evening, and not caring in the least, he bought drinks and drew up another chair.

From there, there was no turning back. Felix had staked his claim. He couldn't imagine how he hadn't see Daphne properly before. How could he have been so blind? Now he had rediscovered her, there was no way he was going to lose her. His whole body ached for her and Daphne could read his desire in his face and in the way he touched her. He was now working at the Air Ministry, and his hours were pretty regular. He drove down to see her every weekend that she wasn't working, and they had long and passionate kisses in the back of his little sports car, but that was all. Daphne never let him take advantage. It had happened to her once and she was determined that this time if an officer got her into his bed, it would be a marriage bed. She remembered the teenage fantasies she'd woven round Felix and the remembrance of them made her laugh.

Felix was an attractive man and Daphne liked him. She had no intention of letting him go. He was her escape from Hackney, saving her from sliding back into a repeat of her mother's life. She was astute enough and worldly wise, now, to know that to have any chance of Felix marrying her, she had to keep him waiting, waiting until there was a wedding ring on her finger. She had been caught once by a lusty and infatuated young officer who'd promised her the world. She'd thought then, in her innocence, that the way to keep him was to share all that she was with him. Now she knew better. She would give Felix absolutely no chance to disappear, leaving her alone and pregnant as her earlier lover had. Felix was her ticket to respectability, to a manor house in the country, to a life of luxury she could never even have imagined in those days before the war.

She didn't love Felix, but she was fond of him. He was thoughtful and attentive and very often made her laugh; she could picture herself married to him, lady of the manor with servants to run the house. Whenever they met she was gentle and loving, her eyes and her lips promising more. She enjoyed kissing him and being kissed by him, she gave herself into the strength of his arms, feeling her body respond, despite her determination not to carry that response to its natural conclusion. Always she held back, and Felix had been brought up to respect his girlfriends. Despite several forays into exciting sex with good-time girls met during the hectic wartime days when each such encounter could well be his last, Felix never forced himself on Daphne. She was shy, he decided, afraid of her own emotions. She was no good-time girl to be used and left aside. He knew she came from a working-class background, but that didn't mean she had no morals. He'd become intoxicated by her, and he'd set aside the knowledge of the garage in Hackney with its alleyway cottage. He didn't plan to marry Daphne, but he did want to sleep with her, to do things to her and with her that made his imagination run wild.

Surely, he thought, with careful wooing, she would eventually relent and allow him into her bed.

But Daphne held fast to her plan and eventually, after several months, it was Felix who finally gave in.

It was a warm August evening and they'd had dinner at the Silver Swan, one of their favourite restaurants. Afterwards they walked along the Thames Embankment, holding hands. A full moon silvered the river and the night air was balmy. They paused for a moment near Westminster Bridge and leaning on the wall, watched the leisurely flow of the Thames as it slipped by, gleaming in the moonlight.

Felix saw the water passing steadily along its course; its smooth surface ruffled eddies of wind into ripples which flashed silver and were gone. His life was passing like that, he thought, flowing steadily, tediously, from day to day and the only flashes of silver were the hours he spent with Daphne. When he held her in his arms, he ached for her with every fibre of his being. Holding her close, as close as she allowed, ceased to be a pleasure and became a torment. He tried to imagine not seeing her, a life of which she was not a part, and found it almost impossible.

The memory of the evening they had first met, so easily forgotten at the time, was etched on his mind. He could remember the tears spilling from her wide, blue eyes at the pain from her ankle; the way she'd clung to him for support, the feel of her body against him as he carried her down into the Tube station. Now it was Felix who fantasised.

'Daphne,' he said, still gazing at the river. 'Will you marry me?'

Daphne had begun to feel a little chilly and about to move on. She was suddenly tense beside him; the moment had come. 'Felix?'

He turned to face her then, putting his hands on her shoulders and looking down into the soft blue eyes that had captured him and now gazed up at him.

'I said, will you marry me?'

'Do you really mean it?' Daphne breathed, hardly able to believe he'd finally asked.

'Of course I mean it.' Felix held her gaze. 'Will you?'

Daphne nearly accepted him immediately, but caution made her decide to tackle the obstacle of her family head on and she said, 'But your parents. They'll want you to marry someone of your own class, not someone from the backstreets of Hackney.'

'My parents will be only too delighted that I've finally met a girl I want to marry. They'll love you, my darling girl, just as I do. I promise you.' And as he said the words, Felix truly believed them.

Daphne gave him an ecstatic smile. 'Oh, Felix, darling, of course I will.' She raised her face to be kissed and Felix held her as if he'd never let her go.

The next time they met, he brought her an engagement ring. As he slipped it on to the third finger of her left hand, he tentatively suggested that they might spend the night together at his flat in Oakley Street.

It wasn't the first time he'd suggested it, but Daphne gave him a warm smile and shook her head.

'Felix, darling, it sounds lovely, but we can't. I want to save myself for our wedding night. I always promised myself I'd come to my husband on my wedding night as a virgin.' She kissed him gently and then drew away. 'And that's still what I want. I want our wedding night to be absolutely perfect.'

'So do I,' Felix somewhat reluctantly agreed. 'So, let's get married straight away.'

The words were music to Daphne's ears. 'Of course, my love. As soon as it can be arranged.'

'We should talk to your parents about a date,' suggested Felix. 'You'll need time to get the wedding organised.'

'No!' Daphne almost shouted the word and seeing his startled expression, said more calmly, 'No, Felix. I just... well, I just want something quiet. You know, a registry office...'

'That's fine,' Felix agreed. He didn't want a flash wedding either. 'But even so, your parents will want to be there, your father to give you away.'

'No,' repeated Daphne. 'No fuss. I just want us to get married, just us and a couple of witnesses. Really, no fuss.'

'I'll have to tell my parents,' Felix said, 'and invite them to be there.'

'If you must.' Daphne sighed. 'But I haven't seen my parents for years, and I don't want to see them now.'

Felix reluctantly agreed, guiltily acknowledging to himself that it would make life easier if Daphne's parents were not there; there need be no revelations about her family background.

Daphne had to accept, however, that Felix wanted her to meet his parents, and now she was sitting in the dining car of the train on her way to Wynsdown. She glanced down at the engagement ring, a deep blue sapphire within a circle of diamonds.

'It was my grandmother's engagement ring,' Felix had told her. 'She left it to me and now I give it to you.'

Daphne would have preferred a solitaire diamond, but she was in no position to complain. Until the engagement ring translated into a wedding ring, she would risk nothing.

Fred Jones was waiting at the station and he greeted Felix with a smile.

'Welcome home, Mr Felix, it's been too long.'

Felix laughed. 'Don't you start, Fred. I'll get enough of that from my mother!' He gestured to Daphne. 'And this is my fiancée, Miss Daphne Higgins.'

Fred touched his cap and said, 'Howdy-do, miss,' before opening the door so that Felix could hand her into the car.

As they drove over the hill towards Wynsdown, Daphne stared out of the window. The gorge through which the road twisted and turned had enormously steep, craggy sides. Thin vegetation clung to the rocks which towered upward against the pale blue of an autumn sky. Eventually they emerged on to the hill top and Daphne found herself gazing out across wide, undulating country, bathed in sunlight. Hedges and moss-covered stone walls marked off fields, patches of woodland broke the skyline, and tucked in the sheltered folds of the land, an occasional farmhouse or barn. The sun struck colour from the hedgerows and the woodland glowed with autumn reds and golds. For someone brought up in the crowded East End of London, where the streets were narrow and houses jostled each other for space, it all looked empty and bleak. Sheep grazed the fields and a herd of cows was gathered at a farm gate waiting for evening milking. Sheep and cows! Where were all the inhabitants?

Fred and Felix were chatting, talking about people she'd never heard of and as they finally turned into the village of Wynsdown she was becoming more and more disheartened. As Fred swung the car round the village green and into the lane that led to the manor, she saw a small group standing outside the pub, the Magpie, watching. One small child waved and Felix waved back.

'Who was that waving?' she asked a little pettishly. She was tired of Felix paying her no attention.

'Haven't a clue,' laughed Felix cheerfully. 'Probably wasn't born last time I was home. Who was it, Fred, the kid who waved?'

'That was little Johnny Shepherd, Billy Shepherd from Charing Farm's lad.'

'Billy's married?'

'Yes, he married that Charlotte, what was a German refugee.' He turned in between some tall stone gateposts and pulled up outside the manor house. 'Now then, Mr Felix, here we are.' As the car crunched to a halt, the front door opened and two Labradors erupted into the driveway, followed a little more slowly by Felix's parents, Peter and Marjorie Bellinger. Daphne stared at them through the car window as Felix jumped out to greet them. They stood side by side in the doorway, waiting, as Felix, shooing the excited dogs away, hurried across to them.

Major Bellinger looked all right, Daphne decided, tall and soldier-straight, his white hair cut short and smoothed across his head, a neat white moustache above his mouth. She could see the likeness to Felix.

That's how Felix'll look when he's old, she thought as he shook hands with his son. He was dressed in grey trousers and a navy-blue blazer over a white shirt and some sort of regimental tie, navy-blue with red zigzags across it. He'll be all right, Daphne thought. She was sure she could win him over, given a little time. Felix's mother, though, was another matter altogether. Daphne watched as Felix hugged her, not at all sure she liked the look of her prospective mother-in-law. She wore a coffee-coloured suit, with a straight skirt, fitted at the waist. The jacket had a neat collar, buttoned down with ornate metal buttons, and four matching buttons down the front. Her lipstick was red, her nose powdered, her grey hair permed into regimented curls.

Mutton dressed as lamb, thought Daphne as she pinned a smile to her lips and taking Felix's hand, eased her legs elegantly out of the car.

'Mother, Dad,' Felix said, proudly leading her forward, 'I'd like you to meet Daphne, my wife to be.'

'Welcome to Wynsdown, my dear,' Peter Bellinger said and held out his hand.

'Pleased to meet you, I'm sure,' trilled Daphne as she shook the proffered hand.

'Daphne, welcome,' said Marjorie, 'we're so glad you could come. Come along in. You must be dying for a cup of tea.' And Daphne followed her through the front door into the house that, one day, could be her home.

Chapter 4

Charlotte and her family were among the group who saw Felix and his fiancée arrive that Saturday afternoon. They were crossing the village green to the vicarage to make the final arrangements for the christening next morning, when Fred Jones's taxi swept round the corner. Johnny waved excitedly at the car, and was delighted when the man inside waved back to him.

'Did you see, Mummy, did you see? That man waved to me.'

'So he did,' Charlotte agreed. 'Wasn't that nice of him?'

'That must be Felix Bellinger and his fiancée,' Clare said. 'Nancy Bright says he looks like Clark Gable.'

'I know,' laughed Charlotte. 'She told me that, too.'

'Didn't see much of *her*, though, did we?' Clare shifted awkwardly, trying to ease the ache in her back. Her first baby was due any time and she was decidedly uncomfortable.

'Fair hair and a hat,' replied Charlotte. 'She'll probably be in church tomorrow.'

Clare's eyes widened. 'Ooh, d'you think she will?'

'I expect so,' said Charlotte. 'Major Bellinger's a church warden, isn't he?'

'And your Edie'll steal the show,' grinned Clare.

'More likely everyone'll be looking at Daphne and no one'll give Edie a thought,' answered Charlotte. 'I bet the vicar'll find his church overflowing tomorrow.'

Charlotte was right. When the christening party reached the church the next morning, a large crowd was standing outside in the sun. Major Bellinger was already there, and for a moment there was a palpable disappointment as the gathered group thought that Mrs Bellinger, Felix and the famous fiancée were not. Billy greeted his parents and Jane who were waiting at the door and then led his family inside. They sat at the back near the font, Caroline and Clare sharing a pew with Uncle Dan; the rest of the family spread through the next two rows. The five-minute bell was ringing and people began to file into the church, some stopping to admire Edie, who, wearing the trailing lace of the Shepherds' family christening robe, looked like an icicle in Charlotte's arms, but as the final tones of the bell began to toll, Marjorie Bellinger walked into the church, followed by Felix and Daphne, and took their places in the manor pew.

Daphne had not wanted to go to church that morning. She was not a church-goer and hadn't thought Felix was either, but to her surprise he insisted that they accompany his parents.

'Do we really have to?' she moaned. 'Can't we just stay here until they get back?'

'No.' Felix was adamant. 'It's only for an hour, and it's expected.'

'Who by?'

'By the village,' replied Felix. 'Come on, darling. The parents will be very disappointed if you don't come, too.'

'Come, too? You mean you'll go without me?'

'Yes,' Felix told her. 'I have to go, and I wanted you by my side.' He kissed her sulky mouth. 'I want to show you off to everyone. I want them to see how beautiful my future wife is. Come on, Daph, put your hat on.'

41

Daphne had given in and as they walked into the church she was aware that all eyes were on her, assessing, admiring, curious. She was pleased that she'd bought a new hat to go with her blue dress specially for this visit. While she sat through the service, her mind was miles away, going over the events of the previous evening.

The manor was not as she'd imagined it at all. She had thought it would be tall, three storeys at least, with high windows and tall chimney pots. It was a disappointment. It was long and low, built of grey stone, with a sloping slate roof. There were chimneys, but they were short, with cowls on the top to discourage birds from nesting, not like the tall, brick-built chimneys she'd seen pictured in books. However, when they entered the house, Daphne found herself in an open hallway with cheerful rugs on its polished wood floor. A staircase curved up to the landing above and through an open door she could see comfortable furniture grouped round the fireplace. Three other oak-panelled doors led off the hall, but they were all closed, and a passageway branched off towards the back of the house, to the kitchen? Or the servants' quarters?

Mrs Bellinger had shown her up to a guest bedroom that looked out over the garden. There was a double bed covered in a white quilt, a chest of drawers, a dressing table and a big old wardrobe. The walls were papered with faded pale green floral paper, and the windows curtained in rather tired dark green velvet. Daphne paused in the doorway, looking round her.

'I think you'll find the bed comfortable,' Mrs Bellinger said. 'The bathroom is next door and the lavatory next again. I'm sure you'll want to take off your hat and wash your hands before we have tea, so I'll leave you to it. Just come down when you're ready.'

The words were friendly enough, but Daphne felt the eyes assessing her and knew that she was under scrutiny.

When she was left alone she went to the window and looked out over the garden. It was large and well kept. A smooth lawn bordered with flowerbeds bright with autumn colour. A rainbow of dahlias filled one flowerbed and there were Michaelmas daisies standing tall along the fence that divided off the kitchen garden. Beyond the garden there seemed to be a paddock of some sort, where Daphne could see two horses grazing peacefully in the afternoon sun.

At that moment there was a tap on the door and when she called 'Come in,' Felix appeared with her suitcase.

'Thought you might need this,' he said, depositing it on the dressing-table stool. 'You all right? My room's just across the landing.'

'Yes, I'm fine,' Daphne said sharply. 'I'll be down in a minute.'

'Good. Tea'll be in the drawing room.' Felix smiled at her and disappeared.

'Drawing room,' she murmured. She must remember to call it 'the drawing room'. She'd only just got used to saying 'lounge' instead of 'front room'.

Quickly she removed her hat and gloves, went to the lavatory and then downstairs. She was determined they shouldn't have time to discuss her with Felix.

In the drawing room, she found them sitting in comfortable armchairs, with afternoon tea laid out on a small table beside Mrs Bellinger. As she came through the door both men got to their feet, and Felix came forward to lead her to the sofa and then sat down beside her.

Daphne let her left hand rest lightly on the arm of the sofa, so that her engagement ring sparkled in a shaft of sunlight.

'That's a beautiful ring you've got there, my dear,' said the major with a smile. 'A beautiful ring for a beautiful girl.'

'Oh, reely, Major Bellinger,' Daphne said with a flutter of eyelashes, 'you shouldn't say such things!'

'It's the one Gran left me,' Felix said. 'It's right it should go to my wife.'

Mrs Bellinger picked up the teapot and looking across at her said, 'Daphne, my dear. How do you take your tea?'

Daphne leaned back on the sofa and said, 'Oh, just as it comes, no sugar, thank you, Mrs Bellinger.'

Mrs Bellinger poured the tea and Felix handed first the cups and then the cucumber sandwiches, small triangles with the crusts cut off.

'The cucumbers come from our own greenhouse,' Mrs Bellinger said, 'and though we cut the crusts off the sandwiches, they're never wasted.' She smiled at Felix. 'Your favourite bread and butter pudding this evening.' Adding ruefully, 'Though more bread than butter these days, I'm afraid!'

Daphne had tried to look interested in this and the other small talk over the teacups. She must do her best to please Felix. She balanced a plate on her knee as she ate the sandwiches and holding the saucer, she raised her cup delicately to her mouth as she'd seen others do. She wanted to show them that she knew her manners.

The rest of the day dragged by. She'd been shown the garden, including the vegetable garden and the greenhouse, where she'd admired the tomatoes and cucumbers; she'd been taken through the stable yard and out to the paddock where she dutifully looked at the horses. One of them came up to the fence where they were standing, he was a big bay with a white blaze down his nose. Daphne took a hasty step back, but Felix stroked his nose and feeling in his pocket gave him half a carrot.

'This one's mine,' Felix said. 'Archie. And the other one, Jester, is Dad's. Come on, let's go back in.' He took her hand and led her in through the back door. Daphne was glad to get back inside the house. There was too much outdoors here for her liking.

Mrs Darby from the village was in the kitchen, cooking the evening meal as she always did, but the moment the dessert was cleared away she would be off home again. Mrs Darby was a treasure and Marjorie Bellinger valued her as such. There had been no live-in servants at the manor since before the war, and it was Mrs Darby working as cook and Mrs Gurney, coming in for the rough work, who allowed Marjorie to keep up appearances.

The dinner was excellent and it was over the dinner table that, at last, the wedding became the topic of conversation. Somehow they had danced round the subject during the afternoon, but as they sat at the table and ate roast lamb followed by the promised bread and butter pudding, it could no longer be avoided.

'Felix says you're going to be married in London,' said Mrs Bellinger. 'Not near your own home?'

Felix knew she was fishing and he cut in quickly, 'I told you, Mother, it's all set for two weeks' time. Chelsea Town Hall, Saturday, the first of October at twelve o'clock.'

'Of course. I look forward to meeting your family, Daphne. Do they live in London?'

'I'm afraid they won't be there, Mrs Bellinger, we're not really in contact any more.'

Marjorie Bellinger raised her eyebrows in surprise and was about to speak again when a fierce and quelling look from Felix changed her mind.

'Yes, twelve o'clock ceremony,' he said, 'and then I've reserved us a table at the Savoy Grill.'

'The Savoy?' cried his mother. 'You are splashing out!'

'The Savoy,' repeated Felix, pleased that his diversionary tactic had worked. 'It's not every day we get married!'

'Well, that must be our treat,' said his father. 'Our contribution to your wedding!'

Felix looked at him with affection. 'Thanks, Dad, that's very generous.'

'Have you found somewhere to live yet?' asked his father.

'For the moment we're going to stay on in my flat,' Felix replied. 'It's a bit small, but it'll do till we can find somewhere bigger.'

'That's very convenient,' remarked Marjorie. 'And where do you live at present, Daphne?'

'I've been in a bedsit in Pimlico for the last few weeks; since I left the WAAFs.'

'You left the WAAFs?' Neither of the Bellingers had known that; things were moving faster than they thought.

'Oh yes! Felix didn't want me working once we was… were… engaged. I was given an immediate discharge to get married.'

Marjorie had the sense not to ask who was paying for the bedsit in Pimlico. 'Everything seems to be arranged perfectly,' was all she said.

'I told you it was, Mother,' Felix said a little impatiently. 'We've no reason to wait and every reason to get on with things.'

'Every reason…?' Marjorie heard the dismay in her own voice. Was he now going to break the news that a baby was already on the way?

But Felix, sublimely unaware of her fears, said, 'Now things are beginning to pick up after the war, why should we wait?'

As she sat in church, listening to the vicar droning on,

Daphne allowed herself a secret smile. Marjorie thinks I'm pregnant and that's why we're getting married quickly. Well, she couldn't be more wrong!

Marjorie wasn't concentrating on the service either. In her head she was replaying the conversation she and Peter had had the previous evening in the privacy of their room. As soon as she'd closed the door, she'd said, 'Well, so that's Daphne.'

'Yes, I'm afraid it is,' Peter agreed. 'Not really who we'd have chosen for a daughter-in-law, but she may improve on acquaintance.'

'On acquaintance,' echoed his wife scornfully. 'She's not going to *be* an acquaintance. She's going to be Felix's wife. Don't you care that he's really going to marry her?'

'Of course I do,' he replied, 'but I don't think there's much we can do about it.'

'Couldn't you speak to him?'

'And say what?'

'I don't know,' said Marjorie wretchedly, 'something to make him think again.'

'I think that would probably do more harm than good. Almost anything we say against the idea is likely to make him more determined.'

'But she's not a suitable wife for him. She's not our sort. She's a working-class girl and I don't think she's even in love with him. I think she's using him as a meal ticket for life.'

'Now, darling, you don't know that. And he's in love with her, or at least he thinks he is, which comes to the same thing, and why not? You can't really refer to her as a girl, she's all woman, and a beautiful one at that, with her big blue eyes and her long blonde hair.' Peter spoke matter-of-factly, but Marjorie looked at him sharply.

'Well, she certainly seemed to win you over at dinner, with her smiles and her wide eyes, and her, "Oh, Major Bellinger, reely?"'

'No, she didn't,' replied Peter soothingly. 'I'm a better judge of character than that, but you have to admit she is an attractive woman.'

'But surely Felix can see past a pretty face?'

'Not at the moment, he can't.'

'And when he can it will be too late,' Marjorie said bitterly. 'At the moment she's all sweetness and light, but there's a hardness under all that charm; she's a calculating…' Marjorie bit back the word 'bitch', it was not in her vocabulary, saying only, 'a calculating little madam. I hope she knows Felix has only his pay to live on. I bet she thinks we're rich and that Felix will inherit the lot.'

'Well,' Peter smiled in an effort to calm his wife's fears, 'he will inherit the lot, but it won't be much of an inheritance, just our problems and our debts.'

'But *she* doesn't know that. Couldn't you just let something slip, you know, in conversation, about our financial problems?'

'No, I couldn't,' Peter answered firmly.

'But it might make her change her mind. You know, go after someone richer. Can't you see what she's after?'

'Of course I can, I'm not a fool, but any sign of antagonism on our part will only cement Felix into his decision. She's his choice of wife. If we seem to criticise her, he's bound to defend her and the situation'll be even worse.'

How could it be worse? Marjorie wondered now as she looked along the pew at her prospective daughter-in-law. There she sat in a smart blue frock with a perky little hat perched on the side of her head. Where'd she got those, and who'd paid for them? Her face at rest was beautiful, her complexion flawless, enhanced by a touch of make-up to emphasise the brilliance of her eyes and the delicate shape of her mouth, but beneath the apparent perfection, Marjorie could see steely resolve. There was nothing she could put her finger on and say, 'There! Look at her. Can't you see…?' But, instinctively, she knew it was there and she wished Felix could see it, too.

When it came to the christening of little Edith Martha Shepherd, everyone turned to face the font at the back of the church and the vicar called the parents and godparents forward. Felix watched the ceremony with interest. He saw the look of love on the faces of the parents, as they presented their baby and named her Edith Martha.

Would he soon be a father? he wondered. It was the first time he had actually considered the question. He glanced at Daphne standing beside him and wondered if she was thinking the same; that they might soon be starting a family, and the idea gave him a jolt of happiness.

Daphne was looking at Charlotte and thinking, she hasn't got her figure back. If I ever get pregnant again, I'm not going to let that happen to me.

All round the church the people of Wynsdown were admiring Mr Felix's fiancée. They made a handsome couple, standing side by side in the manor pew.

'She's a bit of all right, an' no mistake,' Bert Gurney said to Frank Tewson as they gathered in the sunshine on the village green after the service. 'D'you see the arse on 'er? Wouldn't mind a bit of that meself!'

'Dirty ole bugger,' Frank said with a grin. 'She's young enough to be your daughter!'

'Nah, she ain't,' protested Bert, whose children were indeed in their twenties.

'An' I can't see your Mavis liking the idea.'

Nor could Bert. 'No, well, no harm in lookin'. I was only sayin'…'

'Only saying what, Bert Gurney?' His wife had come up behind him unnoticed.

'Nothing, love,' Bert said hastily. 'Just that Mr Felix has caught himself a pretty bird, that's all.'

Mavis Gurney eyed her husband darkly. 'Yes,' she said, 'I thought that would be it.'

It was, indeed, the consensus of the village – Mr Felix had done all right for himself, and Daphne, despite her reluctance to appear at church, found herself basking in the warmth of their attention, her hand tucked into Felix's arm, smiling shyly as she was introduced to the vicar's wife and the doctor's fiancée, who'd stood godmother to the baby.

Felix stood beside her, beaming with pride as various people shook his hand and offered their congratulations, and Marjorie had to concede there was no point in trying to dissuade him from what she was sure would be a disastrous marriage.

The christening party set off up the road to Blackdown House, and gradually the villagers dispersed to their own Sunday lunches. With the christening of Billy Shepherd's baby, with visitors travelling all the way from London to be there, and the arrival of Felix Bellinger and his fiancée, it had been an exciting weekend, and food for village gossip and speculation for the foreseeable future.

When they got back to Blackdown House, Billy started pouring drinks for his visitors; beer for the men, and some white wine that Dr Masters had provided, for the ladies. Clare went into the kitchen with Charlotte to help carry out the food and lay it out on the dining-room table. As they took the dishes of cold meat and salad out of the pantry she said,

'What did you think of the famous Felix then? Don't know what that Nancy Bright was thinking about. He didn't look much like Clarke Gable to me.'

Charlotte laughed. 'No,' she agreed, 'but he is quite good-looking, don't you think? Dark and handsome?'

'Not my type,' said Clare, thinking of her husband Malcolm with his red hair and freckles.

'No, nor mine,' Charlotte said as she glanced through the open door to where Billy stood in the hallway. 'But even so, he's a very attractive man.'

'What about that Daphne? All dolled up for her appearance in church?'

'Oh, come on, Clare,' cried Charlotte. 'That's a bit hard. I bet you'd have dressed up if you were going to church with your future in-laws.'

'Well, maybe,' conceded Clare, ''cept me and Malc ain't got no in-laws.' She laid a hand on her extended stomach and sighed. 'Baby would have liked a nan and grandad. You're lucky to have Billy's parents.'

'I know,' Charlotte said.

At that moment Billy stuck his head round the door. 'Hey, what's going on?' he asked. 'Are we going to get any food?'

'Don't be impatient,' Charlotte scolded, and handing him a dish of ham said, 'Here, make yourself useful and put this on the table.'

It was a cheerful party, everyone enjoying the food Charlotte had prepared. Margaret had made a christening cake, and Dan, a little nervously at first, proposed a toast to Edie, wishing her a long, happy and healthy life. Charlotte unwrapped the presents that the godparents had brought: a silver teaspoon engraved with Edie's initials from Caroline, a china mug and porringer from Clare and a little silver bracelet from Dan. David and Avril had bought her a prayer book, 'For when she's a bit older,' David said with a smile as he handed it to Charlotte.

The afternoon flew by and all too soon it was time for the Federmans to leave to catch their train. Charlotte hugged them all, as they got into John's car to go to the station.

'Thank you for coming so far for such a short time,' she said, her eyes bright with tears. 'I can't tell you what it means to me.'

'Thank you for asking us, Lisa, me duck,' said Dan as he returned her hug. 'I'm right proud to be young Edie's godfather.' Adding, 'Didn't think it would be allowed, me not being a Christian an' that.'

David overheard him. 'You and Naomi did a truly Christian thing, giving Lisa a loving home when she needed one,' he said. 'That was good enough for me.'

'Oh Billy,' cried Charlotte when they'd gone. 'I'm so glad they came. I just wish they'd been able to stay a little bit longer.'

Charlotte's feelings couldn't have been more different from those who sat round the table for Sunday lunch at the manor. Lunch there was another awkward meal; Daphne couldn't wait to leave and Marjorie couldn't wait for her to go. It was a relief to both women when Fred Jones arrived to drive them to the station.

As Felix gave his mother a hug and kissed her on her cheek, he murmured, 'You do like her, don't you, Ma?'

'Well, I don't know her very well yet,' she replied, 'but she seems charming.'

Felix beamed at her. 'I knew you would. We'll see you at the wedding. Not long now!'

'Well,' he said as he and Daphne settled into a first-class compartment, 'I thought that went very well, didn't you?'

'Your father's an old dear,' Daphne said, 'but your mother isn't sure about me, I could tell. Do you know, I think she thought we were getting married quickly because I was expecting.'

Felix gave a shout of laughter. 'Oh, Daph, she thought no such thing! She knows you're not that sort of girl.'

'And she didn't like not knowing about my family.'

'She was just interested, that's all,' Felix said. 'Anyway, I'm the one that's marrying you, not her, so if it doesn't matter to *me* that your father runs a garage, then it doesn't matter to anyone else.'

At least, Daphne thought as she sat back in her seat and closed her eyes, the nightmare weekend is over and Felix seems happy with how it went, which is the main thing.

She knew Marjorie Bellinger hadn't liked her, but that, Daphne decided, was not her problem. She and Felix would be living in London, and her new in-laws would be safely in the country, out of the way.

The day Felix and Daphne tied the knot dawned white with autumnal mist. There was a chill in the air, but as the sun rose higher the mist burned off and it changed into a warm October morning.

Daphne had invited one of her ex-WAAF colleagues, Joan Archer, to be her witness, and Felix had Toby Squires as his best man. The only other guests were Marjorie and Peter Bellinger. They had arrived in London the night before and stayed at a small hotel in Victoria. They all met in Chelsea just before noon, a rather ill-assorted group, gathered outside the town hall, waiting for Daphne to arrive.

Toby was one of the few survivors of Felix's fighter squadron. Together they had come through the Battle of Britain and continued to fly in defence of the skies over London throughout the war. This survival had cemented their early camaraderie into a strong friendship and though Toby was no longer in the RAF, he and Felix remained close.

Joan Archer had been another aircraft maintenance mechanic, working alongside Daphne during the latter part of the war. Though they were not particularly close friends, and Joan had left the air force, she and Daphne had kept in touch, and Daphne couldn't think of anyone else to ask.

'For goodness' sake,' Felix felt exasperated, 'tell your parents we're getting married. Surely they'll want to be there with you on your big day, won't they?'

'No, Felix,' Daphne snapped. 'I'm not going to tell them, so stop asking.'

Felix sighed. He didn't understand, but he did stop asking.

Daphne and Joan arrived in a cab just as the clock began to strike twelve. She was wearing a slim, buttercup-yellow dress that hugged her figure and a matching hat with a tiny veil that covered her eyes. For a moment she looked at Felix, standing waiting for her, handsome in his uniform, and there was a gleam of triumph in her eyes. When they got out of the taxi, Joan handed Daphne her bouquet of yellow and white roses. She looked stunning, standing there, holding her flowers, her golden hair gleaming in the sunshine, and Felix's heart missed a beat. Then he stepped forward and took her hand and they all went up the steps into the town hall.

The ceremony was short, over so quickly it seemed it had hardly begun before Felix was kissing his bride and the registrar was congratulating Wing Commander and Mrs Felix Bellinger on their marriage and wishing them a long and happy one.

Outside on the steps, Daphne accepted kisses of congratulation from Toby and from Felix's parents. Joan had brought a camera and took pictures of them all, before they flagged down two taxis to take them to the Savoy.

The wedding breakfast, as Marjorie insisted on calling it, was not an easy affair. Toasts were made, health was drunk, but despite the best efforts of the best man and the bride and groom, it didn't seem very celebratory. As soon as it was over, it was with relief that Felix's parents left to go to their hotel to collect their luggage and catch their train.

'I hope you'll be very happy, my boy,' Peter said as he clapped Felix on the shoulder. 'Don't leave it too long before you come down and see us again. I need to chat over some things with you, and your mother so looks forward to your visits.'

'Don't worry, Dad, we'll be down to see you again soon,' Felix promised.

Marjorie gave him a farewell hug. 'Be happy, Felix,' she said. 'That's all we want for you.'

Felix returned her hug. 'Don't worry, Mother, I couldn't be happier than I am today.'

On the day Felix and Daphne got married, Vic Merritt disembarked at Southampton and caught the train to London. It was four years since he'd taken ship for Australia with gangland boss, Denny Duncan; both of them travelling on forged papers and both of them wanted by the police. As Vic watched the countryside flash by he considered his options now that he was back. Hiding in plain sight seemed to be the safest. His papers confirmed his new identity and there was nothing to connect him with Heinrich Schwarz, the Jewish refugee who'd fled from the Nazis on a Kindertransport train in 1939, nor Harry Black, the name he'd assumed on his arrival, by which he was known to the English police.

He had plenty of cash with him now, Denny had seen to that. He was well dressed with no hint he'd ever been anything else, so, he decided, he'd find a good hotel, but nothing flash. Once, long ago, he'd vowed he'd march into the Ritz and the commissionaire would touch his hat in salute, rather than chase him away as he'd done before. That day was still to come; today was not the time.

Denny had sent him back to London with a particular commission. He couldn't return himself for two reasons. Firstly, he was still wanted by the police as an escaped prisoner; but the second, more frightening reason, was that he had just been diagnosed with lung cancer. With about nine months to live, he wanted to see his wife and daughter again before he died, so he'd sent Vic to fetch them.

'You won't be running any risks going back now,' Denny assured him. 'You was only small fry, them rozzers'll have forgotten all about you!'

Vic knew he was probably right, though he rather resented being dismissed as small fry.

'Possible the house is still being watched,' Denny had gone on. 'Unlikely after all this time. Still, you never know, so go careful, Vic. Don't want to blow my whereabouts at this late stage.' Vic was to arrange passports and tickets for Dora and Bella and bring them out to Sydney. However, this wasn't his only commission; he had other business of Denny's to attend to.

Since his escape, Denny's empire had been left in the hands of his second in command, Mick Derham, but although Denny still had some clout on the London scene even in his absence, two opposition firms, those of Grey Maxton and Bull Shadbolt, had begun to move in, gradually taking his business and his territory. There'd been no violent takeover, no turf war, just a gradual eroding of Denny's manor.

One of Denny's old associates, Ricky Mawes, had turned up in Sydney. A small, wiry man with a face like a battered ferret, Ricky was an ex-flyweight boxer who'd made extra money on the side, bare-knuckle fighting. He'd had to leave London in a hurry when he managed to kill one of his opponents.

'Mick got me out,' he told Denny, 'but things is going downhill, there, Denny. Mick ain't strong enough to hold off the likes of Maxton's lot, or Bull Shadbolt.' He hesitated before going on, 'Heard it on the street, Denny, your lady ain't being treated with the respect what she deserves.'

Denny exploded with anger, but there was little he could do from twelve thousand miles away. He'd always hoped to slip back into London unnoticed when the heat was off, but it was still too soon. He had five years of a fifteen-year sentence hanging over him and he had no intention of serving it. He was only fifty-four and he'd already spent enough of his life inside. But now this diagnosis of advanced lung cancer was a different sort of sentence and one he knew he couldn't dodge, so he decided to send Vic to collect his wife and daughter and to deal with Maxton and Shadbolt.

On arriving in London, Vic continued to use his Vic Merritt identity, complete with the safety of a new, legal, Australian passport, but once back in the familiar London streets, he reverted in his head to being Harry. Not Harry the cellar-rat; not Harry the streetwise kid and boss's runner; not Harry the enemy alien arrested by the police; not Harry the black marketeer, but Harry, a combination of all these. A man at ease in his own skin, with a confident grasp on his life and ambitious for his future.

He found himself a comfortable hotel near Charing Cross station and booked himself in for three nights. His business would take much longer than that, but he had learned a lot of things from Denny over the years, and keeping on the move was one of them.

After a good night's sleep, Harry dressed with care and walked out into the autumn sunshine, setting off with confident stride along the Strand. He was not a tall man, but there was something about him that made people move aside to let him pass. Well-dressed in a dark suit, white shirt and navy-blue tie, his boots polished to a mirror shine, he was clearly a man of means. He needed to be taken seriously if he were to complete Denny Dunc's business in London and there must be nothing about him to give a glimpse of the runaway lad, Harry Black.

It was a beautiful morning and he decided to walk a while, to soak up the familiar sights and sounds of London before taking a bus to Maida Vale where Dora Duncan lived. He decided on the anonymity of a bus, a taxi being too noticeable. Dora was not expecting him. No message had been sent. Denny, having heard Ricky Mawes's report of the state of things, didn't trust anyone in London any more, not even Mick Derham. Maybe he'd sold out to Shadbolt or Maxton? A rat deserting a sinking ship? Denny could trust no one but Harry who'd been with him in Australia.

Harry had served time with Denny during the war. In the early days of his sentence, Harry, a young lad tossed into the harsh world of prison, had had to fight his corner, but he was a streetwise kid who'd survived the attentions of the Hitler Youth back in Germany. He fought hard and he fought dirty and proving he could handle himself, he came to the attention of gangland boss, Denny Dunc. Denny, seeing something of his younger self in Harry and recognising his potential, took him in hand. Harry, a quick learner, soon acquired skills from other inmates that would stand him in good stead in the jungle that was post-war London, and ensured he'd be useful to Denny once he was back on the outside. On his release Harry was happy to run some errands for Denny who still languished in gaol with several years of his sentence to run. Despite being inside, Denny's influence was such that he'd had no difficulty organising Harry's new identity. With new papers naming him as Victor Merritt, Harry shucked off his police record, and was able to walk the streets of London freely.

Denny Dunc's escape plan, from prison and from the country, had been meticulously planned. The escape itself was carried out on VE Day when the world was thinking about something else, and once Denny was safely hidden in a run-down area of the docks, he sent Mick Derham to find Harry. Denny was taking ship for Australia, planning to stay there until the heat was off. Harry, unknown to him, had always been part of this plan, he was part of Denny's cover. Despite his reluctance to leave London, he had no choice and as George and Victor Merritt, father and son, they had travelled together on a jobbing merchant ship, the *Maiden Lady*, and had arrived in Sydney some eight weeks later. Now Harry was back.

He took a bus to Maida Vale and walked down the street, Marsh Avenue, where Dora lived with her daughter, Bella. He had no intention of going there until it was dark, but he wanted to see the house and its neighbours in daylight.

Marsh Avenue proved to be a small side street of detached houses, each set back from the road, maintaining its privacy behind a walled front garden. The grey stone wall protecting Dora Duncan's home ran the width of the frontage. It was taller than most with a privet hedge behind and above, shielding it from casual curiosity. Halfway along was wrought-iron gate allowing Harry a glimpse of the house beyond. It looked much like its neighbours, double-fronted, with bay windows, the front door protected by an arched porch. Harry took a quick glance through the gate but kept on walking. Marsh Avenue was empty, basking in the October sunshine; there were no parked cars, no pedestrians, no one sitting in the small public garden at the end of the street. On the corner was a pub, the Blue Anchor, and opposite the garden was a parade of shops. Harry went into the newsagent and bought a newspaper before wandering into the garden. He sat down on a bench in the sunshine and opened his paper. From here he could see the front door of Dora's house. He sat there for nearly half an hour, ostensibly reading his paper and enjoying the autumn sun, then he got to his feet, folded the paper and strolled off in the direction of Kilburn High Road. There had been no sign of interest in Dora's house. Denny had been right. The police had given up hope of him coming home.

Early that evening, Harry took a bus back to Kilburn and walked the few hundred yards to the Blue Anchor. As he waited for it to get dark, he had a pint of bitter, sitting quietly in a corner and listening to the general chat going on round him. He heard nothing to interest him, he hadn't really expected to, but another of Denny's maxims was that you should always take the time to look round a neighbourhood you were interested in.

As the twilight faded to darkness, Harry downed the last of his pint and left. No one showed any interest in him as he walked briskly up Marsh Avenue and let himself in through Dora's front gate. He had been concerned that Dora might not believe he came from her husband, might not even open her front door at night.

'She's never met me, Denny,' he'd said. 'How'll she know I'm legit?'

'Don't worry about that, Vic,' Denny replied. 'We have a password, "Thermometer".'

'Thermometer?' Harry sounded incredulous.

'Yeah, for testing the water, ain't it? Not the sort of thing you say out of the blue. If you say thermometer to her, Dora'll know you come from me.'

He rang the bell and waited in the shadow of the porch. After a moment a light came on over his head. There was a spyhole in the door and Harry realised he was being studied from the inside. He waited and then a man's voice said, 'Who is it?'

'Vic Merritt,' said Harry. 'I have a message for Mrs Duncan.'

There was a moment's silence and then the door opened on its chain, and Harry saw Mick Derham peering at him through the crack.

'Vic Merritt,' Harry said again. 'With a message for Mrs Duncan. Come on, Mick, stop fucking about and let me in.'

Mick's eyes narrowed. He knew the name and now that he could see Harry properly he knew the face. He'd been instrumental in Denny's and Vic's escape from London, but he found it hard to equate this smooth-looking bloke on the doorstep with the scruffy lad who used to be called Harry Black.

'Wait there,' he said and closed the door again.

Feeling very exposed standing in the lighted porch, Harry moved into the shelter of its arch. Moments later there was the rattle of chain and Mick Derham opened the door and allowed Harry to step inside, closing it behind him.

'Stand there,' Mick snapped and with quick rough hands he patted Harry down, searching for weapons. Harry submitted to this without comment. He'd have done the same to anyone who'd arrived unexpectedly on his doorstep, but Mick was inefficient. Satisfied that Harry was unarmed, he failed to find the flick knife tucked into his boot. He was certain now that Harry was who he said he was, the lad Denny had taken a shine to in prison, and Mick's resentment of him was as great now as it had been then. He glared at him and said, 'So, what d'you want with Dora?'

Harry held his gaze and said, 'That's between me and her.'

Mick's cheeks darkened at the rebuke and he turned abruptly to knock on double doors that led off the hall.

'Come in,' said a soft voice from within. Mick stood aside and Harry pushed open the doors and stepped into the room.

A comfortable sitting room, with soft lighting, the curtains drawn across the windows against the night and prying eyes, it was warm with a fire smouldering in the hearth.

Harry didn't know what he'd been expecting, but Dora Duncan was nothing like he'd imagined. For some reason he'd pictured her as thin, with lined cheeks and sparse hair, creeping towards old age, bitterness etched on her face from how life had treated her, left alone for so many years. He couldn't have been more wrong. On a sofa, her feet up on a stool, was a late-middle-aged woman, who, Harry thought, if she stood up would be as wide as she was tall. Her permed hair was carefully styled with no hint of grey in the corrugation of its curls. She stared across at him from a pair of coal-black eyes, regarding him shrewdly as he paused in the doorway. Her gaze noted the well-cut suit, the polished shoes and the brushed trilby hat he held in his hand, taking in every detail.

'Thanks, Mick,' she said dismissively. 'I'll call you if I need you.'

Mick glowered at Harry before accepting his dismissal and leaving the room.

'So,' Dora said once the door was closed, 'you're Harry Black. Denny's told me about you. Done well for yourself, by the looks of you.' She waved a pudgy hand towards an armchair on the other side of the fireplace. 'Sit down.'

Harry sat and waited.

'You been with him in Sydney all the time,' she said – a statement not a question.

Harry nodded. 'That's right.'

'And now you're here.'

'Yes.'

'Denny sent you.' Again a statement.

'Yes.'

'This is like drawing teeth, Harry,' she said in exasperation. 'What did he send you for? What's going on?'

'He gave me a password,' Harry said.

'I don't need a password,' Dora snapped. 'I know fine well who you are. Mick said it was you and I only had to look at his face to see it was true! So, what's going on?'

'He sent me to fetch you, you and Bella.'

'Fetch us?' Dora showed surprise for the first time. 'Fetch us where?'

'To Sydney.'

'To Sydney?' she echoed in astonishment. 'But I don't want to go to Sydney. I thought you was going to tell me he's coming home at last.'

'I'm afraid he ain't coming home again, Dora. Not now, not never.'

Dora stared at him for a moment and then asked flatly, 'Is he dead?'

'No,' Harry shook his head, 'but he's not well.'

'What sort of not well?'

'Lung cancer,' Harry replied. 'He was diagnosed a couple of months ago.'

Dora turned pale but went straight to the point. 'How long's he got?'

'About nine months is their best guess, but I don't think they really know.'

'That's a facer.'

'So, he wants you an' Bella to come out to Sydney and he's sent me to fetch you.'

'We ain't got passports,' Dora said. 'If we apply for them they'll know. They'll find him and put him back inside.'

'Don't worry about passports,' Harry said. 'Denny's given me money to sort them out for you… new names.'

'But how quick? And how do we get there?'

'Once we know your new names,' Harry told her, 'I'll get you booked on the next available ship.'

At that moment the door burst open and a young woman of about nineteen came in. She was tall and slim, her blonde hair, swept back off her forehead in a smooth victory roll, tumbled about her ears in fluid curls, her eyebrows were plucked and pencilled into perfect arcs dark above her sea-green eyes, and her wide, inviting mouth was a glossy crimson. She paused on the threshold, looking Harry up and down.

'Mick said someone had come, Ma. Who is he? What's going on?'

'Bella, this is Harry Black. Went to Australia with your dad.'

Harry stared at her, stunned for a moment, before recalling himself and saying, 'I'm known as Victor Merritt now. I've come to see your mother, to see she's OK and to bring a message from your dad.'

'He's dying,' Dora said. 'Got cancer.'

'Dad has?' whispered Bella, glancing at Harry as if for confirmation.

He nodded. 'I'm afraid so.'

Bella sank into a chair and a sob escaped her as she covered her face with her hands.

'Harry's come to take us to see him,' said her mother.

'In Sydney?'

'Yes. He'll get our passports sorted and then we'll go.'

'I'm sorry to bring such bad news,' Harry said. 'But we'll get you both there as soon as we can.'

'Where're you staying?' Dora asked. 'You need a bed here?'

'No, thanks, Mrs Duncan…'

'Dora.'

'Dora. I'm staying at the Kingswood, near Charing Cross.

I'm better staying there until I've sorted all the things Denny has told me to do. It's anonymous-like, no one interested in why you're there, or when you come and go. But thanks for the offer, it would've been nice.'

For a moment his eyes met Bella's and she blushed at the look she encountered.

A sound from the door made them all turn. Mick was standing in the doorway. None of them had heard him come in. Had he heard what they'd been saying? The news of Denny's cancer? Harry hoped not.

'I got a meet,' he said. 'I'll come by tomorrow or the next day, Dora.' He looked meaningfully at Harry. 'See everything's all right.'

'It will be, Mick,' replied Dora. And with that Mick Derham left the room and left the house.

'He don't live here?' asked Harry.

'Lord, no,' cried Dora. 'But he comes round from time to time, checking up.'

'Checking up?'

'Checking up on business. He makes sure we get our money, Bella and me, but I'm not sure I trust him no more,' Dora said.

'Denny don't trust him, neither,' Harry said. 'What's been going on?'

'Things have been going wrong lately.'

'How wrong and how lately?' asked Harry. He hadn't liked Mick's attitude but had assumed it was because of him.

'It was all right at first. Mick ran Denny's businesses, you know, the usual stuff, clubs, girls, protection, gambling. The money come in the same as usual. Everyone thought Denny'd be back soon, but it's been too long now and he ain't the boss no more. Mick's no use. No backbone. When the Orion burned down...'

'Orion?'

'A nightclub Denny owns… or rather owned. Legit business, that was. Anyhow, it burned down crack of dawn one day last month. No one in it, so no one hurt, but the premises gone. Fire brigade called it in as arson. Police suspected us. Word went round that we'd torched it ourselves and so there weren't no insurance money. We was all pretty sure it was down to Shadbolt, but no one's talking. He wouldn't've risked it, not if Denny'd been here, but Mick, Mick's a pushover.

'Then there's been trouble with some of those we protect, and money going missing from the bookies' runners.'

'But hasn't Mick dealt with that? That's basic enforcement, that is. Shouldn't be standing for nonsense like that!'

'Think it's Bull Shadbolt behind all of it,' Dora said, 'and Mick isn't strong enough to take him on. Denny wouldn't have stood for it, that's for sure.'

'Think he's on Shadbolt's payroll now?'

Dora shrugged. 'Could be, wouldn't surprise me. His or Maxton's.'

'Hmm,' said Harry. 'I'll keep an eye.' It was the kind of thing they'd been hearing back in Sydney, though the news of the Orion fire had yet to reach them. It's what he'd been sent to sort out.

'Tell me about Dad,' Bella said suddenly. 'Tell me about him in Australia. I haven't seen him for years. I was a kid when he was arrested and Ma wouldn't let me go into the prison to see him there.'

'Yes,' agreed Dora, keen to change the subject until she could discuss what was going on with Harry in private. 'What happened when you got to Sydney? Den's sent me occasional letters, sent from all over the place. Take months to get to me, some of them do, but he's not much of a letter writer, so I don't know about his life over there.'

'Well, when we landed he made contact with a bloke called Bernie Welbeck; said he owed him cos he'd helped him get out of London in a hurry some years ago. Denny said Welbeck had known we was coming, but not our new names and not when. Didn't trust him. When I asked him why not he said, "Vic, I don't trust no one, son. And nor should you."'

'That Welbeck help you?' Dora asked. 'I remember him, slimy bastard. Den was right not to trust him.'

'Yeah, you're right there,' Harry agreed. 'Denny called in the favour, he let us in on a few bits of business, and Denny took it from there. Had to sort Welbeck out once things got going. Tried to play two ends off against the middle. Never pays, that. Still, Denny eased his way in and gradually built his business up. Took on Mawes, a boxer he'd known in London as an enforcer, collecting payment from some of the small businesses who were under his protection.' Harry smiled at Dora. 'Nothing big, just enough to keep him in the readies. Doing OK, your Denny is.'

'And you, too.'

Harry grinned. 'I'm his right hand. He knows he can trust me.'

Denny had grown his business slowly, with a few illegal grog shops, a string of working girls and an illegal betting ring, but he'd been careful not to tread on too many toes.

'Too old to start any aggro out here,' he said to Harry. 'Too old and too tired.'

Harry could see that there was something wrong with Denny, he was beginning to lose his touch, and with an eye to the future, Harry found himself a lieutenant; one Monty Redfern. Redfern had flown with the Australian air force during the war, and on returning to civilian life, found it decidedly dull. A large, pugnacious man with a lived-in face, he was the sort who tended to hit first and ask questions after. Harry had met him in a backstreet bar on the wrong end of a broken bottle, but once that little matter had been sorted out, ending with Monty on the wrong end of the bottle, they came to an agreement which suited them both. Monty joined the firm; Denny and Harry supplied the brains, Monty supplied the brawn and they all made money.

When Harry had returned to London to collect Dora and Bella, he'd left Monty to keep an eye on the failing Denny.

'No funny business,' he'd warned Redfern, 'and you and me'll have a future. Anything happens to Denny, you'd better make sure I never find you. Capeesh?'

Harry spent another hour with Dora and Bella before slipping out into the night. He had told them what they needed to know about Denny and they were eager to travel to Australia to see him.

'Sit tight,' Harry said as he left. 'Don't trust no one, particularly Mick, and don't tell no one else that I'm here nor that Denny's ill. We don't know if Mick heard me tell you about his cancer, but if he didn't, the longer he don't know nothing about it, the better, cos I've got some other business to see to before we go. OK?'

'Don't you worry, Harry,' Dora said. 'I haven't survived as Denny's wife without knowing how to keep my mouth shut.' And Harry believed her.

When Harry had gone and Bella had locked and bolted the door behind him, she went back into the sitting room.

'Well,' she said as she dropped into the armchair Harry had just vacated. 'What do you think of him, Mum? Can we trust him?'

'I think we have to, Bella, pet. There's no one else and we need to get to your dad as quick as we can.'

'Yeah, but what I mean is, d'you think Dad really is ill?'

'Yeah, I think so,' said her mother quietly. 'I don't think there's any point in Harry making that up. Your dad sent him to get us, so we'll have to go.'

'But we'll come back.' Bella sounded uncertain.

Dora shook her head. 'I doubt it, pet. Once we're there, we're there. There won't be nothing left for us here. One way or another Maxton and Shadbolt'll take us over and that'll be it. Reckon that toerag Derham has already jumped ship, so remember what Harry just said, not a word to him or anybody else about our plans.'

'So we're going to live in Australia for ever,' Bella said.

'Reckon so.'

'And that Harry'll be living there too?'

'Probably.'

'An' he'll look after us when Dad dies?'

Dora winced at Bella's casual acceptance of her father's death sentence, but remembering that Bella hadn't seen her father for over ten years, she simply said, 'I expect so.'

Bella smiled. 'Well, that'll be all right then,' she said. 'He's a good-looking bloke, don't you think?'

Chapter 6

When Harry left Dora and Bella, he returned to his hotel and made his plans for the next few days. The first thing he had to do was to find Freddie, the forger who had produced passports and other necessary documents for himself and Denny. Freddie's work was first class, as had been proved when their papers had allowed them easy access into Australia. There had been no suggestion at any time that they weren't genuine, even when Harry had used his to apply for an Australian passport.

Freddie could usually be found at the Crooked Billet on the Isle of Dogs. He had a photography studio nearby, where he carried on his creative trade. Harry had been there before, but decided to approach Freddie in the pub in case things had changed in the last four years, in case he, or the studio, were compromised. That meant he couldn't see Freddie, at the earliest, until the following evening.

He also had to set up a meeting with Maxton and Shadbolt. He had definite instructions from Denny about his approach to them and he would need to tread carefully. He would make his move with them only once the passports were delivered, so that nothing could prevent Dora and Bella from leaving the country.

This left Harry free to follow an agenda of his own, and the next morning, he'd begin looking for Lisa.

She was special, Lisa was. She and Harry had come from the same town, Hanau, near Frankfurt. They hadn't known each other there, but they'd been on the same Kindertransport train that brought them safely out of Nazi Germany in 1939. Despite the fact that she was a refugee from Hitler, Lisa was still German and when war was declared, she'd had a tough time at school. One afternoon, Harry saw her backed into a corner, surrounded by Roger Davis and his cronies, and decided to step in. He despatched the bullies, and he was soon recognised as her protector and the bullying stopped. They became friends, but the bond between them ran deeper than simple friendship. As Jews they'd both suffered the horrors of Nazi persecution and each understood what no one else could unless they'd been there: the horror of living in Hitler's Germany. They had so much in common: loss of family, loss of home, loss of everything familiar. Lisa had clung to the desperate hope that her family were still alive and one day they would all be reunited, but Harry dismissed this as a vain hope. He was far more pragmatic about their situation; determined to leave his past behind him and carve himself a new life in this new country.

'We got to make our own lives now,' he'd said. 'I learned that the hard way. Got to look after number one. We ain't kids no more. So, we get on with it.'

It was four years since Harry had last seen her and he had no idea where she might be now, but he was determined to find her, and the obvious place to start was the place she'd been working then, the Livingston Road children's home.

Four years ago, on VE Day, they'd been among the crowds out celebrating in London, and when he'd taken her back to Livingston House he'd promised her he'd come back next day, but Denny Dunc had intervened. His plans for them to sail for Australia had prevented Harry from keeping his promise. When Harry had protested that he must visit Lisa before they left, there had been veiled threats with regard to her safety, a suggestion that Mick Derham might pay her a visit, and Harry had quickly backed off. He wanted Mick Derham nowhere near Lisa.

As Harry stepped out of his hotel and headed for Livingston Road, a nondescript young man in workman's clothes who'd been waiting at a bus stop opposite seemed to give up on his bus. He folded the newspaper he'd been reading while he waited and drifted off along the street, wandering aimlessly behind Harry. Hound, as he was known to his friends, had long ago learned to work as a tail, reporting back to whoever had employed him on where the mark went and what he did. He was the best in the business, or so Mick Derham thought. As soon as Harry had appeared at Dora's that first evening, Mick had realised that there were plans afoot of which he knew nothing. He went hotfoot to Rat Ratcliffe to warn him something was going on, and the Hound had been employed.

Unaware of his shadow, Harry took a bus that dropped him at the end of Livingston Road. As he walked along the street looking at the houses on either side, he thought how grey and depressing post-war London looked, so different from the buzz and optimism of life in Sydney. The houses huddled together wearily as if for support, surviving the Blitz but patched and mended and tired.

The children's home, when he reached it, looked exactly as when he'd seen it on VE Day: a rather forbidding three-storey stone house, set back from the road behind a grey stone wall. A flight of steps from an overgrown patch of garden led up to a heavy front door in dire need of a coat of paint and the whole house looked ill-kept and shabby.

Harry paused at the gate for a moment, wondering if the Morrison woman, who'd been in charge of the place, would still be there. Well, now was the time to find out. He'd had a run-in with her about Lisa before and if necessary he was ready to do battle again. He pushed open the gate, marched up the steps and rang the bell. It took a while for someone to come to the door, but when it opened Harry found himself facing a small, dark-haired woman of about thirty. She wore a harassed expression and had tired brown eyes that looked at Harry expectantly.

'Yes?' Her tone abrupt. 'Can I help you?'

'Good morning, madam—' Harry began, but the woman interrupted him.

'I'm sorry,' she said, 'we don't buy at the door.'

'That's all right then,' said Harry cheerfully, 'cos I'm not selling anything. I was hoping to catch up with someone who works here, an old friend, Lisa, Lisa Becker.'

The woman shook her head. 'Sorry,' she said. 'There's no one works here called Lisa anything, I'm afraid.'

'Come to think of it,' said Harry, who hadn't thought of it before, 'I think when she came to work here she was called Charlotte.'

'Was she?' The woman looked a little sceptical. 'Well, we haven't got anyone called Charlotte here, either. Sorry.' She made a move to shut the door and Harry put a hand out to stay her. 'She was working here during the war.'

'Was she? Well, that was years ago, and I'm afraid she's not here now.'

There was nothing for it, Harry was going to have to talk to Miss Morrison if he was going to discover Lisa's whereabouts. He knew she didn't like or trust him, but it was the only chance he had.

'Is Miss Morrison here today?' he asked. 'Miss Caroline Morrison? Could I have a word with her?'

'No, I'm afraid not.'

'When will she be? Will she be here tomorrow?'

'Miss Morrison has resigned as superintendent and has left to get married,' stated the woman firmly. 'My name is Audrey Acton and I am superintendent here now.'

'Oh, I see.' Harry felt deflated. 'Is there anyone else who was here during the war? Anyone who might remember Lisa, I mean Charlotte?'

'Look, I'm very sorry Mr...'

'Black, Harry Black.'

'Mr Black, but I really can't let you in to go interrogating my staff about some girl who might have worked here during the war.'

'She certainly did work here for almost three years. If I could just ask someone who was here too, if they know where she is now...'

'I'm afraid that's impossible, Mr Black,' said Mrs Acton firmly. 'Good morning to you.' And with that she closed the front door, leaving Harry standing fuming on the doorstep. He thought of ringing the bell again, but knew that the door would not be reopened to him. He turned and walked slowly down the steps, thinking hard. Would it be worth lying in wait in the street, hoping to catch one of the staff as she came out for some reason? Or wait for the children to come home from school and try asking one of them? Reluctantly, he decided that neither was a good idea. Either course of action might lead to Mrs Acton summoning the police, and his mission for Denny Dunc was too important to risk being arrested for making a nuisance of himself at a London children's home. He'd have to think of some other way of finding Lisa.

What about those foster parents of Lisa's, who'd lived in Kemble Street? he wondered.

When they'd been bombed out, Harry had appropriated their cellar to store his black-market goods. What was their name? Freeman? Freidman? It would come to him. If he could find them again, they'd be sure to know where Lisa was. Where had they gone? Somewhere in Suffolk, Harry was sure, but where in Suffolk he'd never bothered to find out. It hadn't been important, then. Still, Kemble Street was a lead. He could go back there and see if the foster parents... Federman... that was it, Dan and Naomi Federman... see if they'd returned after the war, and if not, whether any of their neighbours knew where to find them.

Harry glanced at his watch. He had time enough to go to Kemble Street before searching out Freddie. There might be someone there who could help him. With one final glance at the closed front door of Livingston Road children's home, and the wry thought that it was the second time that a superintendent had virtually pushed him back out into the road, he set off for Shoreditch.

From one of the front windows of the home, Audrey Acton watched him go. She'd called Matron down as soon as she'd shut the door.

'D'you know that man?' she asked. 'The one just going out of the gate?'

Chloe Burton had been matron ever since she, Caroline and Mary Downs, the cook, had been bombed out of St Michael's, the children's home where they'd worked before. She was a small, sturdy woman with piercing blue eyes, the sort of eyes the children in her care were sure could see round corners and never missed dirt behind the ears or under the fingernails. Her iron-grey hair was cut short, tucked behind her ears, making her look sterner than she really was. She loved her charges dearly, but she stood no nonsense from any of them. Now she peered out of the window at the man's half-turned face and shook her head.

'I don't think so,' she said. 'What did he want?'

'He wanted to find someone called Lisa who'd worked here during the war. Then he changed his mind and said her name was Charlotte. It all seemed very odd to me. When I said there was no Lisa or Charlotte working here, he asked to speak to Miss Morrison.'

'Did he indeed?' Matron said sharply. 'Did he tell you his name, by any chance?'

'Black,' replied Mrs Acton. 'Harry Black. I told him Miss Morrison had left to get married and I sent him away.'

'Harry Black,' repeated Matron. 'Well, I'm glad you got rid of him. He's always caused trouble. He and Lisa were both German refugees, but he was a scamp. Caroline didn't trust him as far as she could throw him. She thought he had some hold over Lisa, but wasn't quite sure exactly what. She sent him away one evening, but he said he needed to talk to Lisa and he'd be back in the morning. Lisa was her German name, we knew her as Charlotte.'

'This all sounds very confusing,' said Mrs Acton, shaking her head.

'It's a long story,' Matron agreed. 'Suffice it to say, he didn't turn up. Charlotte was very upset, it was the second time he'd promised to come and see her and then disappeared. We were all pleased. She was better off without him. Anyhow, he seemed to vanish into thin air, and we all thought good riddance; even Charlotte herself after a while. She's happily married now, with two lovely kiddies. We certainly don't want that Harry Black to reappear and rock the boat.'

'No, I see that,' said Mrs Acton thoughtfully. 'Well, he'll learn nothing of her from anyone here, will he?'

'No, he won't,' agreed Matron, while thinking privately that if Harry ran true to form, he wouldn't give up so easily.

When the children were in bed that evening, she sat in her work room and wrote to Caroline, care of St Mark's Vicarage, Wynsdown, to warn her that Harry was back and looking for Charlotte.

Harry, meanwhile, still unaware of his shadow, caught the bus to Shoreditch High Street, from where he walked to Kemble Street. It was almost unrecognisable as the street where the Federmans had lived and where he had inhabited their cellar for several months before he'd been arrested as a black marketeer. Most of the houses along the right-hand side were still habitable, though many had roofs patched with corrugated iron and the occasional window was still boarded up, awaiting new glass.

How could all the repairs take so long? Harry wondered as he walked down the road. The war had ended four years ago; surely people must have been able to rebuild their homes by now.

The opposite side of the road, where the Federmans' house had been, was a building site. The terrace of houses that stood there from Victorian times was gone. Destroyed by fire in the Blitz, their blackened remains had now been razed to the ground, and in their place a block of flats was being constructed, rising to four storeys. Blank-faced, built of yellow London brick, they were ugly, utilitarian, towering over the rest of the street, but they would provide homes for twice as many families as the earlier terrace had done, and Harry realised that housing must be at a premium since the end of the war. Something Denny might have taken an interest in,

Harry thought, had he been here to see the opportunities. He'd bear that in mind when he finally got to talk to Maxton and Shadbolt.

He stood for a moment and looked up at the half-finished building and wondered if the Federmans were planning to come back to live in one of the flats when they were finished.

'If you're looking for one of them places, you'll have to be quick cos they're nearly all took,' said a voice behind him. He turned round to find a woman standing on the step of the house opposite.

'Aren't they going to be for the people who lived here before?' Harry asked innocently. 'I mean,' he added, 'don't they get first chance to have one?'

'No, all owned by one landlord, then rented out. First come first served.' She looked at Harry speculatively and asked, 'So you ain't looking to rent one, then?'

'No.' Harry smiled. 'I'm Australian,' he improvised. 'I've just come round here to see if I can find a relative that used to live in this street. Cousin of my mother's, she is, but Ma lost touch with her during the war and hasn't heard from her since. I was over here on business and Ma asked me to look her up.'

'Oh?' The woman looked interested. 'An' who was that then?'

'She's called Naomi Federman,' said Harry. 'Ma's afraid something might have happened to her during the Blitz.'

'Naomi? She went to live in the country when they was burned out.'

'You know her then?' Harry treated the woman to his most charming smile. 'D'you know where she is now?'

'I know where she was,' replied the woman, 'but I don't know if she's still there.'

'Well, perhaps you could tell me that, then even if she's moved on maybe I could track her down.'

For a moment the woman eyed him suspiciously. 'I've known Naomi Federman since we was children,' she said. 'I don't remember she had a cousin in Australia. What's your name, young man?'

'Victor Merritt,' answered Harry. 'You probably never heard of my ma. Her family moved to Australia just after the war, the Great War that is. She'll be thrilled when I tell her that Cousin Naomi is alive and well.' He paused, hoping that the neighbour, whoever she was, would now supply the information he was looking for.

The woman studied him for a moment and then said, 'She moved out to a village in Suffolk. Place called Feneton. Got a live-in job at the local pub, but as I said I ain't seen her for years, so I don't know if she's still there.'

'Well, that's very helpful... Mrs?'

'Newman, Shirley Newman.'

'Thank you, Mrs Newman, you've been a great help. Shall I give your good wishes to Cousin Naomi if I catch up with her?'

'You can, I s'pose,' Shirley said, 'if you find her.'

'I didn't know whether to tell him or not,' Shirley said to her husband Derek when he got home later. 'Him being a complete stranger. Only last time, when that girl Lisa came looking for them and I didn't tell her where they was, that Naomi gave me a right mouthful!'

'I'm sure you did the right thing,' said Derek with a yawn. 'Any tea on the go?'

Harry was delighted with the information Shirley had given him. As soon as he heard they'd gone to a village called Feneton, he remembered the name. Lisa had traced them there when she'd come back to London after the Blitz. Now he had something to go on; if he could find Naomi and Dan Federman, he could find Lisa. He'd follow it up as soon as he'd got all the other business sorted.

He caught a bus back to his hotel and got ready to go to the Crooked Billet in the hope of finding Freddie, the forger. When he reached the pub, he sat in a corner nursing his pint as he watched and listened to the comings and goings in the bar. Other people came in – a young couple took their drinks to another corner table and sat whispering together, an elderly man with a dog on a lead took a place by the fire, a bloke in overalls who bought a half of mild and propped himself up on the bar and chatted to the barmaid – but there was no sign of Freddie. Harry was beginning to think he would have to try the studio after all, when the door opened and Freddie slouched in. Harry recognised him at once. He was a thin man. Everything about him was thin: his pointed nose, his chin, his faded fair hair, his whole body. If you turned him sideways, Harry thought as he studied him standing at the bar, you wouldn't be able to see him!

Harry had remembered that Freddie was skinny, but he hadn't remembered him being little more than skin and bone, skeletal wrists and bony hands poking out from his sleeves and his head no more than a skull perched atop a scrawny neck.

He's dying, Harry realised as he took in the man's grey colour and protuberant eyes. Wonder if he's up to the job? And who the hell am I going to get to do it if he ain't? Who could I trust?

As these thoughts skittered through his mind, he knew he must find out for sure. Swallowing the last of his beer, he went up to the bar for a refill. He pushed his glass over to the barmaid and then, turning casually to Freddie who had already downed half his whisky, he said, 'Get you another one of those, Freddie?' Without waiting for a reply he said to the barmaid, 'And the same again for my friend.'

Freddie look up, fear in his eyes. 'Who're you?'

'Vic Merritt,' replied Harry with a smile. 'You did a bit of work for me and my dad, George, a few years back. Remember that, do you?'

'Never heard of you,' Freddie said, glancing anxiously over Harry's shoulder as if to see if anyone were watching.

'Let me buy you a drink, Freddie, and then we can go to my table over there,' he nodded at the corner, 'where we won't be overheard, and I can remind you all about my dad, George.'

Harry hadn't sounded menacing, but there was something in his expression that made Freddie decide it would probably be wise to do as he was asked. He picked up his glass and downed the rest of his whisky before picking up the refill and following Harry to his table.

'Not looking too well, Freddie,' Harry remarked as he sat down. He raised his glass and said, 'Good health.'

Freddie took a mouthful of his drink and then put the glass down on the table.

'What do you want?' he asked wearily.

'You do remember who I am… and who I work for?'

'Never forget a job I done,' Freddie said.

'Good. Well, now that we understand each other, Freddie, I got another little job for you.'

'I'm retired,' Freddie replied flatly. 'I don't do that stuff no more.'

'Retired?' Harry sounded surprised. 'Why've you retired, Freddie? You had a nice little business going.'

'I'm retired because I'm ill,' said Freddie.

'Well, I must say you don't look too special, Fred,' Harry agreed cheerfully. 'Still, I'm sure you can manage just one more job before you kick the bucket.'

'No, told you, I'm retired. I don't do that stuff no more.'

'That's bad news, Freddie. Really bad news. Thing is, you see, we got to get this job done and my dad, George, he wants you, and only you, to do it.'

'He can't have me,' said Freddie, his eyes swivelling with fear. 'He can't have me no more. I don't work freelance no more.'

Harry looked at him through narrowing eyes. 'Who's took you over, Fred? Shadbolt or Maxton?'

At the mention of the two names Freddie turned even paler and tears started in his eyes. 'I can't do it, Vic,' he whispered. ''S more than my life's worth.'

Harry looked at him in surprise. 'Your life? Want to spend the last months of your life in gaol, do you?' he asked. 'Want the cops tipped off about you and your boyfriend, do you? Know what they do to nancy boys in prison, don't you, Freddie? Be a pity if that happened to you simply because you couldn't help out an old friend one more time. Think about it, Freddie, before you finally decide.'

Freddie gulped the rest of his whisky down in one huge swallow, his whole body rigid with fear.

'I'll get you another one of those, Freddie, while you think about it. You look as if you need it.'

When Harry returned from the bar he set another whisky down in front of the terrified Freddie. 'Now, look here, Freddie, you don't have to worry about Grey Maxton and Bull Shadbolt, I'm here to sort them out. Which was it, by the way?'

'Shadbolt,' whispered Freddie.

'Forget about Shadbolt for now, Freddie. What you have to do is take this little job I got for you, and then you'll have no trouble with any of us no more and you can go home to your friend Eric and die in peace. All right?'

Dumbly, Freddie nodded. He didn't believe Vic could deal with big boys like Bull Shadbolt, but he had no choice. Whichever way he decided, he knew he was in the shit. Bull Shadbolt's minder, Rat Ratcliffe, had been round and told him that from now on, Bull wanted both names of everyone Freddie did an ID job for, old name and new name. He also wanted 25 per cent of whatever Freddie was paid.

'That way,' Rat had explained, 'you won't be troubled by the rozzers, or anyone trying to muscle in on your business. You… and your friend,' he gave a sly wink, 'will be under Bull's particular protection, see? Best thing all round, wouldn't you say?'

Freddie wouldn't say, no, but there was nothing he could do about it if he wanted to protect Eric and himself. He did, very much; and now Vic's threat was the more immediate.

'What's the job, then?' he asked wearily.

'It's a very private one,' Harry said, his eyes holding Freddie until the little man looked away. 'I hope you understand that, Freddie, cos as you know, my dad George can be real mean if he thinks someone's double-crossing him. Know what I mean?'

When Freddie didn't answer, Harry said again, 'Know what I mean?'

At last Freddie nodded.

'Right,' said Harry. 'Here's the deal. He needs new papers for his missus and daughter. OK? The works, like you did for him and me. Them papers, Freddie, was first class. He wants the same for his ladies.'

Freddie was about to speak but Harry raised his hand. 'And he will pay you, Freddie. He will pay you a grand.'

Freddie's eyes flew to Harry's face. A thousand pounds was more than he could have dreamed of. Ever. He and Eric could disappear. They'd get out of London; could go to the seaside. With that much money they could live in comfort for what he knew and accepted were the last few months of his life. And when he died, Eric would not be left penniless. For a thousand pounds it was worth the risk, and with any luck at all, he could be up and gone before the Bull or the Rat knew he'd done one final job for Denny Dunc.

'You're on,' he said. 'But I want half up front.'

'Don't think you're in a position to make demands, Fred,' Harry told him. 'Still, as you've always done good work for Denny, you can have a ton up front, but we need them papers yesterday, so get your arse in gear.'

A hundred pounds was less than he'd hoped, but even with that safely in his pocket he had a chance to make a break for it.

'They'll have to come round my studio, same as you did,' Freddie said. 'You know where, and they'd better come after dark. Bring them tomorrow, when the pubs is closed.'

'You better make sure you've got everything ready, Freddie,' Harry warned, 'because they ain't coming there twice.'

'I will,' promised Freddie, feeling happier than he'd felt since the Rat's visit. 'If there's any problem, the outside light will be on. Make yourself scarce. If it's off, you can bring them on in... with the money, Vic. You won't forget that, will you?'

'A hundred up front, the rest when you deliver the goods,' Harry agreed. Then he got up and was about to leave when he turned back and, leaning across the table, spoke softly.

'If Mick Derham comes sniffing around, he won't be coming from me, right? Whatever he says, tell him nothing, Denny's orders, or the deal's off and you're on your own. Capeesh?'

Then with a nod to the barmaid, he made for the door and walked out into the night. He'd been there too long for comfort, but he'd got the job agreed, and with the promise of enough cash to last him out, he was pretty sure he'd secured Freddie's silence. He had a list of things to discuss with both Shadbolt and Maxton, and now Freddie was one of them. All he had to do now, was to deal with them. He set off back to his hotel, Hound drifting along behind him. It had been a long day for both of them.

Chapter 7

When Harry returned to Marsh Avenue the next morning, it was Bella who opened the door to him, and he felt a stirring in his loins as he saw her again, her beautiful face and her luscious figure only partially concealed by the pink and orange wrap she was wearing.

'Hallo, Harry,' she said, her husky voice seemingly an invitation to some sort of intimacy. 'You're an early bird.' She indicated her informal attire and then smiled. 'We wasn't expecting you so soon. You'd better come in. Ma'll be down in a minute.' She looked at him with innocent eyes and said, 'Can I offer you anything?' adding after a pause, 'A cup of tea? Some breakfast?'

Harry grinned at her. 'Nothing… at the moment.'

She led him into the sitting room and said, 'Make yourself at home, Harry. I'll just go and get dressed.'

Harry sat down and waited. Moments later Dora appeared. She looked a little flustered. 'You're very early, Harry. What's up?'

'I seen the bloke about your papers and I've persuaded him to get on with the job right away. Thing is, he needs photos for the passports an' that. So I got to take you to his studio down the Isle of Dogs so's he can take them. We're going tonight, after the pubs shut.'

Dora shook her head. 'No, we ain't,' she said firmly.

'Me and Bella ain't going anywhere near the Isle of Dogs at night. You get the bloke up here.'

Harry scratched his head. 'Not sure he can do the necessary up here.'

'He did it for Denny, he can do it for us.'

'Did it for Denny?' Harry sounded puzzled. 'You mean he came to the house?'

'No, not this house, Den couldn't come back here once he was out, could he? No, he went to the safe house and done the pictures there.'

'What safe house? The one we was in before we went to Australia?'

Dora shrugged. 'Don't know where it was, do I? Just know the bloke went to Denny and took his picture.'

'An' you want him to come here, do you? To this house?'

'Safer all round,' Dora insisted. 'We're safe enough in our own place.'

'You being threatened?' asked Harry.

'Not directly, no. But we ain't going to take no risks either. You just go and fetch him here, Harry boy.'

Harry thought for a moment; he had been trying to work out the best way to take Denny's wife and daughter safely to Freddie's studio and so far had not come up with anything. Now, he thought about what she'd said. If Freddie came to them under cover of darkness, he could do the job with no one the wiser.

'OK,' he said. 'I'll go down tonight as arranged and pick him up. Bring him back here. But it won't be till late. We got a cabby on the firm?'

'No, but Den's car's in the garage. You can take that.'

'You've still got his car?' Harry was incredulous.

'Course we have,' replied Dora. 'How d'you think we get about?'

'Drive yourself, do you?'

'No, I can't drive, but Mick takes us to where we want to go.'

'Ah! Mick!' said Harry thoughtfully. 'You haven't said anything to him, have you? About going to Sydney, an' that?'

'I wasn't born yesterday, Harry! Course I haven't. He come in yesterday, fishing about you and what you was doing here—'

'An' what did you tell him?' interrupted Harry.

'Nothing, Harry. I told him nothing. Just said you'd brought messages from Denny. He asked what messages and I said they was private ones, just for me and Bella.'

'Who's talking about me?' demanded Bella as she came into the room. She was dressed now, her hair smooth and shining, her make-up perfect. She gave Harry a coy smile as she dropped into the chair next to his.

'No one,' said her mother. 'I was just telling Harry that he could borrow your dad's car.'

'Ooh! Where's he going?' Bella beamed across at him. 'Can I come with you?'

'No,' said Dora before Harry could answer, 'he's on an errand for me.'

Bella looked mutinous. 'Where? Where's he going?'

'Never you mind,' snapped her mother. 'But he'll be back later this evening to have a drink with us. Then he'll tell you where he's been.'

Harry's mind had been whirring ever since Dora had mentioned the car. Use of a car was just what he needed; not just on Denny's business, though it would be useful for that, but giving him the freedom to follow his own plans. He could drive to Feneton in Suffolk and try to find the Federmans; maybe find Lisa there, or at least ask them where she lived now. If they gave him her address he could go and see her.

'Let's have a look at the car then,' he said, getting to his feet. 'Got petrol in it, has it?'

'Yes, Mick took the coupons and filled it up last time. We got more if you need them.'

'What'll Mick say when he sees the car is missing?' he said as they went through the inner door to the garage.

'You leave Mick to me,' Dora said. 'We'll open the garage after it gets dark, so you can drive straight in when you get back tonight. Come in through the kitchen. That way no one won't see who's here.'

Harry left Marsh Avenue at the wheel of the smart black Rover that had been in the garage since before Denny had been sent down the last time. It had been used only when Dora needed to be driven somewhere, but it was polished and cared for and started first touch of the self-starter; the engine purring gently as he backed it out into the street. He watched as Bella closed the doors behind him, and then drove away, delighted to have his own set of wheels. He had business of his own to pursue.

Mrs Burton at Livingston House had indeed been right. Harry wasn't going to give up any chance of finding Lisa, and now he had the time and the means, thanks to Shirley Newman and Dora Duncan, to follow the trail to Feneton.

He stopped outside a newsagent in the nearby parade of shops and bought himself a motoring map.

'Ooh! Lucky you to have some petrol!' said the girl who served him. 'Wish I could go for a spin!'

Harry grinned at her and said, 'Been saving them for a special occasion, haven't I? Going to see my girl.'

'Lucky girl,' replied the assistant wistfully as she watched him go back out to the car.

He sat in the driver's seat and studied the map. There it was, Feneton, just over the Suffolk border. It didn't look very far; he should have plenty of time to get there and back.

It was well over an hour later that he drove into the village. He pulled up outside the Feneton Arms and went inside. The pub had just opened and the bar was empty. At the sound of the door a buxom woman came out of the kitchen and greeted him with a smile.

'Hallo,' she said. 'What can I get you?'

Harry ordered a half of bitter and perched himself on a bar stool.

'Just passing through, are you?' asked the barmaid.

'Sort of,' Harry said with a smile. 'Trying to catch up with a relative of my mother's.' He'd decided to stick to the story he'd told Shirley Newman; it sounded sincere and it couldn't be disproved, at least, not until he found the Federmans. 'I heard she used to work here and I was hoping she might still be around.'

'Work here? At the pub, you mean?'

'Yes. A Mrs Shirley Newman said she moved here in the war.' He retold the story he'd spun to Shirley. 'Naomi Federman's her name. Do you know her? I think her husband's called Dan.'

The barmaid's face broke into a smile. 'Of course I know them. They've just moved into a cottage on the edge of the village. Ivy Cottage, it's called. You'll find it out on the Ipswich road. First house after the church, you can't miss it. How exciting to get a visit from someone all the way from Australia!'

Harry finished his beer, stood up and said with a smile, 'Thank you very much, Mrs...?'

'Dow, Jenny Dow. I hope you find her, she'll be so pleased to see you.'

When Harry reached Ivy Cottage he parked the car and walked through a neatly kept garden to the front door. Through an open window he could hear music, a wireless playing and the sound of somebody singing. Harry raised the knocker and gave a couple of sharp taps. The singing stopped and moments later Naomi Federman appeared at the door, her hands covered in flour. She looked at Harry without recognition, but Harry knew her at once.

'Mrs Federman?' he asked with a smile.

'Yes? Who are you?'

'You won't remember me, but my name's Harry Black and I'm a friend of Lisa's.' He saw recognition of his name flash across her face and he held out his hand. 'You and your husband were kind enough to offer me a bed one night during the war when I had nowhere else to go.'

'Yes,' agreed Naomi, instinctively wiping her floury hands on her apron before shaking the proffered hand. 'Yes, I remember.'

'The thing is,' went on Harry, 'I've been away, in Australia since the war, and I've lost track of Lisa. I wondered if you could tell me where she is.'

Naomi gave him a hard look and then stood aside. 'You'd better come in,' she said.

Harry followed her into the house and she led the way into the kitchen where there was a mouth-watering smell of baking. 'I'm sorry to bring you in here,' she said as she returned to rolling out pastry on the kitchen table, 'but as you can see, I'm baking. I make pies for the pub and cakes for the café in the village. So sit down while I finish these and get them into the oven and then I'll make a cup of tea and we can have a chat.'

Harry sat down in the chair she indicated and watched as she lined and filled four pie dishes before sealing them with the another layer of pastry. It wasn't long before they were safely in the oven and she'd put the kettle on.

If Naomi were honest with herself, she hoped to keep him there until Dan got home. She didn't know whether she ought to tell this Harry where Lisa was living; that she was married, that she had children. She remembered the look on Billy's face when Dan had asked Lisa if she'd heard from Harry. She didn't want to make things difficult for Lisa, which, she decided, they would be if Harry turned up in Wynsdown unexpectedly.

'So, you've been in Australia,' she said as she sat down opposite him and poured the tea. 'How very exciting! Is it as big as they say, just miles and miles of empty country?'

'It's certainly a big country, but I haven't been far outside Sydney. That's a beautiful city, for sure. The harbour's huge and you can go to lots of places by boat. There's ferries going every which way.'

'Bit different from London, I expect,' Naomi said, 'still recovering from the Blitz. You should see Kemble Street.'

'I have,' replied Harry. 'I went there to find you.'

'They've pulled down our house,' Naomi said sadly. 'Building a block of flats, they are. We went to have a look, but it weren't the same; we haven't been back since. Our life is up here now. Our son's at the village school and Dan works at the RAF base.'

'I met a woman there, Shirley Newman,' Harry said. 'It was her told me where to find you.'

'Oh, Shirley,' was all Naomi said.

'She told me where you worked and then the woman at the pub told me where you live.' Harry smiled at her and added, 'Afraid I told a few porkies. Said you was my ma's cousin.'

'You what?' Naomi stared at him.

'Thing is, Mrs Federman, I'm trying to find Lisa. I hoped she might still be living with you. I went to that children's home where she worked, but they wouldn't tell me where she'd gone. The woman what's running the place now said she'd never heard of her.'

'I see,' said Naomi.

'So after that I told people I was looking for you, cos I knew you'd know where Lisa was. Is she here?'

'No,' replied Naomi. 'She don't live with us.'

'So, can you tell me where she is?' Harry was losing patience. 'I just want to see her before I go back to Australia.'

'You're going back?' Naomi tried not to sound hopeful. 'Soon?'

'Yes, very soon,' Harry said. 'Got some business to finish in London and then I'm going back down under.'

At that moment the back door flew open and a boy of about eight burst into the kitchen.

'Mum...' he began and then stopped as he saw there was a stranger sitting at the table with his mother.

'Nicky, say how d'you do to Mr Black,' Naomi said, and turning to Harry said, 'This is our son, Nicholas.'

Nicky looked at the man with interest, saying, 'How d'you do, Mr Black.'

'He's an old friend of Lisa's come to say hallo.'

'I knew her during the war,' Harry told him.

'Lisa isn't here,' Nicky said. 'She lives miles away in Wynsdown. We went to Edie's christening and it was ever such a long way. We went on the train and it took ages.'

'That's enough, Nicky,' said Naomi firmly. 'Wash your hands for dinner, it won't be long.' She stood up and said to Harry, 'I'll have to give Nicky his dinner, he has to be back in school in an hour.'

Harry also got to his feet and said, 'I won't hold you up any more, Mrs Federman. I can see you're busy. Just tell Lisa I was asking for her and that I send my love.'

Naomi heaved a sigh of relief as she saw him get into his car and drive away. He was going back to Australia very soon. Nicky had let on where Lisa was now, but Harry hadn't said he would visit her, he'd simply sent her his love, and that could get lost along the way.

Chapter 8

Harry drove back to London and went to his hotel, parking the car in a side street. Tomorrow, he decided, he'd move somewhere else; better to keep moving.

He ate a quick meal in the hotel restaurant and then set off for the Isle of Dogs, arriving at the Crooked Billet well before it closed. He wanted to make sure that Freddie wasn't being followed. He parked the car outside in the street and watched the door of the public bar. At closing time Freddie emerged with another man, a much younger man, who Harry assumed was his friend Eric, and together they set off down the street towards Freddie's studio. Harry stayed where he was for a few minutes but there was no sign of anyone taking an interest in the photographer and his friend, so he started the engine and drove round to the studio. He reached it at the same time as the two men, and pulled up outside, just as Freddie was opening the door. The man with him turned, his face a mask of fear as the car drew up behind them and another drove past. He touched Freddie's arm and muttered something, causing Freddie to spin round. When he saw Harry getting out of the car, he pushed open the door and beckoned him inside, shutting the door quickly behind them.

'What you come here in a motor for, Vic?' he demanded. 'Not exactly discreet, are yer?'

'You expect me to bring 'em on the bus?' snapped Harry.

'Anyhow,' he went on, 'I come to fetch you. You got to come with me now, Freddie.'

'You ain't got the women with you?'

'No. Dora won't come here. She wants you to come to the house, now. So get your cameras and get in the car.'

'What about the money?' Freddie's friend asked.

'You Eric?' Harry asked.

'Yeah, what's it to you?'

'It's what it's to Fred what counts, mate,' Harry said. 'Now, get your stuff, Freddie, and get in the car. We want this done soon as, so let's get on with it.'

For a moment Harry thought Freddie was going to refuse and he took a step towards him. 'You done it for Denny, now you're going to do it for his missus, so get your arse in gear and get in the car.'

Freddie still looked less than happy. 'The money?' he quavered. 'You promised me a hundred up front.'

'And you'll get it,' snapped Harry. 'Dora's got it, so the sooner you stop pissing about and get in the car, the sooner you'll get the cash.'

Eric, clearly afraid the deal was going to fall through, gave his friend a push. 'Off you go, Fred, you'll be all right.'

Freddie sighed and picked up the things he needed, putting them all into a canvas bag, and followed Harry to the car. He turned before he got in and said to Eric, 'You go home. Lock the door and don't let nobody in till I get back.' Then he got in and slumped on to the back seat, keeping his head down, afraid to be seen riding in Denny Dunc's motor.

When they reached Marsh Avenue it was almost midnight and the house was in darkness but the garage door was open as promised, and Harry drove straight in. He closed the door behind them before putting on the light and tapping on the inner, kitchen door. Bella let them in and led them into the sitting room where her mother was in her usual chair by the fire, her clothes smart, her hair done, her face made up, ready to be photographed. The windows were tightly curtained, showing no light. From the street outside the house was asleep.

'This is Freddie,' Harry said by way of introduction. 'Get on with it, Fred.'

Once Freddie had got his apparatus set up, it didn't take very long to take the pictures of Dora and Bella that he needed. He took several of each of them so that there could be no question of having to do the job again. When he'd finished, Dora thanked him graciously.

'Thank you for coming here, Mr Freddie. I'm sure all our documents will be perfect.' She reached into her handbag and extracted a fistful of notes. 'Here's your advance. Can you tell us when the papers will be ready?'

'You can have 'em Friday,' he said. 'Send Vic down for them Friday night... and don't forget the rest of the money.'

'Certainly, Mr Freddie, he'll be there... and so will your money.'

Freddie nodded and gathered his equipment back into its canvas bag. He looked across at Harry, who had watched the whole proceedings in silence, and said, 'You gonna take me home, Vic, or what?'

'I'll drop you outside the Billet,' Harry replied. 'You can walk from there.'

'Just let me check the street,' Dora said, and heaving herself out of her armchair she went up to the landing window and looked out into the night. The street lay silent and empty, lit by pools of light from the street lamps; there was no sign of anyone.

Hardly surprising, she thought, since it's one o'clock in the morning. 'All clear!' she called down the stairs and Bella led them back through the kitchen.

The two men got into the car and Freddie once again slumped onto the back seat, out of sight. Bella opened the garage door and Harry drove out into the street. As he reached the main road another car fell in behind him but branched off at the next traffic lights, causing him no alarm. The Hound, in the driving seat, realised where Harry was going and left him to it.

When he dropped Freddie off near the Crooked Billet, Harry said, conversationally, 'Don't do a runner with that hundred quid, will you, Fred? You wouldn't like it if I had to come looking for you.'

'Not likely, is it?' demanded Freddie with an unusual spurt of anger. 'Not going to pass up nine hundred quid just to keep a miserable ton, am I?'

'Fair enough,' Harry acknowledged. 'Soon as I got them papers, you'll get your money and then you an' Eric can do your vanishing trick.'

As soon as he'd dropped Freddie off, Harry drove back to his hotel. Dora had told him to keep the car until he collected the new documents on Friday night. It was worth something, Denny's car, and she'd been afraid that Mick might disappear with it.

'If you've got it, Harry, Mick Derham won't know where it is, so he can't get his hands on it.'

Harry parked the car in the side street and went into the hotel. The Hound went home to bed, ready for an early start in the morning.

Harry had three days to kill. He considered taking the train to Somerset, in search of Lisa. He was determined to find her before he sailed again for Australia. He now knew that she was married, that she had a child called Edie, and he realised that there would be no way he could persuade her to leave them behind and come to Sydney with him, but he had a deep-seated need to see her once again. He remembered the name of the village, Wynsdown, that young Nicky Federman had mentioned. Surely if he reached there it wouldn't be difficult to find her. Perhaps there'd be a village pub where he could stay for a couple of days while he searched for her. That being the case, he decided, it would be better to wait until he had collected the documents Dora and Bella needed, and perhaps even concluded the business he had to do on Denny Dunc's behalf with Shadbolt and Maxton. There'd surely be a chance to visit this Wynsdown place and find her again, before he took ship for the other side of the world.

The decision taken to wait, Harry decided it was time to move hotels. Followed by the faithful Hound, he left the Kingswood and set off to find another. He took the Tube to Marble Arch and walked down the Edgware Road searching for somewhere suitable. Nothing grand, he wasn't planning to stay long, but, he decided, he wanted Denny's noticeable car off the street. When he saw the Malvern Hotel, he realised that it suited his purposes perfectly. Standing in a side street, it was an undistinguished, narrow, four-storey building, with steps up to a glazed front door. More importantly, there was an alley at the side, leading to a small yard at the back where he could park the car out of sight. Harry secured a room on the first floor with a view out over the street, and satisfied with this change of address, he returned to the Kingswood, packed his bag and left. When he arrived at the Malvern, the Hound watched him drive the car into the yard and go into the hotel, before reporting that the mark had moved house.

Friday evening saw Harry once again driving Denny Dunc's car to the Isle of Dogs. He was feeling satisfied with the way everything was going. Once he had the documents safely in his possession he could book passages for Dora and Bella to Sydney. He expected to travel with them, but he still had to confront Bull Shadbolt and Grey Maxton and put Denny's proposition to them. As he drove he also gave thought to Mick Derham. He was almost certainly on the payroll of one or other, and should be dealt with accordingly, but Denny had been adamant.

'Don't start a turf war, Vic,' he'd said. 'That won't do no good to nobody. You got to talk to Maxton and Shadbolt and sort things out sensible-like.'

The studio was in darkness when Harry drove past, no lights inside or out. He continued on to the Crooked Billet. It was still open, its windows splashing yellow light out on to the rain-washed street. Harry parked the car in a nearby side road, and walking back to the pub, heard a shout of laughter as the door opened and two men came out. He watched them from the shadows as, unaware of him, they set off up the road, hurrying through the drizzle away from the pub, away from the studio.

A damp Friday night at the Crooked Billet was always busy. The public bar was smoky and noisy. A group of men stood round a dartboard at the back of the room, and there were shouts of encouragement as a tall man stepped forward to throw. Several people congregated at the bar, and two couples sat together at a table near the fire drinking beer and port and lemon. Harry paused at the door, looking round briefly to see Freddie, sitting in a corner by himself, an empty whisky glass in front of him, before approaching the bar and ordering himself a pint of bitter.

When he saw Harry, Freddie's eyes widened, but he made no move to acknowledge him. Harry seemed to ignore him, staying at the bar once his pint was drawn and listening in to the conversations about him, but with an alert eye on Freddie and the door. He had no real reason to distrust Freddie; the man wanted, needed, the money, and the papers he was providing were the bread and butter of his daily life. But he did distrust Mick Derham, and despite Dora's assurance that Mick knew nothing of their plans to leave the country, Harry wasn't so sure. He was anxious to collect the documents and get Denny's ladies booked on to the next available ship going to Australia.

Over the next half-hour, people came and went, but Harry saw nothing to cause him any disquiet. The Billet served a mixed area. From where he sat Harry could see through to the lounge bar, where a few well-dressed customers sat at tables or in the easy chairs grouped round the fire, chatting over their gin and tonics.

When the landlord eventually called time, the customers from both bars wandered out into the street. As Freddie stood for a moment, turning up his collar against a misting rain, which continued to drizzle from the night sky, Harry moved up behind him and laid a hand on his shoulder. Freddie jumped as if he'd received an electric shock.

'Hallo, Freddie,' Harry murmured. 'Can I give you a lift home? You'll get very wet walking.' He took a firm hold of Freddie's arm and led him, unprotesting, to the parked car.

'What you come to the pub for?' Freddie demanded once he was in the car. 'I don't want to be seen anywhere near you. Ain't good for me 'ealth!'

'Nothing's good for your health, Freddie,' Harry remarked genially. 'But you do want the money I've got for you,' he pointed out, 'an' I got to protect Denny's interests, ain't I? Come on, Fred, I'll just come and pick up them papers, check 'em through and pay up. Bob's yer uncle! We got what we want and you're shot of us with a nice little earner in yer pocket!'

Harry started the car and once again Freddie cowered down in his seat. Two minutes later they drew up outside the studio, and Freddie scrambled out, hurrying across to open the door. Harry, with a quick glance along the quiet street, followed him inside. As he stepped through, the door closed behind him and he felt something cold against the back of his neck. He froze. Sudden light flooded the room and Harry saw two of the men who were waiting for them, each with a gun, one trained on Freddie, and knew a third held a pistol against his own neck.

'Good evening, gentlemen,' said Rat Ratcliffe. 'Nice to see you both.'

Harry weighed up his options and decided that there weren't any. Three against two would be difficult odds at best, and he could see that Freddie was going to be worse than useless.

He took a step forward and half turning, saw that it was Mick Derham behind him. Trying to ignore the pressure of the gun, which had shifted to the small of his back, he forced a smile to his face and said, 'Mr Ratcliffe, I've been looking forward to meeting you. I need you to introduce me to Bull Shadbolt.'

'Shut your mouth,' Mick Derham growled in his ear. 'Bull don't want to talk to you. You're just...' His voice trailed away as the Rat raised a hand to cut him off.

'Vic, is it? Or should I call you Harry?' Ratcliffe's eyes were fixed on Harry's face.

Returning his gaze and very much aware of the gun at his back, Harry tried to keep his voice steady and replied, 'I answer to either.'

'Search him, Manny!' Ratcliffe ordered, and while Mick kept him covered, the third man, Manny, searched him thoroughly, removing the knife Harry always carried in his boot.

'Nothing else, boss,' Manny said as he pocketed the knife and turned back to stand over the quivering Freddie.

The Rat was not a big man. He had a round face with a blob of a nose; his receding hair gave him a high forehead and prominent ears, but it was his cold, grey eyes that instilled fear; eyes that spoke of the callous killer.

'Well,' he said, 'Harry it is then. The thing is, Harry, Bull wants to know what you're doing on his patch.'

'And Denny Dunc wants to know what Bull's doing on his,' replied Harry.

Ratcliffe raised an eyebrow. 'Does he now?'

'And he's sent me to find out. He's been hearing that his lady hasn't been treated with the respect due to her. I've got to deliver messages from Denny to Bull.'

'Have you now?' drawled the Rat. 'And what might those be?'

'For his ears only.'

'Maybe he won't want to hear them.'

'Can you risk that?' Harry held his gaze. 'Could be worth Bull's while to listen.'

'What was you and this pillock doing here tonight?' demanded the Rat, with a sudden change of subject. 'What was your business?'

'None of yours,' answered Harry, for which Mick Derham brought the barrel of his gun up under Harry's chin.

'Steady, Mick,' growled the Rat, 'don't want to blow his head off... not yet we don't.' He turned his attention to Freddie. 'Well, dickhead, you gonna tell me what you and Harry boy was up to? I mean, Bull's been good to you, giving you protection an' that. He won't be pleased to hear you've gone back to working for Denny Dunc without so much as a by your leave. Without telling him, without making sure he got his cut.'

'Wanted some papers,' Freddie squeaked. 'For Denny's missus and daughter.'

'Did he now? And what sort of papers was those, Fred?'

'Passports, birth certs, driving licences.'

'And you done them?'

Freddie nodded miserably.

'How much did he pay you?'

'A ton.'

'Only a ton for all that work, Freddie? That's slave rates, that is.' Ratcliffe fixed Freddie with a gimlet eye.

Freddie lost his nerve and said, 'That was up front.'

The Rat gave him a wolfish grin. 'So, what's he owe you, then?'

'Another nine hundred,' Harry said before Freddie could answer. 'I don't care who I pay it to, you or Freddie, but I want them papers.'

'Where's the papers, Fred?' demanded the Rat.

Freddie's eyes flicked to the battered-looking bureau in the corner of the room.

'Better fetch 'em out then.' The Rat jerked a thumb at the desk and Manny, again holding the gun in Freddie's ribs, encouraged the shaking Freddie towards it. He raised the lid, pulled out a brown foolscap envelope and held it out to Ratcliffe.

The Rat took it and tipped the contents out on to the table. Harry could see that all the documents he'd asked for were there. Ratcliffe shuffled through them and then put them back into the envelope.

'You been a bad boy, Fred,' he said conversationally. 'Bull's not gonna be a happy man when I show him this lot.' He sniffed dismissively. 'Tie him up, Manny, gag him and leave him. He won't cause us no more trouble.'

Manny did as he was told and when Freddie was well and truly trussed, the Rat said, 'Now tie Harry-boy's hands and take him out to our motor.' While Mick kept him covered, Manny tied Harry's hands securely behind him. The Rat turned to Mick and said, 'You go and pick up Harry's car and bring it over to the Bull's yard.' He gave Mick a sharp look as he added, 'The money'll be in it somewhere. Make sure it's all there.'

Mick nodded and disappeared.

Harry allowed himself to be hustled out of the studio to a car parked in an opposite driveway. It was past midnight now and the street was deserted. Manny kept the gun pressed into the small of Harry's back, and Harry made no move to break free. He knew he wouldn't get a yard. He also guessed that he was going to be taken to see Bull Shadbolt. The Rat dare not finish him off until Shadbolt had heard whatever message Denny Dunc had sent him. Harry had challenged him to risk it, but he wasn't about to accept that challenge. There'd be time to deal with Harry Black if necessary, later on.

Harry was put in the back seat of the car and Manny and the gun got in beside him. The Rat slid into the front, and started the engine. It sounded very loud in the silent street, but both the Rat and Harry knew that no one in this district would chance looking out to see something they shouldn't.

'Why didn't you top that Freddie bloke?' Manny asked Ratcliffe.

'Too messy,' came the reply. 'Don't want the rozzers involved. We got what we came for, and Freddie won't make the same mistake again. We'll collect that ton off him soon enough.'

Harry watched out of the window as the car drove through the late-night streets. He recognised several places, but still wasn't sure where they were going. Suddenly the car was lit with flashing blue light. Harry turned his head to see a police car close up behind them.

'Shit!' muttered the Rat and pulled over to the side of the road. 'A word from you, Harry, an' you're a dead man.'

Manny's gun was pressed firmly into Harry's ribs now, and Harry, who had for a moment thought this might be deliverance, sat back in his seat with his eyes shut.

A policeman left the car behind and approached the driver's window. Harry heard the Rat wind the window down, though he'd left the engine running.

'Evening, officer,' he said. 'Is there something wrong?'

'No, sir, just checking you knew you've a brake light missing on your car.'

'Have I? No, I didn't know. I'll get a new bulb first thing in the morning.'

'Would be wise, sir,' said the policeman, as he shone a torch into the back of the car, the beam resting on an apparently comatose Harry and a dozing Manny. 'Late-night party, was it, sir?'

'Lat- night cards,' replied the Rat. 'On our way home now.'

'Good night then, sir,' said the policeman, 'and don't forget to change that bulb.'

The Rat put the car into gear and pulled away, leaving Sergeant Unwin standing in the road, watching him.

'Was it who you thought?' his colleague asked as he got back into the car.

'Yes,' replied Unwin, 'Rat Ratcliffe. And he'll know I sussed him when he discovers both his brake lights work. Can't do much about him, he's too canny, but it doesn't hurt to keep him on his toes. Another couple of hopefuls in the back, Manny Parkes and a bloke I didn't recognise. We'll report it when we get in.'

For the rest of the journey Harry kept his eyes closed. It helped him to think. He reckoned he was on his way to meet

Bull Shadbolt and the meeting certainly wasn't going to be quite as he'd planned it. He knew he'd have only one chance to get this right. If it came right down to it, he, like Freddie as far as Shadbolt was concerned, was expendable. He thought briefly about Freddie and wondered when Eric would come looking for him and set him free. They'd be lucky if they could get away before one of Shadbolt's heavies came looking for the hundred pounds Harry had already paid.

The car turned off the road and came to a halt in a yard behind a darkened building. The Rat killed the engine and Manny, opening the back door, prodded Harry with the gun.

'Out,' he growled, 'an' no funny business.'

Harry got out. With his hands tied behind him, he stood waiting in the darkness; pointless to try and make a break, that way he'd wind up dead for sure.

The two men led him across the yard to a door at the back of the building. As they reached it, a second car swung into the yard, its headlights illuminating the place, and Mick Derham joined them as they went inside.

The place appeared to be a pub. Harry was led through a deserted bar and up a flight of stairs. At the top was a landing with three doors off it. A man had been sitting outside one of them and hearing footsteps on the stairs had come to his feet, a gun in his hand, barring the way. When he saw it was the Rat, he pocketed the gun.

'Bull's got company just now,' he said, with a nod at one of the doors. 'You'll have to wait till he's free.'

However, at that moment the door behind him opened and a scantily clad young girl came out. She squeaked as she saw the waiting men and hurriedly disappeared through one of the other doors. Moments later she was followed on to the landing by Bull Shadbolt, tucking his shirt into his trousers.

Gordon Anthony Shadbolt was indeed a bull of a man, well over six feet tall with a barrel chest, tree-trunk legs and the arms and fists of a boxer. His bullet head was as smooth as a billiard ball. 'Bull' suited him and was the name by which he was known everywhere.

He paused on the landing, looking at Harry and his captors, and grinned. 'Who've we got here, then?'

'Harry Black alias Vic Merritt,' replied Ratcliffe. 'Says he's got messages from Denny Dunc. Been doing business with Freddie on our patch.'

'Has he now?' Bull fixed Harry with cold, dark eyes. 'Have to discuss that with him, then.' He jerked his head towards the third door. 'Bring him in the office.'

The office was in darkness except for the moonlight shining through two windows that looked out over the yard. Manny drew curtains across these, and then across a glass door which, Harry saw, led to an iron fire escape. Then, safe from any prying eyes, he switched on the lights. The office was a large room with a desk before the windows, some upright chairs and a couple of armchairs beside an empty grate. There was a bar in the corner and Bull went to this now, pouring himself three fingers of Scotch before seating himself behind the desk. The Rat pushed Harry down onto a chair in front of the desk and leaving Mick to cover him, dropped into one of the armchairs.

'Think you can untie his hands, now, Mick,' Bull said as he settled himself and took a sip of his drink. 'He ain't going nowhere.'

It was with obvious reluctance that Mick cut through Harry's bonds, allowing him to rub his wrists in an effort to get the blood flowing again.

'Now then, Harry,' Bull said. 'Hound says you been a busy little bugger last few days. So, let's hear it... all of it.'

Hound! thought Harry. He'd heard of him. That's how they'd caught him. Bloody fool, he chastised himself, not spotting Hound on his tail.

'Well, Harry? Messages from Denny. What's all that about, then?'

Harry looked across at the big man and taking a deep breath he said, 'Well, the first one is don't trust Mick Derham.' He felt, rather than saw, Mick take a step forward, but a glare from Bull made him retreat again. 'Seems he was right there,' Harry went on. 'So, you don't need him to hear what Denny's suggesting.'

For a long moment there was silence and then Bull said, 'Get lost, Mick.'

Mick stared at him and then said, 'You going to let this little Kraut dictate to you, Bull?'

'No,' retorted Bull. 'Nor you, neither. Beat it.'

Red-faced and furious, Mick turned on his heel and left the room.

'Manny,' said Bull, 'don't need you, neither. Come back in the morning.'

'Right-ho, boss,' and Manny, pocketing his gun, followed Mick out of the door.

'So,' Bull took another slurp of his whisky, 'what's these messages? Denny think he's coming back, does he?'

Harry looked across at him, and for a moment their eyes locked. 'No,' he said. 'Denny ain't coming back. He's got cancer. Six months, tops.'

'Christ!' Bull knocked back the rest of his drink and holding out his glass to the Rat said, 'Get me another.'

Ratcliffe took the glass and refilled it.

'That's why he wants his missus and daughter to go out to Australia,' Harry went on. 'He's in Sydney, but if Dora and

Bella travel under their own names, it might tip off Scotland Yard where he's living. The Australian cops'll find him and he'll spend his last months back inside.'

'An' he's sent you to what…?'

'Denny still has business over here, you know that. Mick was supposed to caretake for a while, but…' Harry shrugged. 'Anyhow, he's got a proposition for you, and Grey Maxton too.'

'Maxton?' Bull Shadbolt's face darkened. 'What's it got to do with him?'

'You know as well as we do that Maxton's been moving in on Denny's territory, same as you. All Denny wants is for his ladies to be taken care of after he's gone. He has a proposal which might suit all three of you.'

'Sounds unlikely, but I'm listening.'

'He knows neither of you wants a turf war. Could well happen if you both lay claim to Denny's manor. He's suggesting that you agree a split. Take over all his businesses between you. Protection, girls, betting, black market, and the couple of legit enterprises for laundering the cash. Maxton's south of the river, you're East End. You two agree a split on the territory, but until Denny dies the profits is split three ways.'

'Now you've told me he ain't coming back,' said Bull, 'what's to stop me simply taking over all his business?'

'Grey Maxton,' replied Harry. 'He wouldn't let you take over, any more than you'd let him.'

'And if Maxton and me agree the split, what's to make us pay out Denny's share?'

'Denny still has clout over here,' said Harry.

'Who says so? Even that toerag Mick Derham has seen where the future lies.'

'With you? You got too much nous to take on a bloke

what's already jumped ship on his boss. So's Grey Maxton. Mick Derham's history.'

'Still, Denny's twelve thousand miles away. Who's going to look after his interest here till he kicks the bucket?'

'He's already sorted out an insurance on that,' retorted Harry. 'He may be dying, but he still knows how to look after his own.'

'An' this insurance is...?'

'If I told you that, it wouldn't be insurance, would it?'

'You been to Maxton with this crazy scheme?'

'Not yet. I was planning to fix a meet with you both, once Dora and Bella was on their way.'

'But you ain't got their papers no more.' The Rat spoke for the first time. 'So they ain't going nowhere.'

'We'll have to come to an arrangement about those,' Harry said. 'If they aren't on the next available boat, then the deal's off.'

'Not sure you're in much of a bargaining position, Harry,' drawled the Rat. 'We eliminate you, the ladies stay where they are, an' we simply move in.'

'It might work that way,' agreed Harry with a cool he was far from feeling. 'But if that happens it'll start a war between you and Maxton, there'll be bloodshed on both sides, and the rozzers'll be all over you. Both firms lose out that way and could leave the field open to someone else. Reckon Bull's got more sense than to get into all that, simply to stop Denny's ladies from going to see him in Australia before he dies.'

'How do we know he's dying?' challenged the Rat.

'You don't,' returned Harry, 'but if he wasn't and anything happened to Dora or Bella, he'd make you regret it.'

'I wonder just how he'd do that?' snapped Ratcliffe. 'You got a lot to say for yourself, but—'

'Shut it, Rat,' drawled Bull. 'Get the boy a drink.'

The Rat stared at his boss and Harry thought for a moment he wasn't going to obey, but with a great show of reluctance he went to the bar and slopped whisky into two glasses. He took a long pull at one before handing the other to Harry, who took a grateful gulp, before he put the glass down, so that Bull wouldn't see his hand shaking.

'This'll take some thinking about,' Bull said. 'What happens to the women when Denny falls off his perch? Won't they be shrieking for their share in all this?'

'No, they'll be took care of in Sydney. New names, new lives and the money Denny's put by for them. You won't never hear from them again once they're on that ship. They can't afford to be associated with you, back here.'

Bull gave Harry a long level look. He admired the young man's brass to bring him such a message.

'If I do decide it's worth doing,' he said, 'we'll have to fix a meet with Maxton. Neutral territory.' He turned to Ratcliffe and said, 'Where's them papers, Rat?'

The Rat held out the envelope and Bull emptied it onto his desk. 'Looks as if Freddie's done his usual good job.' He glanced up at Harry. 'What're they worth to you?'

'Agreed a grand with Freddie,' Harry said. 'I got nine hundred in the car... unless Mick Derham's done a runner with it, but even he couldn't be that stupid.'

'That and another grand and they're yours,' Bull said, getting to his feet. He pushed the documents back into the envelope and locked them in a drawer of his desk. 'Need a bit of compensation for all the trouble you've caused us.'

'I ain't got that much,' Harry said.

'Then you better set about getting it, Harry. You can come back when you have and then, maybe, we'll discuss Denny's proposition. You can take your motor, when you've given Rat the cash out of it.'

Five minutes later, Harry was again behind the wheel of Denny Dunc's car, driving back to his room at the Malvern Hotel. He had survived, but he knew that the evening could have ended very differently.

Chapter 10

It was Saturday and Charlotte had an afternoon with no children, a rare thing. Margaret had suggested that they should come to her for the afternoon to give Charlotte a little time to herself. Charlotte had accepted with alacrity and Billy had taken them over for their dinner and would bring them back in time for bed.

'What will you do with yourself?' he teased as she got the children ready to go. She smiled across at him as she put two bottles and some nappies in a bag for Edie.

'The ironing, of course!'

'Ironing! You're supposed to be having an afternoon to yourself!'

'Silly,' laughed Charlotte. 'I shall go over to Clare's and admire her baby. I haven't seen her yet and I've got a little present for her. We'll be able to have a good old chinwag.'

'Sounds more like it,' Billy said and picked up the bag. 'Come on, young man,' he called to Johnny who was already waiting by the door. 'Let's go and see Gr'ma.'

Charlotte watched them going out into the lane, Johnny helping to push Edie in her pram, and waved when they turned back to wave to her. Then she went back into the house to pick up the little matinée jacket she'd knitted for Clare's new baby. She stood in the strangely silent house for a moment. A whole afternoon to herself; she could hardly believe it.

Well, make the most of it, she told herself, and putting the jacket into her bag, she set off for Clare's.

It was a perfect October afternoon, the air crisp and cool, the sun shining from a periwinkle sky. Charlotte walked with a spring in her step as she left the village green and strode along the lane leading to the little farm cottage where Malcolm and Clare lived. A whole afternoon to herself.

As she passed the ornate gates of the manor house she heard someone shouting, calling her name, and turning she saw Marjorie Bellinger rushing down the manor drive, frantically waving her arms in the air.

'Charlotte! Charlotte! Help!'

Charlotte ran to meet her calling, 'Mrs Bellinger! What on earth's the matter?'

'It's Peter,' Marjorie cried, a sob in her voice. 'He's collapsed! I've tried to ring Dr Masters, but our phone seems to be out of order. Can you go for him? Tell him to be quick!'

'I'll find him,' Charlotte said at once. 'You go back to the major. I'll be as quick as I can.'

She turned and ran back along the lane, crossing the village green to the square, red-brick house set back from the road where the doctor lived and had his surgery. She ran up to the front door and banged hard on the knocker. Her heart was pounding. She'd done just this when she'd found Miss Edie lying on the floor all those years ago. 'Come on! Come on!' she muttered when there was no response, the sound of the knocker echoing away into the silence of the house. She pushed open the letter box and peered through. The hall was empty. There was a stillness about the place and she was certain that there was no one at home; it was Saturday after all, Dr Masters could be anywhere, but she ran round to the back garden, just to be sure he wasn't at work in his vegetable patch. A fork was stuck into the ground at the end of a row of potatoes, but there was no sign him.

What now? thought Charlotte, at a loss for a moment. Then she was running back across the green and pounding on the vicarage front door.

Avril Swanson opened the door and finding her on the step said, 'Charlotte, how lovely! Come on in.'

'Major Bellinger's collapsed,' Charlotte said breathlessly. 'Mrs Bellinger's with him but their phone's out of order. Dr Masters is out. Can you ring for an ambulance?'

'Of course!' Avril turned back indoors, calling to her husband, David, to come quickly. Charlotte followed her inside and as Avril rang 999, Charlotte told the vicar what had happened.

'I'll come at once,' he said, picking up his coat and slipping his prayer book into his pocket.

'They're coming,' Avril said as she put the phone down. 'They'll be here as soon as they can.'

All three hurried down the lane to the manor to see if there was anything else they could do, and to be with Marjorie while she waited for the ambulance. The front door stood ajar and Avril pushed it wide, calling to Marjorie as she did so.

'Marjorie! We're here. The ambulance is on its way.'

'In here!'

They found Marjorie in Peter's study. Peter was lying on the floor, his eyes closed, his breath rasping in his throat.

'I can't get him up,' Marjorie said, her face rigid in her effort not to cry. 'I can't get him up off the floor. We should get him onto the couch.'

'We'll help,' Avril said, 'easy now.' And between the four of them they managed to lift the inert form of Peter Bellinger off the floor and lie him on the sofa in the corner of the room.

He was still struggling for breath. Marjorie set a cushion under his head and then sat down beside him, holding his hand.

'What happened?' Avril asked softly.

'I don't know,' murmured Marjorie, still fighting her tears. 'I was in the kitchen getting lunch and I heard a crash. I called out to see if he was all right but he didn't answer so I came in to see what had happened and there he was.' Her lip trembled. 'He looks awful! Do you think the ambulance'll be long?'

'They said they were on their way,' Avril said. 'I'm sure they'll be here soon.' She took Marjorie's other hand and squeezed it encouragingly. Charlotte stood by the window, looking out in the hope of seeing the ambulance, and David sat in the corner, his eyes closed in quiet prayer. Silence fell around them, a silence made more profound by Peter's stentorian breathing.

'I'll go out onto the green and watch for them,' Charlotte said, unable to endure the tense silence any longer, and leaving the Swansons with Marjorie, she hurried back down the lane to wait.

When she reached the green she sat on a bench, watching the road into the village, and she thought again of the day she'd found Miss Edie on the floor. She'd run for Dr Masters then, but it had been too late. At least, she thought, Major Bellinger is still alive.

The steady clang of the ambulance's bell brought her sharply back to the present and a moment later it swung round the corner, bell still clanging, blue light flashing on its roof. Charlotte flagged it down and directed the driver along the lane to the manor. She was aware of people coming out onto the green to see what was going on, but she kept her head down and hurried after the ambulance before they could ask questions. Village gossip would catch up with what had happened soon enough.

Back at the house the ambulance men hurried indoors to where Peter lay on the sofa.

'Looks like a stroke, ma'am,' one of them said to Marjorie. 'Hospital for him. We'll be taking him straight to Bristol. You can ride with him in the ambulance if you want to. No time to lose, though.'

Gently they moved him onto a stretcher and carried him out to the ambulance and Marjorie, grabbing her handbag, hurried after them.

'What about Felix?' Avril called to her as she scrambled in beside her husband.

'I don't know where he is,' Marjorie called back.

'Ring us when you know how things are,' David said. 'And when you want to come home, I'll come and fetch you.'

One ambulance man got into the back with his patient and the other climbed up into the cab and started the engine. The back doors slammed shut and Avril, David and Charlotte watched as the ambulance drew away, its bell clanging its urgency.

The Swansons locked up the house and then, paying no attention to those still gathered, wondering, on the green, the three of them went into the vicarage. Avril put the kettle on and they all sat down at the kitchen table to discuss what else needed to be done.

'The first thing is to get hold of Felix,' Avril said. 'We have to let him know what's happened.'

'Isn't he still on his honeymoon?' asked David. 'Do you know where they were going?'

Avril shook her head. 'No, but Marjorie may do, once she thinks about it.'

'We still may not be able to contact him,' David said. 'How long were they going for?'

'Only a week, I think,' said Avril. 'When they got home from the wedding last weekend, Marjorie said something about Felix only being allowed a week away from the Air Ministry.'

'And you can't remember where she said they were going?'

'I'm not sure she knows. I think Felix was keeping it a secret.'

'Hmm,' said David. 'Well, if it was only a week, that probably means he'll be home today or tomorrow.'

When they'd finished their tea, Charlotte left the vicarage and went back along the lane to visit Clare and her new daughter, as promised. There was nothing more to be done until Mrs Bellinger phoned with further news from the hospital.

'I began to think you wasn't coming,' Clare said when she opened the door. She led the way inside and Charlotte was taken to peep into the little crib where the baby was fast asleep.

'I'm sorry,' Charlotte explained, 'I was on my way, but Major Bellinger has had a stroke or something and Mrs Bellinger sent me for the doctor.'

'Is he all right?' asked Clare, immediately interested. The Bellingers had fostered her husband, Malcolm, when they had all been evacuated from London. Neither Clare nor Malcolm had had any family to return to after the war, and they had both stayed on in Wynsdown. 'Is there anything Malcolm or I can do?'

'I should think you've got your hands pretty full here,' Charlotte said. 'Mrs Bellinger went with him in the ambulance, so when she phones the vicar we shall know more. The Swansons are going to try and get hold of Felix and let him know. We think he's back from his honeymoon today or tomorrow. Just hope he's back in time.'

Clare looked at her, wide-eyed. 'D'you think he's going to die?'

Charlotte shrugged. 'I don't know, do I? All I can say is

that he looked pretty awful and sounded worse.' Changing the subject to happier things she pulled out the matinée jacket from her bag and handed it to Clare. 'Here,' she said, 'I made this for her. Have you chosen a name yet?'

'Agnes,' Clare replied, 'after my nan.'

'Well, this is for Agnes, then,' Charlotte said and laid the little coat on the bottom of the crib.

For the next hour or so they chatted about babies in general and their babies in particular until Agnes awoke and demanded her next feed. Charlotte looked at her watch and gave an exclamation.

'Look at the time! Billy'll be home with the children soon. I must dash.'

As she passed the vicarage she saw Avril at a window and waved. Avril waved back, but she didn't come out. There was clearly no more news.

She had been in the house only a quarter of an hour when her family arrived home, full of the day's doings.

Billy carried Edie indoors. 'Hallo, love,' he said as he handed her over to Charlotte. 'How were Clare and the baby? Had a nice peaceful afternoon?'

'Anything but,' Charlotte told him and with a nod to the children said, 'I'll tell you all about it over supper.'

Johnny, as always, still seemed to be bursting with energy and rushed into the kitchen, hugging her round the knees and crying, 'I did riding again, Mummy. Gramp says I'm getting gooder every time! And Daddy let me see Rustler and give him a sugar lump.'

Charlotte looked at Billy in alarm. 'Billy, you didn't let him go near Rustler, did you?'

'Don't worry, Char,' Billy reassured her. 'I was holding on to the horse. Johnny simply gave him the sugar.'

'It's all right, Mummy,' Johnny said earnestly, 'I put my hand flat like Daddy said. Rustler liked the sugar. His lips was all tickly.'

Charlotte, trying to set aside her fear of Billy's hunter, Rustler, managed a laugh as she returned his hug and said, 'Well done you, Johnny. It sounds as if you've had a lovely time.'

'And we had eggs for tea,' Johnny told her. 'Well, not Edie cos she's too little, but Gr'ma made me toast soldiers and they got all eggy.'

'So did you, young man,' Billy grinned. 'Come on, bath-time for you. Mummy's got to feed Edie.'

'So, at the moment no one knows how to get hold of Felix,' Charlotte explained later. 'The Swansons think he may still be on his honeymoon, he was only married last week.'

'Surely his mother'll know where he is?' said Billy.

'She probably does,' agreed Charlotte, 'but, as you can imagine, she was in a dreadful state when she got into the ambulance. I expect she'll remember when things calm down a bit.'

The news was soon round the village and by the next morning it seemed that everyone had heard. People gathering outside the church before the service were discussing what had happened, what they'd seen and heard, what they thought they'd seen and heard. By the time the five-minute bell fell silent and the latecomers scurried into church, poor Peter Bellinger had had a heart attack, had broken his neck in a fall, had had a stroke, was dead and in his grave.

'Reminds me of when Miss Everard died unexpected like,' Nancy Bright whispered to Sally Prynne, next to her in the pew. 'She were found dead on the floor like that.' Then she clapped her hand to her mouth as she saw Charlotte coming into the church.

During the service, the vicar took the opportunity of setting the story to rights, before offering up prayers for the major's swift recovery.

'I'm sure you've all heard the sad news that the squire had to be rushed to hospital yesterday afternoon. Mrs Bellinger went with him and has gone back to the hospital again this morning. The news I've received from her by phone this morning is that though he hasn't regained consciousness yet, he's in a stable condition. I'm sure you all wish him a speedy recovery and will be thinking of poor Mrs Bellinger as she waits for definite news. Let us pray.' There was a whispering and a scuffling among the congregation as they all knelt to join with his prayers.

After the service Avril took Charlotte to one side. 'He really isn't very good at all,' she confided. 'Poor Marjorie stayed until nearly midnight last night, when David went to fetch her. There'd been no change in his condition by the time she left, and when she got there again this morning, he was as she'd left him. I just wish we could get hold of Felix.'

'Doesn't Mrs Bellinger really know where he is?' Charlotte asked.

Avril shrugged. 'She thinks they went to Paris.'

'But doesn't she know when they're getting back?'

'She thinks they'll be back in London today, but they haven't got a phone, so she can't get hold of him until tomorrow when he gets back to the Air Ministry. She'll try and ring him there first thing in the morning.'

★

Felix had been quite glad to get back to work that Monday morning. He carried with him a vague feeling of disappointment. His wedding night and his honeymoon had not been quite as he'd imagined them, and as the days passed he found that he and Daphne had little to say to each other. He still found her very attractive, her smile made his heart skip a beat and the thought of taking her to bed each night made him harden in anticipation, but he knew she didn't enjoy his lovemaking. He kept telling himself she'd come to enjoy it, that when she got used to him, she'd derive the same pleasure from him that he did from her, but somehow everything had been a bit of an anticlimax.

When he'd arrived in his office that morning he'd been greeted with a few sly smiles and comments; how tired he looked, after his holiday! What on earth had he been up to? All this he took in good part. He was glad to be back among people he'd been working with for months, friends and colleagues with whom he felt comfortable.

His secretary, Miss Dixon, followed him into his office with her notepad.

'Good morning, sir,' she said with a smile. 'I hope you had a good holiday.'

'Yes, thank you,' Felix said, returning her smile. 'What's been going on here?'

'I've sorted all the correspondence and memos that came for you while you were away, sir,' she replied. 'It's in three piles on your desk. Left to right, most urgent, less urgent and not urgent at all. Shall I leave you to it? Oh, and Group Captain Hague wants to see you in his office at ten.'

'Does he? Know what that's about?'

'No, sir, he didn't say. Just that there was a meeting that he wanted you to attend.'

Felix shrugged. 'Oh, well,' he said, 'no doubt I'll find out.'

He started going through the papers and was about to call Miss Dixon back in to take dictation when the phone on his desk rang.

'A trunk call for you, Wing Commander,' said the switchboard girl. 'Putting you through.'

Wondering who on earth would be ringing him at the ministry, Felix said, 'Wing Commander Bellinger!'

He was answered by a woman's voice, one he didn't recognise. 'Felix? Is that you?'

'Felix Bellinger speaking.'

'Felix, this is Avril Swanson, the vicar's wife in Wynsdown.'

'Mrs Swanson?'

'I'm so sorry to phone you at the Air Ministry, but we didn't know how else to get hold of you. It's bad news, I'm afraid. Your father's had a stroke, on Saturday afternoon, and is in hospital in Bristol. Your mother's with him, of course, and she asked us to contact you and let you know.'

'Saturday afternoon.' Felix's mouth went dry. 'How,' he cleared his throat, 'how bad is he?'

'I'm afraid he hasn't regained consciousness since, and to be honest with you, it doesn't sound very good. We think you should come as soon as you can.'

'I see.' Felix felt winded, as if he'd been punched in the solar plexus. His father, an ever-present, indestructible part of his life, was dangerously ill. He drew a deep breath and said, 'Thank you for letting me know. Please tell my mother I'll get there as soon as I can. Give her my love and say we're on our way.'

'Of course,' Avril said. 'And when you get here, if there's anything we can do…'

'Thank you.'

The pips went and the call was over.

Felix replaced the receiver and sat back in his chair. He must go at once, today. As he pushed his chair back and got to his feet, there was a quiet knock on the door and Miss Dixon came in.

'Just to remind you, sir, that you're due in the group captain's office in ten minutes.'

'What did you say?' Felix looked at her blankly.

'Just reminding you, sir, about your meeting with Group Captain Hague.' As she took in his distracted air and pallor, she looked at him with concern. 'Is everything all right, sir?'

'Yes... no. While I'm with the group captain, will you please consult Bradshaw and find me the times of trains from Paddington to Bristol for the rest of the day.' And with that, he strode out of the room and headed for Group Captain Hague's office.

The meeting did not go well. With Avril Swanson's words, 'We think you should come as soon as you can,' echoing in his ears, he pre-empted whatever it was that Hague had been going to discuss with him and asked for immediate compassionate leave. His request was not well received, but Felix pressed his case and was finally granted leave for the rest of the week, starting at once. He returned to his office and having briefed Miss Dixon on what was happening, picked up the list of train times she had prepared for him and went home.

Chapter 11

That Monday morning, Daphne lay in bed until she heard the door of the flat close, then she got up and peeped out of the window to watch Felix striding off down the street. She was filled with relief that he'd gone. It was his first day back to the Air Ministry after their week's honeymoon in Paris; the first time she'd been alone since they were married.

When they'd left the Savoy they'd taken a taxi back to the flat in Oakley Street where Felix insisted on carrying Daphne over the threshold, and without putting her down, he carried her through to the bedroom. The moment that they'd both anticipated, Felix with desire, Daphne with dread, had arrived.

Felix set her down gently and as she stood still and silent looking at him, reached to remove the combs from her hair, allowing it to tumble free about her shoulders. Murmuring endearments, he began, slowly, to undress her, stroking her neck and shoulders as he unzipped her dress, letting it slip to the floor. She stood unresisting as he removed her bra, allowing her breasts to fall free.

'You are so beautiful,' he breathed as he bent to kiss first one then the other. Gently he removed the rest of her underwear until she stood, naked, her pale skin golden in a shaft of afternoon sunshine. Then he gathered her up in his arms and carried her to the bed. Quickly he stripped off his own clothes, tossing them aside, and slipped onto the bed beside her. He'd waited so long for this moment, dreaming of how her skin would feel against his own, how her lips would open to him, how her body would respond, how their passion would build, but now that he was holding her, kissing her, Daphne's body was stiff and tense.

Felix felt her tension and thought he understood. She's frightened, he thought. It's her first time and I'm rushing her.

'It's all right, darling,' he whispered into her hair. 'It's all right, just try and relax.' And with a great effort, he tried to restrain himself.

Daphne was frightened, frightened that Felix would be able to tell that she wasn't a virgin. She tried to respond to his lovemaking, returning his kisses and allowing his hands to rove all over her body, but all she wanted was to get it over with. She remembered little of her previous encounter with the subaltern, except that it had hurt and it seemed to be an altogether messy business. She'd pretended to enjoy it, but he was rough in his excitement and when he'd finished her whole body had felt bruised and she was extremely sore between her legs. He was an officer, she'd thought him a gentleman but when he returned to his unit the next day, her letters went unanswered and she never heard from him again. He'd left her aching, miserable and pregnant.

Now it was all happening again. Even though Felix was a little more gentle, there was an urgency about his lovemaking that made her recoil. She kissed him as she had all through their courtship and tried to return his caresses, but when, thoroughly aroused, he tried to enter her, it was all she could do not to push him away.

'It's all right, my darling,' Felix whispered as he drew away from her. Raising himself on one elbow, he looked down into her face, gently rubbing himself against her, smoothing her silky skin with his own. 'Don't be afraid, sweetheart, I won't hurt you.' He bent his head and kissed her neck, flicked his tongue into her ear and then made a trail of butterfly kisses down to her breasts, teasing her nipples with the tip of his tongue.

Daphne felt a faint, answering arousal, but all she could think was, For God's sake, Felix, get on with it. Get it over.

This time, when he tried to enter her, Felix found no resistance at all. She lay almost quiescent in his arms as his need for her built and when he finally exploded, he collapsed against her, for the moment satisfied. After a minute she pushed at him.

'Get off, Felix. You're too heavy, I can't breathe!'

Felix slid off her but kept his arm around her, nestling against the warm curves of her body.

'You're beautiful, Daphne,' he whispered. 'My beautiful wife. Don't worry, sweetheart, it'll be even better next time. We'll take it more slowly. We've got all night! Every night!' At this thought Felix felt himself start to harden and he began caressing her breasts again.

Next time? thought Daphne. All night? 'Felix,' she said with a sigh, 'dearest, it was wonderful, but I must sleep, we've got a long day ahead of us tomorrow.' She took his hand to remove it from her breast, but as she did so he grasped it in his and carried it downward to press against his throbbing erection.

'No,' she wanted to scream. 'No, not again, not yet!' But he was inside her again, gripping her behind with both hands as he raised her up against him, pushing deeper. His mouth found hers, his kisses deep, his tongue probing and she almost gagged.

When he finally came, she couldn't wait to push herself free of him, to curl up so there could be no further invasion of her body.

They had lain side by side, bodies not touching but each aware of the other. Daphne afraid he might reach for her again and Felix afraid to do so. It was not an auspicious start to their married life.

Next morning, they took a taxi to Victoria and caught the Golden Arrow to Paris. Neither of them mentioned the night before and there was an awkwardness between them that had not been there previously. As they crossed the Channel on the ferry, Felix went up on deck, keen to be out in the fresh air. Daphne stayed in the passengers' lounge, happy to be alone with her thoughts. She had been surprised at her own reluctance in the bedroom. She found Felix attractive enough, but when it came to the act of consummation, she had shied away from the intimacy. The only good thing about their wedding night had been that Felix hadn't noticed that she wasn't the virgin she'd pretended. She knew she was going to have to get used to the sex, to make more effort to respond to his lovemaking, but the thought of him on top of her again, hot and sweating, made her shudder. On the other hand, she told herself, it was the price she was going to have to pay for the security of his name, the comfort of his home and freedom from financial worries. She had set out to catch him, and having done so, she couldn't risk losing him by being cold and unresponsive.

Out on deck, Felix stood looking over the ship's rail. The crossing was calm and as he watched the French coast emerge from a bank of low cloud, he, too, was thinking about his wedding night. He couldn't believe that Daphne had had no knowledge of what happened in the marital bed. True, she'd never been with a man before, but surely she must have realised what it entailed. Was she frigid, or was she just shy, needing to be wooed and gentled into enjoying sex as much as he did?

I must be patient, he told himself. I must teach her to find pleasure in what I'm doing... what we're doing... together.

When they landed at Calais each had made a new resolution, and as the train steamed towards Paris, though still aware of the gap that had opened up between them, they began to talk to each other, the talk of acquaintances as they watched the French countryside rush by, but at least some conversation, and by the time they arrived at the Gare du Nord, communication between them had been some-what restored.

The days in Paris passed well enough, but after days of exploring the city, walking hand in hand along the Seine, climbing the Eiffel Tower, visiting the Louvre and taking a taxi out to Versailles, when they returned to their hotel Felix expected to take Daphne to bed and explore the magic of her body with as much delight as they'd explored the magic of the city.

Daphne submitted, she could do little else, but though on occasion she felt an answering arousal, most of the time she simply waited for him to finish and then rolled over and went to sleep.

Felix never expressed his disappointment, simply kept trying all the ways he knew to teach her to respond. She's not used to this, he kept telling himself. I must give her time. Her occasional response encouraged him to keep trying.

On the last morning in Paris Felix said, 'Let's go out for breakfast, Daphne. We'll be on the train all afternoon and it'll be a great way to end our time here.'

They'd found a small café and had been served croissants, warm and buttery, with a basket of fruit and bowls of hot coffee.

This is more like it, Daphne thought as they sat at a table in the window and watched the people going about their Sunday-morning business. This is how it'll be, married to Felix. And she put her distaste for the physical side of her marriage out of her mind as she spread jam onto her croissant.

'It's been a lovely week, hasn't it, Felix?' she said, smiling across the table at him. 'It'll be hard to go back to dreary old London, won't it?'

As always, Felix responded to the warmth of her smile, still loving her, still wanting her, still prepared to wait. It *had* been a lovely week and reaching for her hand, he said so. She returned his grasp and they smiled into each other's eyes.

Being married will take some getting used to, Felix thought, but it's surely worth the effort.

Back in London they had fallen into bed, exhausted from their journey home, but in the morning Daphne was awakened by Felix's lips on her neck and his hands caressing her as he began, gently, to make love to her. It wasn't too bad this time, Daphne thought as she felt a short spasm of pleasure between her legs, perhaps she would get used to it and even begin to enjoy it in time.

Now that she was sure he'd left, she went into the bathroom and removed her diaphragm, douching with soap and water just to make sure. Daphne had no intention of falling pregnant again. She and Felix had not discussed starting a family, but she had already decided that she didn't want children and didn't mean to have any.

Today, she intended to go to Hackney to see her family; to tell them, at last, that she was married. She hadn't mentioned the visit to Felix; he might have suggested that he should come too, but it was something she wanted to do on her own. She wanted to impress them with her new status: well-to-do married woman. She looked through her new wardrobe, clothes bought with the generous allowance Felix was giving her, and chose a pale lilac suit. The jacket's wide shoulders and fitted waist emphasised her slender figure, three-quarter sleeves displaying the elegance of her arms. The skirt fell to below her knees, and as she stood before the bedroom mirror and considered her reflection, she twirled on her heel, enjoying the graceful movement of the skirt about her legs. She applied a little make-up and then smiled at herself in the mirror as she perched a small pillbox hat on the smooth sweep of her hair. She looked well dressed, sophisticated, and the knowledge that she would turn heads when she stepped out into the street gave her the confidence she needed for a visit to her family. One final glance in the mirror and she picked up her gloves and went out to hail a taxi.

It was the first time she had actually flagged down a cab on her own, but when she stepped into it she said in a casual voice that hid her nervousness, 'Barrack Street, Hackney, please, cabby.'

If the taxi driver was surprised at her destination he made no comment, simply let in the clutch and set off. Daphne looked out of the window, and as she was driven through the once familiar streets of the East End, it was if she were seeing it all for the first time. She stared at the dirty, grey and still-battered buildings, the narrow streets with their shops and terrace houses. Open bomb sites cleared of rubble, but sprouting weeds, willowherb and self-seeded buddleia, had become playgrounds for the London children; once-handsome blocks of flats now dark with grime loomed above the crowded streets, and defiant spires of blitzed churches stood tall amid the slowly recovering city. Suddenly Daphne realised with new understanding just how far she had come from the girl she had been before the war. Now she had left all this behind her; she didn't belong to these streets any more. She would never again know the poverty that had surrounded and regulated her childhood. She very nearly leaned forward to tap on the glass and tell the driver that she'd changed her mind, but something held her back and she allowed him to drive her to the end of the street where she'd been brought up.

'This will do, cabby,' she called and he pulled in to the side of the road. She got out and paid the fare, and as he drove away, she stood and watched him go, wondering if she should have asked him to wait for her.

Too late now, she thought, and resolutely turned her steps towards the garage at the end of the street.

She paused as she reached the end of the alley and looked up at the familiar sign, 'Higgins Garage. Motor Repairs', that still swung above the entrance to the yard.

That needs repainting, Daphne thought. The whole place looks pretty run-down.

She glanced into the yard and saw a car jacked up and the overalled legs of someone lying on his back underneath it. She considered going in, hoping to see her father before going indoors to face her mother, but, afraid that her beautiful lilac outfit might get dirty, she turned away and walked up the alley to the house. The back door stood open and without knocking, Daphne pushed it wider and stepped inside. Her mother, Ethel, stood at the kitchen stove, looking to Daphne as she always had done, her brown skirt, cream blouse and yellow cardigan covered with her old flowered overall, her greying hair scraped back off her face and tied in a scarf, turban style. When she heard someone at the door she swung round and when she saw who it was, her jaw dropped.

'Well,' she said, 'look what the cat's brought in.'

'Hallo, Mum,' Daphne said. She hadn't been expecting a warm welcome, but the ice-cold expression in her mother's faded blue eyes chilled her. 'Thought I'd come and see how you was all doing.'

'How kind of you!' replied Ethel, and turning back to the pot on the stove she said nothing more, leaving Daphne standing awkwardly in the doorway.

At that moment she heard footsteps running along the alley and turned to see her daughter, Janet, now almost eleven, coming home from school for her dinner. She stopped abruptly when she saw Daphne on the doorstep. She hadn't seen her for nearly four years, and the last time she had, Daphne had been in uniform. Seeing her now in an elegant lilac suit, it took a moment for her to recognise who it was.

'Hallo, Janet,' Daphne said, also surprised. She knew her daughter must have been growing steadily since she had last seen her, but somehow she'd expected her to be the same, shy child she'd been four years ago, not the confident eleven-year-old she saw now.

Janet looked at her for a moment and then turning on her heel, dashed back the way she'd come, shouting as she did so, 'Dad! Dad! Come quick. That Daphne's come home.'

'That Daphne!' Daphne could hear her mother's voice in those words. It must have been how she'd been referring to her and the child had picked it up. She stood, irresolute, in the doorway. Perhaps she should leave, now, before things got worse. Her mother was still ignoring her, stirring the pot on the stove, humming to herself as if Daphne weren't there.

Daphne heard the tuneless hum. Mum was humming! Mum didn't hum or sing. Grumbling was what Mum did, all the time… about everything.

'Mum…' Daphne tried again; no answer and the humming continued.

Janet reappeared again at the run, closely followed by her father.

'See, Dad,' Janet was shouting. 'Told you, didn't I?' The girl pushed past Daphne into the kitchen and flopping down on a stool by the table said, 'What's for dinner, Mum?'

The humming stopped and Ethel turned round to answer Janet's question. 'Hotpot,' she said. 'Go and wash your hands.'

Janet did as she was told, going to the sink and running her hands under the tap.

'With soap.'

Janet used the soap and then dried her hands on a roller towel on the back of the door, before returning to her place at the table.

Daphne watched her as she did so, thinking, It's just the same as it was when I was a kid. Mum at the stove when I got in from school for my dinner. Being told to wash my hands.

At that moment her father, Norman, reached her and awkwardly took her hand in his. His hand was large and oily from his work under the car in the yard, and instinctively Daphne drew back, saying, 'Careful, Dad!' The last thing she wanted was oil on her suit.

'Sorry, love,' he said, letting her hand fall. 'Don't want to get oil on your lovely frock.'

He edged past her and made his way to the sink where he scrubbed at his hands with a nail brush. Looking across at her he said, 'So, how've you been keeping, Daph?'

'Dinner's on the table,' her mother interrupted, as she

doled out three steaming plates of hotpot. The smell assailed Daphne's nostrils and took her straight back to her childhood. It was the smell of home, of the kitchen where they all sat to keep warm in the winter. Mum's hotpot had always been a family favourite.

Her father sat down at the table and waved to the chair opposite. 'Come on, Daphne, sit up to the table and tell us what you've been up to.' He nodded at her suit and added, 'Doing well for yourself, whatever it is, by the looks of you.'

Ethel sighed. She knew she couldn't simply ignore Daphne any more and reluctantly she ladled another portion of hotpot onto a plate and setting it down on the table, motioned to her to take her place.

For a few moments they ate in silence, the three because they were hungry and this was the main meal of the day and Daphne because she didn't quite know how to broach the subject of her marriage.

After a while her father wiped his plate with a piece of bread and said, 'Well, come on, Daph. To what do we owe the pleasure?'

Daphne extended her hand to show her engagement and wedding rings. 'I came to tell you that I got married,' she blurted out.

'Married? Did you now?' Her mother sounded sceptical. 'Did you have to?'

'No!' Daphne snapped. 'No, I didn't.'

'Who's the lucky man, then?' asked her father.

'His name's Felix Bellinger. He's an officer at the Air Ministry.'

'Did he buy you that dress?' asked Janet, reaching out to touch her sleeve, taking it between her fingers and rubbing the soft material. Daphne resisted the urge to pull away.

She simply nodded and said, 'He did. He's very generous, he gives me an allowance to buy my clothes.'

'You still in the WAAFs, are you?' asked Norman.

'No, I left when we decided to get married. Felix doesn't want me to work any more.'

'He must be very rich,' Janet marvelled, staring at the rings Daphne wore.

'I think his family is well off,' Daphne said, 'but he has a good salary at the Air Ministry. He's a wing commander,' she added with a touch of pride.

'And what do they think of him marrying a girl like you?' asked Ethel.

'Who? The Air Ministry?'

'His family.'

'He took me down to Somerset to meet his parents. They live in a village called Wynsdown,' Daphne said, adding defiantly, 'and they made me very welcome.'

'That's nice,' said her father, pushing his plate aside. 'So when are we going to meet your husband? What did you say his name was? Felix?'

'I don't know.' Daphne shrugged. 'Before long, I expect. He's very busy.'

'Didn't ask us to your wedding, I notice,' remarked Ethel. 'Ashamed of us, was you?'

'No, course not, but it was just us and witnesses at the registry office. Anyway, he knows all about you. You've already met him, Dad.'

Her father looked startled. 'I have?'

'Yes, and you too, Mum. He knows where we live, he's been here. It was Felix what brought me home that time when I sprained my ankle, remember? That night in the air raid.'

'You mean the officer what brought you home in a taxi?'

'Yeah, he's the one.'

'An' you been seeing him ever since?' Her mother sounded incredulous.

'No, course not. I met him again at the end of the war.'

'And he remembered you?'

'No. But I remembered him.'

Ethel glanced up at the clock on the kitchen mantelpiece and gave a cry.

'Janet, look at the time! Off you go, you'll be late for school.'

'But I want to talk to Daph, Mum. I want to hear about Felix.'

'School!' repeated Ethel. 'An' get a move on.'

When Janet had gone, Norman said that he needed to get back to work as well. 'Got to get that Morris back on the road tonight,' he said. 'Bloke's coming back for it later.' He smiled across at his daughter. 'Pity you're in your posh frock,' he said, 'or you could've come an' give me an 'and.' Never a demonstrative man, he gave Daphne an awkward pat on her shoulder, saying, 'Come and see us again soon, Daph, and bring this Felix with you next time.'

'Yeah, Dad, I will,' promised Daphne, knowing it was a promise she had no intention of keeping.

When they were alone in the kitchen Ethel poured them each a cup of tea and then sat down opposite Daphne and fixed her with an unwavering stare.

'Sounds as if you've landed in clover, then,' she said at last.

'Yes.' Daphne took a sip of her tea.

'You're a lucky girl,' went on her mother. 'Him knowing the sort of family you come from. Not many officers would marry beneath them like that. You quite sure you ain't in the family way again?'

'Quite sure,' snapped Daphne.

'Good,' said Ethel. 'Now then, what are you going to do about your daughter?'

Daphne stared at her. 'What do you mean, what am I going to do about her?'

'Well, I'd have thought, now as you're married, you'd want to take her into your own home and look after her yourself.'

'Take her into my home?' Daphne echoed faintly.

'Why not? It's where she ought to be, ain't it? With her mother? An' now you can provide for her properly like, well it stands to reason she should come and live with you.'

'But… Mum, I can't! I mean, what would Felix say?'

'I can't see why he'd mind,' said Ethel mildly as she saw Daphne's panic-stricken face. 'I mean, he already knows about her, don't he?'

'And Janet wouldn't want to come,' Daphne said, ignoring the comment about what Felix did and didn't know. 'She'd want to stay here with you and Dad. You're her parents… at least she thinks you are. I'm just her big sister. How would we explain to her why she was having to leave you?'

'He doesn't know about her,' Ethel said flatly. 'You haven't told him about Janet, have you?'

'Course I have,' Daphne retorted. 'We was only talking about her the other day.'

'But he don't know she's yours, do he?'

'At the moment he thinks she's my sister, yes, but he wants kids, so he won't mind when I tell him. Just got to pick my moment, haven't I?'

'He may want kids,' replied Ethel, 'but he'll want them to be his own, not some sailor's by-blow.'

'Mum!' cried Daphne. 'You shouldn't call her that!'

'Why not? It's what she is.'

'She's your granddaughter!'

'She is my granddaughter and I've seen to it that she's never gone without, but she's your daughter. She's your responsibility. I took it on when you was in no position to look after her yourself, but now you are. Never a penny your dad and I had off you towards her upkeep, even when you was earning good money in the air force. You could have helped out then, couldn't you? But did you? No, not you. You left it all up to us. Well, my high and mighty lady, now it's going to stop. Now it's your turn.'

'Mum, stop! Let's think this through,' begged Daphne. 'Let's work it out the best way for Janet.'

'Oh yes, the best way for Janet,' agreed her mother in a voice thick with sarcasm. 'How do you propose to do that then?'

'The thing is, Mum, that if Janet came and lived with Felix and me, well she'd be uprooted, wouldn't she? She'd have to go to a different school, and leave all her friends behind. She'd miss you and Dad dreadfully. I know, I know, you keep telling me I'm her mother, but she doesn't know that...'

'We could tell her,' pointed out Ethel.

'She thinks you and Dad are her parents, she loves you and Dad far more than she'll ever love me, or Felix.' She saw her mother was about to interrupt again and held up a hand to stop her. 'I think it would be far better if she stayed here with you, where she knows, where she's at home and comfortable, so I got a suggestion. I'll take my responsibility seriously but in a different way. I'll give you the money you need for her to have the best. It'll help with your housekeeping, you can buy her nice clothes, and give her little treats. I can come and see her sometimes, as her big sister, bring her presents and the like.'

Unsurprised at this suggestion, Ethel looked at Daphne hard and long. 'We could do it that way,' she said at last. 'It might work better. Course, she'd come and visit you from time to time. Big sisters like to have their little sisters to stay, don't they?'

'Yes.' Daphne gratefully grabbed hold of her mother's agreement. Anything not to have to tell Felix that she'd lied to him all this time, that he wasn't the first man to make love to her, that she had an illegitimate daughter.

'I mean,' went on her mother, 'I'm sure he'd understand that you wanted to make your sister a small allowance so that she could have a few of the things that your dad and I can't afford. How much does Felix give you a month?'

'Ten pounds,' replied Daphne and immediately regretted that she hadn't halved the amount.

Ethel's eyes widened. 'Does he indeed? Obviously a very generous man. That's £120 a year. Well, suppose we say that you give me five pounds a month for Janet. That'll be enough to give her a few extras.'

'Oh, Mum, I can't,' Daphne cried. 'It's too much!'

'Too much, is it? I can see it might be. Well then, I think the best thing would be for me to come and meet your Felix and explain the whole situation.'

'Mum, you wouldn't!'

'I'm sure, as an honourable man,' Ethel went on as if Daphne hadn't spoken, 'he'll want to do what's right, and when he learns that Janet is your daughter, he'll help all he can.'

'That's blackmail,' muttered Daphne mutinously.

'No, it's taking responsibility,' said her mother. 'Shall we agree five pounds a month, to be going on with?' She gave her daughter a hard look. 'Now,' she went on, 'you write down your address. I want to know where I can find you. And don't think you can disappear into the blue, my girl, cos I swear to you if this address is wrong, I'll go and see your husband at his office. Air Ministry you said, didn't you?'

When Daphne left to take a bus back to the West End, Ethel Higgins sat in her kitchen and thought about the arrangement they had come to. She looked at the address Daphne had scrawled on a piece of paper. Oakley Street. She didn't know where it was exactly, but she could find it if necessary. She'd had no intention of letting Janet be uprooted to move in with Daphne, nor had she any intention of telling Janet about her true parentage, ever. She'd banked on the fact that to avoid that happening, Daphne, secure in her new-found prosperity, would pay a good deal towards Janet's upkeep from now on. It was clear as day that she hadn't told Felix the full story about her family. They had not been invited to the wedding because Daphne was ashamed of them. Well, Ethel could live with that, but she was devoted to her granddaughter and prepared to go a long way to make her life better than her own had been, and Daphne? Daphne was the key.

Daphne, sitting on a bus heading back to Chelsea, fumed at how she'd been outmanoeuvred by her mother. Five pounds a month! Half her monthly allowance from Felix. Could she ask him for a bit more? she wondered. He gave her housekeeping money as well, perhaps she could syphon off some of that to pay for Janet's keep. That was certainly a possibility. She'd have to be careful but with a little clever budgeting she ought to be able to manage that.

She had no intention of going back to Barrack Street for a very long time and she'd agreed to send her mother a postal order for five pounds on the first day of every month. The matter was settled and Daphne could put it out of her mind. She might tell Felix she'd made the visit, she might even admit to giving her parents a little cash from time to time, to make their lives easier, but she would pick her moment; perhaps after one of their more successful lovemaking sessions. But when, after changing buses three times, she finally reached Oakley Street and pushed open her front door, all thoughts of telling him anything about her visit to her family went out of her head as she was greeted by a fuming Felix, with the words, 'There you are, Daphne! Where the hell have you been?'

Daphne stared at him. 'I been out,' she said. 'What's up?'

'My father's had a stroke, that's what's up. There's a train in three-quarters of an hour.'

'A train, where?'

'My father's had a stroke, Daphne. We're going down to Wynsdown.'

They arrived at Temple Meads station and took a taxi straight to the hospital. Following directions from a receptionist in the entrance hall, they found Marjorie sitting on a chair in a small office outside one of the wards. She was alone, staring sightlessly at the floor.

'Mother!' Felix hurried to her and dropping down beside her, took both her hands in his. 'Mother?' he said again, gently, but now, as Marjorie lifted her eyes to his and he saw that they were wet and red-ringed, he realised the worst. 'I'm too late,' he whispered.

'He died this afternoon,' Marjorie said, her voice cracked with emotion. 'He never regained consciousness.' She tightened her grip on Felix's hands. 'Don't blame yourself, Felix, he wouldn't have known that you were with him.' She stifled a sob as she said, 'He didn't know I was.'

'Where... where is he now?'

'They've taken him to the hospital mortuary. They said they'd tell me when I could go and see him.'

'Were you with him?' Felix hardly dared ask, but he didn't want to think of his father being alone as he died.

'I was holding his hand,' replied his mother, 'but he didn't know I was.'

'You don't know he didn't, Mum,' Felix said. 'Somewhere inside he may have known you were with him and drawn comfort from it.' Fighting his own tears he said, 'But I wasn't.'

His mother raised his hand to her cheek. 'Darling,' she said. 'You came as soon as you could.'

And Felix wished that it was true, that he hadn't waited for Daphne to get back from wherever she'd been, that he'd left her an explanatory note and simply gone straight to the station.

Daphne stood at the door of the little office and watched as mother and son shared their grief and tried to comfort each other. She felt awkward and embarrassed. She had never been comfortable with overt emotions, and here were Felix and his mother both in tears. She felt no grief for her dead father-in-law, she hardly knew him, but she knew that she'd have to show at least a degree of sadness, later, for Felix's sake. Now she turned away and went back out into the corridor. Felix heard her go, but didn't follow her. He simply knelt on the floor beside his mother's chair and held her hands.

A few moments later a nurse came into the office. 'Mrs Bellinger, I can take you down to see your husband now.' She looked at Felix and asked, 'Is this your son? I'm Sister Deben, I was looking after your father. If you'd like to come with me…'

Felix stood up and helped his mother get to her feet. She rose stiffly and clutched his arm for support. She'd had virtually no sleep in the last forty-eight hours and felt that if she let him go, exhaustion would take over and her legs would fold beneath her; she'd simply collapse back into the chair.

'Follow me.' Sister Deben led the way out of her office and along the corridor to some stairs leading down. Daphne, seeing them moving off, left the window where she'd been standing looking out at the courtyard below and trailed along behind them. Felix paused and turning said, 'We're going to see my father now. Will you come with us?'

Daphne's expression of horror was answer enough and when she shook her head, he simply said, 'Well, never mind. Wait for us in the entrance hall.' Sister Deben pointed along the passage to another set of stairs and murmured, 'It's that way. We'll come and find you there,' before leading Marjorie and Felix down the staircase in front of them.

Daphne watched them go, her relief making her almost light-headed. Why would anyone want to go and look at a dead body? She could think of nothing worse, and she only hoped that Felix would understand why she didn't, couldn't. He wasn't *her* father, though she knew in her heart that even if he had been, she wouldn't have gone. Still, there was no need to say that to Felix. She went down the stairs that the nurse had pointed out and found herself in the open foyer through which they'd passed when they arrived. There was a row of seats along one wall and taking one of these, she settled down to wait. Surely they wouldn't be very long viewing the body.

Felix and his mother followed Sister Deben along another corridor, and paused when she did outside a door.

'We've laid him out in here,' she said, opening the door. 'Stay as long as you like.' And with that she stood aside to let them in, gently closing the door behind them.

Peter Bellinger was laid out on a bed. He was still wearing the pyjamas that Marjorie had brought in for him. Lying on the bed with his hands at his sides and his eyes closed, for a moment he looked to Felix as if he were asleep, but there was a stillness about him that made it clear he would never awake again. A chair had been placed on either side of the bed, and when he'd settled his mother in one, Felix took the other. He reached forward and took his father's hand. It was cold, the skin already with a different texture and feel. Felix had seen death before, many times during the war –

death of friends, death of companions, young lives, often brutally cut short, in air raid or battle – but never the quiet, end-of-life death of someone so close to him. He looked down at his father's peaceful face and saw the lines of worry – which he'd noticed but dismissed as ageing – were smoothed away, and Felix realised just how much he loved him and how great his loss was going to be. He'd left it too late to talk to his father as a man. He'd been away in the air force, fighting a war, at a time a young man might begin to learn the true character and being of his father. He'd left the family home as a youth and returned to it only when necessary, not often from choice. There'd always been plenty of time in the future to do that, but now, suddenly, there wasn't. The future had been cut off, abruptly and irrevocably. Silent tears spilled down his cheeks. He hadn't realised when he'd said goodbye to his father the afternoon of his wedding day, when he'd been glad to see his parents leave and return to Somerset, allowing him and his new bride to forget them and begin their married life in London, he hadn't known that he would never see him again. Of course he hadn't! He hadn't said a proper goodbye, just a clap on the shoulder and a vague promise to visit soon, a promise, he now acknowledged, he hadn't intended to keep in the very near future.

He looked across at his mother and saw that she had dried her tears and was simply sitting holding her husband's other hand, her eyes closed as if in prayer. Was she praying? Felix wondered. Should he be praying too? Prayer had meant little to him during the war years. It had seemed pointless to him to pray to a God that let his friends die, shot down in flames by an implacable foe. Too late, Felix thought, to pray for his father now as he lay still and silent on an October evening in the bowels of a hospital.

They sat for nearly half an hour in the silent room, lost in their own thoughts.

'He loved you very much,' Marjorie said, finally breaking the silence, 'and he was very proud of you.'

Felix nodded. 'I know,' he said softly, 'and I loved him, but I never told him so.'

'Men don't,' replied Marjorie, 'but he knew it, all the same.' She released Peter's hand for the last time and stood up. Gently she leaned forward and kissed his cold forehead.

'Goodbye, my darling,' she whispered. 'You were the love of my life and I will miss you, every minute of every day.'

Felix stood, too, gently replacing his father's hand at his side.

'Goodbye, Dad,' he murmured. 'Don't worry, I'll look after Mum.' He placed a kiss on his fingers and pressed it to Peter's cheek, then turning he took his mother's arm and they left the room.

They found Daphne waiting impatiently in the foyer. When she saw them come up the stairs, she got to her feet and bustled over to them.

'Everything all right?' she asked. 'You took a long time.' And then reddened as Felix simply shook his head at her.

'What are we going to do now?' she went on, trying to cover her confusion.

'We're taking Mother home,' Felix said.

'To Wynsdown?'

'Of course to Wynsdown,' Felix snapped. Then he asked Marjorie, 'Where did you leave the car?'

'Outside in the street.'

They collected their suitcase from the receptionist and walked out into the October night.

'You drive, Felix,' Marjorie said. 'I'm too tired.'

Felix helped her into the front passenger seat, and with

Daphne installed in the back with their case, Felix went round to the driver's side and got in.

The journey back to Wynsdown was a silent one. Marjorie and Felix were busy with their own thoughts and Daphne was wondering how long they'd have to stay. At least until the weekend, she supposed, and with a silent sigh, set herself to put up with four days in the country in a house where a body might lie.

As they swung into the manor's drive, they saw that there were lights on inside, and as the car came to a halt, the front door opened and Avril Swanson stood on the step.

Felix helped Marjorie from the car and Avril came forward, her expression questioning.

'I'm afraid my father died this afternoon,' Felix said, adding with a slight shake of his head. 'I was too late.'

Avril's eyes filled with compassion and she reached a hand to each. 'Oh, Marjorie, Felix, I'm so sorry. He was such a good man.' Then with a brisk shake of her head she went on, 'Anyway, come on in. You must be exhausted.' She stood aside to let them into the house. 'The fire's alight and there's hotpot in the oven.'

'I am tired,' Marjorie admitted. 'All I need is my bed.'

'You should eat something,' Avril said gently. 'You've got to keep your strength up.'

'I'll sleep first,' Marjorie said. 'Tomorrow I'll eat. Just now I'm too tired.'

Daphne had got out of the car and now walked in through the front door. Avril had forgotten that she would be there with Felix and turning to her said, 'Oh, Mrs Bellinger, come into the warm. What a sad day it is. I'm Avril Swanson, the vicar's wife. We did meet last time you were here.'

'Yes, I remember,' Daphne replied before saying, 'Our case is in the car, Felix. Will you bring it in?'

Half an hour later Marjorie was in bed and Felix and Daphne were seated at the table eating Avril's hotpot. Avril herself had gone home to break the news of Peter Bellinger's death to her husband.

'David'll be round to see you in the morning,' she promised as she left, 'to make arrangements…'

'What arrangements?' demanded Daphne when she'd gone. 'Surely you and your mother make those.'

'For the funeral, of course,' Felix said. 'It'll have to be this week, before we go back to London on Sunday. I doubt if I can get any more leave for the foreseeable future.'

Sunday, thought Daphne, six days to stick it out here.

'There'll be a lot to do,' Felix was saying. 'I'll have to have a look through Dad's papers, speak to his solicitor about his will and that sort of thing.'

Despite her tiredness, Marjorie lay awake in the bed she'd shared with Peter for nearly forty years. Their bedroom had always been her favourite room in the house. It was their sanctuary, private to them. Their bed was the one Peter had been born in, the dressing table had been her mother's, brought to the house on her mother's death. In the winter they would undress in front of the flickering flames in the fireplace, the only source of heat in the room. The fire was alight now, Avril had tried to ensure that the bedroom was warm and welcoming, but as Marjorie lay under the bedclothes she still felt cold, and with no Peter snoring gently at her side, the room was empty. She pulled the pillow from his side of the bed towards her and turning her face into it, cried herself to sleep.

*

In the guest bedroom next door, where a fire also burned, Felix and Daphne got undressed and slid into bed.

'It's freezing,' Daphne complained as she pulled the blankets up to her chin. 'Isn't there central heating in this house?'

'No,' replied Felix, as he got in beside her. 'But I've banked the fire up and it should still give us some warmth until the morning. Here,' he said as he reached over and pulled her into his arms, 'I'll warm you up.'

Daphne stiffened a little, but he made no further move to make love to her, simply curled himself round her, sharing his warmth with her, and thus she fell asleep in his arms. Felix, himself, did not sleep for several hours and lying there with his wife's body warm against him, he had never felt more lonely in his life.

David Swanson arrived the next morning as promised and Felix explained the need to have Peter's funeral as soon as possible.

'Shouldn't be a problem,' David told him. 'He died in hospital so there shouldn't be any problem with the death certificate, and he'll be buried in the family grave, here in Wynsdown. I suggest we go for Friday. It'll give you time beforehand and another day with your mother afterwards.'

'I'll get on to the undertakers this morning,' Felix said and added it to his list of things to do. 'Perhaps you could discuss the actual service with my mother. I know she'll have very definite ideas of what she'd like to be included.'

'Of course,' the vicar agreed. 'Perhaps she'd like to come over to the vicarage and we can talk it through.'

That afternoon, the bright autumn of the previous day turned to grey skies and driving rain. Mrs Darby had come in as usual to cook the meals, and Mrs Gurney, having lit the fires and washed the breakfast dishes, was busy in the washhouse, ironing. Daphne felt like a spare part. There was nothing for her to do. She had thought of going out to explore the village, but the heavy rain put paid to that.

'What am I to do?' she asked Felix, and it was, he had to concede, a fair question.

'I don't know,' he said. 'Perhaps there's something you could help Mother with. I'm busy going through all of these.' He waved a hand at the piles of paper in front of him.

Marjorie thanked her politely for her offer of help, but said there was nothing for her to do at present, and that she was just going across to the vicarage. Bored and fed up, Daphne drifted off into the drawing room and seating herself on the window seat, listened to the rain rattling against the casement. She stared out into the rainswept garden, and the paddock beyond. Under the lowering grey sky it all looked dreary in the extreme.

How could anyone want to live here? she wondered. What is there to do in a backwater like this?

As far as she knew, the nearest big town was Bristol and it had taken them nearly an hour to get home from there in the Bellingers' car last night.

At least it's warm in here, she thought, and turning away from the bleak aspect outside, sat down by the fire to wait to be called to lunch.

When the vicar left, Felix telephoned Mr Thompson, his father's solicitor in Cheddar, to apprise him of his father's death and to make an appointment to see him.

'The funeral will be on Friday,' Felix told him, 'and I have to return to London on Sunday afternoon, but I would like to meet you before Friday if possible just to go over what's in my father's will and any of the estate business that needs immediate attention.'

'Of course, Wing Commander,' said Mr Thompson. 'Would you like to come here to my office, or would you prefer for me to call to the manor?'

'Well, there seem to be a great many papers in my father's study,' Felix said. 'I haven't had a chance to look at them all yet. I will over the next couple of days, but I think it would be easier if you came here, where all the paperwork will be at hand.'

'I agree with you,' Mr Thompson said. 'Did Major Bellinger discuss any of the estate business with you recently?'

'No,' Felix said, 'though, last time I saw him, on my wedding day, he said we needed to have a chat.'

'I see.' Mr Thompson sounded thoughtful. 'Well, in that case I think we should certainly meet, sooner rather than later. May I suggest that I come to see you tomorrow morning?'

'If that suits you,' Felix said. 'Don't know if I shall have been able to have a look at it all by then. You've got Dad's will, I assume.'

'Yes, indeed,' replied Mr Thompson. 'I have the original, but there should be a copy amongst his papers. It's fairly straightforward.'

'That's fine. I'll have a look for it and we can go over it tomorrow when you come.'

When they'd rung off, Felix went into his father's study. For a long moment he stood looking round the room where his father had spent so many hours. It was all so familiar, and yet coming into it now made Felix shiver. There was no fire in the fireplace, but that wasn't what made the room feel so chilly.

His father's leather armchair was at the empty fireside, the couch where they had laid him still had a blanket draped across it. Floor-to-ceiling bookshelves covered one wall, a big roll-topped desk stood against another and his work table, where he spread his paperwork, filled the bay window that overlooked the garden. The room smelled of pipe tobacco, a smell that had accompanied his father ever since Felix could remember. There was a rack of pipes on the wall, a tobacco jar on the mantelpiece, an ashtray on the work table. On the small table beside the easy chair were a pair of spectacles and another ashtray with the pipe still lying in it. It was all as it had been, but it would never be the same again.

Felix gave himself a shake and put a match to the ready-laid fire, before turning his attention to the roll-topped desk. When he opened it he'd expected everything to be neatly pigeonholed in his father's usual meticulous fashion and was surprised when a pile of papers cascaded out on to the floor. He picked them up and took them to the table in the window. Still inside the desk were a couple of large envelopes, labelled with the names of the farms leased to farmers on the estate: Charing Farm where the Shepherds lived and Newland Farm, worked by Richard Deelish. Felix set them aside to look at later and picked up a narrow brown envelope with the word 'Will' printed on it. He pulled it out and with it came a smaller, white envelope with his name on it.

Leaving the will aside for the moment, he opened the envelope and found himself staring at a last letter from his father, dated 9 April 1949, just six months ago.

DEAR FELIX,

I hope you never have to read this letter. It will mean that I have died before I have got everything sorted out. I'm afraid

I have to tell you that we are in some financial difficulty at present. Unfortunately your grandfather made some bad investments before the war and many became worthless in the depression of the early thirties. I have to admit culpability for some of this. I should have looked harder at where our money was invested, but while it was giving a reasonable return I wasn't too concerned. Much of our capital, in the funds, has gone. James took his half of our shared inheritance as cash, leaving me the house and the estate. Unfortunately, he also advised me to invest in a South African mining company, an investment that failed in 1937. During the war, to raise money for the estate, I decided to take out a mortgage and thinking I could soon pay it off, I put the house up as collateral. We still had a small portfolio of shares left but the income from these fell and was not enough to cover the repayments. Things went from bad to worse and I was about to default on payment, so rather than lose the house, which has been ours for four generations, I decided to sell off some of the property. The four cottages in Oak Lane have gone, bought by a Bristol man as an investment, but with the sitting tenants. What he intends to do with them if and when they become vacant I don't know. I paid off the mortgage with the money from those sales and I have since put the house into your mother's name, so that she'll never be without a roof over her head. I'm considering selling Charing Farm to John Shepherd and Newland Farm, over the hill, to Richard Deelish if they can raise the cash. When approached, both of them were keen to have the freehold of the land they were farming and both hoping to raise the money to buy their farms outright. So, Felix, you'll find that the estate is in trouble. We still own Havering Farm, but it is small and the return is too little to alleviate our financial troubles. I intend to offer it to my foster son, Malcolm Flint, when old Martin Flower gives up. He has no one to take it on and Malcolm, who has been working for John Shepherd for several years now, deserves a better chance in life than he's been given so far. I know you will honour this intention if it is not already accomplished.

I intend to keep Home Farm going myself as I have been these last years, but am looking at alternative use of the land, something that may bring in a better return than we're getting at present. With this in mind you'll see that I have planted a small plantation of conifers for their timber. Clearly this is a long-term project, but if successful I intend to plant more so that in years to come, it produces a steady income.

It is my hope that I shall be able to recoup our losses to some extent and die in the knowledge that our estate, what's left of it, is on a firm footing and will continue in our family for your children and theirs. It pains me that things should have come to this, but God willing we shall come through.

I know you'll do your best with what is left, you are a man of great character and strength, a son to be proud of, and I know I can rely on you to see that your mother never goes without.

God bless you, Felix.
DAD.

Felix read and reread the letter. He could hear his father's voice in every word, and as what he was reading sank in he realised what his father had wanted to discuss with him. Now it was too late for that too. Tomorrow Mr Thompson would be able to put him in possession of the full facts. He stared at the bundles of papers and the two envelopes with the names of the farms on them. All the details of the sales must be in those. If things were as bad as his father intimated they could well lose everything. Felix felt sick to his stomach. He sank into his father's armchair and buried his head in his hands.

Chapter 13

Charlotte heard the news about Major Bellinger when she went to the post office on Tuesday morning.

'Very sad, isn't it?' said Nancy Bright. 'Poor Mrs Bellinger, so sudden, such a shock.'

'It always is a shock somehow,' Charlotte agreed, 'even if you have been expecting it.'

'Which she wasn't, poor lady!' sighed Nancy. 'Well, at least she's got Felix down with her now, though I did hear he was too late to see his father alive. Come down by train, he did, yesterday, with his new wife. She'll be a great comfort to him, won't she?'

'I expect she will,' agreed Charlotte. 'I'll have a book of stamps, please, Nancy.'

'Ooh! Writing lots of letters, are you? I love getting letters, don't you? Something exciting or unexpected coming in through your letter box.'

Clearly Nancy was hoping to hear to whom Charlotte was writing, but Charlotte didn't enlighten her. She simply smiled and called Johnny away from the window.

'But, Mummy,' he said, 'there's Auntie Caro.'

Charlotte looked out and saw Caroline Morrison crossing the green from the vicarage, where she was staying until her marriage with Dr Masters in ten days' time.

'So she is,' said Charlotte. 'Let's go and say hallo to her, shall we? Bye, Nancy.'

Outside, she found Caroline cooing to baby Edie, who was tucked up in her pram.

'Caroline,' called Charlotte as she came out into the street. 'Lovely morning!'

'Hallo, Charlotte, just saying good morning to my god-daughter.' She turned to Johnny who was pulling at her skirt. 'And hallo to you, young monster,' she said and bent to give him a hug.

'I not a monster,' Johnny informed her. 'I'm a hunter!'

'Are you indeed?' laughed Caroline, before turning to Charlotte and saying, 'Have you got time for a cup of tea at Sally's?'

'Of course,' said Charlotte, 'that'd be lovely. Come on, Johnny, if you're good you can have some milk and a sticky bun.'

Together they walked across the green to Ye Olde Tea Shoppe. There was nothing 'olde' about this tea shop. It was a new venture of Sally Prynne's. Since her daughter, Sandra, had married and moved to Weston-super-Mare, she'd found herself with nothing to do. She persuaded her husband, Arthur, that she should use the front room of their cottage as a tea room.

'There isn't nowhere for anyone to get a cup of tea and have a chat in this village,' she said. 'I'm going to give it a go.'

'There's the Magpie,' said Arthur.

'That's a pub, not a tea room. What this village needs is a nice little caff where you can take the weight off your feet, have a cup of tea, a piece of cake an' a chat.'

'Suit yourself, girl,' Arthur said. 'Can't do no harm to try, like.'

He painted a sign to hang over their front door, though anything less like 'an olde tea shoppe' than Sally Prynne's front room, Billy'd said when he first saw it, would be hard to imagine. But surprisingly it had taken off and most mornings Sally had customers sitting at one of the two tables in her front room, drinking tea and exchanging gossip.

Johnny was given his promised milk and sticky bun and then sent out to play in the Prynnes' backyard.

'It's very sad about Peter Bellinger, isn't it?' said Caroline as she poured the tea. 'Avril told me that it was you who raised the alarm.'

'Well, I ran for Dr Masters…'

'And we weren't there. We'd gone to Bristol to collect Henry's wedding suit from the tailor's. Poor Henry, he felt awful that he wasn't there to render first aid.'

'I don't think it would have made any difference,' Charlotte said. 'The major hadn't moved again when the ambulance came.'

'I hear the funeral's on Friday,' Caroline said. 'David went round there this morning.'

'You are up with the news,' Charlotte laughed, 'and I bet it'll be just the same when you're Mrs Doctor!'

'Actually, Charlotte, I do have a piece of news that may interest you. You remember Matron at St Michael's and Livingston Road?'

'Of course I do,' replied Charlotte. 'I'm never likely to forget anyone who looked after me. What about her?'

'Well, I had a letter from her yesterday.'

'Did you? Is she keeping well? Is she still at Livingston Road?'

'Yes to both those questions,' Caroline said. 'But more important, she wrote to me about you.'

'Me? Why me?'

'Apparently someone came looking for you last week and Mrs Burton remembered him well.'

Charlotte's eyes opened wide. 'Harry?'

Caroline nodded. 'Harry.'

'Did she tell him where I am?'

'No. He spoke to the new supervisor, Mrs Acton, and of course she'd never heard of you. She insisted that whoever you were, if you had been there during the war, you weren't any more. Harry was still at the gate and Mrs Burton saw him. At first she didn't recognise him, but when she heard his name was Harry, she knew exactly who he was. She's written to me to warn you that he's looking for you. He may never find you, but she thought you ought to know.'

Charlotte took a sip of her tea and then put down her cup and looked earnestly at Caroline.

'I think he will find me.'

'Do you? Why?'

'I had a letter this morning. From Aunt Naomi.'

'And?'

'And somehow, Harry had found her. He just turned up on her doorstep and asked if I was there.'

'And she told him where you are?' Caroline sounded surprised. All Charlotte's friends knew how casual Harry had been about his friendship with Charlotte, or Lisa as he still called her, and few of them would have wanted her to revive a contact that had caused her so much sadness in the past.

'Not exactly. She knows that Billy doesn't like him and so she'd decided to say she didn't know. Trouble is, young Nicky came home from school for his dinner. She told him Harry was an old friend of mine and Nicky told Harry how they had been to Wynsdown to baby Edie's christening. She didn't enlarge on what Nicky had said, but she thinks the damage was done.'

'So you think he'll turn up here?'

Charlotte shrugged. 'I don't know. Aunt Naomi said that

he's been in Australia ever since the end of the war. Remember, he wanted me to go with him?'

Caroline nodded. 'I remember.'

'Well, Aunt Naomi says that he's going back, but he'd hoped to see me again before he went. He sent me his love.'

'Hmm,' Caroline gave a sigh, 'he's certainly been looking for you. Do you want to see him?'

'I don't know. Yes. I s'pose so. I know Billy won't like it if he turns up, but, well, Harry has always been sort of special, you know?'

Caroline nodded, she did know Harry was special, even though she wished he weren't. 'So,' she said, 'are you going to warn Billy that he might just appear?'

'I don't know.' Charlotte looked confused. 'He *won't* like it if he does, but if I say he might and then he doesn't, well, I'll have upset Billy for nothing. Aunt Naomi says she doesn't think he will come. He doesn't have an actual address.'

'Do you think that will stop him? We're talking about Harry, remember.'

'I don't *know*,' cried Charlotte, an edge of panic to her voice. 'And I don't know what to *do*. What do you think? Wouldn't it be better to say nothing for the time being? No need to rock any boats needlessly?'

Caroline, remembering how her interference in things between Harry and Charlotte had caused trouble before, said, 'It's a decision you've got to make for yourself, Charlotte. I can't tell you what to do.'

Silence rested between them for a moment and then Caroline said, 'Billy has nothing to fear from Harry, has he, Charlotte?'

'No!' responded Charlotte fiercely. 'Of course he hasn't.'

'Then maybe you should tell him about your aunt Naomi's letter. Show it to him. I mean, if you don't and then Harry does appear, and Billy thinks you knew he was coming, well, then he might feel you'd been hiding it from him for a reason. That there *was* something to hide.'

Charlotte looked at her with mute appeal and Caroline reached forward and took her hand. 'Only you can make the decision, Charlotte. I shall say nothing about the letter from Mrs Burton to anyone else, I promise, so if you decided to say nothing there's no reason for anyone else to know.'

At that moment, Johnny appeared in tears. 'I felled over,' he said, 'and my leg's hurt.' He displayed a graze on his knee, and when suitable sympathy had been shown, he allowed Charlotte to take him into Sally's kitchen to bathe the knee.

'It doesn't need a plaster,' she told him as she patted the knee dry.

'It does!' Johnny assured her earnestly. 'It does, there's blood. Blood needs a plaster.'

'Well, we haven't got one here, so we'd better go home and find one, hadn't we?'

'Don't worry about Harry,' Caroline said as they stood together on the green. 'If he does turn up, well, sufficient unto the day...'

Charlotte walked home with the children and when the plaster had been applied, lunch had been eaten and they were both in their beds for their afternoon nap, she sat down in the kitchen with another cup of tea and reread Naomi's letter.

> Ivy Cottage
> Feneton
> Suffolk

DEAREST LISA

How are you all down there in Wynsdown? I hope you're all keeping well as we are here. We have moved into our new home now, I've put the address at the top, and are very happy here. It's ever so nice having our own home again. A place just for us where we can shut the door on the world outside. Dan was real chuffed when you asked him to be little Edie's godfather. We all wish you were living a bit closer so we could see you more often. Still, never mind, eh?

I thought you might like to know that that lad what you used to know in the war, Harry Black, turned up here the other day. He said he was trying to find you and was you living here with us? I told him no, so then he asked where you was living. I wasn't going to tell him without asking you first because I know your Billy ain't too keen on him. Anyhow Harry said he'd been in Australia and was home in London on business and wanted to see you. I think he's been looking for you at Livingston House and Kemble Street which was how he found us. That nosy cow Shirley from across the road, told him where we'd moved to, and so he'd come looking.

I wasn't going to tell him where you was but then young Nick come home from school for his dinner and he spilled the beans. Said we'd been to see you in Wynsdown for Edie's Christening. I don't know if Harry knows where Wynsdown is, but I thought I ought to warn you that he's looking for you and he might show up. He told me he was going back to Australia soon, so he may not have time. I hope he goes there for good. He may have looked after you at school, but you've got your Billy to look after you now.

Do write me a line sometime soon and let us know how you're going on. I bet young Johnny is shooting up. It won't be long before he goes to school, will it?

Uncle Dan's at work just now, but if he was here I know he'd send you all his love and a special kiss for little Edie.

Love from AUNT NAOMI.

Dear Aunt Naomi, thought Charlotte, still trying to look after me. I wish they lived nearer, too.

She sighed and folding the letter again, put it back in its envelope and slipping it into the dresser drawer turned her attention to preparing the vegetables for supper.

Chapter 14

Felix had considered discussing the financial difficulties he'd discovered with his mother, but decided that he would wait until he'd had his meeting with Mr Thompson. He didn't know how much his mother knew about the state of affairs he was faced with, and with her grief still so raw, he didn't want to add to her misery. He said nothing to Daphne, either. He knew that she was finding it difficult here in the house. There was little she could do for Marjorie, little she could do for him, and the kitchen was in the hands of the redoubtable Mrs Darby. When they'd retired to their bedroom that night he'd put his arms round her, folding himself into the warm curves of her body.

'At least it was quick,' Daphne murmured by way of consolation. 'He didn't know nothing, anything, about it. He didn't suffer.'

No, his father probably hadn't suffered, but those he'd left behind were; suffering from shock, from grief, from the emptiness of his going.

Felix had lain awake long after Daphne had fallen asleep, his mind churning with what he'd discovered. What was he going to do? What could he do?

Eventually, he, too, had drifted off into an uneasy sleep, to wake in the early morning, unrested and with no solution to his problems.

Mr Thompson arrived punctually and when he'd given his condolences to Marjorie, Felix led him into the study and shut the door. Together they sat down at the work table in the window, and Mr Thompson opened his briefcase.

'I assume you've looked at the will,' he said.

Felix shook his head. 'No,' he said. 'I haven't.'

'Isn't there a copy among the major's papers?'

'Yes, there is,' Felix replied, 'but in the same envelope was a letter addressed to me.' He picked it up from the desk and handed it to the solicitor. Mr Thompson put on his glasses and read it through.

'Well,' he said as he handed it back, 'that pretty much sums up the situation.'

'The house belongs to my mother?'

'It does, as does Eden Lodge.'

'Eden Lodge?' Felix looked puzzled. 'You mean the Miss Mertons' house?'

'Yes, your maternal grandfather owned it and left it to your mother when he died. It's been rented to the Miss Mertons ever since their father died in the 1930s. Of course, Miss Rose died during the war, but Miss Violet is still there.'

'So, Mother has some income from that?'

'She has,' answered Mr Thompson, 'but not much. The rent has been the same since the doctor died.'

'It's never been increased?'

'Your mother always said she didn't need the money and the Mertons couldn't afford to pay any more.'

'Well she's going to need the money now,' said Felix. 'It may be her only income.'

'It's certainly something we can look at,' agreed the solicitor.

'In his letter, my father mentioned he was considering selling off the farms. How far did he get with that?'

'He's spoken to Mr Shepherd and Mr Deelish, but there has been no agreement as yet.'

'And if we did that...?'

'It would mean you still owned, or rather that your mother still owned the house and garden. You'd own all the land that belongs to Home Farm, which includes the paddock and the twenty-acre field. Also Havering Farm, which as your father has pointed out brings in a small but regular income. Mr Flower has already written his determination to give up the tenancy next Lady Day. The major apprised me of Mr Flower's intention though I haven't seen the actual letter. I assume you'll find it somewhere among your father's papers. If you're in agreement with your father's wishes, that tenancy can then be offered to Malcom Flint.' He pulled an envelope from his briefcase and extracted a document which he passed over to Felix. 'Here's your father's will. I can read it formally on Friday after the funeral if you wish, but you need to know the contents now.'

Felix took the will, the last will and testament of Peter Michael Bellinger, dated 1 April 1949. Felix glanced up at Mr Thompson.

'This is a very recent will,' he said as he glanced at it. 'Tell me the main points.'

'The major decided to remake his will in the light of all the financial arrangements he was making. It is relatively simple. Your mother already has the house. The estate, such as it is, is left to you. The shares in the portfolio will be transferred to you, but he asks that any dividends will be hers until she dies. This is a request, not a legal requirement. There is a life policy which pays out on your father's death, the beneficiary being your mother, which should supply her with sufficient funds to continue living here for the foreseeable future. He reiterates his wish that Malcolm Flint should be offered the tenancy of

Havering Farm, but this is also only a stated wish and is not legally binding upon you as heir to the estate.' The solicitor looked over his spectacles at Felix. 'Your father has left you with a good deal of discretion here. He told me that he had implicit trust in you to do as he asked.'

'All this has come as a complete surprise,' Felix said. 'I had no idea of the financial problems he was facing.'

'I have to say, I did encourage him to discuss these things with you some time ago,' Mr Thompson said, 'and I understood that he intended to do so. Perhaps he had no opportunity.' There was no criticism in the solicitor's voice, but Felix knew it was his fault. The infrequency of his visits to his parents in recent years was the reason no opportunity had occurred. 'I suggest,' Mr Thompson went on, 'that when the funeral is over and things have settled down again, you discuss everything with your mother. She's an extremely sensible woman and she may have suggestions to contribute as to the way forward. I'm here and happy to deal with any legal matters that may arise, but for the moment, I suggest that you do nothing. The aftermath of a sudden death is never the time to make hasty decisions.'

The church was overflowing for Peter Bellinger's funeral. Almost the whole village had turned out to see the squire laid to rest. Though thought, by some, to be rather aloof, he was generally acknowledged to be a kind man and a generous employer. There was a whispering and a rustling as the congregation waited for the arrival of the coffin. Heads were turned when the major's brother and his wife walked in and took their places in the reserved pew at the front. James Bellinger was dressed in a dark suit, his shirt a startling white against his carefully knotted black tie. His wife, wearing a black coat and skirt and a smart black hat, was of particular interest to many of the village ladies. They hadn't see 'Mrs James' for several years now and were interested to see her dressed in the latest London fashion.

David Swanson was at the church door to greet Marjorie and her son and daughter-in-law while they waited for the coffin to be unloaded from the hearse, only going into the church himself moments before it was carried in. Marjorie insisted on walking behind the coffin alone, leaving Felix and his bride to follow slowly up the aisle in her wake as, led by the choir, the congregation sang 'Abide with Me'.

Earlier that morning, Marjorie had gazed out of her bedroom window at the autumn garden, a view she'd loved and looked at every morning of her married life. She fought back the tears that sprang to her eyes; today she had to show a brave face to the world. Tears were for tomorrow.

Now, as she followed the coffin, she held her head high. Wearing a simple black coat over a plain black dress and black hat from which hung delicate lace, veiling her eyes, she was dignified and strong. She moved into her pew and reached for Felix's hand as he came in beside her. She would listen to James speak in praise of his brother. She would hear Felix read the passage she'd chosen from Corinthians, a favourite passage of Peter's, ending with the words 'And now abideth faith, hope, charity, these three; but the greatest of these is charity.'

She would listen, but she would not hear. The only way she could get through the service was to distance herself from the proceedings; to retreat behind her veil and be with Peter. To remember Peter, her own Peter, not the one everyone else knew. Peter as she'd first seen him at Maud Hathaway's twenty-first-birthday dance nearly thirty-six years ago. He'd come through the door, glanced across the room and smiled at her... and she'd known she was his.

As the service progressed, she tuned in to James telling the congregation of Peter's exemplary war record and then tuned out again as her thoughts went to their wedding in July 1915, when Peter was home on leave. Their wedding and their three-day honeymoon before he returned to the front. Felix had been born nine months later; a honeymoon baby whom Peter didn't meet for another two and a half years.

Felix gave her hand a squeeze, bringing her back to the present, and she watched him go up to the lectern, heard him, with a slight tremor in his voice, read the passage from Corinthians. Dearest Felix, she thought. In his own way he's grieving as much as I am.

She looked along the pew at Daphne, also decked out in black. Her face was blank as if her mind were also elsewhere. Marjorie found that she didn't blame her. After all, she and Felix had been married less than a fortnight, and here she was at her father-in-law's funeral where she really knew no one except Felix.

Daphne was indeed thinking about other things. She was almost counting the minutes till they could leave Wynsdown, catch the train back to London and get on with normal life. The whole week had been very difficult, with Felix virtually ignoring her as he dealt with the business things which had to be done.

I might as well have stayed in London, she thought angrily. And then to top it all, the major's brother and his awful wife, Freda, had arrived yesterday evening. With Felix and Daphne already ensconced in the main guest room, the smaller, blue guest room, that looked out over the drive, had been prepared. It was clear Freda wasn't best pleased with this arrangement, but James had said, 'Come on, Kitten, it's only for two nights.'

Kitten! thought Daphne as she glanced across the aisle to where James and his wife were sitting. With her permed iron-grey hair, her rouged cheeks and her down-turned mouth, anything less like a kitten than Freda would be hard to imagine.

Dinner had been a difficult meal. Daphne had been introduced and having looked her up and down, Freda had asked, 'And who are your people, Daphne? Would we know them?'

To her surprise Marjorie had answered her before Daphne had time. 'Daphne has no close family, Freda, we're her family now.'

'Oh.' Freda was undeterred. 'Still, we might have known them from somewhere.'

'It's very good of you to come, James,' Marjorie said, changing the subject.

'Well, couldn't not be here,' he replied awkwardly. 'My only brother. Like to say a few words about him at the service, give him a good send-off, and that.'

Marjorie looked round the church as David Swanson began the final prayers. It was a good send-off, she supposed. In the row behind her stood Malcolm Flint, the evacuee they'd taken in seven years earlier. Both she and Peter had become very fond of the two boys who'd come to live with them. Fred Moore had returned to his family in London at the end of the war, but Malcolm had no family left. He had grown to love his foster parents and he'd stayed on in Wynsdown when peace broke out, working at Charing Farm. He'd married fellow evacuee Clare Pitt the previous summer and Peter had let them move in to one of the estate cottages.

The day after they heard the news of his death, Malcolm and Clare had been to visit her. Clare, quiet and reserved, showed nothing of her emotions; Malcolm was clearly affected by Peter's death as he awkwardly took her hand and offered his condolences. She had surprised them both by giving him a quick hug and saying, 'Thank you for coming, Malcolm. Peter thought very well of you.'

After the service, now almost at an end, everyone was invited back to the manor for refreshments. Mrs Darby had been amazing and had produced plates of sandwiches, cakes and biscuits, now covered with linen clothes, waiting in the kitchen for their return. Daphne was to help carry the teacups and pass the plates. Felix would dispense something stronger to those who wanted it. Marjorie hoped that people wouldn't stay too long. She well knew that many of the local people would want to have a look at the inside of the house, but most of them would not be particularly comfortable hobnobbing with people like Peter's brother James and his wife. Her heart sank as she remembered that they were staying another night, before going back to London.

Marjorie had never got on very well with James, or his wife. Though he was the younger of the two brothers, he'd always assumed a superiority because he lived in London and held some important job in the War Office. He'd married the Honourable Freda Berwick, and they had come to regard Peter as something of a stick-in-the-mud. No 'Honourable' for him; he'd married the daughter of another local landowner, and was still living in the family home where he and James had been born and brought up.

'You should get up to town more,' James had said on more than one occasion. 'Always stay with us, you know.'

But they hadn't. Neither Marjorie nor Peter liked London and visited it as seldom as possible. Peter had done all he could for the war effort, ensuring the estate produced as much food as possible and organising the Home Guard, but he'd felt sidelined, while James was doing something hush-hush at the War Office.

Before the war, Freda would occasionally bring the children, Clive and Christine, to visit Wynsdown in the summer holidays.

'So good for the children to have some clean country air,' she'd enthuse as they all piled out of James's new Lanchester. 'And they so love coming to Wynsdown.'

That at least was true; Felix and his cousins got on well and all three of them looked forward to the visits. Their mothers, however, merely put up with each other, distantly polite as they waited for the visit to end. Their fathers seldom met.

Generally, the James Bellingers had little time for the Wynsdown branch of the family, and now here they were, all solicitude, and going to stay for two nights. Marjorie, who was aching for solitude in her own home, could hardly bear it.

Later that evening, when the three women had gone to bed, Felix and James sat in the drawing room, each with a large whisky beside him.

'So, Felix,' James said, as he stretched his feet to the fire, 'what are you going to do?'

'Do?'

'Well, I mean are you going to resign from the RAF and come back here to live? Take over the running of the estate?'

'There is no estate as such,' Felix said. 'We're virtually bankrupt.'

'What!' exclaimed James. 'How can you be bankrupt? You've got this house, the land, the outlying farms. They must bring you a pretty substantial income, and what about the cottages in Oak Lane?'

'They've been sold,' Felix said flatly. 'And it probably won't be long before the farms are, too.'

'But where's the money gone?' demanded James.

'I believe,' Felix said carefully, 'that you took your inheritance from your father in cash.'

'That was agreed at the time,' James said hotly. 'Peter had a house and the estate. I had neither, and I had to buy my house in London. It was not handed to me on a plate!'

'My father received the estate,' Felix agreed, 'but little money for its upkeep. He had to mortgage the house to keep the estate running during the war. He had to sell the Oak Lane cottages to repay that mortgage. The income from the three farms is insufficient to cover the upkeep of the house and the general living expenses. The estate needs investment and there's no cash to invest.'

'And you're blaming me for all this?' James's face flushed beetroot red. 'You think it's my fault?'

'No,' said Felix, though in truth he did, 'but you can see Dad has been struggling over the last few years.'

'And you intend to sell off the farms?' James sounded horrified.

'Dad was considering it, and so am I. We may not have much choice.'

'What about the house? That must be worth a pretty penny.'

'The house is my mother's home,' said Felix. 'Dad put it into her name after the war, so that she would always have somewhere to live.'

'But if you can't afford the upkeep…'

'I've been discussing various options with Mr Thompson, Dad's solicitor, and when we've thought them all through, we'll decide what to do.'

'And what are these options?' demanded James.

'I'd rather not say at the present time,' replied Felix.

'But perhaps I can advise you,' James suggested.

'Like you advised Dad to invest in those South African mines?' Felix couldn't keep a trace of bitterness out of his voice.

'Well, that wasn't a very good investment,' admitted James. 'I lost some money in that venture, too.'

'Yes,' agreed Felix flatly. 'But you could afford the loss. Dad couldn't.'

'But I warned him,' said James angrily. 'I told him to sell.'

'Maybe you did, but if so, it was too late. All I know is that he lost much more than he could afford.'

'Perhaps I can help out with your plans, if you'd only tell me what they are.'

'When we've come to a decision,' Felix said, 'I'll keep you informed.'

'Well, in that case,' James picked up his glass, and tossing off the last of his whisky, got to his feet, 'I'm for my bed,' he said. 'Good to have a chat with you, Felix. I'll see you in the morning before we go. Goodnight.'

Felix poured himself a second much-needed whisky and sat for another half-hour, thinking. Would he indeed have to resign his commission and return to live here in Wynsdown? What could he do here that he couldn't do from London? Look after his mother. She would be desperately lonely without his father, but her home was here in Wynsdown. It was here that she'd spent the happiest days of her life. It was here she belonged with her friends about her.

After the service, Malcolm Flint had come up to him to shake his hand. 'I owe everything I am now to your father and mother,' he said. 'They took me in after I'd lost my parents in the Blitz. If there is anything I can do to help you or your mother, please ask.'

Felix had never actually met either of the evacuees who'd lived at the manor, but as he shook Malcolm's hand he was struck by the sincerity with which the younger man spoke. He remembered his father's intention of offering him Havering Farm when the tenancy came up and knew he must give it serious consideration.

'I'll remember,' he said, 'and I know my mother will be grateful for your care.'

When James and Freda had departed next morning it was as if the house itself had heaved a sigh of relief. Marjorie felt as if a weight had been lifted from her shoulders. Her loss, reborn each morning as she awoke to the emptiness in the bed beside her, was no less, but the blessed comfort of her own home was returned to her. Felix and Daphne would be leaving tomorrow morning, and though she felt guilty admitting it even to herself, she was ready for them to go. She needed the house to herself. Felix had been wonderful, tackling the piles of paperwork in the study, dealing with the solicitor, but now all that could wait. She knew Felix had to be back at work on Monday, and it was quite clear that Daphne, a fish out of water, couldn't wait to leave.

At lunch Marjorie decided to take the bull by the horns and said, 'I think you should catch the evening train back to town, Felix. There must be things you have to do before you go back to the office on Monday, and I shall be quite all right here on my own.'

As she spoke she saw the light of hope flicker in Daphne's eyes and added, 'Poor Daphne's hardly been in her own home since you got back from your honeymoon. That's where you should both be now, together in your own home.'

'There's still a lot to sort out, Mother,' Felix said.

'Darling, it can wait. I know things are in a dreadful state, but you need time to go through it all. You can come down for another weekend in a couple of weeks' time and we can talk things through properly.' She gave a sad smile and went on, 'To be quite honest with you, darling, I'm not quite ready to go into it all now.'

Nor was Felix, and to Daphne's delight, they caught the early-evening train.

It was almost ten o'clock when Felix and Daphne got back to the Oakley Street flat. They'd had some dinner on the train and were both ready to fall into bed and sleep. It had been an exhausting week.

Daphne had heard Marjorie saying that things were in a dreadful state, but she'd not expected these 'things' to relate to her. What worried her more was that it sounded as if her mother-in-law expected them to visit her again very soon. Daphne, however, had no intention of going. If Felix needed to go, well that was up to him, but Daphne hated the country, disliked her mother-in-law and found the house cold and uncomfortable.

If Felix feels he has to go, he can go by himself, she decided, and closing her eyes, she slid into a dreamless sleep.

Tired as he was, Felix found it difficult to switch his brain off and sleep. He'd told James that he had some ideas which he hoped might help the estate finances, but that was all they were, ideas. He hadn't a clue if they were really viable. What he needed to do was to go back down to Wynsdown and spend time with all the people concerned to see if they could thrash something out between them. He knew Daphne wouldn't want to go there again yet, but there was little he could do about that. Tomorrow he'd have to explain to her how things stood with regard to the estate and his father's will and the effect it was going to have on them; it was a conversation to which he was not looking forward.

On Sunday morning, as they sat over a late breakfast, Felix

said, 'We've got to have a chat, Daph. Things have changed in the last week and they affect us as well as Mother.'

Daphne looked startled. 'What d'you mean?' she demanded. 'What things?'

'Well, as you know, I was going through my father's papers while we were down there and I discovered that the estate is in financial difficulty.'

'So, how does that affect us? We don't live there.'

'No, but you know in my father's will the estate comes to me, and so now I'm responsible for it… and its debts.'

'Debts? Why can't you pay them off with some of the money your father left you?'

'There wasn't much for him to leave and most of what there was goes to my mother.'

'You mean there ain't no money?'

Felix had noticed before how Daphne lapsed back into her childhood speech when she was angry or upset. Sometimes he teased her about it, but now was certainly not the time.

'No, I'm afraid not, well, very little anyway.'

'So we get nothing?' Daphne sounded incredulous and Felix saw just how difficult the rest of the conversation was going to be.

'It's not quite like that. There are some stocks and shares, but they'll have to be transferred to my name and that'll take a while.' No need, Felix thought, to mention that any dividends would be going to his mother. Maybe Daphne wouldn't know about dividends… he could only hope.

'I expect I'll have to go down there quite a lot in the next few months,' he continued. 'I have to get things back onto an even keel, and that won't be easy from here.'

'But what about your job at the Air Ministry? They won't give you any more leave, will they?'

'I don't know,' admitted Felix. 'I'm going to explain the situation and ask for some extended leave, but I may not get it. It'd probably be unpaid anyway.'

'Unpaid!' squeaked Daphne, beginning to worry for the first time. 'If you don't get paid what are we going to live on?'

'I've got some savings,' Felix said, 'but whatever happens we're going to have to tighten our belts for a while.'

'But what about me?'

'What about you? We're both in this together, Daph, and I know you'll do your best to manage on less. I'm sorry, but for a little while at least, I shan't be able to give you the allowance I promised.'

'But you *did* promise!' cried Daphne. 'You know I ain't got no money of my own! I need that allowance!'

'And you'll have one, Daph. It's just that it'll have to be a bit less than you thought, that's all.'

'How much less?' Daphne demanded. 'You promised me ten pounds.'

'I'm afraid, in the circumstances, it'll be more like five.'

'Five pounds! But that's only half!'

'I know, my darling girl, but for now it's all I can afford. It's just till I'm sure my mother has enough to live on.'

'Oh, I see,' snapped Daphne, 'she's more important than me.'

'Don't be silly, darling,' Felix scolded gently. 'Of course she isn't, but she's in more need than you just for the moment, and she's my mother and I have to make sure she's looked after. She'll have money coming through in the next few months, but until it does I'm going to fund her from my pay. Don't worry, I'll still give you housekeeping.' He looked across at his wife's mutinous face and forced a smile. 'Come on, Daph, it won't be for ever. Just till we get the finances sorted.'

He hoped it was true, but he knew better than to go into more detail now.

'It's all right for you,' sniffed Daphne. 'You don't have to try and run a home on nothing. It's me what's got to do the belt tightening.' But even as she spoke she knew a wave of relief. He might be cutting her allowance, but she still had the housekeeping and surely she'd be able to scrimp five pounds over the month from one or other to pay off her mother. She had already sent the first postal order. She'd intended to send it as soon as she got home on the day she'd visited Hackney, but she'd been rushed off to Wynsdown. However, while she'd been hanging about in Wynsdown, with little to do, she had been to the post office, bought and posted the necessary postal order. At least that would keep her mother at bay till next month.

'I'm sorry,' she said now. 'I didn't mean you shouldn't be looking after your mother, it's just, well I'm not used to being married yet and I don't want to share you.'

'You won't have to share me,' Felix assured her. 'You'll always come first, but I do have to make sure Ma's OK. She and Dad were married nearly thirty-five years. It's a long time to live with someone and then suddenly find they aren't here any more. I have to look after my mother, Daphne. You know that.'

Suddenly Daphne realised that Felix had given her the perfect opportunity to explain her need for the money she'd been expecting.

'I *do* know. You're right. Of course you are.' She smiled across at him. 'And there's something I was going to tell you, Felix, only with your dad dying an' that it went completely out of my head.'

'Oh? What was that then?' Felix sounded wary.

'Well,' Daphne had just seen how to make sure she didn't lose out on her allowance. 'The day he was took ill, I went to see my parents.'

Felix's eyes widened. 'Did you? You didn't tell me.'

'No, well, I didn't really get a chance. When I got back, we rushed off down to Wynsdown, didn't we? And since then, well, you've had other things to think about, haven't you? Anyhow, that day I'd been to see them at dinnertime, lunchtime,' she corrected herself. 'I knew they'd all be home then, so I went as a surprise. And, well, I told them about us getting married.'

'What did they say?'

'They said they was, were, very pleased for me and looked forward to meeting you one day.'

'I see. And they didn't mind that we hadn't asked them to the wedding?'

'No, of course not. I knew they wouldn't. I told them it was very small, just us and witnesses.'

'And my parents.'

'And them. And anyway, what I was going to say was, well, I understand that you have to look after your mother, of course you do. The thing is, Dad's still got his garage. It's doing OK, but business is tough just now, so I said I'd help them out a bit. Not every month like,' she went on hurriedly, 'but occasionally with a bit of cash. They was, were, very grateful. I told them how generous you've been to me, and that you'd quite understand that I wanted to help them.' She turned her big blue eyes on Felix now and said, 'And you do, Felix, don't you?'

It was the last thing Felix could afford to do now, look after his in-laws on a regular basis, but he'd put his mother's claim on him so strongly that it was difficult to say so.

'Of course I understand,' he said. 'But I'm serious, Daphne, we really are going to have to pull our horns in now. Small economies will add up, like not going first class when we go down to Wynsdown on the train, and not going out as much as we have been. We've got to pay cash for things and not run up bills.'

'No, of course not.' Daphne thought of all the clothes she'd bought before the wedding with the dressmaker's bill still unpaid, and decided not to mention that yet. Felix would have to take care of it if it became pressing. Her allowance for the present month was long gone and the postal order she'd sent to her mother had come out from the last of the cash he'd given her to stock up the flat for when they got home from their honeymoon.

'And I think we'll have to give Mrs Barton notice,' Felix went on. 'I'm afraid we shan't be able to afford her for a while.'

'But she only comes in three mornings a week,' cried Daphne in dismay. She'd known she was going to have to shop and cook, but had thought that at least the flat would be kept clean by the redoubtable Mrs Barton. She'd been cleaning for Felix three mornings a week ever since he'd taken the flat. Daphne had been delighted to inherit her. 'And only for three hours. She'll be awfully cut up. I expect she relies on the money we pay her.'

'I know it's not ideal for any of us, Daphne, but I'm sure you can cope on your own. Other housewives have to. It's not as if I'm asking you to go out to work, just to do your own housework.'

'Well, you can give her notice,' snapped Daphne. 'I ain't going to.' And with that she flounced out of the room. Moments later Felix heard the front door slam.

Chapter 15

It was three nights later that Harry met Bull Shadbolt and Grey Maxton in a back room of the Golden Eagle pub in Soho.

'Grey's prepared to meet,' Bull had told Harry when he returned with the extra money and retrieved the papers Freddie had prepared for Dora and Bella. 'Neutral territory. Wants to hear Denny's idea.' The Golden Eagle had been agreed.

Bull Shadbolt had brought the Rat and Manny Parkes with him. They came into the room and found Grey Maxton already there. He had a long, narrow face, his pale, almost yellow eyes close together above a sharply pointed nose, his mouth a drawn line beneath a pencil-thin moustache. His thinning, salt-and-pepper hair was a sandy grey, carefully smoothed over the sloping baldness of his head. He looked, Bull Shadbolt thought, not for the first time, like a disgruntled, vicious ferret. Smoking a cigar, he was seated at a table, a full whisky glass in his hand, and he was accompanied by his second in command, Ray Holden, and his minder, Big Frank. Bull paused on the threshold before nodding to Grey and crossing the room to a table on the opposite side where a whisky bottle and glasses stood waiting. He sat down and poured himself a generous measure. The Rat and Manny took up station behind him, one on either side, their eyes firmly fixed on the opposition. Silence enveloped the room, stretched wafer-thin as the two sides eyed each other with great suspicion.

Moments later the door opened and as Harry stood aside, Dora Duncan walked in.

'What's she doin' 'ere?' growled Grey Maxton, and the atmosphere, already tense, tightened another notch.

'I'm here,' Dora replied coolly, 'to discuss Denny's proposition.' She looked round the smoky room. 'I see you gentlemen have brought friends with you; I've brought Harry. You've no objection, I assume.' She walked across to the empty table in the middle and sat down. She opened her handbag and producing a silver cigarette case, took out a cigarette which she fitted into a slim, gold holder, and glanced round as if in search of a light. Harry pulled a lighter from his pocket and flicked it into life. Dora held her cigarette to the flame, drawing on it deeply, taking smoke down into her lungs before breathing it out again in one long, smooth breath.

'Now then, gentlemen,' she said, looking round at the ill-assorted group. 'Shall we get down to business? First, I must apologise that Denny's second ain't here, but as I think you know, Mick Derham no longer works for this firm. I've taken Denny's businesses into my own hands now as, I have to admit, I should've done soon after he left. So, in answer to your question, Mr Maxton, that is why I am here.'

'I thought young Black was here to speak for Denny,' Maxton sneered.

'Harry's worked for Denny in Australia for the last four years,' Dora said. 'Denny's trusted him with messages for me and for you. He's here on Denny's say-so, to sort out what's going to happen to them businesses I just mentioned.' She looked at the two men, seated as far apart as possible, and went on. 'You know my Den's got cancer; Harry told you. He wants me and Bella out there before he dies, and that's what we want, too. We leave in two weeks' time and that, gentlemen, will be the last you see of us.' Her words were greeted with silence and she went on. 'We sail on *The Pride of Empire* and we ain't coming back.'

'So, we just split Denny's patch straight down the middle,' sneered Grey. 'Nuffink you can do about it.'

He glanced at Bull for confirmation, but Bull kept his eyes on Dora. She should have taken over sooner, he thought, as he saw the determination on her face. She's got more balls than Derham.

'Because,' Dora replied, 'if that's the way you choose to play it, you'll be starting the father and mother of a turf war. There'll be blood and cops and arrests. You know the cost of tit-for-tat, Grey. You don't pay Denny his share, we'll fight. Make no mistake about that. No Mick Derham, well rid, but we still got plenty on our payroll only too happy to take you on.'

'With Denny dying in Australia and you gone, who's gonna make a fight of it?'

'Me.'

All eyes turned on Harry. 'The deal Denny's offering you makes everyone a winner. No one makes waves. You two quietly increase your business, no one the wiser, and for six months, maybe less, Denny gets his dues. After that,' Harry gave an expressive shrug of his shoulders, 'Denny'll be in his grave, his ladies'll be in Australia, and you two can slog it out between you.' Harry turned to face Grey Maxton, feeling he'd already convinced Bull or they wouldn't even be discussing the idea. 'But if you fuck him about, it won't be a quiet takeover, no one hurt, it'll be what Dora said. Total war... an' we don't fight clean.'

It was clear Grey Maxton didn't want to lose face in front of his own men, and even more so in front of Bull Shadbolt. He swallowed the last of his whisky and poured himself another before saying, 'How'll we know when Den's kicked the bucket? You could go on milking us for years.'

Harry had been ready for this question. It was an obvious one and certainly one he'd have asked himself if faced with the same proposal. 'Denny knows how long he's got,' he replied. 'After six months the payments stop.'

'Stop even sooner if we tip Scotland Yard where Denny is,' suggested Grey.

'But in that case, you won't be taking any of his business,' Harry replied calmly. 'You'll be dead.'

That Harry's got balls an' all, Bull thought, wondering if he could persuade him to join the firm. However, a glance at the Rat, glowering across the room at Harry, made him think again. No point in starting war within his own ranks.

'So, if we go for this bullshit plan,' Maxton was saying, 'how does it work?'

It was Dora who answered. 'Bella and I leave as planned. Harry'll stay here in London as the go-between.'

Harry and Dora had discussed this point long and hard before coming to the Golden Eagle that evening.

'We can't trust 'em, Harry. If you come back with us as planned, we might as well kiss goodbye to the money we got over here.'

'Denny said I was to bring you,' reiterated Harry. 'He won't be pleased if I send you out on your own.'

'Chrissakes, Harry! What do you think I am, a school girl? Whatever can happen to me on board a ship? And anyway, I shan't be on my own. Bella'll be with me. No, you have to stay, check on everyone who works for us. Stan Busby'll put you in the picture now Derham's gone. Your job? Get rid of any other Derhams, and collect the money as usual. *You* collect the cash and keep our share. Give *them* the rest. They'll fall out over it before very long, but maybe, just maybe, we can keep them off our backs while you salt away as much as you can. Yeah, they know about us, but we know just as much about them. There's stuff Denny put in our safe over the years. Names. Dates. Photos. Our insurance, remember? They don't know exactly what we know; which cops're in our pocket, who we can call in favours from. We'll have plenty of ammunition if we need it. Just hope we don't.' A sentiment with which Harry heartily agreed.

Grey Maxton still hadn't accepted the plan when they left the Golden Eagle.

'It's still on the table, Grey,' Harry said as he got to his feet. 'For now.'

Grey made no reply. He sat slumped in his chair as first Bull, the Rat and Manny left, slipping out into the narrow street and disappearing into the night, quickly followed by Harry and Dora, hurrying to where they'd parked the car.

'Will they go for it?' Harry wondered as he pulled away from the kerb. 'Or will they simply carve us up?'

'To be quite honest with you, Harry,' Dora said, 'I don't give a shit. If I can get out there to see my Den once more before he dies, that's all that matters to me.'

He glanced across at her and in the light of a street lamp, saw the bitter expression on her face.

'It's a mug's game, Harry,' she went on. 'Always has been. Denny and I been married for nigh on thirty years and how many have we lived together? Ten, maximum, and that in bits. That's not married life.' She shook her head as she spoke. 'It's not the life for anyone, and certainly not for my Bella.

I seen the way she looks at you, Harry, an' I know you have too. Seen the gleam in your eye an' all. Well, you can think again, Harry Black. You play fast and loose with my girl and you'll have me to reckon with. Once we get to Australia, all this business of Den's is over. If you think you're going to step in an' take over from him, well, that's up to you. Be your funeral, maybe literally, but if you do, I ain't gonna let you within a mile of my daughter. You just remember that, Harry Black.'

As he finally lay in bed that night, Harry considered Dora's warning. He knew she was right. Bella clearly found him attractive and given any encouragement from him, would easily be enticed into his bed. It was tempting to try, she was after all an extremely attractive young woman, but he realised that it would be disastrous if Dora found out. He was pretty sure Bella wasn't as inexperienced as her mother seemed to think. The signals she'd been sending out were pretty clear, but she was not a priority and he put her out of his mind.

Lisa, however, was another matter. Since he'd returned to London, Lisa had crept back into his thoughts, lingering in the shadows of his mind, slipping to the forefront at unexpected moments. Now, since he wasn't going straight back to Sydney as he'd thought, maybe he'd have the chance to find her. Perhaps, when Dora and Bella were safely on their way, under their new names of Doreen and Belinda Cartwright, he could go and find this village where she lived.

Grey Maxton finally agreed a deal with them and Shadbolt. Denny's dues would be collected by Harry with an escort from each of the others, and immediately divided into three equal shares.

Dora owned the Maida Vale house, and she'd already put it on the market.

'You can keep the car,' she said to Harry, 'an' live in the house till it's sold. But when it is, that money's mine. Not for sharing with them other two. You make sure I get it, Harry. Stash it an' bring it with you when you come.'

They decided to visit all Denny's 'businesses', together, before Dora left.

'Need to make sure everyone's on board,' Dora said. 'Let 'em know that you're the man, and what you say goes.'

'Important that Mick don't cream off any more cash,' Harry said. 'Make it clear that he's working for someone else now.'

By the end of the week, Dora had done the rounds of all Denny's businesses, legitimate and otherwise. When she realised how many there were – a gambling den, a snooker club, a couple of brothels, an upmarket escort agency and a restaurant, not to mention the bookies who ran their books from his pub, the Jolly Sailor, and the street markets where many of the traders, financed at some stage by Denny, paid him a percentage of their weekly takings – she also realised that she'd been receiving only a proportion of the monies due. Denny's firm provided protection to jewellers and furriers, posh clubs and West End pubs; anyone who wanted to be safe from police raids and shysters, robbery and violence. They paid up regularly and remained untroubled. When questioned, firmly, by Harry, they all said that they'd been paying their dues as always.

'Mick Derham and one of his heavies come round every week, Mrs Duncan,' said Midge Cowell who ran an intimate club for gentlemen with particular proclivities. 'We paid up as usual, even when the rate went up.'

Dora's brow darkened. 'Well, Mr Cowell, it'll be Harry you pay now, an' no one else. Got it?'

Midge, a small man, afraid of any form of physicality, nodded vigorously, muttering 'Yes, Mrs Duncan, yes, yes.'

'So, that's where it's all been going,' remarked Dora, later. 'Derham has either got a nice little nest egg tucked away somewhere, or he's been taking his cut and then passing on our cash elsewhere.' Her expression hardened. 'I shoulda taken over, soon as Den went,' she groaned. 'Was scared the cops'd be watching me, and I'd be nabbed, too.'

'They probably were,' Harry said. 'Better not to get involved until the heat was off. Don't worry about Mick, Dora. I'll sort 'im out. Tell Denny I'll finger 'im for something before I leave.'

'Good. You do.' Dora spoke with satisfaction. 'An' from now on you make sure no one else is ripping us off. Down to you, Harry boy. Denny built up his business, he's entitled.'

Two weeks later on a Friday evening Felix again caught the train to Somerset. Unable to ask for further leave, he'd left the office at the end of the day and gone straight to the station. Daphne did not go with him. She'd put her foot down and refused, point-blank.

'No, Felix,' she said when he told her they had to return to Wynsdown. 'You go if you have to, but I'm not coming with you.'

'But, darling,' he said in a conciliatory tone, 'you know I have to go. I have to try and sort out the financial mess that my father's left behind. The sooner I get that sorted out, the sooner we'll be able to get back to normal.'

'But you don't need me to come with you,' insisted Daphne. 'There's nothing for me to do down there and I'll just be in the way.'

Felix had known a guilty sense of relief at her decision. It would be so much easier to discuss things with his mother if it were only the two of them in the house. He wouldn't have to worry about Daphne being bored, or, he had to admit, getting on his nerves with her complaints about the house and the village and having to be there.

He arrived late in the evening and when he climbed out of Fred Jones's taxi, his mother was waiting at the door to greet him with a hug.

'Darling,' she cried, 'it's lovely to see you again so soon.'

They went indoors and Felix felt a comforting warmth as he entered the house; not simply because it was welcomingly warm after the cold of the October night outside, but because it was home, the home of his childhood. He dumped his grip in the hall and followed his mother into the kitchen.

'Mrs Darby's left a pot of stew in the oven,' she was saying. 'I thought we'd eat it in here. The dining room's a bit cold at the moment.'

Felix saw that the kitchen table was laid for two, and said, 'You shouldn't have waited for me, Mother, you must be starving.'

'I thought it'd be nice to eat together,' she said as she put the dish of stew onto the table and went back to the oven for two large baked potatoes. 'I'm tired of eating meals by myself.' There was no self-pity in her voice, but Felix recognised the loneliness in her words. He wasn't surprised she'd stopped eating her meals in the oak-panelled dining room; how depressing to be sitting alone at the big dining table, facing his father's empty chair.

He sat down at the table and Marjorie served the food before sitting down opposite him.

'How's Daphne?' she asked.

'She's fine,' Felix replied. 'Sends her love.'

'Thank you,' Marjorie said, without believing a word of it.

'She thought we'd be better on our own this weekend,' Felix said, 'and I think she's probably right. We've lots to discuss and she's got plenty she can do in London.'

Actually, Felix hadn't a clue what Daphne proposed to do while he was in Somerset; he hadn't asked and she had said nothing.

'Let's not start on anything tonight,' Marjorie said, 'you

must be exhausted and I'm certainly too tired to think straight.'

After their supper, they carried their coffee cups into the drawing room where a fire still smouldered in the grate. Marjorie poked it back into life while Felix poured them each a brandy. For a while they sat in companionable silence and it came to Felix as he looked round the familiar room, warm in the lamplight, that he couldn't remember when he'd last sat alone with either of his parents.

'I'm sorry I didn't come down to visit more often,' he said. 'I should have.'

His mother smiled sadly. 'Perhaps,' she said. 'But it wasn't easy during the war and since then, well, you've had your own life to lead. It's what children are supposed to do, you know, fly the nest. I remember my mother saying to me, "First you give them roots and then you give them wings." It's what we tried to do for you.'

'Definitely wings in my case,' Felix said.

'Yes,' agreed his mother, 'but at least you survived it all. It was difficult for us during the war, always dreading the telegraph boy's knock at the door. Let's hope your children won't have to go to war. Two generations running is quite enough.'

Felix thought about this conversation, later, as he lay in bed. His mother had made up the bed in the guest room where he and Daphne had slept last time they'd come, but it felt odd sleeping there alone and he wished he were in his childhood bedroom along the landing.

'Let's hope your children won't have to go to war,' his mother had said.

His children, his and Daphne's. Felix hadn't really given children much thought. He'd assumed that they'd come along in due time and that he'd be pleased to be a father, but as he considered the idea now, he found he wanted it to happen sooner rather than later. Children of his own to love and cherish.

'Love' was a word that had always faintly embarrassed Felix, particularly when his mother had used it with regard to him. Saying they loved each other wasn't what his family did. They loved each other, of course they did, but it wasn't something they put into words.

Perhaps we should have, he thought as he lay in the darkness. But he wasn't sure he could say it to his mother, even now. He couldn't say it, but he could show it.

Next morning he went back into his father's study and spread out the notes he'd made on the work table. Marjorie followed him in and pulling up a chair sat down beside him.

'Now then,' she said. 'Let's work out what we're going to do.'

Felix laid out the figures. 'It won't be long before you get Dad's insurance money,' he said, 'so you should be able to live quite comfortably on that. The house is already yours, but the upkeep isn't going to be cheap. I'm afraid Dad let the repairs it needs go for too long.'

'What does it need?' asked his mother.

Felix shrugged. 'I don't know, but I do think we need to get someone to look at the place, properly. There are certainly tiles missing from the roof and there's that damp patch at the far end of the landing.'

'Right,' said Marjorie. 'Let's make a list of what we need to do.' She drew a piece of paper towards her and wrote, *Get builder to check roof.*

'We have to make some economies and maybe sell—'

'Before you go any further, Felix, I want to tell you what

I think we should do and then, when we've considered that, we can discuss what you think of the idea and any other options you have in mind. All right?'

Felix looked at her in surprise, but there was a firmness in her voice that brooked no argument. He sat back in his chair and nodded. 'Fine,' he said. 'Go ahead.'

'Well, I've given the situation a lot of thought,' she began, 'and I've spoken at some length with Mr Thompson about this, so these are no spur-of-the-moment suggestions.' She drew a deep breath and went on, 'I think I should move out of the manor— No, hear me out.' She held up her hand to halt the interruption already on his lips. 'I think I should move out of the manor and move into Eden Lodge. Miss Merton is now virtually bedridden and is being moved into a nursing home. Eden Lodge is, as I think you know, already mine. It is smaller, easier and cheaper to run. If I stay here I shall rattle round the place.'

'But it's your home,' protested Felix. 'Your home with Dad.'

'But Dad's not here now,' Marjorie said softly, 'and it doesn't feel like home without him. I need to make a new home, a home of my own, somewhere else.'

'But what would you do with the manor?'

'Well, as I see it, there are three possible options,' replied his mother. 'The first is that I could sell it.'

'Sell it!' exclaimed Felix. It wasn't one of the options he'd seriously considered, for he'd been assuming she would continue living there.

Ignoring his interruption Marjorie continued, 'The second is to let it. Mr Thompson thinks that it might let quite well, perhaps to some businessman who lives in town but would like a country retreat.' She looked at Felix enquiringly. 'What do you think?'

'I think, Mother, that you'd absolutely hate to see someone else living here, you know you would.'

'Yes, I probably would,' she agreed, 'but I could cope with it if I had to. The third option is for me to give it to you.'

'Give it to me?'

Marjorie smiled at his surprise. 'Why not? After all, it's your home too. If it were yours, *you* could sell it, or let it, or… live in it.'

Felix buried his head in his hands. 'Mother,' he said, 'you've thrown me completely! I have to think about this.'

'Of course you do, darling. I just wanted to let you know what was in my mind, that's all. You have to consider what's best for you and Daphne and then we can decide the best way to achieve it. Whatever we decide about the manor house, I've made my decision. I shall have Eden Lodge modernised a little, and then move in there.'

Felix found it difficult to concentrate on the other things they needed to discuss after this bombshell, and Marjorie, seeing his confused state, said, 'Let's forget about all that for now and look at what else we need to sort out. What about the farms? Are you thinking of going ahead with the sales that your father had set in motion? Mr Thompson says you're not committed to anything yet. The talks had only been exploratory.'

'I shall need to visit both John Shepherd and Richard Deelish to see if they still want to proceed. I had a look at the paperwork, as far as it went, while I was here before, but what I want to know is what you think about it?'

'I don't know enough about the deals that are being considered,' replied his mother. 'Your father didn't discuss them with me. All I feel is, if we sell off those farms, the estate will be reduced to about a third of its original size.

Only Havering Farm and Home Farm will be left. Dad was coping with Home Farm all right, and as you know he wants Malcolm to take on Havering.'

'I know, Mother, but we need an injection of cash for machinery and general maintenance to make the place viable. That could come from selling either Charing Farm or Newland, or both.'

'But do we need to sell? The working of those farms is not our responsibility, and they do provide rent. Surely, with the men we've got working for us at present, we can keep Home Farm running as it is.'

'Trouble is, Mother, we have to modernise and make economies. As far as I can see we can't afford to keep on all five men at Home Farm, and even if we could, we'd need a farm manager to do what Dad was doing and we can't afford him, either.' He sighed. 'I'm happy enough to let young Malcolm Flint take on Havering Farm, as that's what Dad particularly wanted, but he can't have it until Lady Day and if he does decide to take over, he won't be in any position to pay any rent for it for several months. I'll need to talk to him, too.'

After a morning spent indoors rereading the papers that already dealt with the possible sale of the two farms, Felix felt the need to get out and stretch his legs. He ate a scratch lunch of home-made soup and sandwiches at the kitchen table with his mother, and then set out for Charing Farm. He knew John Shepherd better than Richard Deelish, and feeling that he needed to start somewhere, he decided he would start with him.

The afternoon was bright, but chilly with a wind sweeping across the hills and chasing the last of the leaves in scurrying eddies along the drove. Despite the problems he'd been considering all morning, Felix felt his spirits lift as he strode along the familiar track and then cut across the field past Charing Coppice and down into the fold in the hill that protected Charing farmhouse from the prevailing west wind. The sun on his face and that indefinable smell of the country gave him a lift he hadn't felt since his father's death. He reached the farm and went through the yard to knock on the back door. His arrival was greeted with a chorus of barking from the farm dogs and John Shepherd appeared from the stables to see who was there.

'Felix,' he cried, coming forward with hand outstretched. 'Good to see you. I didn't know you were home again. I was just seeing to the horses. Come in out of the wind while I finish up and then we'll go into the warm.'

Felix followed him into the stables where two fine-looking horses – one a grey, the other a chestnut – and a diminutive pony were all contentedly pulling at their haynets. When he had admired them all, stroking silky noses and offering apples from a barrel in the corner, he said, 'Will you be hunting this year, Mr Shepherd?'

'Hope so,' John replied. 'There was none in the war, of course, but we started up again a couple of years ago and gradually we've built up our numbers, and people are keen to get going properly again. The Boxing Day meet is here this year, at the Magpie. If the weather's anything like, it should be well supported. Will you be coming down to hunt, do you think?'

Felix shrugged. 'I don't know. I doubt it. I'll probably have to sell our horses. Can't have them eating their heads off and nobody riding them.' He looked across at John and said, 'Might you be in the market for either of them?'

'To be honest, I doubt it, Felix. I've still got old Hamble, here, getting on a bit, but he's still a goer, aren't you, old feller?' He stroked Hamble's grey nose. 'The chestnut belongs to my Billy. Bought him at the Michaelmas Fair last year. He hunted him towards the end of the season and he's worked hard with him ever since. He's planning to hunt him again this winter.'

'Whose is the pony?' asked Felix as he gave Barney half an apple.

'My grandson is learning to ride him,' John said with pride. 'He's rising three and his legs stick out like matchsticks, but he loves it. You'll see him in a minute when we go indoors.'

John finished settling the horses and was about to lead the way inside when he stopped and turned back to Felix. 'Tell you what I will do,' he said. 'If you want to bring your father's horses over here, I'll keep them in our stables, just for a while, until you decide what you're going to do, keep them yourself or find a buyer.'

Felix stared at him. 'I can't ask you to do that,' he said.

'You haven't,' said John. 'I've offered. Somebody needs to be responsible for them and it'll stop your mother worrying about them.'

'It'd have to be on a business footing,' Felix said. 'I'd have to pay you.'

'If you think you must, you can pay for their feed.'

'You're very generous,' said Felix.

'Your father and I have been friends and neighbours ever since I can remember,' replied John. 'You can say I'm doing it for him. Between us Billy and I can exercise them enough for the time being. We'll both enjoy that. Now, if that's agreed, let's go indoors and get warm.'

The farm kitchen was welcoming as ever. A small boy was sitting at one end of the kitchen table busy with chalks and paper. His grandmother was at the other, rolling out pastry for an apple pie.

'Here's Wing Commander Bellinger come to see us,' John said as they walked in through the door. 'And this is my grandson, Johnny. Say hallo to the wing commander, Johnny.'

The little boy looked up, staring solemnly at Felix, but saying nothing.

'We've been putting the horses to bed,' John said, 'and the wing commander gave Barney an apple.'

Mention of Barney brought a smile to Johnny's face. 'I rided him this afternoon and Gramp said I was good at riding today.'

A little at a loss, Felix managed, 'Well done, young man.'

'Was this a purely social call, Felix,' John asked, 'or shall we go into the farm office for a chat?'

'The farm office, I think,' replied Felix, 'if that's all right.'

'I've got the kettle on,' Margaret Shepherd said. 'Come back in for a cup of tea when you've finished talking business.'

John led the way across the hall to the small room he used as a farm office. He went across to the desk, which was piled high with papers, waving Felix to a chair beside it.

'It must have been an awful shock when your father was struck down like that,' he said. 'We were all shaken by it. Peter and I were much of an age and it brings one face to face with one's own mortality.'

'It certainly was a shock,' said Felix. 'I'd only seen him the week before and he seemed absolutely fine. Even more of a shock for my poor mother, finding him on the floor.' He looked across at John Shepherd, a man he'd known all his life, and sighed. 'I'm afraid the estate finances are in a bit of a mess. I know he approached you about buying out your farm, and I wondered if that was still in your mind.'

'If I can raise the money,' John said, 'it's certainly something

I'd like to do. It would give security to my wife if anything happened to me, and a future for Billy and his family. You know he's married and has two children? Little Johnny out there is his son, and there's a baby, Edie. I want my family to be able to stay here at Charing Farm, where we've been for the last three generations. Owning rather than leasing the farm would secure that.'

Felix nodded. 'So if I wanted to sell, would you still be in the market?'

'Definitely,' John replied, 'but I certainly wouldn't be able to proceed until Lady Day at the earliest.' He smiled across at Felix. 'That'd give you time to reconsider if you want to. I know you're probably under some financial pressure, but if you'll take my advice, Felix, you won't make any hasty decisions. If at any time you want to discuss anything with me,' he went on, 'I'll be happy to listen. Your father and I became good friends over the years.'

"Thank you,' Felix said, genuinely grateful for John Shepherd's attitude and advice. 'I'll bear that in mind.' He reached over with outstretched hand and John grasped it firmly.

'Good,' he said. 'Now let's go and find that cup of tea.'

They returned to the kitchen to find Charlotte seated in a chair, her baby in her arms. She looked up as they came in and smiled.

'Hallo, Gramp,' she said. 'Johnny said you'd come in.'

'Have you met my daughter-in-law, Felix?' Margaret said as she picked up the teapot from the hob. 'Charlotte. This is Felix Bellinger.'

'We haven't met,' said Felix, 'but wasn't it your baby that was christened not long ago? I saw you all in the church.'

'Yes, that's right,' Charlotte answered. Nancy Bright was

right, she thought, as she smiled up at him. He does look like Clark Gable!

Felix returned her smile, thinking, as he accepted a cup of tea from Margaret, that Billy was a lucky bloke to have such an attractive wife; and not just physically attractive, there was an air of serenity about her as she sat there, gently rocking the baby.

At that moment Billy himself came in and was greeted with delight by his son. Felix saw him exchange a quick smile with his wife, the warmth in their eyes apparent for all to see. Billy washed his hands and then turned to Felix.

'Wing Commander Bellinger,' he said by way of greeting.

'Bit of a mouthful,' remarked Felix easily. 'Felix'll do. After all, we've known each other since we were kids.'

Billy shrugged. 'Felix, then.'

'Felix is home to see his mother,' John said. 'We're glad he found time to come and see us, too. He was asking if we'd be hunting this year.'

'I've been admiring your horses,' Felix said. 'That chestnut of yours looks good.'

A little more warmth came into Billy's expression. 'Rustler? Yes, a bit headstrong still, but he's a goer. Looking forward to riding him to hounds and maybe a bit of point-to-point, as well.'

The conversation became general, but John Shepherd made no reference to their talk in the farm office, and Felix wondered if Billy knew about the possible deal they'd been discussing.

Billy drank his tea down and then got to his feet. 'Still got a bit to do before it gets dark,' he said.

'I think I'll go home straight away, Billy,' Charlotte said. 'I've got things to do and I want to be back in the daylight.'

'All right. I'll be home as soon as I can.' Billy reached down and kissed the top of her head. 'Go carefully.'

'I must go, too,' Felix said. 'There's still lots to do at the manor, and I'm only here until tomorrow evening.'

'Then I'll walk with you,' Charlotte said, 'if you can just wait while I gather up all our things.' She turned to Margaret. 'Thanks for giving them their dinner,' she said. 'I really appreciate an hour or two on my own.'

'I love having them,' Margaret returned. 'And Johnny loved his riding lesson with Gramp.'

Ten minutes later, with Edie safely tucked up in the pram and Johnny dressed in his warm coat and wellington boots, they set off along the lane towards the village.

'It was you who ran for help when my mother found Dad, wasn't it?' Felix asked, suddenly remembering.

'I just went for the doctor,' Charlotte said. 'He wasn't there, so we rang for an ambulance.' She gave a sigh. 'I know what it's like to find someone you love collapsed on the floor. Several years ago I found my foster mother like that, but I was too late. She was dead.'

'Your foster mother?'

'I was evacuated from London during the Blitz,' Charlotte explained. 'Miss Everard took me in.'

'Miss Everard!' exclaimed Felix. 'At Blackdown House? She was a weird old bird.'

'She was no such thing,' retorted Charlotte hotly. 'She was lonely, and she was kindness itself to me.'

'I'm sorry,' Felix apologised hastily. 'I didn't mean to be rude about her, but when we were kids we were all scared stiff of her. We thought she was a witch.'

'Well, she wasn't,' Charlotte snapped, and for a while they walked on in uneasy silence.

'Whereabouts in the village do you live?' Felix asked.

'Blackdown House,' replied Charlotte.

'But...' Felix began.

'She left it to me.'

Another awkward silence enfolded them as Charlotte man-oeuvred the pram over the uneven ground. Johnny, running on ahead, was kicking up leaves and splashing through the puddles that had collected in the ruts and potholes of the drove.

'He's a bright boy, your son,' Felix said in an attempt to heal the breach that had opened up between them.

Charlotte, accepting the proffered olive branch, laughed. 'He's certainly a bundle of energy,' she said, 'he never stops.'

As she spoke, Johnny slipped on a patch of mud and with a cry, landed on his bottom in a puddle. Charlotte let go of the pram and rushed forward to pick him up, cuddling him against her as she soothed him, wiping away his tears. Felix took hold of the pram and pushed it to where the pair of them were sitting on the ground.

Johnny's sobs gradually subsided to hiccups, but he still clung to his mother, his face buried in her neck.

'Cheer up, darling,' Charlotte was saying. 'You're not hurt and it's only mud.'

She tried to stand him on his feet, but he wouldn't let go. 'Come on,' she encouraged. 'Let's get home so we can get you clean and dry.'

'Would you like to ride on my shoulders?' offered Felix. 'I could be your horse.'

Still clinging to Charlotte, Johnny looked up at him. Then he nodded.

'Come on, then, up with you.' Felix held out his arms.

'Oh please, don't worry,' Charlotte said. 'He's awfully wet and muddy.'

'A bit of mud won't hurt me,' grinned Felix. He reached down and swung Johnny up onto his shoulders. Johnny, his tears forgotten, gave a crow of delight as he settled himself, and clutched a fistful of Felix's hair to steady himself. Felix grasped his dangling legs and with Johnny urging him onwards, set off at a trot along the track.

Laughing, Charlotte followed. She was used to pushing the pram over the bumpy ground, but even so she couldn't keep up with Johnny and his mount. She found them waiting for her where the track emerged onto the lane into the village, Johnny still perched on Felix's shoulders.

'Johnny, you must get down,' she cried. 'Poor Mr Bellinger!'

'Poor horse!' agreed Johnny as Felix lifted him down and set him on his feet.

'Thank you,' Charlotte said, smiling at Felix. 'That was very kind.'

Felix smiled back at her. 'Not a problem,' he said and turning to Johnny said, 'You'll have to walk from here, old chap.' He pointed up the manor drive. 'This is where I live.'

'Oh, don't worry, we'll be fine from here,' Charlotte assured him. She reached for Johnny's hand. 'Come on, Johnny, let's get you home and dry.'

Dusk was stealing the afternoon light as Felix watched them continue down the lane into the centre of the village. He could still feel the scrabble of Johnny's fingers in his hair, and it made him smile. Reluctantly, he turned in through the gate. There were more discussions to be had; more decisions to be made, and none of them was going to be easy.

Chapter 17

Harry escorted Dora and Bella to Southampton and saw them aboard the ship. Before he walked back down the gangway, Bella flung her arms around him and kissed him long and deep on the mouth and Harry found himself responding. Bella tasted and felt as good as he'd always imagined she would.

'You make sure you come out to Australia and find me,' Bella said fiercely when, breathless, they finally broke apart. 'I'll be waiting for you.'

Under the steely gaze of Dora, they kissed again and for a moment Harry found himself wishing that he was going with them.

'Goodbye, Harry,' Dora said, her voice cool and impersonal. 'Keep your wits about you... and remember what I said to you, *not within a mile.*'

Harry went ashore and waited on the quay until, with Bella still waving from the deck, the ship steamed slowly out of the harbour. He felt a weight lift from his shoulders. They'd gone, and there had been no last-minute hitches. Doreen and Belinda Cartwright were on their way to join Denny in Sydney.

Back in London, Harry went straight to the Jolly Sailor where he found Stan Busby, with two of his sidekicks, brothers Alf and Eddie Shaw, waiting for him.

'Any sign of Derham?' Harry asked as he sat down in Denny's chair.

'Nope,' replied Stan. 'Hasn't shown 'is face round 'ere.'

'Right,' said Harry, 'an' that's the way it's gonna stay. You and me, Stan, are gonna do the rounds again, just to make sure everyone knows who's looking after Denny's interests now, right? Eddie, you stay here and mind the shop. Alf, you come with us... so's there's no misunderstandings.'

There had been none and at last Harry had time to give real thought to his search for Lisa. He had the car, and Dora had given him the last of her petrol coupons. There were also several cans of petrol stashed in a lock-up half a mile away. He had the means, he had the opportunity. It was time he went to find this Wynsdown place, to find his Lisa.

In Wynsdown, Charlotte and Johnny were in the kitchen, making biscuits together. As Charlotte slid the tray into the oven, Johnny got down from the chair he was standing on and went to the back door.

'When can we go to the bomb-fire?' he demanded. 'I want to go to the bomb-fire and see the fireworks.'

'And so you shall,' Charlotte said, 'but it's not time yet. They don't light the bonfire until it's dark, so it won't be until Daddy and Gr'ma come home.'

Johnny was beside himself with excitement. He had watched the bonfire growing bigger every day when they'd walked into the village. People were continually adding bits and pieces to the pile and now it stood nearly ten feet high.

'When will they light it?' he'd demanded. 'Can we watch?'

'They'll light it on Saturday,' Billy said, 'that's Firework Night.'

'What's fireworks?'

Billy explained and Johnny's excitement increased. 'But Edie won't go,' he said with great firmness. 'She's too little. She won't like fireworks.'

'No, but that's all right, Gr'ma is coming to sit with her, so that we can go and she can stay at home. You'll be staying up very late, young man, so you'd better behave yourself!'

Harry arrived in Wynsdown that same Saturday afternoon. He'd found the village on a road map, and using the last of Dora's petrol coupons had driven down to Somerset. He parked the car outside the Magpie and walked into the pub. The landlord, Jack Barrett, had just called time and the regulars were downing the last of their pints before moving out of the warm fug of the bar and heading home for their dinners.

'Sorry, sir,' Jack said, as Harry approached the bar. 'Afraid I just called time.'

'That's all right,' Harry said. 'I was looking for a bed for the night. You do rooms, do you?'

'Yes, we got rooms,' replied Jack, and glancing back over his shoulder, called through a door at the back of the bar, 'Mabel!' Then he turned back to Harry. 'Just for the one night, was it?'

'Yeah,' Harry said, 'just the one.'

A buxom woman with a mass of red hair exploding round her head came through to the bar and greeted Harry with a smile.

'Can I help you Mr...?'

'Merritt,' supplied Harry, his Australian accent loud and clear. 'Victor Merritt. I'm from Sydney in Australia.' Best to establish his Australian identity, he'd decided, until he saw how things were in this village.

'You're a long way from home, Mr Merritt,' replied the landlady. 'What brings you to our part of the world?'

'Just a few days away from London,' Harry replied airily, glad he'd mentioned Australia. Clearly, strangers coming to stay were few and far between and he'd a shrewd idea his arrival at the Magpie would be round the village in no time.

He was shown upstairs to a room with a tired-looking iron bedstead, a washbasin and an armchair. He went across to the window and peered out into the street below. Some boys were walking round the car, stroking its paintwork and peering in through its windows. One, a little braver than the others, put his hand on the driver's door handle, about to open it.

Harry flung open the window and roared at him. The little group scattered. Behind him he heard Mabel laugh.

'That your motor, is it, Mr Merritt? We don't get many flash cars up here, I can tell you. It won't only be the local lads wanting to have a look, it'll be their dads, as well. Now, then, does the room suit?'

Harry dumped his grip on the bed and said, 'Yes, it's fine. As I said to your husband, I'm only passing through.'

'It's a good night to be here,' replied Mabel. 'Bonfire Night. The whole village'll be out on the green for the fireworks when it gets dark.'

'Fireworks?'

'Yes, love you, it's Guy Fawkes tonight, isn't it?'

'Oh, yes, of course,' Harry said. 'I'd forgotten.'

'There'll be sausages and baked potatoes at the bonfire,' Mabel told him, 'but I'll do you some dinner in here after, all right?'

'Yes, thank you.'

Harry nodded absently, and Mabel said, 'I'll leave you to it then,' and left the room. Downstairs, she found Jack finishing the clearing up and said, 'That Mr Merritt's a rum'un. Says he's just passing through. Who passes through Wynsdown, I'd like to know? It ain't on the road to anywhere.'

Jack shrugged. 'None of our business, Mabel. We've let the man a room, that's all.'

'I know that,' replied Mabel. 'I just think it's odd, that's all. I was just wondering what 'e's up to.'

'Well, stop wondering, woman, and help me get the tables set out on the green for this evening.' Mabel did as she was asked, but she couldn't help wondering why the strange Australian had come to Wynsdown.

Upstairs, Harry was sitting in the armchair and considering what Mabel had told him. He wasn't sure what Bonfire Night was about, but whatever it was, Mabel had said the whole village would be there. So, Lisa might be there, too.

He decided to stretch his legs and take a quick walk around the village. When he stepped out onto the green, he saw the huge bonfire, waiting for the torch to set it aflame. People were busying about, clearly getting things ready for the evening. Two men were roping off a wide area around the bonfire, and two more roping another area, where posts had been set into the ground. Several of them glanced at Harry with interest and he saw one or two eyeing him up and then speaking to Jack Barrett as they helped him heave out the old metal trough they used as a brazier; Jack glanced across at him as he answered. Harry wasn't near enough to hear the exchange, but he guessed it was about Victor Merritt, a stranger, who was in their midst.

As darkness fell and the festivities started, Harry wandered out of the Magpie and joined the throng on the green. He saw her at once, standing in the crowd who were watching the fireworks. Her face, so familiar, was half in shadow, lit only by the flickering flames of the bonfire, but he'd have known her anywhere. Her long, dark hair, swept upward, was tucked into the woollen hat pulled down over her ears and she wore a black coat against the November cold, over slacks tucked into wellington boots. She was just as he remembered... only different. He watched her for some time, trying to discover what that difference was, and at last it came to him. She'd grown up, of course she had, but that wasn't it, or not the whole; now she stood, an adult young woman, with the maturity and confidence that had come with marriage and motherhood. Gone was the diffidence that had marked her out, unsure of herself and of her place in the world. Now, she was comfortable, comfortable as herself. Beside her stood a tall man with a small boy perched on his shoulders. Harry recognised the man, too. Billy Someone, who'd got in the way and stolen his Lisa. He knew from Naomi Federman that Lisa was married, had children, and he'd realised her husband must be Billy. He'd been there to pick up the pieces when Harry had disappeared off to Australia without being able to tell Lisa he was going or explain why. He watched, now, as they oohed and aahed at the cascades of golden rain, the spinning Catherine wheels, and craned their necks to watch the rockets exploding into the sky. He felt a sharp stab of jealousy as he watched Billy lift his son down and light a sparkler for him to hold. The boy cried out in delight as he waved the sparkler, drawing circles in the air as it fizzed and spat.

Lisa turned and laughed at something that Billy said, before bending down to speak to the child. Then she nodded and leaving them watching the fireworks, walked over to the makeshift brazier where Mabel Barrett was cooking sausages. The fireworks continued to fizz, whizz and bang behind her as she stood chatting with Mabel, waiting for the sausages.

Harry watched her for a few moments and then, after a quick glance to see Lisa's husband and son still enthralled in the firework display, he strolled over to join her.

'Hallo, Lisa.'

Charlotte froze. She knew that voice so well.

'Aren't you going to say hallo, then?'

Slowly she turned round, and there he was, Harry.

'Harry?' she breathed. 'Harry?'

'Good to see you, Lisa.'

For a moment everything receded and all she could see was Harry – older and broader, but with the same eyes, dark and fierce, the same thick, dark hair, cut short to his head – looking at her with the half-smile she remembered so well. Last time she'd seen him he'd been angry; not with her, but there'd been no smile, his face had been dark with anger, his eyes narrowed in rage. He'd stormed out of the house and never come back. And now, suddenly, here he was: Harry, who'd waltzed in and out of her life throughout the war, so that she never knew where he was or whether she'd see him again.

Harry's face split into a grin. 'Your face!' he exclaimed. 'Aren't you pleased to see me?'

'That'll be sixpence, Charlotte.' Mabel's voice seemed to come from miles away and brought Charlotte back to the present with a jolt. She felt in the pocket of her coat and pulling out a coin, handed it to Mabel and took the sausages, wrapped in bread, that she was holding out.

'Of course,' she managed to say as she moved away from Mabel's enquiring eyes. 'You surprised me, that's all.' She looked over her shoulder and saw Billy was still watching the fireworks with Johnny. 'Just a minute.' She darted across to where they stood and handed Johnny the sausages and said something to Billy, who nodded.

Harry had followed her away from the brazier and stood waiting at the edge of the green, in the shadow of the church hall. Charlotte came back to join him and this time she held out her hands to him. He took them and pulling her towards him, hugged her close.

'It's so good to see you, Lisa,' he murmured. 'You haven't changed a bit.'

She pulled free, laughing a little self-consciously. 'Of course I have,' she said. 'Two babies make you a different shape!'

'Well, whatever it is, it suits you,' Harry said.

'What about you, Harry? How have you been?' What a stupid question, she thought, even as she asked it. He'd walked out on her, and now here he was turning up like the proverbial bad penny and expecting her to be pleased to see him. Suddenly she was serious and asked, 'Where did you go, Harry? One day you were there and the next you'd vanished.'

'It's a long story—' Harry began, but she cut him short.

'I'm sure it is,' she retorted, 'and I'm sure none of it was your fault, it never is, but you disappear for years and then turn up again out of the blue and expect me to be delighted to see you.'

'Aren't you?' Harry asked with a quizzical smile. 'Aren't you pleased to see me?'

'No!' Charlotte snapped, and then looking at his dear, familiar face, her shoulders slumped a little and she said, 'Yes, of course I am. At least, I'm glad you're alive and haven't forgotten me.'

'Lisa...' Harry took her hands in his again, 'I'm never gonna forget you, am I? I've come to find you, haven't I? An' I tell you what, it ain't been easy, neither. Come on, give us a kiss and make up.'

He suited the action to the words and pulled her back

into his arms, seeking her lips with his. For a second her lips parted and then she struggled to push him away, saying, 'No, Harry. Don't!'

'It's only a kiss, Lisa.'

'Well, I don't want it, Harry.' She pulled free and turned away.

'Charlotte? What's going on?' Billy emerged from the shadows, holding Johnny by the hand. 'I thought you were going to the ladies.'

'I was, I am...' Charlotte felt the colour rise in her cheeks, burning hot. 'It's just...' Her voice died away. It was just... what?

'Billy, ain't it?' drawled Harry. 'Think we met at the end of the war.' He extended his hand. 'Harry Black.'

'Yes,' Billy's voice was icy and he ignored the outstretched hand, 'I remember.' He bent down and picked up Johnny, hoisting him up onto his shoulders. 'It's time to go home, Charlotte. Johnny's getting cold.'

'I'm not cold, Daddy,' Johnny protested. 'I'm hot. I want to see the fireworks.'

'The fireworks are finished, old chap, and poor Mummy's cold even if you're not. So, it's time to go home.' He held out his hand to Charlotte, who took it and moved to his side.

'It was nice to see you again, Harry,' she said. 'But we have to be going now.'

'Can I come and see you tomorrow?' Harry asked. 'Just to chat, you know, before I go back to London?'

'No.' It was Billy who spoke firmly. 'I'm afraid we're spending tomorrow with my parents.' And with that he turned and walked away, Charlotte at his side. She glanced back once, her eyes bright with unshed tears, and Harry put his finger to his lips. A sign to say nothing? A last blown kiss? She didn't know, but she walked away with her husband

and her son and left him standing alone, a dark shape in the flickering flames of the bonfire.

'He was definitely kissing her,' Mabel confided to Nancy Bright from the post office.

'But who is he?' wondered Nancy, a gleam of excitement in her eyes as she smelled gossip.

'He's Australian,' answered Mabel as she handed Nancy her sausage. 'His name's Victor Merritt. He's taken a room with us, at the Magpie.' She looked round to see if they were being overheard and then added softly. 'He told us his name was Victor Merritt, but *she* called him Harry.'

'Well, that just shows, doesn't it,' marvelled Nancy. 'He's in... inco... not using his own name! I should keep an eye on him, if I was you. You can't never trust a foreigner, can you.'

'He's Australian,' Mabel reminded her. 'They're very free and easy in their ways.'

'Maybe,' Nancy said darkly. 'But even if he is, that makes him a foreigner, so you can't trust him.'

Billy and Charlotte walked home in silence and when they got there Billy's mother was anxious to hear how the evening had gone. Johnny was full of excitement, chattering on about the bonfire and the fireworks.

'I held a sparkle and it was very bright and I had a sausage Mrs Barrett cooked outside. It was wrapped in bread and very hot. And then Mummy met a man and then we came home. I didn't want to, cos the bomb-fire was still going, but Daddy said we had to because Mummy was cold. I wasn't cold, I was hot.'

'Come on, darling, it's late,' Charlotte said. 'Way past your bedtime. Say goodnight to Daddy and Gr'ma.' Johnny hugged his father and his grandmother and Charlotte took him up to bed.

As Billy walked his mother back to Charing Farm, Margaret asked him about the 'man' Johnny had mentioned. Billy answered that it was an old friend of Charlotte's from London, during the war.

'And he's come to see her?'

'He's always turning up, upsetting Charlotte,' Billy muttered.

'But why does it upset her?' Margaret was mystified. 'Who is he?'

'His name's Harry Black. They came from the same town in Germany and met up when they were both refugees in London at the beginning of the war. She was getting bullied at school and he saw off some anti-German bullies.'

'I seem to remember you doing the same thing yourself, here in Wynsdown,' remarked Margaret. She glanced across at her son's face, but was unable to see his expression in the darkness. 'I think it's you who's upset, Billy, not Charlotte.'

'I saw them together at the bonfire,' Billy said miserably. 'He had his arms round her.'

'And is that so bad?'

'She was hugging him back.'

'So what Billy? That's what old friends do.' She waited, but he said no more, so she asked, 'How long is he here for?'

Billy shrugged. 'I don't know. Just a day or so, I expect. He said he was going back to London.'

'Then forget about him, son. He's an old friend of Charlotte's, that's all. It's you she loves. You've got nothing to fear from him.'

'*If* she loves me.'

'For goodness' sake, Billy, pull yourself together. You know she does, it's pretty obvious, to everyone else if not to you!'

When they reached Charing Farm Billy saw his mother

to the back door. She looked at him in the porch light and seeing his misery, she took his hand and drew him into a hug. 'Don't doubt your Charlotte,' she said softly. 'Trust her as you always have. Now, you go straight home and tell her you love her.'

Billy didn't go straight home, he headed for the pub. As he plodded back to the village, his mind was in turmoil. It wasn't Charlotte he didn't trust, it was Harry. When he reached the village green he found it deserted and he realised that most people had adjourned to the Magpie. He paused outside for a moment and then with sudden resolution, he pushed open the door and marched into the bar. He'd have it out with Harry Black, once and for all.

Seeing Harry sitting at the bar, Billy plonked himself on the bar stool next to him. He ordered a pint with a whisky chaser and then glancing over at Harry, nodded to Jack to replenish his glass too.

Jack poured Billy's drinks and then said, 'Same again, Mr Merritt?'

'Yeah, thanks.' When his whisky glass had been refilled, Harry raised it to Billy and deliberately speaking German, said, '*Prosit!*'

Billy scowled at him and took a long pull at his pint. 'Mr Merritt, is it? What happened to Harry Black, then? Life too hot for you with that name, is it?'

'Not at all,' replied Harry easily. 'I use them both.'

'What did you come here for?' Billy demanded.

'I came to see Lisa.'

'Her name's Charlotte.'

'She'll always be Lisa to me.'

'She won't be anything to you, if I have anything to do with it.'

'Up to her, don't you think?'

They drank, enclosed in an angry silence, while the hubbub of a village night out swirled round them. The bonfire had burned to embers and the November night was cold. Those who had no children to take home to bed had moved into the warmth of the pub.

'Time you went back to London, or Australia or wherever you've sprung from,' Billy said as he finished his pint and downed the whisky chaser. 'Leave my Charlotte alone. You're not part of her life any more and we don't want you hanging round. Time you got lost!'

Harry's eyes hardened. 'That's for her to tell me, not you!'

'I'm her husband and she's the mother of my children. We're a family and you don't belong to it! You're *nothing* to us and I speak for both of us.' Billy slammed his glass down onto the bar and got a little unsteadily to his feet. An interested silence fell on the pub as, watched by Mabel, Jack and more than half the village, he stalked out into the night, leaving Harry sitting alone at the bar. For a few moments the bar remained hushed and then the chatter and laughter returned. Harry knocked back the last of his drink and with a quiet 'goodnight' to Mabel, he went upstairs.

With Johnny now safely tucked up in bed, and Billy walking Margaret home, Charlotte was on her own at Blackdown House. She sank into an armchair, feeling thoroughly miserable. Harry had come back, as he always did; always on his own terms, his own inimitable self. Hearing his voice, seeing him smiling at her, she recognised the bond that had always been between them, strengthened when as refugees they had struggled with life in a country which was at war with their own. Their lives had moved on, diverged, and yet when she heard him say her name, the name he knew her by, she had felt the familiar tug of affection. She hadn't wanted him to kiss her, she'd had no thought of that, and yet when he had, she'd known a fleeting response before she'd pulled away. Had Billy seen that embrace? She didn't know. If he had, would he confront her with it? She didn't know. If he did, would she be able to convince him that though she was fond of Harry, it was he, Billy, whom she loved with all her heart. She didn't know.

It was some time before she heard Billy coming in through the back door. Longer than the walk to Charing Farm and back. He came into the kitchen and it was immediately clear he'd stopped off at the Magpie to have a drink or two on his way home.

'Sorry I've been so long,' he said as he flopped down onto a chair. 'I've been having a drink with your beau!'

'With Harry?'

'Oh, so you know who I mean, then?'

'Don't be silly, Billy, he's not my beau, as you call it, and never has been.'

'He thinks he could be.'

'Well, he couldn't.' She fixed Billy with a stare. 'And you know it.'

'Looked to me as if you were pretty pleased to see him. "Just going in to the ladies,"' he mimicked. 'Just going to meet your boyfriend, rather!'

'Billy, my darling, listen. I was getting Johnny his sausage and he just came up behind me. I didn't know he was here until he spoke to me.'

'But you knew he was coming.'

'No, I didn't.' She reached for Billy's hand. 'I admit, I did know he was looking for me. Aunt Naomi wrote to me and told me he'd been to see her, trying to find me.'

'You didn't tell me that,' scowled Billy.

'I didn't because I knew it would upset you. I didn't think he'd actually turn up, without any warning. Aunt Naomi said he was going back to Australia soon. I didn't think he'd come here and so there was no point in upsetting you.'

'I'm not upset,' snapped Billy. 'I'm angry. I saw you, you were in his arms. I expect the whole village saw you.'

'He gave me a hug,' Charlotte said. 'A hug and a kiss as any old friend might. It meant nothing and you know it. It's you I love, Billy. It always has been, right from the day you stood up for me against Tommy Gurney when I was just fourteen. I've never loved anybody but you. I'm fond of Harry, you *know* I'm fond of Harry, he's been an important part of my life, but it's you I love. Love with every fibre of my being. You are my best friend, my lover and my husband and you know it... don't you?'

Billy nodded, and getting to his feet, he pulled her into his arms.

'I love you, Char, more than anyone in the world,' he murmured with his face against her hair. 'And d'you know something else? I'm sorry for Harry.'

'Sorry for Harry?'

'Because you love me and not him. Come on, my dearest girl, let's go to bed.'

Back at the Magpie, Harry lay on his bed, smoking a cigarette and listening to the noise downstairs. He'd found her. He'd seen her with her family, and he knew, much as he hated the fact, that Billy was right. He ought to leave, to disappear once again and let her get on with her life, but he also knew he couldn't simply walk away for ever. What lay between them was too strong. Like a piece of elastic, he thought. I can stretch it just so far before it brings me back to find her. He wanted to see her once more before he left; to tell her that if ever she needed him, she only had to call, but he knew Billy wouldn't let him near her again... this time.

It was the next morning, after a night of fitful sleep, that he awoke with the answer. When he got back to London he would write to her. He would write her a letter and send it, sealed, to Caroline Morrison at Livingston House. She wasn't there any more, but they would surely have a forwarding address and the letter would reach her eventually. Harry knew that Caroline had withheld one of his letters before, and maybe she would do so again, but, he decided, it'd be worth a try.

Chapter 18

Caroline Masters picked up the post from the mat and carried it back into the dining room, where she poured herself another cup of coffee. Henry was already in his surgery and she set his letters aside for him to open later. There was only one for her and it had been sent on from Livingston House. Addressed to her as Miss C. Morrison, it had been redirected to her new name and address in a different hand. She picked up a knife and slit the envelope open. Inside was another envelope, wrapped in a folded paper. The second envelope was simply addressed to Mrs Charlotte. There was no surname, but plenty of space to add it and an address. On the paper that had been wrapped round it was a scrawled note.

DEAR MISS MORRISON.

Please send my letter on to Lisa. I don't know her address, but I do know she is married to Billy. Last time I wrote to her you kept the letter back. Please do not this time as I mean her no harm. If you do not send my letter on I will go back to Wynsdown and see her again for myself. Billy won't like that.

Thank you.
HARRY BLACK

Caroline stared at the sealed envelope for a long moment and then set it aside. She knew that Harry had been in Wynsdown on bonfire weekend and the trouble that had caused. Like everyone else in the village, she'd heard the rumours circulating about Charlotte and her 'lover'.

Caroline and Henry had not been at the bonfire party, and had not seen Harry, but thanks to the good offices of Nancy Bright and Mabel Barrett over the past week, Caroline had heard various stories of what was supposed to have happened that evening. These ranged from Charlotte being caught in a passionate embrace with Harry, who apparently was posing as an Australian, Billy dragging his wife away from the bonfire party by brute force, Harry and Billy having a punch-up in the bar of the Magpie and Harry overheard threatening dire revenge on his lover's husband.

'Nasty piece of work,' she'd heard Nancy say to Mavis Gurney in the post office. 'Well, Australians are, aren't they?' replied Mavis, who'd never met one.

'Surprised at Charlotte, though, carrying on behind Billy's back.' Nancy shook her head at the thought of it.

'Well, she's a foreigner, an' all, ain't she?' returned Mavis. 'Two stamps, please, Mrs Bright.'

'Yes,' agreed Nancy, as she handed over the stamps and took Mavis's money. 'We tend to forget that now, don't we?'

'You saw all this happening, did you, Nancy?' interposed Caroline, unable to control herself any longer.

Nancy looked at her in surprise. 'Well, no,' she admitted, 'not myself, but Mabel saw them hugging and kissing in the shadows where they thought no one could see them.'

'And my Bert was in the pub when Billy come in, later that night,' put in Mavis. 'He said Billy was raging at this Vic bloke and telling him to leave his wife alone.'

'Who's Vic?' asked Caroline, confused.

'Well, this Australian, of course,' replied Nancy. 'Like I was saying, Mabel saw them kissing and she says his hands were all over her. Mabel says they were hiding in the shadows, so's not to be seen.'

'Mabel seems to be saying a good deal,' remarked Caroline with asperity.

'Well, she was right there, weren't she?'

'She was in the shadows with Charlotte Shepherd and some unknown man?' Caroline raised a quizzical eyebrow.

'No, course not. But she saw them, Charlotte and this bloke.'

'And his name was Vic, was it?'

'Well, Mabel said it was. He stayed at the Magpie for the night, so she should know.'

'My Bert says,' Mavis Gurney went on, anxious not to be left out of the story, 'that they nearly came to blows in the bar, him and Billy Shepherd. "Don't blame Billy," my Bert says. Says he'd have fetched the bloke a swipe if he'd laid a finger on me.'

Caroline suppressed a smile at the thought of anyone laying a finger on the redoubtable Mavis Gurney. She was a large woman in every particular and, Caroline thought as she watched her leave the post office, it'd be a brave man that would try, even if he wanted to, which, she thought uncharitably, is most unlikely.

'Course, you've known that Charlotte since she was a kid, haven't you?' Nancy said to Caroline. 'You must be surprised as me at such behaviour. And her with two young kiddies, too. That baby can't be more than four months and there's her mother—'

'There's her mother meeting up with an old friend from the war, who gave her a hug and, possibly, a kiss.'

'You didn't see them!' Nancy said pointedly.

'Nor did you,' snapped Caroline. 'You're just a vulgar gossip. It's you who should be ashamed of yourself, spreading rumours like this. How would you like *your* name dragged in the mud?'

'I wouldn't do anything like that,' said Nancy self-righteously.

'No,' said Caroline acidly. 'I doubt if you'd get the chance.' And with that she turned on her heel and swept out of the post office, her letters still in her hand.

Bother, she thought ruefully, now I'll have to get Avril to go in and buy me some stamps.

When she told her sister about her confrontation with Nancy, Avril laughed. 'Well done you,' she said. 'But I'm afraid the rumours are still going round and people are saying there's no smoke without fire. Poor Charlotte, several people have cut her dead. David noticed it at church on Sunday, people turning away. He made a point of greeting her very publicly after the service, but I heard Sally Prynne say, "Well, he's got to, ain't he? He's the vicar!"'

Poor Charlotte indeed! Caroline had thought. And now, here was a note from the troublemaker himself, Harry Black, asking her to send on a letter to Charlotte and threatening to come back to Wynsdown if she didn't.

It was clear from the fact that he'd sent her the letter addressed to Livingston House, that Harry didn't know where she herself was.

He probably doesn't know we live in the same village now, Caroline thought. I can simply take Charlotte the letter and we can talk about what she wants to do about it.

Her mind made up, that morning she set out for Blackdown House. She found Charlotte feeding Edie, and Caroline happily took over the bottle while Charlotte made coffee for them both. Johnny was playing with some soldiers on the kitchen floor.

'The ones in red are the goodies, Auntie Caro,' he explained. 'The blue ones are the baddies.' He swept a hand across the line of blue soldiers and they all fell over. 'The goodies have won!' he shouted in triumph and began to set them up again for a second battle.

Once Edie was settled in her pram for her morning nap, Charlotte and Caroline sat down with their coffee.

'This is nice,' Charlotte said. 'I'm glad you came. I haven't been out much the last week or so.'

'No, well I heard you'd been having a difficult time,' Caroline said.

Charlotte looked at her sharply. 'What d'you mean?'

'Charlotte, you know there are rumours about you and Harry going round the village.'

'Oh, those.' Charlotte forced a half-hearted laugh. 'We haven't been paying any attention to them. Just stupid, they are.'

'What does Billy say?'

'Same as me,' replied Charlotte. 'We pay them no mind. Harry was here, he came to the bonfire party and said hallo. We had a hug, that's all there was to it.'

'I'm sure it was,' smiled Caroline. 'And I'm sure it'll all die down very soon. Nancy'll find something else to gossip about.'

'Oh, her!' Charlotte dismissed the postwoman with a wave of her hand. 'My poor mother-in-law had a run-in with her yesterday. Mrs Shepherd gave her a piece of her mind, I can tell you, told her she was a spiteful troublemaker.'

'She's right, and I told her the same,' Caroline said.

'Let's talk about something else,' Charlotte said. 'How's Henry? Enjoying married life?'

'I hope so,' laughed Caroline. 'He's fine and busy. The waiting room was full this morning... just the way he likes it!' She was suddenly serious and said, 'Charlotte, I'm sorry, but we have to go back to Harry for a minute. This came in the post today.' She reached into her pocket and pulled out the letter, still in its outer envelope.

Charlotte took it and looking at it, said, 'Who's writing to you at Livingston House?'

'Open it,' Caroline said.

Charlotte pulled out the inner envelope and the paper wrapped round it and read what Harry had written. She looked up to find Caroline watching her face.

'I didn't know whether to give it to you or not,' Caroline said. 'But I know you were angry with me last time, so I'm not interfering now. The main thing that struck me was his threat to come back and see you again. With the rumours circulating... well, I didn't think it would be a good idea at all.'

'No,' whispered Charlotte. 'No, he mustn't do that.'

'Why don't I play with Johnny for a while and you can go and read what he says to you, in peace?'

Charlotte nodded wordlessly and went upstairs to her bedroom; then feeling that she shouldn't read a letter from Harry in the bedroom she shared with Billy, she went into the bathroom, locked the door and sat down on the closed lavatory seat. For a long moment she held the unopened envelope. Perhaps it would be best simply to destroy it, unread. If she did that Harry would be cut out of her life for ever... except that he might not be. He might come to Wynsdown again as he threatened and cause yet more trouble. She had convinced

Billy that there was nothing between her and Harry except a deep and abiding friendship, born of shared troubles, at least she thought she had, but would this conviction survive another visit from Harry? Billy had been as robust in his defence of her reputation in the village as his mother and Caroline had been, but how would the scandalmongers react if Harry put in another appearance?

At least I should read what he's written, she thought. I owe him that.

She knew Billy would say she didn't owe Harry anything, but she also knew Billy would never quite understand the bond that existed between them.

She slipped her finger under the flap, tore the envelope open and extracted Harry's letter.

DEAR LISA,

I'm back in London now, but for reasons you know why I couldn't come round your house and say goodbye. I don't even know which your house is, so I'm sending this to Miss Morrison so she can send it on to you. Your Billy won't worry about a letter coming from her. I shall be here for the next few months and after that I'm going back to Australia.

I wanted to take you with me, but I can see that ain't going to happen. You got your family here now. Just write to me at this address to tell me the Morrison woman sent it on and I'll stay away. But if you ever need me, Lisa, write to me here. I'll get the letter in the end, even if I've gone back to Sydney. Address it to Victor Merritt, that's my new name, but as you'll always be Lisa to me, I'll always be your Harry.

Charlotte read and reread the letter. The address at the top was a pub, the Jolly Sailor in Shoemaker Lane, wherever that was. Charlotte had no idea, but here was the chance, if she wanted it, to maintain a thin thread of contact with Harry.

After a while she put the letter back into its envelope. She had several options. She could ignore it and risk Harry reappearing in Wynsdown. She could send an answer to him at the Jolly Sailor and that would be the end of it. Perhaps that's what she should do. Or she could tell Billy, show him the letter and let him read her reply; that thought made her feel sick with apprehension. What should she do for the best?

I'll have to think about it. She felt the panic rising up inside her. And I can't think about it now.

In the meantime she needed to keep Harry's letter some-where safe, somewhere Billy wouldn't come across it by mistake. She went back downstairs, but before joining Caroline and Johnny in the kitchen, she went into the living room and slipped the envelope in among the music stored in her piano stool.

Back in the kitchen, Caroline and Johnny were sitting on the floor with the soldiers again lined up for battle.

'Auntie Caro's the baddies,' announced Johnny as his mother came in, and began marching his men forward, knocking over those in blue as he went. 'I winned,' he cried in delight as the last blue soldier fell.

'So you did,' laughed Caroline, getting up from the floor. 'Again!'

She didn't ask Charlotte what was in Harry's letter, simply raised her eyebrows in silent query.

'Just saying goodbye,' Charlotte said. 'Off back to Sydney.'

Caroline nodded. 'That's good,' was all she said.

Later that afternoon, Charlotte walked down into the village to visit Clare.

'I wondered if you'd have Johnny for me for half an hour,'

she said when Clare opened the door. 'I just want to go and tidy Miss Edie's grave.'

'Yeah, sure.' Clare stood aside for Johnny to come in and Charlotte followed him, carrying Edie.

'I've brought some paper and crayons,' she said, taking them out of her bag. 'Johnny'll be quite happy doing some drawing while I've gone. I'll take Edie with me in the pram. She's wide awake just now.'

Leaving Johnny happily established at the table with his drawing, Charlotte put Edie back in the pram.

'I'll have the kettle on for a cuppa when you come back,' Clare promised as she closed the door. Charlotte went back up the lane to the churchyard and pushed the pram across the grey winter grass, past the newly erected headstone for Peter Bellinger, to the yew tree in the corner that shaded Miss Edie's grave.

Tears filled her eyes as she stood looking down at the headstone. 'I don't know what to do, Miss Edie,' she whispered. 'People in the village seem to think I've been unfaithful to Billy. I haven't! I wouldn't! Billy's the world to me. Billy and the children.' She dashed a tear from her cheek. 'But Harry's special, too. He hugged me and I hugged him back. Is that so wrong? It's tearing me apart.' But she knew in her heart that what was tearing her apart most of all was the knowledge that when Harry had kissed her, just for a fraction of a second, she'd responded. She knew it, but could hardly admit it, even to herself. She didn't want Harry as a husband... or as a lover. She'd pushed him away, but he'd known and she'd known, that her response had been there.

'He's written to me,' she went on. 'And if I don't answer his letter, he's threatened to come here again. I can't let that happen; he mustn't do that! But if I write back to him and

Billy ever finds out, it'll break his heart. I don't know what to do.' Her tears were flowing freely now, and she picked up Edie, holding her close, feeling the comfort of her warm little body in her arms.

Gradually her tears dried and she put Edie back into the pram. Taking out her handkerchief she blew her nose. She couldn't leave Johnny with Clare for too long, Clare had Agnes to think about. As she turned to retrace her steps to the lane, she saw Marjorie Bellinger standing at her husband's grave. Marjorie looked up as Charlotte approached and, seeing her tear-streaked face, put out a hand to her.

'Are you all right, Charlotte?'

'Yes.' Charlotte managed to conjure up a smile. 'Yes, I'm fine.'

'It never gets any easier, does it?' She gestured towards Peter's grave.

'I'll be fine in a minute,' Charlotte assured her. 'Just hits me sometimes, specially when I feel I need her advice.'

'Anything I can do?' Marjorie asked softly. 'I know it's been difficult for you this last week or so.'

Charlotte didn't pretend not to know what Marjorie was talking about. She shrugged and said, 'Oh, I suppose it'll all blow over in the end.'

'Bring the children for tea one afternoon,' Marjorie suggested. 'I'm rattling around in the manor and would love to have some young company.'

'Thank you, that would be nice.' Charlotte sounded a little doubtful.

'No, I mean it, Charlotte. Come tomorrow. I'll get Mrs Darby to make a cake.'

Recognising the appeal in Marjorie Bellinger's invitation, Charlotte smiled. 'That sounds lovely,' she said. 'We'll come when Johnny wakes up from his afternoon nap.'

A night's sleeplessness had finally decided Charlotte on her course of action. She would write back to Harry and tell him she'd had his letter. She'd say goodbye and wish him well in his new life in Australia. A short letter, breaking the thread. Then, she'd put the whole incident behind her.

As soon as Billy had left for Charing Farm, she wrote her letter.

Blackdown House

DEAR HARRY,

I got your letter. I'm sorry we didn't get to say a proper goodbye, too.

You have to believe that I'm very happy here with Billy and my children and I wouldn't change my life for any other.

I hope you'll be happy living in Australia and that you find someone there who'll make you as happy as Billy makes me.

Though we'll never meet again, I'll never forget you.

LISA

She read it through several times before she put it into an envelope and addressed it, as instructed, to Victor Merritt at the Jolly Sailor. Picking up another letter that she'd written to Naomi the previous day, she put both in her bag, ready to post. She needed stamps and so, on her way to have tea with Marjorie at the manor, she took her courage in both hands and went into the post office.

'Writing to someone special, are you?' asked Nancy Bright with a coy smile.

Charlotte faced her with a steady look and then answered, 'Yes, to my Aunt Naomi.' She held up the letter addressed to Naomi and Dan. 'Would you like to read it, Miss Bright?'

'Certainly not,' snapped Nancy, looking affronted. 'I don't read other people's letters.'

'No?' replied Charlotte. 'And there was I thinking you take great interest in other people's business.'

'Really! How dare you?' spluttered Nancy.

'Oh dear!' cried Charlotte, her hand to her mouth. 'I must have got that wrong. I must make sure I don't pass it on to anyone else!'

She picked up the stamps. 'Sorry,' she said, 'I must fly, we're on our way to have tea with Mrs Bellinger. So kind of her to invite us, don't you think? Come along, Johnny, there's a good boy.' And with that Charlotte stalked out of the post office, leaving a scarlet-faced Nancy Bright, for once at a loss for words. Once outside, she stuck a stamp on each of her letters and dropped them into the pillar box, before crossing the green and taking the lane towards the manor.

Chapter 19

W hen Felix had arrived back from his visit to Wynsdown, late that Sunday evening, Daphne had already gone to bed and he found the flat in darkness. He switched on the hall light and went through to the living room where he poured himself a stiff whisky and dropped into an armchair. One way and another it had been a long weekend. He and his mother had spent several hours discussing the possibilities, and he'd been over to see Richard Deelish at Newland Farm. He, like John Shepherd, was still interested in buying his farm outright, but he, too, expressed doubts about when he might be able to raise the money. Money everywhere was tight, and though he'd have the farm to put up as collateral for a mortgage, he was hesitating. If he did nothing, he would still have a farm to work and a living to make. If he bought the farm and it failed, he would lose everything.

Felix could understand his indecision. He was filled with all manner of doubts himself. The main thoughts that exercised his mind were the ideas Marjorie had floated with regard to the manor house itself. Although she had not said in so many words, Felix knew that she was hoping that he would not only accept her gift of the house, but also that he and Daphne would leave London and come and live there permanently. He was glad that Daphne was asleep when he crept into bed beside her, he didn't want to broach the subject until he had allowed it to simmer in his own mind. Lying beside her, he was aware of the warmth of her body, but as he pulled the covers over them, she muttered in her sleep and turned away. Better that way, he thought, than questions.

Felix need not have worried. Daphne seemed entirely uninterested in how he'd spent his time in Wynsdown that weekend. She asked no questions, and for this he was grateful. After much consideration, he had come to the conclusion that he couldn't keep the estate going without living there himself. Either he sold the whole estate, manor house, farms and land, or he had to move in to the manor and take up the reins himself as his father had done; and for this he would have to resign his commission and leave the RAF. It was a big step. Staying in the air force would provide him with a regular salary, but not enough to fund the improvements necessary on the estate.

He didn't think Daphne would be very keen on the idea of moving to Somerset, but even so, he wasn't quite prepared for her reaction when he finally broached the idea.

'You want to what?' she cried. She stared at him as if he were crazy. 'You have to be joking! I'm not going to bury myself in the country. I'm a Londoner, not a country bumpkin.'

'Not everyone who lives outside London is a bumpkin,' Felix pointed out, in an effort to lighten the mood.

'Everyone I've met down there is,' snapped Daphne. 'What on earth would I do all day? Make jam? Keep hens?'

'You could do either,' said Felix mildly.

'For Christ's sake, Felix...'

'Please don't use that language, Daphne, it doesn't become you.'

'I'll use what language I like,' shouted Daphne, her anger rising and the East End returning to her voice. 'You can't tell me 'ow to speak. An' I'll tell you this, Wing Commander Felix Bloody Bellinger, I ain't gonna live in Somerset, neither.'

'Where *are* you going to live, then?' asked Felix.

Daphne stared at him, brought up short. 'Well, here, of course.'

'Afraid not,' Felix said. 'I'm giving notice and we'll have to move out by the first of Jan.'

'An' you didn't think to discuss this with me first?'

'I'm discussing it with you now.' He saw how angry she was and said, 'I'm sorry, Daphne, I'm sorry. Perhaps I should have told you what I had in mind, but I didn't want to worry you before I'd thought it through.'

'Worry me? You didn't want to worry me, so you've made this decision, what affects me as much as you… without even consulting me?'

'Circumstances have made the decision for me,' Felix said. 'I'm truly sorry. I realise now that I should have spoken to you first—'

'Yeah, you bloody well should,' retorted Daphne. 'You've decided we're moving and that's it, is it? No talking it through?'

Felix looked at her in dismay. He realised now that he was in the wrong. He'd been so concerned how the big decision would affect him and the estate, he hadn't given much consideration to what Daphne might think. She was his wife and he'd simply assumed that she'd be happy enough to move with him wherever he had to go. It's what wives did. But Daphne was having none of it.

'It's ridiculous, Felix,' she went on. 'We can't just up sticks and move to Somerset. Even if we really wanted to, and I don't, we'd have to have somewhere in London as well.'

'Daphne, dearest,' he reached out and took her hand,

'you really haven't been listening to what I've been telling you this past month. We can't afford to live in London while we have a house in Wynsdown. The manor is going to belong to me. There'll be no rent to pay. I shall manage Home Farm, make it pay, and we shall be able to live within our means in a beautiful part of the country.'

'We don't have to go. If the manor's yours, you can sell it, we'd have money then, wouldn't we? You could stay in the air force, and we can stay living up here.'

'Darling, I can't sell it, certainly not while my mother's still alive. It's been in my family for more than a century and I want it to be there for my children... our children. Think about it, darling, it'll be a great place to bring up a family.'

'A family? Who said anything about a family?' demanded Daphne, snatching her hand away. 'I ain't gonna go, Felix, and that's all there is to it.'

'I'm resigning my commission,' Felix ignored her interruption, 'and moving to Wynsdown in time to spend Christmas with my mother. It'll be her first Christmas without Dad, and I don't want her spending it on her own.'

'It'll be our first Christmas together an' all,' Daphne said. 'Thought about that, 'ad you? Thought about me an' my Christmas?'

'We'd all spend Christmas together,' Felix cried in frustration. 'I want us to make it special for her.'

'Well, you can make it special by yourself,' retorted Daphne. 'I ain't coming.'

'That's up to you,' Felix said with a patience he didn't feel. 'We have this flat until the new year, and after that we have to be out of it.'

Daphne's eyes narrowed. 'You've given notice already, ain't you?'

'No, I haven't, but I shall in the next few days. A month's notice is all he needs.'

'I'm your wife,' Daphne almost snarled at him. 'You have to provide for me.'

'I know,' replied Felix, 'and I'm doing so. I'm providing you with a home and the means to run it. If you choose to live somewhere else, well, that's up to you. I'll continue to give you your allowance…'

'Ten pounds a month?' she scoffed. 'What good's that?'

'It's a lot more than many young wives get to spend on themselves,' answered Felix. He sighed and stretched his hand to her again. 'Come on, Daph, don't be like this. We can't afford to live here. My job is to make the estate in Wynsdown pay; your place is with me. We love each other, don't we? You're my wife, we should be a team; we should be together, to support each other if there are problems.' His shoulders slumped. 'Don't look at me like that, darling. It's not my fault that things are in such a mess, but I do have to try and put them right.' He thought about the dressmaker's bill that had arrived in the post the previous day, but he didn't mention that; it was not the time to remind her about the economies they were supposed to be making, and would continue to make, wherever they lived.

'Mother is moving into Eden Lodge as soon as the plumbing's sorted and the decorators have finished,' he went on. 'Then the manor will be ours. You'll be the squire's wife, lady of the manor. I'd have thought you'd like that.'

At one time the idea would, indeed, have thrilled Daphne, but that was before she had visited the manor and been disappointed. It had not been at all as she'd imagined, no grand entrance hall and high-ceilinged rooms; no servants to wait on her, just a couple of women from the village to do the housework and cook. Still, she thought reluctantly, it did have a certain cachet to it.

Was it that which finally persuaded Daphne to agree to move with him? Felix wasn't sure, but if it was, he hoped she wouldn't be disappointed.

Once the decision was made, Felix expected Daphne to let her parents know that they were moving to the country. Daphne, however, had other ideas. If they moved away, her parents wouldn't know where they had gone. Had she ever told them the name of the village where Felix came from? She racked her brains. She wasn't sure, but she didn't think so. If they simply disappeared, she could stop paying what she called the blackmail money. Mum had threatened to tell Felix everything if she stopped paying, to go and see him at the Air Ministry, but now he wasn't going to be at the Air Ministry any more. Daphne, however, had reckoned without Felix.

'Have you told your parents we're moving?' he asked one evening over supper.

'Oh, yes,' replied Daphne airily, 'they're fine about it.' And Felix knew at once that she was lying. He'd never understood her reluctance to reintroduce him to her parents – after all, it wasn't as if he didn't know her family background – and he felt it was important that she wasn't entirely cut off from them.

'Shall we go over there, to see them? Say goodbye before we go?' he suggested.

'No need,' Daphne replied. 'I been to see them, told them where we'll be. I'm meeting up with Joan tomorrow,' she said, changing the subject. 'Thought we'd have a girls' day together before I move too far away.'

'Good idea,' Felix answered absently, while in his mind he was planning his own tomorrow.

There had been many changes taking place at the Air Ministry, and when Felix had been to see his commanding officer to discuss resigning his commission, there seemed to be little problem.

'Responsibilities elsewhere,' agreed Group Captain Hague when Felix explained about his father's death and the problems he'd left behind. 'Duty calls. Wish you luck, Bellinger. We shall miss you, but you're right to go.'

They're actually quite pleased to get rid of me, Felix thought when the deed was done and he walked back into civilian life.

It meant he was free in the daytime for the week before they moved, and while Daphne was out with Joan, Felix caught the bus and headed for Hackney. He found Norman Higgins's garage with little trouble. It looked pretty run-down, a yard with ramshackle buildings and the carcases of two long-dead cars rusting in a corner. His father-in-law had his head under the bonnet of an elderly-looking vehicle, unaware that anyone had come into the yard.

Felix coughed, and Norman Higgins emerged from the bonnet to see a tall, good-looking young man standing just inside the gate.

'Help you?' he asked, wiping his oily hands on an equally oily rag.

Felix stepped forward, and despite Norman's begrimed hands, offered his own. 'Mr Higgins?' he said. 'I'm Felix Bellinger.'

Norman stared at him for a moment and then a look of recognition crossed his face. He gave his hand another surreptitious wipe on his overall and then took Felix's extended one. 'You're our Daph's bloke.'

Felix smiled. 'Yes,' he said. 'I thought it was time we met properly.'

For a moment Norman was at a loss, then he said, 'Well, yes, good. We better go up to the house and see Ethel.'

He led the way out of the yard and up the alley that Felix remembered from the night he'd brought Daphne home.

'Ethel,' Norman called as they reached the door. 'Come and see. Look who's 'ere! It's Daph's husband.'

Ethel met them at the door, staring for a moment at the man who was with Norman, before standing aside to let them into the house.

'How do you do, Mrs Higgins?'

Felix held out his hand and Ethel touched it briefly, murmuring, 'Fine, I'm sure.'

'Well, aren't you going to offer the man a cup of tea?' said Norman. 'Sit down, Wing Commander, do.' He pulled out a chair from under the kitchen table.

'We should go into the front room, Norman,' hissed his wife.

'Not at all, Mrs Higgins,' Felix said quickly, 'but I'd love a cup of tea if you've got the kettle on.'

'Always got the kettle on, haven't you, Eth?' said Norman, taking a seat across the table. He turned back to Felix. 'Daphne not with you today, then? That's a pity. We miss 'er, you know.'

'I'm afraid she's out somewhere with a friend. I didn't tell her I was coming to see you. Came on the spur of the moment, or I'm sure she'd have come too.'

Ethel brought cups and saucers to the table and then made the tea. She had said little, leaving Norman to struggle with the conversation. She was wondering why Felix had suddenly turned up on their doorstep. Why had he come without Daphne? Had he found out about Janet? And if so, what was he going to do about her?

She poured the tea and handed Felix his cup. There was an awkward silence and then she decided to take the bull by the horns and find out why he'd come.

'It's nice to meet you properly, Wing Commander,' she began.

'Please, do call me Felix,' Felix said. 'Wing Commander doesn't apply any more, anyway. I've left the air force now.'

'Left the air force?' echoed Ethel.

'Why's that, then?' asked Norman.

Felix had been right. Clearly Daphne hadn't spoken to them about the move, or if she had, she hadn't told them the whole story.

'I'm afraid my father died a few weeks ago,' he explained. 'He had property in Somerset which has come to me, now. We've decided to move down there, so that I can take it over properly.'

'So you're moving out of London, then?' Ethel knew at once that Daphne hadn't been going to tell her.

'Yes, we move just before Christmas. I'm anxious my mother shouldn't spend her first Christmas without my father, on her own.' Even as he said the words he realised how they must sound. They were moving to be near his mother, when they never saw or seemed to bother about Daphne's family, and colour flooded his cheeks.

'You're a good son to your mother,' Norman said without a hint of irony. 'That's as it should be.'

'So, where is it you're going?' asked Ethel.

'Wynsdown,' replied Felix. 'It's a village on the Mendip Hills ... in Somerset,' he added as it was clear from the Higginses' blank looks that they had no idea where the Mendips were. 'I'll write down the address before I go, so that if ever you need us, you'll know where we are.'

Ethel thanked him with a satisfied smile. She remembered that Daphne had mentioned a village in Somerset, but hadn't been able to remember its name. Now she knew where to find her if the money she was sending for Janet should ever dry up.

As Felix was about to leave, Janet came running up the alley, home from school for her dinner.

She stopped short in the doorway when she saw Felix standing in the kitchen.

'Hallo,' she said in surprise. 'Who're you?'

'Janet, this is Felix, Daphne's husband,' said Norman. 'Say how d'you do.' He turned to Felix. 'This is our Daph's sister, Janet.'

Felix tried to mask his surprise and said, 'Hallo, Janet. How nice to meet you.'

'How d'you do, Felix,' Janet said, adding hesitantly, 'Can I call you Felix?'

'Of course you can,' Felix replied with a smile, 'you're my sister-in-law!'

Janet's face broke in a grin. 'Am I?' she cried. 'Your sister-in-law!'

'You certainly are,' Felix assured her. 'And I'm your brother-in-law. Tell you something else, too, you look very like your sister.'

'Do I?' Janet was surprised. 'But she's so pretty!'

'So are you,' smiled Felix. 'Isn't she?' He looked across at her parents for corroboration.

Norman nodded. 'Just like Daph used to look at your age, Janet.'

When Felix had taken his leave, the three Higginses sat down to their midday meal.

'I like him,' Janet enthused as she tucked into the fish pie in front of her. 'Isn't Daphne lucky to have married him!'

'Too good for her by far,' murmured Ethel, which drew a disapproving look from Norman.

'I hope we see him again soon, Mum,' Janet said.

'I don't expect we will,' replied her mother. 'They're moving to Somerset.'

'Oh! That's not fair!'

'Never mind, duck,' said Norman. 'Who knows, you might be able to go and see them down there, one day.'

'Really!' Janet's eyes sparkled at the thought.

'Maybe,' said Ethel with a quelling look at her husband. 'Now, get on and eat your dinner, or you'll be late back to school.'

When she had the kitchen to herself again, Ethel took out the scrap of paper on which Felix had written the Wynsdown address... and telephone number. She gave a secretive smile as she looked at it.

The Manor House, Wynsdown, Somerset... and even a phone number.

'Got you, my girl,' she said to the empty kitchen, and taking from the cupboard the old cash box where she kept all the family papers, she put the address inside, relocking it for safety.

When Felix got back to the flat, Daphne was already home.

'Hallo!' he said in surprise. 'I thought you were out for the day with Joan.'

'Decided to make it just for lunch,' was all Daphne said flatly and Felix realised that for some reason the day had not been a success, but he knew better than to ask what had happened. As if to change the subject, Daphne asked, 'Where've you been?'

'Me?' he replied casually, fearing her reaction to his visit to her family, but knowing he wasn't going to hide it. 'I went to see your family.'

'You what?' Daphne's voice was icy.

'Went to see your family.'

'Felix!' Daphne almost shrieked. 'How dare you go behind my back!'

Apparently unperturbed by this outburst, Felix went on. 'And I met your sister, Janet.'

'You saw Janet?'

'Yes, she came home for lunch. What a lovely girl she is.'

Daphne seemed suddenly deflated. 'Oh, Felix, why did you have to go?'

'Because I knew you hadn't told them we were moving... and they have a right to know, Daph, they really do.' He smiled placatingly. 'It's all right. I didn't let on that I didn't know you had a sister. She looks very like you, you know. She'll be a beauty one day, too.'

Ignoring his rather heavy-handed compliment, Daphne groaned, 'Why do you have to interfere with my family?'

'Because, as we're married, my darling, so now they're my family, too.'

Clearly Daphne was angry that he'd been to see her family, and she hardly spoke to him for the rest of the day, but he was relieved that she said no more about it.

Daphne, in turn, was relieved that he thought Janet was her sister. At least Mum hadn't spilled the beans.

But she wouldn't, Daphne thought bleakly, or she'd have no hold over me.

Still, she was angry with Felix for going; now she'd still have to pay up. So, it was going to cost him money, and serve him right!

Felix had been thinking of ways they could cut down their expenditure and as one of his economies, he sold his open-topped car and bought a small Standard.

'Why've you got to sell the car?' Daphne wailed when he told her what he was going to do.

'Because it's impractical and expensive to run,' he replied. 'We're going to need a car, but we don't need anything flash, just something to get about in. The buses from the village are few and far between.'

He brought the new car home the week before they were due to leave. Daphne stared at it in horror. 'Felix, it's not even new!'

'No,' he admitted, 'but it'll have to do.' He gave her a mischievous grin. 'I thought you, as the family mechanic, could give her the once-over. Don't want to break down on the way, do we?'

Daphne glowered at him, but the next day she donned her old overalls, tied her hair up in its familiar turban and spent a happy hour or two under, not only the bonnet, but also the chassis. When she emerged, her hands black with oil and a smudge across her nose, Felix felt his heart do a flip. She was the Daphne he'd seen working on Spitfires at the air base, the Daphne he loved.

'She's actually not in bad shape,' Daphne conceded. 'Won't be long before we'll need new brake pads, but I've changed the plugs and given the engine a spring clean. She'll do for a bit.'

Felix and Daphne moved into the manor on the Monday before Christmas. It had not been an easy decision to make and had caused a good deal of heartache and friction between them, but Felix was still sure it was the right one. They had rented the flat furnished, and there was little to pack apart from their clothes and the few small personal items they had bought together. Everything had been packed into two trunks and sent on by train, luggage in advance.

On their last Saturday night in London, Felix, with one last burst of extravagance, took Daphne out for dinner to her favourite restaurant. The Silver Swan was a small, intimate restaurant in a corner of Soho; tables tucked into booths, candlelight glinting on silver and cut glass, where they had often eaten while Felix was courting her. Indeed it had been after an evening there that Felix had proposed, and they'd begun to think of it as 'their place'. The head waiter greeted them by name and showed them to a secluded table in an alcove. When they'd ordered their food, Felix poured the wine and, raising his glass to hers, said, 'To us, my darling. And to our new life as the squire and his lady.'

Daphne clinked his glass. 'I suppose this'll be the last time we'll ever come here,' she sighed. 'I wish we wasn't going.'

Two days later, they packed their last bits and pieces into the Standard and set out for Somerset. It was chilly in the late afternoon of a dull December day when they arrived in Wynsdown, cold and tired. As they turned into the manor's driveway, Felix pipped the horn and Marjorie emerged to greet them.

'Welcome home,' she said as she kissed Daphne's cheek and then gave Felix a hug. 'I hope you'll be as happy here as your father and I were.'

'I'm sure we will, Mother,' Felix said, returning her hug.

Daphne said nothing, simply walked through into the drawing room, where a fire snapped and crackled in the hearth, offering welcome warmth after the cold of the December afternoon outside. She took off her coat and dropped it onto an armchair before turning to face her mother-in-law who had followed her in. 'At least it's warm in here,' she remarked, and crossed to the fireplace to hold out her hands to the flames.

'You must be dying for a cup of tea,' Marjorie said. 'The kettle's on the boil, I'll just go and make some.'

Felix carried the tray into the drawing room and they all sat by the fire, drinking their tea and eating slabs of cake, left by Mrs Darby.

'A warm house and a cup of tea,' sighed Felix. 'Nothing better.'

'Mrs Darby's left you a cottage pie in the kitchen, too,' Marjorie said. 'All you need to do is pop it in the oven and it'll be ready for your supper whenever you want it.' She put down her cup and got to her feet. 'Well, I'll leave you to it,' she said, and went out into the hall. Taking her coat from the stand she shrugged it on. 'I had your trunks put upstairs when they arrived and I'm sure you'll want to get settled.'

'Mother, you don't have to go?' protested Felix.

'Yes, Felix, I do. I've got a pie for the oven too, and you and Daphne'll want your first night here to yourselves.'

'Well, at least let me walk you back to Eden Lodge,' Felix said.

'No, I'll be fine,' Marjorie said, but Felix insisted and together they set off down the drive.

Daphne closed the front door behind them and stood for a moment in the silence of the hall and as she did so, the house seemed to sigh and settle round her. A sudden vision of her childhood home assailed her, rough, cramped and ugly. How squalid it seemed; life lived in the kitchen, no hot water, outdoor privy in the small backyard. She shook her head to dispel the thought and looked round the hallway of her new home; doors opening to dining room, study, drawing room. She had a drawing room! The thought made her laugh out loud. No real servants as she'd first imagined, she knew that now, but she assumed that Mrs Darby and Mrs Gurney would still be employed as they had been before. Perhaps it wouldn't be so bad living here, after all.

There were rooms she hadn't seen on her previous visits and now it all belonged to her, she wanted to take possession of it, explore it, discover it on her own. She decided to make a tour of the rest of the house before Felix got back. She was already familiar with the downstairs rooms so, deciding to start upstairs, she climbed the carved oak staircase to the first floor. The door to the bedroom she and Felix had occupied before stood open, and going into the room she found it warm and welcoming, ready for occupation. A fire smouldered in the hearth, the green velvet curtains were drawn and a bedside lamp shed warm, yellow light onto the bed, ready made up, where the clothes had been turned invitingly back.

The two trunks they'd sent down ahead of them were standing in a corner, but Daphne wasn't interested in them or their contents; plenty of time to unpack those. All the time in the world.

Further along the landing she came to Marjorie's bedroom, a room she'd never entered before. Now she flung open its door, and switching on the lights, stepped inside. She found herself in a large, almost empty room. The curtains at the bay window stood open to the darkening sky and the dank winter garden spread out below. It was cold. There was a fireplace, but no fire, laid or lit. A heavy mahogany wardrobe stood against one wall, and standing in the middle of the room was a large wooden bedstead, a pile of blankets, neatly folded, on the bare mattress; apart from a large Turkey rug providing an island of softness in an otherwise austere room, there was no furniture at all.

Daphne stared round angrily. This is the main bedroom, she thought. This should be *our* bedroom. Where's all the furniture? There must have been more than this! His wretched mother's taken it with her! So what are we supposed to use?

She marched across to the wardrobe and threw open the doors. Apart from a few wooden coat-hangers that rattled together as they were disturbed, it contained nothing.

She went out onto the landing again, going from room to room. There were four more bedrooms, one of which had been Felix's as a child, another the blue guest room where James and Freda had slept when they came for the funeral, and two others, furnished but clearly disused. At the far end of the passage were narrow back stairs leading down to the kitchen and a door, behind which Daphne discovered a further flight of steep wooden stairs, leading to three tiny bedrooms in the roof: the servants' rooms, unused for years, dusty and festooned with cobwebs.

By the time Felix got home again, she had been into every room in the house including the kitchen, the scullery and the huge walk-in pantry. There she had found the pie Marjorie had mentioned, and some cabbage, chopped and ready to cook. She left them where they were.

Finished with her exploration Daphne was sitting by the drawing-room fire with her feet up when Felix came in.

'She's taken the furniture from the bedroom,' she said as soon as he came in through the door.

'What?' Felix looked confused.

'Your mother! She's taken the bedroom furniture!'

'Well, it's hers,' said Felix mildly.

'So what do we use, then?' demanded Daphne. She had been thinking about the almost empty bedroom for the past half-hour and was spoiling for a fight.

'There's plenty more furniture in the house,' Felix said as he dropped into the armchair on the opposite side of the hearth.

'We'll just move it around a bit.' He looked across at her angry face and hoping to change the subject asked, 'Did you put the pie in the oven?'

'No!' snapped Daphne, who hadn't finished fighting yet.

'Never mind,' Felix said easily. 'I'll go and put it in.' He waved towards a small trolley standing in the corner of the room. 'Why don't you pour us each a drink? I think we've earned one.'

Later, as they lay in bed in the warm bedroom prepared for them, Felix slipped an arm round her, one hand cupping her breast, the other gently massaging her bottom.

'No, Felix. Not now!' Daphne pulled away from him. 'It's the wrong time of the month.'

Felix withdrew his hand and sighed. 'Pity,' he said. 'You should always make love on the first night in a new house.'

'It's not exactly new to either of us, is it?' Daphne replied.

'No,' Felix conceded, 'but we've never made love here. I do love you, Daphne.' He pulled her close against him, nuzzling the back of her neck. 'Let's just have a cuddle, then.'

Daphne sighed and relaxed against him. She could feel his erection against her back and felt guilty for her lie. 'Only a couple of days,' she said, 'then I'll be fine.'

Chapter 20

'I thought you might like to come over to me for Christmas Day itself,' Marjorie suggested a few days later over a cup of coffee. 'I'm all settled in now, I've even got a Christmas tree.'

'Wouldn't you rather to come to us, Mother?' asked Felix, surprised at her suggestion.

'No, not really, darling,' she said. 'The last few Christmases it was just Dad and me at the manor. I think I'd rather do something quite different this year.' She turned to Daphne who, for the first time, had come with Felix to visit her at Eden Lodge. 'Would you like to cook the Christmas dinner, Daphne, or shall I ask Mrs Darby to come in? I don't think she'll mind just for an hour or so.'

'To cook what?' Daphne sounded very apprehensive. While they'd been in London, she and Felix had been living on a diet of chops and sausages, fried fish, liver, eggs and bacon. She could manage the basics, dishes she'd watched her mother make over the years, but her family's Christmas dinners had been whatever the butcher could supply, cheap cuts, cooked long and slow in the oven.

'I've got a chicken coming up from Home Farm,' answered Marjorie. 'Hope you don't mind, Felix, I asked Donny Day to kill one. Mrs Darby's going to pluck and draw it for us, but I thought Daphne might want to do the cooking.'

'No,' Daphne spoke firmly. 'Ask Mrs Darby.'

She had been more than a little annoyed when Felix had told her that Mrs Darby was going to continue working for his mother.

'But I can't cook!' she exclaimed. 'I'm a hopeless cook.'

'Mother needs her and anyway, we can't afford her.' He grinned reassuringly at Daphne's horrified expression. 'And you can cook, you know you can, and now we're living in the country, you'll find far more food available than in town. We've eggs from Home Farm and grow our own vegetables, don't forget, so there's usually something extra to bring to the table.'

When they had first arrived, Felix had also decided that they could dispense with the services of Mrs Gurney.

'You should continue to employ her, Felix,' Marjorie said. 'I don't need her more than twice a week in this little house, so I'm sure she'll be glad to come to you at the manor the other three days. Otherwise she'll miss the money.'

'I'm not a charitable trust, Mother,' stated Felix. 'I'm sorry if she'll be missing some of her money, but I can't afford to be giving her any of mine!'

'I know,' Marjorie said soothingly, 'but it's a big house for Daphne to run on her own, you know. I couldn't manage it on my own, remember.'

It was the first time that Daphne had ever felt gratitude to her mother-in-law when, after further discussion, Felix relented and they finally agreed that Mavis Gurney should come two days to each house.

The first morning she arrived, she walked in through the back door, hanging her coat on a hook and shedding galoshes on the scullery floor as she shouted, 'Morning, Mrs Felix.'

Daphne, who had not yet met her, came into the kitchen

and found herself facing a tall woman, her ample bosom constrained in a cross-over apron, her hair tied up in what looked like a yellow duster. Broad-shouldered, her large forearms tapered to rough, capable hands. She stood, hands on hips, in the scullery doorway.

Daphne stared at her uncertainly. 'Mrs Gurney?'

''S right,' she said. 'I'll get on with what I usually do, shall I?' Her expression darkened as she added, 'Course, now you cut me hours, I won't get as much done as what I used, but I 'spect you'll be able to pick up what's left.'

'And—' Daphne was horrified to hear her voice come out as a squeak. She cleared her throat and started again. 'And what is it that you usually do?'

'Four hours a day. I go home at one for me dinner.'

'And the afternoons?'

Mrs Gurney folded her arms and raised her chin. 'I don't do afternoons.'

Trying not to be intimidated, Daphne said, 'And you do what, in those hours?'

'Mondays, I light the fire under the copper an' put the wash on. Get it hung out if the weather's kind. Clear the fireplaces, bring in the coal. Clean the kitchen and the scullery. Dust the hall and drawin' room. Bring in the washing before I leave. Tuesdays, well now, Tuesdays I ain't comin' no more. Going to Mrs Bellinger at Eden Lodge. Wednesday I'll do the upstairs and give the kitchen a quick once-over. That suit?' This last was posed as a question, but Daphne could see that it wasn't. Mrs Gurney had stated her terms, thinking that the new Mrs Felix would agree to anything to keep her.

'Sounds fine,' she said faintly. Then, giving herself a mental shake she asked, 'What did you normally do the rest of the week?'

Mavis Gurney looked thoughtful for a moment and then said, 'Tuesdays was ironing and cleaning silver. Thursdays was windows an' floors. Fridays change the beds and if guests was coming prepare the guest rooms and then whisk right through the house ready for the weekend.'

'I see,' Daphne said and then added, 'Where will you start today?'

'Today's Wednesday, so upstairs and spruce the kitchen.'

'The thing is, Mrs Gurney,' Daphne said, 'we're only using one room upstairs just now, so perhaps when you've done our room and the bathroom you could come down and do the drawing room today, as well as the kitchen.'

Mrs Gurney pursed her lips. 'Suppose I could,' she said grudgingly, 'just this once. I don't like having me routine changed.' The two women stared at each other for several moments and to her own surprise it was Mavis who turned away, saying, 'I better get on, then.'

Daphne left her to it and went into the study to find pencil and paper. She sat down and made a list of all the things Mrs Gurney was supposed to do on a Monday and Wednesday and another list of things she said she used to do on the other days.

When he came in for lunch, she showed them to Felix. 'I don't know what she used to do when, but it looks to me as if she's picked the jobs she doesn't mind doing and left me the others, the ones she doesn't like. Ironing, cleaning windows, scrubbing floors, polishing the silver.'

'Well, you're employing her to do what you want done, not what she wants to do,' pointed out Felix. 'So, you tell her. Let's face it, Daph, it's no different to dealing with an insubordinate aircraftswoman, and you used to do that with your eyes shut. Have a chat with Mother and see what she says Mavis is supposed to do.'

'She says it's cos we've cut her hours.'

'Call her bluff and tell her we'll cut them some more if she doesn't do what she's asked.'

'Suppose she calls *our* bluff?' Daphne said.

'She won't, but if she does, well, we'll deal with that when the time comes.'

Christmas Day, falling on a Sunday, meant that Mrs Gurney was not due to put in another appearance at the manor until the following week. Daphne did as Felix suggested and went to see Marjorie.

'Mrs Gurney isn't the easiest,' Marjorie said with a wry smile. 'She was here this morning and I had to listen to her moaning about the shorter hours. But actually, she's a good worker and she gets things done. Stand your ground, Daphne, tell her what you want her to do. She can't afford to lose the job. Stick to what you want, but make a few concessions so that she thinks she's got the better of you, and you'll get on fine.'

Daphne knew it was good advice and she intended to take it when Mavis Gurney arrived the next Wednesday.

The following morning, Felix walked over to Charing Farm to retrieve his horses. John Shepherd greeted him cheerfully as he walked into the stable yard.

'Felix!' he cried. 'Good to see you. I heard you'd arrived. Settling in all right?'

The two men shook hands and John led the way into the stables. When he opened the door the horses looked out with interest from their loose boxes. Felix crossed at once to Archie, his hunter, who whickered a welcome. 'Hallo, boy,' he said, gently stroking his nose. 'I've come to take you home.'

'The local hunt's meeting here on Boxing Day,' Felix told Daphne that evening. 'John and Billy Shepherd will be going and I thought I'd ride out on Archie, give him a run.'

'I thought you were going to sell the horses... since we're "economising".'

'I shall sell Dad's if I can find a buyer,' Felix said, 'but I'll keep Archie.'

'Just so you can go hunting, I suppose,' sniffed Daphne.

'No. Well, that too,' conceded Felix, 'but actually, I'll be riding him round the estate.' He smiled. 'We'll both enjoy the exercise and it means I shan't need to use the car so much. We can save our petrol, so you'll be able to use the car yourself if you need to.'

That's more like it, Daphne thought. If keeping the horse meant that she was going to be able to use the car more often, she wasn't going to argue. She'd found an old bicycle in one of the outhouses and had spent the afternoon cleaning it up, checking it over. She, like so many others, had used a bike continually during the war, and she'd been determined to have some means of transport to get out of the village. The bike had seemed her only option, but if Felix was intending to ride his horse everywhere, she could have the car.

'So, what happens at this meet thing?' she asked.

'Everyone who wants to hunt with us is welcome. Most of the village turn out to see us off. It's a great gathering.'

Felix and Daphne spent Christmas Day with Marjorie as planned and though Daphne had not been looking forward to it, it wasn't as bad as she'd feared. In the morning, despite Daphne's unwillingness, Felix had insisted that they both went to church.

'Why do we have to go?' she demanded petulantly. 'I don't believe in God... and nor do you!'

'You don't know what I believe,' answered Felix mildly. 'But that's not the point here. We've come to live in the manor, my family home, and we have a position to maintain in the village. You want to be regarded as the lady of the manor and that demands certain behaviour, which, I'm afraid, includes going to church. It's expected.'

'Well, they'll be disappointed.'

'Daphne, we're living here now. We have to become part of the village.'

'Easy enough for you,' muttered Daphne, 'you was brought up here.'

'Exactly,' Felix said. 'You're going to have to make an effort.' Seeing her mutinous expression he smiled and said, 'Come on Daph, it's only for an hour. Put your best bib and tucker on. It's Christmas Day!'

Daphne sighed, but she went back upstairs and changed into one of the new outfits she'd bought when Felix was last away in Wynsdown, visiting his mother. She heard him say that money was going to be tight, and now that clothes rationing had been lifted, she'd decided to make the most of her last few weeks in London and add to her winter wardrobe. She had the bills sent to him.

The church was full when Daphne and Felix walked in just before the service began. Dressed in a smart green costume with a fur collar and a matching hat with a curled green feather, Daphne walked up the aisle on Felix's arm, well aware of the interest she was stirring among the women of the congregation.

It was almost worth coming to see the envy on their faces as she, Mrs Felix Bellinger of The Manor, Wynsdown, joined her mother-in-law in the manor pew.

She paid little attention to the service, but she found she

enjoyed singing the carols she'd learned as a child, so that when it was over and they led the congregation out of the church, she decided that perhaps Felix was right. She should show her face, and her clothes, to the village. Let them see who was squire now that the major had passed away, and who the squire's lady. Not old Mrs Marjorie Bellinger, wearing a drab blue overcoat and tired felt hat, now residing at Eden Lodge, but young Mrs Daphne Bellinger, dressed in the latest fashions, living at the manor and taking her rightful place in the local community.

As always, after the service, the congregation gathered outside the church to chat and wish each other Merry Christmas. As the grown-ups greeted each other, the children rushed round the green, pleased to be released from the restraint of church, boasting of what Father Christmas had brought and what they hoped was still to come. Marjorie led Daphne and Felix over to a young couple, who were talking to the vicar's wife. The woman was rocking a baby in a pram, and Daphne realised she looked vaguely familiar. Then she remembered the christening during the service that she and Felix had attended on their first visit. This was the mother of the baby. Not exactly plain, Daphne thought as they approached. Nice enough face, and thick dark hair, but straight, no style to it. If my hair was like that I'd be putting in curling papers every night. Surely, she could make much more of herself if she tried.

'Daphne,' Marjorie said as the couple turned towards them, 'I want you to meet Charlotte and Billy. Billy's family have Charing Farm, just across the hill, but Charlotte and he live in the village, so you'll probably be seeing quite a lot of her. Charlotte, my dear, I don't think you've met my daughter-in-law, Daphne.'

'No, I haven't.' Charlotte extended her hand. 'How nice to meet you. I did meet your husband last time he was here and now Mrs Bellinger tells me you're coming to live in the manor.'

'Already moved in,' said Daphne. 'Still getting straight.'

'Well, I hope you'll be very happy in your new home,' Charlotte said and then turned to greet Felix with a smile. 'Merry Christmas, Felix,' she said as she shook his hand. 'Welcome home!'

'Thank you.' Felix returned her smile. 'Merry Christmas to you, too. And it does feel like coming home.'

Billy stepped forward to meet Daphne and for him she turned on her brightest smile.

His face creased into a grin, his eyes warmly appraising. 'How d'you do,' he said. 'Welcome to Wynsdown.'

Marjorie, watching, wondered how it was that some women, women like Daphne, had that effect on every man they met. Had Felix noticed, and if so did he mind?

At that moment Henry and Caroline Masters walked up and the conversation became general. Felix turned to Billy and asked, 'You riding out with the hunt tomorrow, Mr Shepherd?'

'Certainly am,' said Billy, and for the first time looked at Felix with some warmth, before adding, 'And it's Billy. You called me Billy when I was a kid, no reason to change that now.'

'Felix, then, since we're going to be even closer neighbours than before. Hear you live in Blackdown House now; old Miss Edie's place.'

'It's Charlotte's house,' replied Billy, 'and we're lucky to have it. So, you hunting tomorrow? Dad said you'd taken Archie back and that you might.'

'Yes,' replied Felix. 'Looking forward to it. Will it be the first time you've taken your new horse out?'

'Hunted him last year,' replied Billy, 'but it'll be the first time this year.'

'Beautiful horse,' said Felix and was rewarded with a wide smile.

'Isn't he just?'

Over the table at lunch Marjorie said, 'I'm glad you got the chance to meet Charlotte, Daphne. She's such a nice woman. You know it was Charlotte who raised the alarm when Peter collapsed.'

'No,' answered Daphne, 'I didn't.'

'She went for Dr Masters, but when she found he wasn't there, she went to the vicarage and got them to ring for an ambulance.'

'But why hadn't you rung for an ambulance?' asked Daphne.

'I tried, of course, but our phone was out of order, I couldn't even get through to the exchange. Peter was lying there on the floor; I was panicking and ran out to fetch the doctor. I saw Charlotte in the lane and she went instead. Anyway, living where we do, it's nearly always better to call the doctor first. It takes some time for an ambulance to get here, you know, and at least he can do his best until the ambulance arrives.'

She took a sip of her wine. 'I remember Dr Masters being called out to a wounded airman during the war. Legs shattered, in an awful mess. It was Billy and his father who rescued him from the tree where his parachute had caught. He was taken to Charing Farm as it was nearest, then Henry Masters was called. He did his best, but he reckoned the boy would lose one leg, maybe even both.'

'How dreadful!' cried Daphne. 'Was he all right?'

'We don't really know,' replied Marjorie, 'he was shipped off under guard.'

'Under guard?'

'It was a German pilot, shot down after a raid on Weston.'

'German!' exclaimed Daphne. 'Why didn't they just shoot him?'

'Because he was a wounded boy, hanging in a tree. He wasn't a danger to anyone,' replied Marjorie drily. 'I'd like to think that if Felix had been shot down over enemy territory and wounded, someone would have done the same for him. Peter was the commanding officer of the local Home Guard. He had to deal with the remains of the plane. There were no other survivors. The lad was only very young and in great pain. They got Charlotte to come and interpret for them.'

'Charlotte? Does she speak German, then?'

'Charlotte *is* German,' replied Marjorie. 'By birth, anyway. She came to London as a refugee at the age of thirteen, but she's naturalised British now, of course.'

Felix had listened to the whole story in silence, his face pale. He knew only too well that the German pilot's fate could so easily have been his; so many of his friends had returned wounded and maimed, or not returned at all.

'She promised the boy that she'd try and contact his parents through the Red Cross,' Marjorie went on. 'He told her his name and address before they took him away and Peter did his best to get Charlotte's letter sent. There was no reply, of course, no way of even knowing if it got through. The last we heard of him he was being taken to hospital in Exeter.'

'Where did the plane actually come down?' Felix spoke at last.

'In that worked-out quarry, near Newland,' replied his mother. 'Dad went over there, but it was burnt out. Three men, didn't stand a chance. The lad on the end of the parachute was the lucky one.'

'She didn't sound German this morning.' Daphne's thoughts had been proceeding along entirely different tracks from those of Felix and his mother. 'When I talked to her, she didn't have an accent. Strange to find a German living here, in the village, so soon after the war.'

'She's been living in England for the last ten years, Daphne,' Marjorie reminded her. 'She's married to an Englishman and her children were born here in the village. Charlotte doesn't think of herself as German, and neither should you. The Nazis killed her entire family.'

'Still—' began Daphne.

'Still nothing,' snapped Felix. 'Let's change the subject.'

'Good idea,' agree his mother. 'It's not a subject for Christmas lunch. Will you pour us some more wine, Felix? I brought a couple of bottles over from the cellar at the manor, I didn't think you'd mind.'

Felix picked up the bottle and topped up their glasses. He, too, had brought some wine from the cellar his father had laid down over the years and with the turn of the conversation he felt in need of another glass.

'But, is she…' Daphne seemed about to ignore the change of subject, but as she opened her mouth to speak, she received such a glare from Felix that she closed her mouth again and said nothing, simply picked up her wine glass, took a large mouthful and glowered back at him over the rim.

Ignoring her, and maintaining the change of subject, Felix said, 'I think your Christmas tree looks really lovely, Mother.'

'It does, doesn't it,' smiled Marjorie. 'I got it from Cheddar. There's a man there who's been planting them… you know…

as a crop. It gave me an idea. Is that something you might do? Grow Christmas trees?'

Felix shrugged. 'I don't know. Dad had planted some trees for timber, but that's very long-term. Be worth looking into it, I suppose.'

The meal finished, Marjorie made coffee and they all moved into her drawing room. Still a drawing room, Daphne noted, despite it being half the size of the one at the manor.

'We're to leave all the clearing up till tomorrow,' Marjorie had explained. 'Mrs Darby says she'll come in again first thing to wash up.'

They listened to the King on the radio, but as soon as they'd had tea and some of Mrs Darby's special Christmas cake, Daphne suggested that it was time for them to be going. It was clear that Marjorie had hoped they'd stay a little longer, but she made no demur when Felix finally allowed himself to be dislodged from the armchair by the fire, and after the business of hats and coats, they set out to walk home. As they passed the vicarage, Avril Swanson waved from the window, and irrationally, Felix felt as if he'd let his mother down by returning home before the end of the day. He might well have felt so even more if he'd known that Avril had immediately phoned Eden Lodge to invite Marjorie to join her and David and the Masters for a supper of cold ham and potatoes in their jackets. Marjorie declined, but it warmed her heart that she'd been invited. She was disappointed that Felix and Daphne hadn't stayed a little longer, but she could understand that they wanted to get back to their own fireside and have a little piece of Christmas, just the two of them. It's what she'd have wanted with Peter in similar circumstances.

The manor was cold when they got in and Felix spent the first twenty minutes lighting fires in the drawing room and their bedroom. He drew the curtains against the night, so that when they finally went upstairs, the room would be warm and welcoming. They were still sleeping in what had been the guest room. He'd promised Daphne that they'd move into the main bedroom as soon as they'd sorted out some more furniture, and in the meantime, she had to admit, to herself if not to him, that the green guest room was a good deal warmer.

'I wish you wouldn't side with your mother against me,' she grumbled, when, with another glass of wine, they were indeed sitting at their own fireside.

'What d'you mean?' asked Felix.

'I mean, if your mother and I disagree, you shouldn't take her side against me.'

'Did I?' Felix was surprised. 'What about?'

'About the German girl.'

'What about her?'

'That it's strange to find an enemy alien in our little village community. Your mother didn't seem to think it odd at all, and when I was asking about her, you glared at me and said to change the subject.'

'Oh, that. Well, to be quite honest, I was fed up with that conversation altogether. It was Christmas lunch. I didn't want to be hearing about finding my father dead on the floor, or about German pilots being burned alive in their crashed plane, or about the fact that Charlotte Shepherd is German. Yes, I tried to shut you up, but I was shutting my mother up as well. Let's face it, Daph. You saw our boys coming home with absolutely dreadful injuries; you saw them with wrecked bodies and wrecked lives. All that could have happened to me. I wouldn't wish those injuries on anybody, enemy or not, and I certainly didn't want to discuss it over Christmas lunch.'

It wasn't often Felix spoke to her like that and Daphne said no more. She made them cheese sandwiches for supper and then Felix said, 'I'm just going out to the stable to see that Archie's all right. It's a big day for him tomorrow.'

'What is?' For a moment Daphne looked at him blankly and then light dawned. 'Oh, you mean the hunt. Well, I just hope you don't kill yourself, that's all. I'm going to go on up.'

'I won't be long,' Felix said.

By the time he came back into the house, Daphne was undressed and in bed. She knew he would want to make love and couldn't think of a reason to deny him. It wasn't too bad these days and she'd developed a strategy for dealing with it. She'd always had an eye for an attractive man even though she'd kept them at arm's length and now, when Felix began to touch her in the bedroom, she would imagine it was someone else, someone attractive but non-threatening; someone who she knew and could imagine stroking her breasts and caressing her thighs. Anyone but Felix. Why she could cope with the idea of someone other than he, she didn't know, but provided she visualised another face poised above her, other eyes looking down into hers, she managed not to pull away, and even, on occasion, derived some satisfaction from the encounter. On one occasion in London she'd thought of Toby Squires, she'd always found him attractive. Tonight she found herself thinking of Billy Shepherd, whom she'd only met today. He was tall and his face with its generous mouth and wide blue eyes made him so entirely different from Felix. Fair curly hair springing in disorder, rather than straight dark hair cut close and smoothed against the head; so *not* Felix that it gave her quite a frisson. With her eyes shut she pictured Billy Shepherd, and reached a shuddering climax. Felix, satisfied at last that he'd reached her, his Daphne, came a moment later, and they both fell asleep, their bodies close, but their dreams a mile apart.

Chapter 21

Charlotte and her family were up and about early on Boxing Day morning. Johnny, still filled with Christmas Day excitement, was longing to set out the farm animals his grandparents had given him.

'Breakfast first,' Charlotte said firmly. 'Daddy's got to go and fetch Rustler from the farm.'

'Can I go, too?' Johnny tugged at his father's hand. 'Can I come and fetch Rustler with you, Daddy?'

Billy looked down at his expectant face. 'We'll see,' he said. 'Come on, eat your breakfast.'

After they'd finished Charlotte said, 'I'll bring Edie down here, Johnny, and then you can set up your farm on the kitchen table while I feed her.'

'But I want to go with Daddy,' wailed Johnny. 'Daddy, I want to come with you.'

'I'll take him,' Billy said. 'You'll be busy with Edie. He can come with me.'

Johnny gave a squeal of excitement, but his mother looked at Billy doubtfully. 'Oh, Billy, are you sure? How will you get him home again?'

'We'll ride, won't we, old chap?'

'On Rustler, Daddy?' Johnny gasped in delight. 'Will we ride Rustler?'

'If you're good and do what I tell you. Now, go and put your coat on.'

Johnny rushed off to find his coat but Charlotte said, 'Are you sure, Billy? I don't like him up on that big horse.' Her eyes were full of fear and Billy leant over to kiss her.

'He'll be fine. He'll just sit up in front of me and I promise I'll walk Rustler all the way home. We'll be back within the hour and then it'll be time to go.' Billy touched her cheek. 'Honestly, love, we'll be fine. Are you going to come down to the green to see us off?'

'Yes, of course, Johnny'd never forgive me if we didn't. Anyway, we're going back to the farm with your mother afterwards.'

'Then we'll see you there. Johnny'll be all yours after that.'

Billy and Johnny walked over to Charing Farm, Johnny running ahead one moment, swinging on his father's hand the next. The sun was breaking through Boxing Day's early mist, bathing the countryside in pale winter sunshine.

Billy felt his spirts lift. He loved the seasons, each in its turn, but sunlight on the muted colours of a winter landscape always gave him a sense of peace; the earth asleep under a blanket of sun, resting before the energy of spring burst forth.

It's going to be a perfect day, he thought as they neared the farm. Just a perfect day.

When they arrived in the farmyard they found John already in the stables preparing Hamble for the hunt. Billy went in to join him and Johnny ran into the kitchen to see his grandmother.

'Daddy's going to let me ride home on Rustler,' he told her importantly.

'Is he indeed? Aren't you the lucky one?'

'Will you be coming in to see us set off, Mum?' Billy asked when he came indoors to fetch his son.

'Oh yes, I'll be there. Boxing Day's a special one. And afterwards Charlotte and the children are coming back here for their dinner.' She gave her grandson a hug and said, 'I'll see you on the village green in a little while. Have a nice ride with Daddy.'

Billy led Rustler out of the stable and mounted him in the yard. John picked up the excited Johnny and set him in front of Billy.

'Now, you sit quite still for your dad,' he said, 'and I'll see you at the Magpie. I won't be far behind you.' And he stood back and waved as they rode out of the yard.

Billy held Johnny close against him, his arm tightly round the little boy's body. As he felt Johnny lean back trustingly against him, Billy felt an overwhelming wave of love for him. His son. His Johnny. His to protect, and he felt humbled with the enormity of the responsibility, his arm tightening instinctively.

'Daddy!' Johnny squeaked. 'You're squashing me.'

'Sorry, Johnny. Just making sure you don't fall off!'

'I won't,' Johnny assured him. 'Can we trot now?'

'No,' replied Billy. 'I promised Mummy that Rustler would walk all the way.'

'That's not fair.'

'Better than all three of us walking, don't you think?' laughed Billy.

When they reached the village green Charlotte was already there with Edie propped up in her pram, watching all the activity around her. Billy dismounted and lifted Johnny down. Charlotte was visibly relieved when she saw her son safe and sound with his feet on the ground.

A crowd was gathering outside the Magpie. Several other horsemen had arrived, including Sir Michael Bowden the Master who, with some friends, was just getting out of his

Rolls Royce parked on the far side of the green. Their horses had already been brought over from his home in the village of Upper Marystoke and were standing patiently waiting with his groom. Seeing Felix ride up on Archie, Sir Michael left his friends and walked over to him.

'Morning, Bellinger.'

'Good morning, Master,' Felix replied.

'Sorry to hear about your father,' Sir Michael said as he reached out his hand. 'He'll be sadly missed round here. Came to the funeral, but couldn't stay.'

'Thank you, sir,' replied Felix, returning the handshake. 'As you can imagine it was a great shock to us all.'

'Hear you got married,' went on Sir Michael. 'Congratulations. Wife hunt, does she?'

'No, sir, afraid not. She doesn't ride.'

'Doesn't ride?' Bowden sounded astonished. 'Oh well, you can soon teach her, no doubt. Is that your mother over there? I must go and have a word.'

Felix turned to see his mother walking across the green. She waved to him, but was almost immediately waylaid by Sir Michael. More riders began to gather, farmers from all round the area; a few strangers, horsemen and -women visiting friends for the Christmas holiday. Felix saw Billy mounted on Rustler and edged Archie over to him.

'Looks a good turnout,' he said.

Billy grinned. 'We always get more when the meet's here rather than at Upper Mary. See Sir Michael's here with a crowd.' He indicated three beautifully turned out gentlemen and a lady being served a stirrup cup by Mabel Barrett. He waved to Mabel and she came over to them.

'Billy,' she said as she passed up a small glass of port. 'Mr Bellinger.' Felix received his port and downed it in one.

'Thanks, Mabel,' he said, 'just the thing to set us up on a winter morning.'

'Better still when you get back again on a winter's evening,' Billy laughed. 'Nothing like a hot whisky or brandy to warm the cockles.' He handed Mabel back the glass. 'Cheers, Mabel. We'll be back for another, this evening!'

At that moment Billy's father rode up and joined them. 'Thanks, Mabel,' he said as she handed him a glass. 'Your good health.'

'Good morning, Felix,' he said. 'Perfect day for it.'

Felix greeted him with a handshake and agreed. He looked round at the gathered riders. 'This is something I've really missed while I've been living in London,' he said.

'Daphne coming to see us off?' asked Billy, looking round.

'Doubt it,' Felix said ruefully. 'She doesn't understand hunting. She thinks it's cruel to the fox.'

'Let's hope she doesn't say so here this morning,' Billy said with a grin. 'Don't think it'd go down too well.'

John Shepherd went across to Sir Michael. 'Good morning, Master,' he said.

'John Shepherd,' Sir Michael said. 'Good to see you still hunting. Perhaps you'd care to ride with my guests.'

'I'd be delighted, Master, thank you.'

'Come over, I'll introduce you.' And John, with a wave to Billy and Felix, went across to meet Sir Michael's guests.

As more and more people rode up the general excitement on the village green grew. Many of the villagers came out to watch the spectacle and there were children everywhere, shouting, laughing and jostling, but most of them kept well away from the horses by anxious parents. To his indignation, Charlotte had a firm hold on Johnny's hand.

'I want to go and see Daddy,' he cried.

'You can see Daddy from here,' replied Charlotte firmly. She was surprised to see several children mounted on ponies ride up to join the throng. 'Surely they're too young to hunt!' she exclaimed to Margaret, who had just strolled over to join her.

'No, not really,' Margaret replied. 'Billy's been hunting since he was eight. They don't go over the big jumps, they're expected to keep back and if necessary open gates to go through. There are other non-jumpers too, who use gates and go round obstacles, but they gallop with the best of them when they can.' She looked down at Johnny's angry face and smiled. 'Never mind, Johnny, it won't be long before you can go, too!'

Not if I have anything to do with it, Charlotte thought vehemently. But she said nothing; that was an argument for some future day.

The hounds had been brought over from Upper Marystoke and were now corralled in the backyard of the Magpie, waiting to move off, the restless sounds from the pack indicating that they at least were ready. Matt Trinder, the huntsman, sat on his horse outside the yard gate and Colin French, the whipper-in, shooed inquisitive children out of the yard as they prepared to move out.

The Master looked at his watch and, mounting his horse, held up his hand. The surrounding hubbub gradually dropped to a general muttering as he spoke.

'I just wanted to extend our thanks to our hosts today,' Sir Michael said. 'Mabel and Jack Barrett who've provided us with an excellent stirrup cup and refreshments. Always good to come to Wynsdown and meet at the Magpie.' Then he turned in the saddle and raising his voice called, 'Hounds, please.'

The gathered riders moved apart, allowing him to proceed towards the lane where Matt Trinder drew alongside him and with a blast of his horn allowed the hounds, already giving tongue in excited anticipation, to stream out of the pub yard behind them.

Sir Michael led the field away from the green and out along the lane to a drove that led up onto the hill. Billy turned to wave as he and Felix followed in their wake. Johnny waved back, his arms whirling with excitement, as the last of the horsemen trotted out along the lane to the drove.

'Will they catch a fox?' he demanded of his mother. 'Mummy, will they?'

'I don't know, Johnny. We'll have to hope so, won't we? Or Daddy'll be disappointed.'

'They're hoping to draw covert up by Charing Coppice,' Margaret said, raising a hand to John as she watched them go.

It was as they were riding out that Daphne arrived on the village green. Though the green was still crowded, the last of the horses were disappearing up the lane and there was no sign of Felix. She paused and looked about her. All country locals, she thought dismissively; but then she saw the Rolls parked under the trees and her eyes brightened. Well, at least there's someone of consequence, she thought, and looked around again to see who it might be. It was then that she saw Charlotte, standing with her children, talking to a matronly-looking woman in dungarees and rubber boots. She watched them for a moment before wandering across to join them.

'Hallo.'

Startled, Charlotte turned to find Daphne standing behind her. 'Oh, hallo, Daphne. They've just gone. Did you come to see Felix off?'

'Not really. I just wanted to see what all the fuss is about. Seems very cruel to me, all those dogs chasing after one poor little fox.'

'You wouldn't call him a poor little fox if you'd seen what damage he causes round here.' Margaret turned abruptly to see who had spoken. 'Kill for pleasure, foxes do. Murder a whole run of chickens and leave the bodies strewn about. Vermin, that's what they are.'

Daphne's eyes widened as she took an involuntary step back.

Charlotte thought Margaret had been unnecessarily sharp and did her best to smooth things over. 'Mrs Shepherd,' she said, 'I don't think you've met Daphne Bellinger, Felix's wife, have you?' Adding, 'Daphne's from London,' as if that explained everything. 'Daphne, this is my mother-in-law, Mrs Shepherd.'

'Nice to meet you, I'm sure.' Daphne held out her hand and Margaret took it, but her expression didn't soften. She looked at the woman standing beside her wearing a fitted overcoat and floppy hat, brown leather gloves and a pair of high-heeled leather pumps, and, instinctively, disliked her.

'Of course, you're a town— come from London,' she said. 'I don't expect you've come down in the morning and found your entire flock of hens lying beheaded in your yard, have you?'

'No, of course I haven't,' replied Daphne stiffly.

'Well, when you have, you'll understand why I'd hunt those vermin to extinction. Only good fox is a dead fox!'

'Only good fox is a dead fox,' parroted Johnny happily. 'Dead fox. Dead fox.'

'That's enough, Johnny,' said Charlotte repressively.

The village green was beginning to clear as people went back to their houses. One or two walked out to the drove, following the mounted hunt on foot, and a couple more set off to follow on bikes, but for most of them the excitement of the meet was over.

At that moment Marjorie Bellinger came across to where they were standing. 'Daphne, my dear, come to see what it's all about, have you? Wonderful sight, isn't it? Better still if you see them in full cry. I wondered if you'd like to walk up onto the hill and watch from there?'

'No, I wouldn't,' said Daphne rudely. 'I'm going home.' And with that she turned on her high heels and teetered off along the lane towards the manor.

'Oh dear,' said Margaret guiltily, 'I'm afraid that's my fault, but she called foxes "poor little". I was rather sharp with her.'

Marjorie smiled ruefully. 'Don't worry about it,' she said. 'I'm afraid she's got a lot to learn about the country.'

'We're going back to the farm for our dinner,' Margaret said. 'Would you like to come too? There's plenty.'

Marjorie's eyes brightened. She hadn't been looking forward to going back to her empty house. 'I'd love to,' she said.

Out on the hillside the hounds were now drawing Charing Coppice, but although one hound spoke, nothing came of it. Having drawn a blank there, the hunt moved on, out across the open hillside towards another covert.

'Surprised we had no joy there,' Billy said to Felix as they trotted up the hill. 'I know there's been an earth there.'

'Not much scent,' said Felix. 'Looks as if we're headed towards the old quarry.' He was silent for a minute as they rode, then he said, 'Was it there you found the crashed plane? Mother said you and your father saved an injured pilot.'

'Yes, we did. Hanging in a tree in Charing Coppice. The plane actually crashed and burned out in the quarry, though. It was your father who went there.'

'Don't suppose there's anything to see there, now, is there?'

'No, nothing. The crew are buried in the churchyard, the burned-out plane was removed soon after the war.'

As they rode across the hillside and approached the next covert, a hound spoke again and with a blur of chestnut and a flash of white-tipped brush, a fox broke cover and streaked away across the hillside.

Matt Trinder's horn was at his lips. *Gone away!* As the hound music filled the air, the mounted field poured out over the hill and away.

Felix grinned across at Billy as they kicked their horses to a gallop and flung themselves into the exhilaration of the chase. Neck and neck, they careered over the winter turf, following the pink coats of the field master and the huntsmen ahead of them. As they reached the top of the rise they were confronted by a long dry-stone wall. The two horses rose together, landed together and galloped on. The fox sped across another field before it jinked at right angles towards a stand of trees, diving into a bank of scrub and disappearing. The sweating horses and their riders gathered at the edge of the covert to take a breather; and while Colin French whipped-in the hounds, Matt Trinder walked the ground, looking for another exit. He found one some thirty yards away, emerging beneath a mass of brambles, but given away by the well-worn path to its mouth.

'Damn thing should have been stopped last night,' he muttered, before blowing his horn for the terrierman.

A pair of terriers were brought and they dived through the undergrowth. Colin kept the hounds close and within a few moments the fox was bolted and streaked away across the open hill. *Gone away!* The hounds released, the chase was on again.

Felix moved up the field to ride with John Shepherd, close behind Sir Michael and his friends, the hounds streaming out in front of them. Billy, still aware of Rustler's relative inexperience, stayed back a little, mid-field. All were galloping, riders and horses exhilarated by the speed, following the lead of the field master as he jumped a gate and led them across a patch of open ground and down into a valley. Billy and Rustler cleared the gate with ease, but as the field began to spread out, Billy found himself beginning to gain ground on the field master. At the end of the defile they were streaming back up the hillside. He could see Felix and his father jumping another wall, but as he followed them he was suddenly aware of another rider coming up close beside him; too close. The man careered past, almost out of control, forcing Billy to change direction, to approach the wall at a slightly lower section. The man cleared the wall, somehow managing to stay in the saddle, then continued flat out, up the hill on the other side. Billy checked Rustler a little as they approached the wall, and knew a moment's exhilaration as he felt Rustler lift, clearing the wall easily; a moment's exhilaration, a split second's horror as he saw a heap of fallen stones on the far side. He shortened his reins, trying to turn the big horse in mid-air, but his momentum was too great. Rustler's front feet landed on the fallen stone and with a terrified grunt he somersaulted into the ground, flinging Billy high and wide, cartwheeling him, arms flailing, onto the debris of the collapsed wall.

Hooves thundered past as the rest of the field jumped the original part of the wall in safety and continued on up the hill. Some of them saw a man down, but riders often fell and they left him to get to his feet again and galloped on. Only the non-jumpers, who were going to use the gate further down, paused before the wall and opening the gate, trotted through, ready to canter on up the hill. One of them saw the fallen horse and gave a shout. As they reached the place where Rustler lay on the ground, he tried to regain his feet but staggered as his forelegs gave way beneath him. For a moment they stared in horror at the horse before they saw his rider, spread-eagled and unmoving on the ground.

Chapter 22

The hounds reached the trees. Felix and John grinned at each other as they rested their horses outside the copse.

'Good run,' said John.

'Fantastic,' Felix agreed. He turned in the saddle and looked out across the country, spread patchworked below them, bathed in winter sun, and he knew a moment of deep satisfaction. He'd made the right decision. This was where he belonged. He turned to say as much to John, but found him looking about him, searching the field for the sight of his son.

'Can you see Billy?' he said, a note of anxiety in his voice.

'Said he was going to hold back a bit,' Felix replied, 'though I doubt he needed to, Rustler seemed settled and was going well.'

'Can't see him,' said John.

'Someone coming up the hill now,' Felix said, 'not Billy though.'

A rider was galloping up the hill and John knew a sudden stab of fear. He didn't recognise the man, but he could see the panic on his face as he started shouting.

'Man down! Horse down!' bellowed the man. He reined in his horse and approached the Master, who'd turned abruptly at the sound of shouting. 'Man down!' panted the man. 'Man and horse. It's bad!'

'Who?' demanded Sir Michael.

'Don't know him!' cried the man. 'Big chestnut horse. Broken front legs. Needs to be shot.'

'And the man?'

'Don't know, sir. But he ain't moving.'

'It's Billy!' cried John, and wheeling Hamble about, headed off down the hill.

Felix paused only to say, 'Sounds like Billy Shepherd, sir,' to Sir Michael, before he, too, set off back down the hill.

They reached the wall and found another rider, dismounted, standing over the still form of Billy.

John leaped from Hamble's back and knelt down beside his son. Billy was lying face down on the ground, his head and upper body resting on the pile of stones that had once been part of the wall, one of his arms bent back at an impossible angle.

Taking his other hand, John felt for a pulse. He found one, but it was faint.

'Billy,' he said, looking down at Billy's bruised and lacerated face. 'Billy, son, can you hear me?'

Billy gave no response, simply lay, as unmoving as he'd been found.

'There's a pulse,' said John, looking up at Felix. 'He's still alive.'

'Andy Lawrence has ridden over to Dunns' farm, yonder, to call for help,' said the man, whom John now recognised as Sam Burns, a butcher from Cheddar. 'And Barry Linton, who was here with his children, he's taken them back home. It's Horace what rode up to warn the Master and I...' he glanced down at the inert Billy and shivered, 'I waited with him.'

'We need to get him to the farm,' John said. 'It's the nearest place.'

'May not be a good idea to move him,' Felix ventured as

he bent down and picked up Billy's riding hat which lay some feet away. 'He's obviously out cold, so he's had a knock on the head. There may be other injuries we don't know about.'

'We can't leave him here,' John said. 'It's too cold to leave him here.' He looked round about him and saw a pile of sheep hurdles, stacked by the gate. 'We can carry him on one of those,' he said.

Felix and Sam fetched one of the hurdles and laid it on the ground. John took off his jacket and Felix did the same. They laid them on the hurdle.

'How best to lift him?' asked Sam. 'He may have broken ribs, landing on them stones.'

'Best to move him while he's still out,' John said. 'Won't feel the pain.'

At that moment Andy Lawrence came galloping back. 'Rang 999,' he shouted. 'Ambulance on its way. Coming to the farm. Mrs Dunn phoned Doc Masters, too, and he's coming over.'

He looked at Rustler, now lying on his side, his eyes blank with pain. 'I'll deal with him, poor bugger,' he added. 'Mrs Dunn loaned me this.' He took a shotgun from his saddle bag and turning his attention to Rustler said softly, 'All right, old boy. All right. All over now…' and pulled the trigger.

The other horses shied at the sound and once they'd been quietened again, Sam said, 'Right, I'll deal with these.' He led the horses down to the gate and hitched them to its top rail. 'I'll come back and fetch they when we got Billy to the farm,' he said.

At the sound of the single shot, Billy had twitched, but didn't regain consciousness. Together they managed to move him onto the makeshift stretcher, covering him with Sam's and Andy's jackets. Carefully, the four men took a corner each and lifting the stretcher, set off across the fields towards the farmhouse half a mile away. Twice they had to put him down; twice they picked up the hurdle and moved on. Somewhere at the back of his brain, John Shepherd knew he'd done this before, carried a man on a sheep hurdle, but that time the burden was another man; that time Billy'd been there, young and strong, taking his share of the load.

As they reached the farmhouse and carried Billy indoors, Dr Henry Masters drove into the farmyard. He followed them inside to the front room where Billy was set down, still on the hurdle, on the floor.

'He's still unconscious, Henry,' John said. 'He hasn't moved. How bad is it?'

'Let me have a look,' replied Dr Masters calmly. 'Why don't you ask Mrs Dunn to make us all some tea while I examine him, eh?' Gently he shooed them from the room and then turned his attention back to Billy.

He carried out some routine checks, taking his pulse and blood pressure. He could see that Billy's face was bruised, one of his cheeks badly grazed, mud and blood mingling. Superficial injuries to his face which would heal in time. More worrying was the blood that oozed from his ears. Dr Masters stared down at the battered and bruised body and there was a chill in his heart. He'd brought this young man into the world and he was, he knew now, in grave danger of being with him when he left it again.

With a gentle finger he lifted each of Billy's eyelids and, looking for a reflex to the light, shone a torch into his eyes. One pupil responded, slowly, but the other was fixed and dilated. He pressed the nerve above the eye and was rewarded with a twitch. Pinching the earlobe produced the same response, giving him some indication of the level of Billy's unconsciousness; deep, but perhaps not perilously so. He made no effort to remove any of Billy's clothes. He realised that his arm was broken and assumed that he probably had broken ribs as well, but those could wait until he reached hospital. There were other, more important, injuries to worry about.

He sat down on a chair and looked at the boy lying at his feet. Not a boy any more, but a young father with a wife and children to look after. Henry Masters thought of Charlotte and her two youngsters, waiting in Wynsdown for Billy to come home and, hardened as he was to life and death, he found unexpected tears in his eyes. That girl's already had enough to bear, he thought.

The door opened and John Shepherd came back in. He was carrying a mug of tea which he passed over to the doctor.

'How is he?' he whispered. 'Is he going to be all right?'

'He's badly injured, John,' replied Dr Masters. 'We need to get him to hospital as fast as we can. The ambulance can take him to the Bristol Royal Infirmary. They have all the latest equipment there.'

'How bad?'

'I think he has a fractured skull. They'll know for sure when they X-ray him. He has other injuries too, but they, in themselves, probably aren't life-threatening.'

'But his fractured skull...?' John left the sentence hanging.

'Could be,' said Dr Masters.

John sank into a chair and put his head between his hands. He felt numb. His throat ached with the effort of fighting tears, of not breaking down, of remaining in control of himself. Henry Masters rested a hand on his shoulder for a moment. 'When the ambulance arrives,' he said, 'I think you should go with Billy. I know he's unconscious but even so, if you talk to him quietly as you go, who knows, at some level he may hear, know you're there with him.'

'I can't do that,' murmured John. 'I have to go back and tell Charlotte what's happened. I have to break the news to her… and to Margaret.'

'I can do that, John,' Henry said firmly. 'You should go with Billy. I'll break the news and then drive Charlotte to the hospital.'

'I'll need to get back to Margaret,' John said.

'I know,' Henry nodded, 'and I'll drive you back again when I've brought Charlotte in.' He tried to sound reassuring. 'They have the best equipment at the BRI, John. Once they've X-rayed they'll know the extent of the damage and can decide what treatment is best.'

Within ten minutes they heard the ambulance bell in the distance and moments later it turned into the farmyard, pulling up beside Dr Masters's car. Two men jumped out and were greeted by Henry Masters, who introduced himself as the local doctor.

'What have we got, then?' one of them asked.

'Man thrown from his horse onto a heap of stone-walling,' replied Dr Masters. 'General injuries from such a fall, but head injury as well. Deeply unconscious and bleeding from the ears, which suggests to me a basal fracture of the skull. Hope I'm wrong, but he needs to get to the BRI immediately. His father's here and will travel with him in the ambulance. I'm going to fetch the wife and bring her into Bristol.'

'Where is he now?' asked the ambulance driver.

'Indoors. They brought him in from the field on a makeshift stretcher. Despite the danger of moving him and making things worse they decided it was far too cold to leave him waiting there.'

'Get the stretcher, Ed,' said the driver, 'and bring it indoors, sharpish.'

'Right-ho, Mac,' called Ed and disappeared inside the ambulance. Moments later the two men were in the front room, looking down at their patient. Gently they transferred him from the hurdle to the stretcher and carried him carefully out to the ambulance, strapping him securely to the stretcher and the stretcher to its rest. Ed placed small bags of sand either side of Billy's head in an effort to keep it immobile for the journey to Bristol.

John still hesitated, feeling it should be he who broke the news of the accident to Billy's family. As he stood uncertainly in the yard, Felix came out and said, 'Sam's gone to fetch the horses, John. I'll take Hamble back with me. He can stay in our stables overnight and you can come and fetch him when you're ready. All right?'

There came a call from Mac, the driver, already in his seat. 'If you're coming with us, Mr Shepherd, better get in. We need to get going.'

Henry gave John a little push. 'Go with Billy, John. I'll tell them… and I'll bring Charlotte.'

Still somewhat in a daze, John clambered in through the back door of the ambulance; Ed shut it behind him and moments later they were heading out into the lane and taking the road to Bristol.

Dr Masters stared after them for a moment and then turned and went back into the farmhouse. The three men and Mrs Dunn were gathered in the kitchen.

'Did anyone see what actually happened?' he asked as he joined them. 'Did anyone see the actual accident?'

'Not the fall, but we think we know what happened,' said Sam. 'We were at the back with the Linton children, but there was a bloke who came charging past us and right through everyone in front of him, as well. Completely out of control, he was. Barry had to haul the kids out of his way. Flung hisself at the wall, he did. Lucky not to kill hisself!'

'Probably pissed,' put in Andy. 'Saw him at the meet. He was knocking back Mabel's stirrup cup outside the Magpie and I saw him swigging from a hip flask when we was waiting for the hounds to speak, up at Charing Coppice.'

'But who was he?' asked Felix. 'Did you recognise him?'

'Not really, but reckon I'd know him again. Fat barrel of a man in a tweed jacket and a flat cap.'

'Not a hunting cap?' suggested the doctor.

'No,' said Sam. 'You're supposed to wear 'em, but lots of folk don't.'

'On a skewbald, he were, hanging on for dear life,' said Andy. 'Shouldn't be difficult to find.'

'You think he caused the accident?' asked the doctor.

'Can't say, not for certain,' admitted Sam, 'didn't see Billy actually fall. But maybe someone else saw what happened, one of them he burst through.'

'I'll speak to the Master when we get back,' Felix said. 'You'll have to tell your story to him and we'll see where we go from there.' He turned to Sam. 'Thanks for fetching the horses back, Sam. I'll take John's with me.'

Dr Masters thanked Mrs Dunn for the loan of her house. 'It was very good of you to let them bring him here,' he said.

'Oh, Doctor, that weren't no problem. Where else could they have taken the poor boy? Just sorry my Ernie weren't here to lend a hand. Gone down to Bridgwater to look at a bull.'

Felix thanked her too, and then went out into the yard where Archie was standing patiently with Hamble, hitched to a fence. Felix mounted Archie and taking hold of Hamble's reins set off across the fields, to hack back to Wynsdown. He heard Dr Masters's car pass by on the road and shuddered.

Don't envy him the job breaking the news to Charlotte, or to Billy's mother, he thought. The sun had gone now and the air was dank and chilly. He quickened his pace, trotting along the bridle path that led across the hills to the slopes above Wynsdown. Felix had retrieved his jacket from where Billy had been lying on it. It was muddy and bloody and he didn't put it back on, simply slung it over his saddle and shivered his way home.

When he reached the village he could hear the noise and laughter coming from the Magpie and guessed that several members of the hunt had ended up there, probably completely unaware of the severity of Billy's fall. Sir Michael's car had gone. Clearly he hadn't realised the seriousness of the situation either and had gone home. Felix walked the horses quietly past and went straight back to the manor. There was a light on in the hall, but otherwise the house seemed to be in complete darkness. The afternoon had slipped from dusk into darkness, and a rising wind had brought the temperature right down.

Felix dismounted in the stable yard and led the two horses into the warmth of their stable, where he rubbed them down, fed them and refreshed their water. Archie whinnied as Felix gently stroked his neck.

'You were going well, today, old boy,' Felix murmured. 'What a dreadful end to the day.' He remembered Billy's Rustler still lying out in the field. I'll get him moved in the morning, he thought. No one to do anything about him tonight.

With a sigh he left the stable and crossing the yard went in through the back door.

'Daphne,' he called. 'Daph, are you there?'

There was no reply and he wandered through into the

drawing room where the fire was laid, ready for a match, in the cold fireplace. Felix struck the match and watched to make sure the flames caught the prepared kindling before going into the dining room and pouring himself a large whisky. He picked up the glass and bottle and returned to the drawing-room fire. He had no idea where Daphne could be, but for the moment he was pleased to have the house and the whisky bottle to himself.

As soon as Dr Masters reached the village he went home to find his wife. Caroline was sitting by the fire listening to the radio when he came in, but one look at his grey, drained face made her leap to her feet.

'Henry!' she cried. 'Dearest, whatever has happened? Who was thrown? Is it bad?'

'About as bad as it could be,' Henry replied wearily. 'It's Billy Shepherd. He's critically injured. If my diagnosis is right he's a basal fracture of the skull.'

'What does that mean?' Caroline asked.

'It means that he's broken his skull at its very base. It will have crushed down on to his spinal cord.'

Caroline stared at him in horror. 'You mean he may be paralysed?'

'If he survives he'll be paralysed from the neck down.'

'If he survives!' she echoed. 'Oh my God! Poor Billy! Poor Charlotte! She doesn't deserve any more sadness.'

'I've sent John Shepherd in the ambulance with him,' Henry told her. 'I said I'd go and tell Charlotte. I thought perhaps you might come with me, offer her whatever comfort you can. I'm going to take her into Bristol to the hospital as soon as I can.'

'Who'll have the children?' wondered Caroline.

'Margaret, I assume.'

'But she'll want to go with you. Does she know yet?'

'No, I told John I'd break it to her, too.'

Caroline got to her feet. 'Come on then,' she said. 'We'd better get it over with.'

They got into the car and drove the few hundred yards to Blackdown House, only to find it in darkness.

'They must be out somewhere,' Caroline said when they'd knocked and rung just to be sure there was no one in. 'Probably over at Charing Farm. We'd better go there.'

They got back into the car and drove out of the village, taking the road that led to the farm. It was almost dark when they got there, and the light from their headlamps sweeping into the yard brought Margaret to the back door to see who it was.

'Dr Masters,' she greeted him with a smile, 'and Mrs Masters! This is a surprise. Come your ways in.'

Dr Masters placed a hand on her arm, stopping her at the back porch. 'Is Charlotte here?' he asked.

Margaret's smile faded and she said, 'Yes, she and the children. What's happened, doctor? Is it John?'

'It's Billy,' replied the doctor. 'I'm afraid there's been an accident.'

The colour drained from Margaret's face and she sank down onto the bench beside the back door. 'How bad?' she whispered.

'Bad enough,' said the doctor. 'He's on his way to the BRI in an ambulance. John's gone with him. I said I'd come and tell you and Charlotte; take Charlotte straight there.'

Margaret gripped the edge of the bench for a moment and then drawing a deep breath got to her feet and said, 'We'd better go and tell her, but not in front of Johnny. Take her out of the room.'

They went into the kitchen and Margaret said, 'Look who's come to see us!'

Charlotte and Johnny were sitting at the kitchen table with a snakes and ladders board out in front of them and both looked up with pleasure as they saw who had arrived.

'Auntie Caro!' cried Johnny in delight. 'We've been playing snakes and ladders and Mummy slid all the way down a snake and I winned!' Caroline seized the opportunity and said, 'Can I play?'

Johnny nodded vigorously and said, 'But I shall win.'

Charlotte smiled at her friend. 'Good luck,' she said. 'He always seems to win!'

Caroline sat down at the table, and as Johnny put the counters back to the beginning Margaret put a hand on Charlotte's shoulder.

'Dr Masters wants a word. Shall we go into the sitting room?'

Charlotte looked up in surprise, suddenly aware of the rigid pallor of her mother-in-law's face.

'What's happened?' she said, her eyes wide with anxiety. Margaret took her hand and led her from the room, followed by Henry Masters.

It seemed to Charlotte, when she looked back later, that her life had been fractured at that moment; life where she and her family sat in a warm kitchen, playing snakes and ladders, snapped short and a dark, unknowable future loomed in front of her.

Dr Masters made her sit down and then, briefly, told her what had happened. She stared up at him, her eyes enormous in her ghostly pale face.

'Is he dead?' she asked.

'No,' replied the doctor. 'He's been taken to the Bristol Royal Infirmary. His father's with him and I've come to take you there.'

'Will he die?'

'I don't know, Charlotte,' Dr Masters replied gently. 'All I can tell you is that he's badly hurt, but that he's in the best place possible.'

'I must go…' Charlotte got to her feet and headed for the door, before turning back, 'but I can't. I can't leave the children.'

'Don't worry about them,' said Margaret softly. 'I'll look after them. They can stay here till you get back.' She gave her a gentle push. 'Go. Go with Dr Masters. Billy needs you.'

'Caroline will stay here with you if you'd like her to,' the doctor suggested to Margaret. 'When I've taken Charlotte to the hospital, I'll bring John home with me.'

Charlotte walked back into the kitchen, a smile fixed to her lips. 'I'm just going out with Dr Masters,' she told Johnny. 'Auntie Caro and Gr'ma will be here with you.'

'I'm winning,' cried Johnny, shaking the dice vigorously, unaware of the change in his mother. 'Six!'

Charlotte held herself together all the way to Bristol. She was determined not to cry. If she once started she might never stop and she knew she had to be brave for Billy. He wouldn't want to see her with a tear-streaked face. If he were asleep when she got to the hospital she would simply sit by his bed and be ready with a smile when he woke. She didn't ask any questions, she simply sat beside Henry Masters in the car, staring out into the darkness. Henry, recognising her need to try and assimilate what she'd just heard, drove in silence. On this cold Boxing Day evening there was almost no traffic on the roads until they reached the outskirts of the city and they were nearing the hospital before Charlotte suddenly asked, 'Henry, where's Rustler? What's happened to him?'

'I'm afraid he broke his legs,' answered Henry. 'They put him out of his misery.'

When they reached the hospital they went straight to Casualty, where they found John, sitting, waiting. When they walked in he got to his feet and enfolded Charlotte in his arms. For a long moment he held her and then, keeping hold of her hand, sat back down and she sat down beside him. Dr Masters raised an interrogatory eyebrow.

'They've taken him for X-rays,' John said. 'The doctor said they'd know more when they'd seen those.'

'No change in the ambulance?'

John shook his head. 'I did what you said, Henry, and talked to him all the way.'

'That was good,' said Henry. 'Now it's just a question of waiting to see what they've found. I don't suppose it'll be long.'

'You've told Margaret, I suppose.'

'Yes, they were all at the farm. She and Caroline are looking after the children. When you're ready to go, I'll drive you home.'

'They put him in that end cubicle when we got here,' John said. 'It's full of the latest stuff. The nurse told me he'd be brought back there when they'd finished. Think I'll wait until we hear something.'

They sat in silence, waiting for Billy's return. A nurse came and spoke to them and told Charlotte that she'd be able to sit with Billy once he was comfortable.

'Dr Smart'll come and talk to you as soon as he knows anything. He told me your husband wouldn't be going up to the ward straight away. We'll have to keep a very close eye on him for a while and that's easier down here. Would you like a drink of tea? I could make some for you in the ward kitchen.'

Charlotte shook her head, the thought of swallowing anything seemed impossible, and the two men declined as well.

It seemed an age before the doors swung open and two porters wheeled Billy in on a trolley. He was taken into the end cubicle where the nurse joined them. Not long after, the doors opened again and a doctor came in. He walked across to where the three of them were sitting.

John got to his feet. 'Doctor, this is my daughter-in-law, Billy's wife.'

'Dr Smart,' said the doctor, extending a hand to Charlotte. 'Perhaps you'd like to come into the office so we can have a chat.'

Charlotte stood up and followed him in to a glassed-off office at the end of the ward. At the door she said, 'Come too, Gramp, and you, Henry.'

'We've had a look at Billy's X-rays,' said Dr Smart when they were all inside. 'He's got a couple of broken ribs and his arm is broken in two places. Those things will heal. What concerns us is the injury to his head. He's fractured his skull, low down at its base. That has crushed the spinal cord, and the fracture has spread outward and upward. I have to tell you that I'm afraid there is little or nothing we can do for this.'

Charlotte's hand went to her mouth, stifling a cry of anguish. Dr Smart looked at her with compassion, knowing what his words were telling her.

'Is he going to die?' She asked the question John dared not ask and to which Henry already knew the answer.

'I can't say, for sure,' replied Dr Smart. 'All I can tell you is that he's deeply unconscious. We shall monitor that to see if there's any change, but in my opinion, I think he's unlikely to recover consciousness, and if he does, he will be quadriplegic; that is, paralysed from the neck down.'

Charlotte stared at him. She had been prepared for Billy to have a long and painful recovery from his injuries, perhaps to have difficulty with walking, but she had not really faced up to the reality of just how badly he was damaged.

'I'm sorry,' Dr Smart said. 'I can't tell you more because I don't know. We shall do our best for him.'

'Can I see him now?' Charlotte asked, her voice breaking on a sob.

'Of course,' replied the doctor. 'Come with me.' He led the way to the cubicle where Billy lay and stood aside to let her in.

Charlotte stood in the doorway and looked at her Billy, dressed in a hospital gown, lying motionless on the bed. His eyes were closed and his face was the colour of alabaster, blotched with purple bruises, and there was a gauze dressing across one cheek. One of his arms was in plaster, and a drip line went into the other. His head rested on a pillow, supported by small pillows on either side.

The tears she had fought for so long welled in her eyes and flooded silently down her cheeks. After a long moment she stepped forwards and took a seat at the side of the bed. She took his uninjured hand in hers and raised it to her wet cheek. His skin was warm against her own; somehow she'd expected it to be cold. She heard John's voice outside the cubicle. He'd said he was going home to Margaret when they'd spoken to the doctor. She gently replaced Billy's hand on the bed and having dried her eyes and cheeks, she went back through the curtains.

'Come in and see him,' she said softly. John nodded and edged past her to the bedside.

She could hear him murmuring to Billy, though not the words he said, and she hoped that somewhere, deep inside, Billy could hear his father's voice and knew he was there.

'Are you going to take John home now?' she asked Henry. 'I'm not coming. I'm going to stay here, with Billy.'

'Of course you are,' replied Henry. 'I'll take John back and then I'll bring them both here in the morning. Don't worry about the children. Caroline'll take care of them while Margaret's with Billy.' He took her hand and gave it a gentle squeeze. 'Be brave, Charlotte, brave as you've always been.'

Charlotte nodded wordlessly and as John emerged from the cubicle, she went back in and took her place at the side of the bed.

'Billy,' she whispered. 'I'm here. Don't leave me. Whatever we have to face, we can face together. I need you, Billy. The children need you. How will Johnny learn to ride properly without you? Edie needs her daddy, Billy. Don't leave us, my darling. Stay with us and watch your children grow.'

She continued to hold his hand, smoothing his skin with her fingers. Can he feel this? she wondered. Remembering Henry had told John to keep talking to him, Charlotte continued to talk to Billy, lying so unresponsive on the bed.

'We had a lovely afternoon,' she told him. 'We all had dinner at the farm and Marjorie Bellinger came too. Your mother found your old snakes and ladders board; Johnny soon got the hang of that and we played it most of the afternoon. He'll want to play with you when you get home again.'

The curtain was pulled aside and the doctor came in. 'Don't move,' he said. 'I just need to check his reflexes.' Charlotte watched as he lifted Billy's lids and shone light into his eyes; saw him pinch his ears. Billy didn't move.

Beyond the curtains came the sounds of people coming and going as the rest of Casualty went on round her, other people with problems of their own, but in the cubicle all she could hear was Billy's rapid, shallow breathing.

When the doctor had disappeared again, Charlotte continued to talk. She reminded Billy of their life together; how they'd first kissed at the summer dance in the village back in 1942; how they'd climbed through the wreckage of a bombed house to rescue a woman and her baby; how Billy had nearly been killed as the building collapsed round him. 'You survived that, Billy,' she told him firmly. 'You can survive this. Come on, my darling, come back to me.'

She spoke of their wedding day; of the day Johnny was born and Billy'd first held his son in his arms, afraid he might break! 'Edie's going to be beautiful when she grows up,' she told him. 'You'll be so proud at her wedding.'

The doctor came in twice more, each time smiling encouragingly at Charlotte. 'You should think of going home and getting some sleep,' he said the third time.

Charlotte shook her head. 'No, I'm not tired. I'll just sit here with Billy.' But she was tired and without meaning to she began to doze, jerking herself awake each time she found her head drooping towards the bed. Forcing herself to stay awake, she continued to hold his hand cradled in hers. Outside, the sounds died away, and the nurse they had seen before put her head through the curtains.

'Are you all right?' she whispered, as if she might wake Billy up.

'Yes, thank you,' Charlotte replied, 'we're fine, aren't we, Billy?'

'That's good,' said the nurse and went away again.

Silence slipped round them, Billy and Charlotte. Still stroking his hand, Charlotte suddenly recognised it for what it was. The silence of death. Billy was no longer breathing. Though he hadn't been moving, a new, deep stillness settled over them and she knew that her Billy had left her. She and her children were on their own. She laid her head down on the bed beside him and wept.

Dr Smart found her, half an hour later, with Billy's hand still in hers, tear-streaked but now dry-eyed. She looked up as he came in and he knew for certain that there was nothing more he could have done. Billy's death warrant had been signed from the time he'd landed, head first on a heap of age-old stone that had once been a wall.

Chapter 24

It was much later that Felix awoke, stiff from dozing in his chair, and began to wonder where Daphne was. The fire was dying in the grate, the gentle plop of a last coal falling into the embers rousing him, and it was a moment before he remembered the dreadful happenings of the afternoon, bringing him back to the present with a jolt. The much depleted whisky bottle standing on the table and the empty glass at his hand bore witness to how he had tried to blot out the events of the day; time had passed, though he didn't know how much, and still the house was silent. Where was Daphne? Where could she have gone? Apart from his mother, she knew no one in the village. Could she have gone to the Magpie? It was unlikely that she'd enter a pub on her own, especially in a place where she had no friends or acquaintances. Perhaps she'd come home while he'd been dozing. Felix struggled to his feet, the tilting of the room reminding him how full the whisky bottle had been when he'd carried it through to his chair. He made his way unsteadily to the hall and switching on the landing light, called Daphne's name. There was no reply. Slowly, he began to negotiate the stairs, holding fast to the banister as the hall threatened to spin out of control. When he reached their bedroom he paused in the doorway. He could hear breathing, punctuated by occasional snorts and snores, emanating from the darkness. He pushed the door wider, allowing the light from the landing to flow in. What it revealed brought him up short. Daphne was lying, fully clothed, flat on her back across the bed, her eyes shut, her mouth hanging open, breath rasping from the back of her throat. On the bedside table stood empty bottles: one gin and several tonic. His first instinct was to cross the room and shake her awake, but as her snores and snorts continued, he changed his mind. Daphne had, for some reason, drunk herself into a stupor and he doubted he could drag her from its depths.

He went back onto the landing and into his own room. He had to admit he was drunk, too, and any confrontation now would almost certainly escalate into a blazing row. Better to wait until morning when they'd both slept it off. Before he collapsed onto his bed, he went to the bathroom where he drank off two tumblers of water. Standing at the basin he looked into the mirror. Peering back at him was a haggard face, pale, with red-rimmed eyes and a darkening five o'clock shadow, though as he screwed up his eyes to focus on his watch, he was amazed to find it was almost eleven o'clock. He thought he'd got home sometime around six. Where had the intervening hours gone? He didn't know and just now, he didn't care. He went back into his room and stripping off his soiled clothes, he followed Daphne's example, falling onto the bed and into a heavy, troubled sleep.

He awoke several hours later to the sound of Daphne next door, throwing up into the lavatory. Felix felt he should go to her, hold her head if nothing else, but the room still revolved disconcertingly when he tried to sit up and so he closed his eyes against its swirl and stayed where he was.

When they finally made it downstairs that morning, both

of them were still struggling with hangovers. Daphne sat at the kitchen table, her head in her hands. Felix brewed a pot of strong coffee and poured them each a cup.

'How are you feeling?' he asked.

'Pretty much as you look,' she replied tartly. 'What time did you eventually get in? I thought you'd be home long before it got dark. In the Magpie, I suppose, celebrating the murder of a fox!'

'No,' Felix said and drank some coffee to steady him. 'No, there was an accident, I had to stay and help.'

'Oh,' Daphne said dully. 'Somebody fell off, did they? What a shame!'

'Billy Shepherd,' answered Felix. 'He's been rushed to hospital in Bristol.'

'Billy Shepherd?' Daphne screwed up her eyes in concentration.

'You met him outside church on Christmas Day.'

Daphne's eyes widened. 'The fair-haired man with the German wife?'

'Yes, him.'

'Yes, I remember. Will he be all right?'

'I don't know, Daphne. Doc Masters said it was bad; he could end up paralysed.'

'But that's awful!' cried Daphne. She picked up her coffee cup, drained it and poured herself more.

'So, what happened to you?' Felix asked, not wanting to speculate further on Billy's injuries. 'You seem to have had a party all by yourself.'

'And why not?' snapped Daphne. 'You were out hunting and short of spending the rest of the day with your mother, there was no one else to party with.'

'But a whole bottle of gin?' Felix was incredulous.

'It wasn't a whole bottle,' Daphne replied defensively. 'It wasn't full when I started.'

'As near as dammit!' retorted Felix.

Daphne glared at him. Her curse had been late and she'd had some idea of encouraging its arrival with large quantities of gin. It seemed to have worked, too, but that wasn't an explanation she could offer him.

'I got bored,' was all she said. 'Bored! Bored! Bored!'

The row was on the horizon, the thunderclouds of recrimination building and the storm might have broken but for an insistent ringing on the doorbell.

Felix got to his feet to answer it and glancing out of the window saw a Rolls parked in the drive.

'I think it's Sir Michael,' he said.

Daphne, now dressed only in a bathrobe, made a dash for the stairs, scooting up them at great speed as Felix struggled with the bolts that secured the front door. On opening it he found it was, indeed, Sir Michael standing on the doorstep.

'Ah, morning, Bellinger,' he said, and without waiting for an invitation, he stepped into the hall.

'Sir Michael.' Felix was very much aware of still being in his dressing gown, with tousled hair and an unshaven chin. 'Come in.'

He led Sir Michel into the drawing room, pulling back the curtains to allow grey daylight to seep in.

'Come to ask you what happened yesterday,' Sir Michael said without preamble. 'John Shepherd's been on the phone. I hear young Billy's been taken to hospital and his horse had to be shot. Bad business all round. Can you throw any light on it? Couldn't ask John, he was just leaving for the hospital.'

The two men sat down on either side of the cold fireplace

and Felix put the Master in possession of the details as he knew them.

'And you think this man on the skewbald caused the accident? Young Shepherd was hunting a novice horse, you know.'

'He'd hunted him before, several times at the end of last season,' Felix said. 'And he was settled and going well yesterday.'

'Still, he can't put the blame on someone else for his own fall.' It was clear to Felix that Sir Michael intended to distance the hunt and anyone who'd been riding with it from any involvement with the accident. 'How is the boy?' continued Sir Michael. 'D'you know?'

'I haven't heard this morning,' answered Felix, trying to control his anger at the Master's attitude. 'I shall ring the doctor in a while.'

'The doctor? Why the doctor?' Sir Michael sounded surprised. 'Surely the people to ask are his parents when they get back from the hospital... or his wife.'

'I really don't think you understand the severity of Billy Shepherd's injuries,' Felix said tightly. 'To be quite honest with you, Sir Michael, I don't think there'll be any news yet, and if there is, I doubt it's going to be good.'

Before Sir Michael could reply, the drawing-room door opened and Daphne appeared. In the fifteen minutes since Sir Michael had arrived she had managed to dress, put on her make-up and brush her hair into flowing waves about her face. She paused, framed in the doorway, then her hand flew to her mouth as she said, 'Felix, darling, I didn't realise we had a guest. I heard the doorbell, but I thought it was the paper boy.'

The hell you did! thought Felix as she stepped forward and extended her hand to Sir Michael.

'How d'you do? I don't think we've met. I'm Daphne Bellinger.'

Sir Michael was on his feet in an instant, returning her smile and introducing himself. Felix, amazed at Daphne's unexpected appearance and her transformation, all signs of bleary-eyed hangover masked with skilful make-up, hair shining and smooth, suddenly realised that he should have performed the introductions and said lamely, 'I don't think you've met my wife, have you, Sir Michael?'

'No, indeed,' beamed Sir Michael, falling prey to Daphne's wide blue eyes and shy, tentative air. 'I hear we're going to have to teach you to ride, my dear,' he said, still holding her hand in his own.

'Oh, Sir Michael, I'm not sure—'

'Sir Michael came to find out what happened to Billy,' Felix interrupted, and as if suddenly remembering himself, Sir Michael let go of Daphne's hand.

'Oh, such a dreadful thing!' wailed Daphne. 'I do hope the poor man will soon be better.'

'Oh, you mustn't worry too much, my dear,' began Sir Michael. 'Lots of us who hunt take a tumble from time to—'

He was interrupted by the shrill of the telephone. Daphne sank gracefully into an armchair, and without looking at Felix, said, 'Answer that, darling, will you? I'm sure it'll be for you.'

Felix strode into the hall and snatched up the receiver.

'Felix Bellinger.'

'Felix? It's Henry Masters.'

Felix caught his breath. 'Any news?' he managed to ask.

'Yes, I'm afraid there is. Billy died at five o'clock this morning.'

'What?' Felix's voice was a croak.

'Charlotte was with him.'

'But the hospital? The doctors there…'

'Could do nothing for him. It was as I feared, he'd a broken skull. Felix, if he hadn't died, he'd have been totally paralysed from the neck down. I hate to say this and I certainly wouldn't say it to Charlotte or any of the family, but for Billy it was best. The Billy we all knew and loved wouldn't have wanted to spend the rest of his life unable to move, entirely dependent on someone else for the slightest thing.'

Felix couldn't speak, he simply nodded into the telephone. Knowing he was still there, Henry Masters went on, 'I told John I'd let you know. There'll be an inquest, of course, but I'm sure it'll bring in accidental death or death by misadventure.'

'Thank you for letting me know,' Felix managed. 'Tell them I'll deal with Rustler, get him picked up by the meat wagon.'

'That would be kind,' said Henry. 'I'll tell them.'

Felix stood in the hall, the weight of the news bearing down upon him. Billy was dead. His wife was a widow and his children would have to grow up without a father. He wanted to shout out loud against the unfairness of it all. Yesterday, Billy had been laughing and joking, declaring it a perfect day; it had turned out to be anything but. Felix drew several deep breaths before he'd collected himself enough to return to the drawing room. As he came through the door, Daphne was laughing at some remark Sir Michael had made. They both looked up as he came in.

'Who was it, darling?' she asked, as if she really wanted to know.

'Billy Shepherd's dead,' said Felix tonelessly. 'There'll be an inquest.'

★

Charlotte was still dry-eyed when Margaret and John arrived at the hospital in the morning. She had continued to sit with Billy for a while, and when they had come to take him away, she had waited until he was laid out on a bed in a small room in the basement, and then gone back to sit with him again. But now it wasn't Billy who lay there, so still and pale, his eyes closed as if asleep. Not her Billy whose eyes were bright blue, wide with laughter and the joy of life, with his halo of blond curls springing up round his head, with his generous, mobile mouth. Not her Billy, lying so still and silent. Later, a nurse came in and told her that Billy's parents had arrived and were waiting outside.

'They've spoken to the doctor,' she said. 'They know he's passed away.'

Charlotte nodded and letting go of Billy's hand, leaned over and kissed his face for the last time before walking out of the room, rigid with self-control.

Her parents-in-law, drawn-faced, went in and took her place at the bedside while Charlotte went upstairs and waited. They were about to leave when Jane appeared. She hurried across to them, her face pale with anxiety.

'I only just got your message,' she cried. 'Tell me it's not true!' But one look at the trio standing by the main entrance told her it was, and her face crumpled.

'What happened?' she whispered. And quietly her father explained.

'You should have called me sooner,' she said bitterly, and Charlotte knew it was true. She should have thought of Jane, working in this very hospital, but she hadn't. Her entire being had been focused on Billy.

'I'm sorry,' she said.

'So you should be.'

'Now, Jane,' said her father gently. 'We're all upset. Charlotte's been up all night.'

Jane said no more, but with an angry scowl went down to make her own farewells to her brother.

Caroline was looking after the children, and Charlotte had phoned, to tell her the news and to ask her not to tell Johnny what had happened. 'I'll tell him when I get home,' she said. 'I need to tell him myself.' Caroline understood and though she had taken them back to Blackdown House, where everything she needed for the care of Edie was at hand, she'd simply told Johnny that Mummy would be home again soon and suggested that he set up his farm animals. Once Edie was fed and comfortable, Caroline joined him at the kitchen table, helping him to build fences for his fields and paddocks with forks and spoons from the cutlery drawer. They were just building a farmhouse with some of his bricks when Charlotte got home. John and Margaret had brought her back from Bristol and dropped her off at the end of the lane.

'Wouldn't you like us to come in with you?' Margaret had protested, but Charlotte had held firm.

'No, thank you. I need to be with the children in our own home.'

'Well, if you're sure…' Margaret had sounded a little put-out.

'I'm sorry,' Charlotte was adamant, 'I have to do this by myself.'

Margaret seemed about to pursue the subject, but John put a hand on her arm and said, 'Leave her, Meg, Charlotte has to do this her own way.' Charlotte gave him a look of gratitude and he went on, 'She knows we're here to help her in any way we can.'

So Charlotte got out of the car and without looking back, walked up the lane to her home and her children.

'Mummy!' cried Johnny in delight as she came in through the back door. 'Look, me and Auntie Caro have made a farm with my an'mals.'

Charlotte forced a smile and said, 'So you have, Johnny. Well done.'

'I'm going to show it to Daddy when he comes home. He'll like it, too, won't he, Mummy?'

Caroline looked across at Charlotte, not knowing how to respond. Charlotte bent down and hugged Johnny fiercely to her. 'Of course he will, it's a lovely farm.' Her eyes were bright with unshed tears as she said, 'Caro, will you take Edie out for a breath of fresh air?'

'Of course.' It was a relief to Caroline to scoop up Edie and put her in the pram.

'Can I go, too?' demanded Johnny. 'Are you going to the playground, Auntie Caro? Can I come?'

'No, darling,' Charlotte replied. 'You and I are going to finish building your farm.'

When Caroline had left, Charlotte settled herself at the table and watched Johnny for several moments, not knowing how to tell him.

'This is the pigsty,' he told her, as he pushed three forks together and put one of the pink pigs into its sty. 'She going to have piglets soon. Daddy says they need lots of space when they're about to farrow.'

Charlotte's heart contracted with love for him, so much Billy's son, already a farmer at heart. She reached out a hand and said, 'Johnny, come here, darling. Come and sit on my knee for a minute.'

The seriousness of her voice must have got through to him, for he put down the pig and looked at her for a moment before taking her hand and clambering onto her lap.

'Darling, you know Daddy went out hunting yesterday—' she began.

'He was riding Rustler,' Johnny interrupted. 'He's the bestest horse in the world, isn't he?'

'He was a lovely horse,' Charlotte agreed, blinking back her tears, 'but yesterday there was an accident. Poor Rustler fell over and Daddy fell off.'

Johnny glanced up at her. 'Poor Rustler,' he said and then added, 'Poor Daddy. Where is he?' He looked round as if expecting to see his father walk in the door. 'Did he hurt himself?'

'Yes, Johnny, I'm afraid he did. He bumped his head very badly. He went to the hospital, but the doctors couldn't make him better.'

'Why not?' asked Johnny, still unaware of the enormity of what she was trying to tell him.

'He was too badly hurt. Darling, poor Daddy couldn't get better.' Charlotte pulled her son tightly against her, burying her face in the fair curls that were Billy's. 'Poor Daddy has died, Johnny. He won't be coming home any more.'

'But I want to show him my farm!' Johnny cried.

'I know you do, darling, but you can't. Daddy's not coming home again.' She took a deep breath and overcoming the lump in her throat that threatened to choke her, went on, 'Johnny, darling, I'm afraid Daddy's dead.'

'Like Mitzi was dead?' Johnny asked with a frown, remembering the still form of his grandmother's cat who had died a few weeks earlier.

'Yes,' Charlotte said. 'Like Mitzi.'

Johnny looked up into her face and tears came to his eyes. 'But I don't want Daddy to be dead,' he wailed.

Their tears mingled as she held their son, hers and Billy's, close against her. 'No, my darling,' she whispered. 'Nor do I.'

Chapter 25

Felix had insisted that Daphne come with her to Billy's funeral.

'But I didn't really know him,' she protested. 'I only met him once.'

'That's not the point,' retorted Felix. 'We go to the funeral to show respect for Billy and to support his wife and family.'

'I don't know them, either.'

'Then bloody well stay at home!' exploded Felix, his patience finally gone. 'I shall go without you, and it'll be clear to all and sundry that you couldn't be bothered to come.' He stormed out of the room, leaving Daphne staring, open-mouthed, after him.

Since the morning when Sir Michael had called and they'd all heard the news of Billy's death, she'd been aware of a change in Felix. She knew he'd been among those who'd found Billy on the ground, who'd carried him to Dunn's farm to await the ambulance, but she couldn't see why that should make him so grouchy. He hadn't been like that when his own father had died. Then he'd been quiet and sad and buried himself in the paperwork his father had left behind. But he had no responsibility for Billy Shepherd, so why was he so upset? He hadn't caused his accident, he hadn't even seen it. The man was dead and that was very sad, but Daphne couldn't for the life of her think why Felix was so badly affected.

When Felix had put down the phone and told them Billy had died in the night, Sir Michael had assured them both that it was a dreadful accident.

'Very occasionally these things happen when the hunt is out,' he said. 'There's always a risk, but, really, a very small one.'

'What about the man who caused it?' demanded Felix.

'My dear boy, no one caused it. It was an accident.'

'The man on the skewbald?'

'What about him? We don't know he had anything to do with Billy's fall. No one saw it happen. It was just a dreadful accident.'

Daphne had actually tried to say that perhaps if men, horses and dogs didn't chase wildly across country after poor little foxes, then accidents like this wouldn't happen, but Sir Michael turned such stern eyes on her that she realised her mistake and faltered into silence before she was halfway through her comment. Sir Michael Bowden was the sort of person Daphne was anxious to cultivate. A man who drove a Rolls Royce clearly moved in elevated circles locally and she'd turned on the full blast of her charm in the hope of getting to know him and perhaps receiving an invitation to Marystoke Hall.

Sir Michael had been charmed, managing to overlook her stupid ideas about foxes, putting them down to the fact that she came from London and had yet to learn the ways of the country, and he held her hand a fraction longer than necessary when he took his leave.

'So nice to meet you, my dear. I hope we'll meet again soon.'

'Is he married?' she asked Felix as they closed the front door behind him.

'No, why?' Felix sounded surprised.

'I just wondered if he had a wife who I could meet. You know, invite them over for dinner one evening.'

'Sorry,' said Felix, who was in no mood for such thoughts, 'you'll have to do without him.' He sighed. 'Oh, Daph, I feel so helpless. I wonder if there's anything I can do for Charlotte. She must be completely devastated.'

'Go round and ask her.'

'Don't be stupid, Daphne. This isn't a time to intrude. It's just, well, I wish there'd been more we could have done at the time.'

'Like what?'

Felix shrugged. 'I don't know. Just something that might have made a difference.'

'You did say you were going to deal with his horse,' Daphne suggested, realising at last that it wasn't the time for suggesting entertaining and dinner parties.

'You're right,' said Felix, pulling himself together, 'I did. I'll ring the knackers now and then I'll go out and see to Archie and Hamble.'

'Archie and Hamble?' Daphne looked confused. 'Who're they?'

Felix simply shook his head and said, 'Horses, Daphne.'

News of Billy's demise had sobered Felix up far more efficiently than any number of pots of coffee and he made his phone call and then went out to the stables.

Dr Masters's expectation that the coroner would bring a verdict of death by misadventure proved to be right. It was clear to all that it was a hunting accident. Felix, John Shepherd, Andy Lawrence and Sam Burns were called as witnesses, but as there had been no eyewitness to the actual fall, they could only tell of what they had seen and the aftermath. Tom Jeavons, the man riding the skewbald, had been the guest of one of the farmers at the meet. When he was called he told the court that he'd jumped the wall well ahead of the man on the chestnut, and had no knowledge of the accident until he'd heard about it later in the day.

Dr Masters gave evidence of the injuries Billy had sustained and what he had been able to do to offer first aid; Sir Michael testified that he knew that there'd been an accident, a fall, but had no idea of its severity until the following morning when he'd heard that Billy was dangerously ill in hospital. Nobody was at fault, except, by inference perhaps, Billy. The coroner pronounced Death by Misadventure and offered his condolences to the Shepherd family.

Charlotte was sitting at the back of the court. The Shepherds had suggested that she need not go, but she knew she had to; she needed to hear what was said. She listened to all the witnesses, but knew the actual verdict didn't matter to her or the children. Billy was dead and nothing would bring him back.

Billy was laid to rest in the churchyard, his grave next to Miss Edie's beneath the old yew tree. The church was packed for his funeral, the susurration of the gathered congregation as they waited for the service to begin fading to silence as Charlotte, Margaret, John and Jane followed the coffin and took their places in the front pew. The children were not there, they were with Caroline. She had offered to look after them and Charlotte had accepted with gratitude. She had been adamant that the children should not go to the service, despite her sister-in-law's expressed outrage at this resolve.

'They need to say goodbye to their father properly,' Jane said hotly when Charlotte was telling John and Margaret of her decision.

'Edie will know nothing about it,' Charlotte said, 'and I want Johnny's memories of Billy to be of him when he was alive; of the fun they had together. I do not want him to see Billy lowered into a hole in the ground and be left with that as his final memory.'

'Well,' sniffed Jane, 'I think you're wrong, but it's your decision.'

'Yes, it is,' replied Charlotte, and she stuck to it.

She had already visited Miss Edie's grave and it was here, sitting on the cold ground, that she finally gave way to her grief.

'How am I going to live without him, Miss Edie?' she'd cried as the pent-up tears flooded her cheeks. 'How will the children grow up without a father? Johnny knows he's dead, but he doesn't understand what that means. He still talks of showing something to Daddy, or telling him something when he comes home. And Edie. Edie will never know him. She won't have a single memory of her father.'

Charlotte had been determined that Johnny should not see her cry. She had to be strong for him, but sitting here beside Miss Edie's resting place, feeling her close, she could allow herself the luxury of the tears she would not shed at home. Miss Edie would understand her agony. She, too, had lost the man she loved; but had never allowed herself the relief of tears. At her graveside, Charlotte wept for them both.

David and Avril Swanson had been as supportive as the Masterses, and it was David who had suggested that Billy should lie next to Miss Edie in the churchyard. Charlotte had been grateful, as if having them close to each other somehow kept them closer to her.

She stood at the graveside and as Billy's coffin was lowered into the ground, Charlotte knew she had been right not to let Johnny see this. It was almost impossible for her to bear, to think of Billy lying under the weight of the winter earth, and she closed her eyes for a moment to shut out the sight. When she opened them again, David was saying the final prayers. Charlotte looked round at those who'd gathered with her, people who had known Billy Shepherd all his life, who'd been at school with him, who'd chased him when he'd been scrumping apples, who'd served with him in the Home Guard, who'd seen him grow up into the kind and generous man they all knew. For a moment her eyes rested on Felix, standing with Daphne. She saw his eyes soften in the faintest smile of encouragement and remembered that it was only weeks since he'd been standing at his father's graveside.

What had finally persuaded Daphne to attend the funeral was the thought that Sir Michael would almost certainly be there. Perhaps she'd have the chance to engage him in conversation again, remembering to keep well clear of the subject of hunting. So, she told Felix that of course he was right and she would definitely go with him. On the morning of the funeral she dressed carefully in her dark overcoat and small black hat, a suitably sober outfit, and accompanied him to the church. It was a cold day with rags of grey cloud scudding across the sky in the blast of a north-easterly wind, threatening rain, and she shivered as they stood at the graveside. Charlotte Shepherd seemed entirely oblivious of the cold. She stood with Billy's family, her pale face empty, as if she were trying to blank out what was going on round her. Daphne saw her close her eyes as the coffin was lowered into the ground and she shuddered. She didn't want to look either. She glanced up at Felix and found he was watching Charlotte, a gentle compassion on his face.

Daphne felt a flush of anger run through her. We've only been married five minutes, she thought, and already he's looking at other women. Well, let him look. He's married to me, and it's going to stay that way.

The mourners began to move off, back to the welcoming warmth of the Magpie, and at last it was only Charlotte, standing with Billy's parents and Jane.

'Will you come back to the farm?' Margaret asked her.

'No,' Charlotte said. 'No, thank you. I'm going to go home to the children. I need to be with them, now,' adding to soften her answer, 'but perhaps I could bring them tomorrow.'

Margaret nodded. 'Yes, of course.' But her eyes were full of sadness and disappointment, and Charlotte saw John put a comforting arm round her shoulder as they turned and walked across the churchyard.

As they moved away, Jane held Charlotte back. 'Don't forget that we've lost Billy, too,' she said fiercely. 'It isn't just about you and the children. My parents have lost their only son and I've lost my brother!'

'Do you think I don't know?' Charlotte replied bitterly. 'But my first concern is my children. You all understand what's happened, but they don't. I have to make life as normal for them as possible. I've said I'll bring them over to the farm tomorrow.'

'I shan't be there tomorrow,' snapped Jane. 'I have to go back to work.'

'I'm sorry,' said Charlotte, but she knew in her heart she wasn't. She didn't want to have to spend the rest of this dreadful day, or the next, with Billy's sister, determined to make her feel like an outsider.

That night, when both the children were tucked up in bed, Charlotte sat down and reread the letter she'd received from Aunt Naomi in reply to her own, breaking the news.

MY DEAREST CHARLOTTE,

Dan and I were very sorry to hear about Billy's dreadful accident. You said in your letter that no one quite knew how it happened but his horse fell. It must have been an awful shock. I'm sure you're being very brave for the children, but it can't be easy on your own. You said not to try and come down for the funeral and I'm afraid we can't, but we want you to know that we shall be thinking of you that day.

Your Billy was a lovely fellow and it gave us so much pleasure to see the happiness he brought you. You have his children, they're his legacy, and you've got to be strong for them. I know you will be, you're one of the strongest people I know.

Don't forget, if ever you want to bring the children up to visit us, we'd love to see you all. I know it's a long way, but perhaps when they're a little older. In the meantime we'll keep writing as usual.

Dan and Nicky send their love and lots from me, too.

AUNT NAOMI

Despite telling her foster parents not to come all the way to Somerset for the funeral, a small part of her had hoped that they would. She was surrounded by friends here in the village. Caroline had been a tower of strength, the vicar and Mrs Vicar would always be there if she needed them, Clare had called to see her and offered to look after the children if that would help, but somehow she felt as alone as when she'd arrived in the village as a refugee; before she met Billy.

Everyone was telling her how strong she was, how brave, but she didn't feel strong or brave, she felt utterly wretched with an aching loneliness that threatened to engulf her. How could she be strong and brave? She'd only been brave and strong before because Billy was at her side, giving her courage and strength. Now he was gone and she felt that courage and strength had faded away with him.

Entirely unbidden, Harry slipped into her mind. Should she tell him what had happened? She had an address for him, somewhere in London, written in his last letter. That was still hidden in her music stool. Perhaps she should destroy it now. It seemed disloyal to Billy to keep it, but the fact that she had it couldn't hurt Billy any more. As far as she was concerned there'd been no contest between them. It was Billy she loved, heart and soul, but Harry was still special, special in a way that Billy had never been able to understand. Harry's letter would remain where it was, but she wouldn't destroy it, not yet. It was her last link with him and her childhood.

The rest of my life starts tomorrow, she thought miserably, and for the children's sake I have to make the most of it.

The first step would be in the morning when she took them over to Charing Farm to see their grandparents.

Henry Masters had given her something to help her sleep, but Charlotte had decided not to take it. She must wake up properly if either of the children awoke in the night and needed her. Before she went to her own bedroom, she looked in on Johnny. He'd thrown off his covers and was lying, one arm flung out above his head, the other clutching his panda bear close against him. She stood for a long moment, watching him as he slept, his eyelashes fluttering with dreams, his fair curls untidy on the pillow.

Very gently Charlotte drew the eiderdown back over him

and bent to kiss his forehead. 'Goodnight, my darling,' she whispered, and stole out of the room, leaving him to sleep.

She had already moved Edie's cot into her own room, hers and Billy's. She wanted to be sure of hearing her in the night, but even more she wanted the comfort of hearing another human being breathing softly beside her. As she climbed into the bed she could hear the comforting snuffle from the sleeping Edie, and despite her churning thoughts, she slipped into a deep, exhausted slumber and awoke only when Edie did, as daylight filtered through the curtains to announce the new day.

After breakfast she got the children dressed and ready and, as promised, set out for Charing Farm. It was a step she had to take, a place she had to confront without Billy, and the sooner she did it, the better. As they walked the familiar path to the farm, the path Billy had taken every morning and evening, a weak winter sun broke through the clouds, casting its pale light across the hillside, finding colour in the hedgerow and glinting off the puddles in the rutted, muddy track. Johnny splashed through them, and as the water sprayed over his wellington boots he turned back to his mother and cried, 'It's all right, Mummy, I've got my boots on.'

Charlotte forced a smile to her lips and said, 'Yes, it's all right when you're in your wellies.'

Billy'll never walk this path again, she thought miserably. He'll never see Johnny jumping in the puddles, or Edie learning to do the same.

These thoughts assailed her with a stab of pain, but she instantly pushed them away. Everything around her reminded her of Billy and she couldn't allow such thoughts to invade her mind, couldn't afford to break down; she must force herself to look forward.

Their arrival in the farmyard was greeted, as always, by the barking dogs. Margaret and John both came out to meet them and Johnny ran to hug his grandfather.

'Can I do riding today, Gramp?' he asked. 'Can I ride Barney with you? Daddy's not here, but I could ride him with you.'

John swung him up into his arms, saying, 'We'll have to see about that, old son. Maybe when Gr'ma's found us a drink and a biscuit, eh?' As he held the little boy close against him, Charlotte could see the unshed tears in the old man's eyes. She'd never thought of her father-in-law as old before, but now it seemed as if he'd aged ten years in the last ten days.

Margaret was standing at the back door and as Charlotte turned to her, she held out both hands. For a long moment they held each other and then Charlotte said shakily, 'If we're having drinks and biscuits, I know Edie'd like a rusk.' She reached down into the pram and lifting her daughter, passed her over to Margaret. Cuddling the baby against her, Margaret carried her indoors and they all followed her into the kitchen.

'Can I ride Barney now?' Johnny asked as he swallowed the last of his milk.

John looked at Charlotte for guidance and she gave a brief nod. She knew that there was no way she could stop Johnny riding, and that it was something she was going to have to get used to.

'You can,' replied John, 'but first we have to see if the hens have laid any eggs and feed the pigs. I waited till you got here to do that.'

Johnny slid down off his stool and caught at his grandfather's hand. 'Come on, Gramp, they'll be hungry.'

They went out into the yard and Charlotte could hear Johnny's piping voice as he swung on John's hand and they headed for the hen house.

Edie was sitting in the high chair, gripping a rusk in her fingers and happily smearing it round her face. Margaret looked across at Charlotte and asked, 'How're you doing? Are you coping all right?'

Charlotte gave a faint smile. 'It's not easy,' she admitted. 'Sometimes, when I'm doing something mundane, Billy ambushes me and it's as if I'd just heard the news all over again.' She sighed. 'I try not to let the children see I'm upset, particularly Johnny.'

'You know we're here to help, if there's anything we can do.'

'I do know, thank you. I know it's devastating for you, too.'

Margaret reached for her hand. 'Yes,' she said. 'It's very difficult for all of us, but we have each other and in time… maybe…' Her voice trailed off.

Thinking of Jane's comment in the churchyard Charlotte said, 'I don't mean to push you away, it's just…' Her voice trembled and she took a deep breath to steady herself. 'It's just that I have to deal with Billy's death in my own way.'

'Of course you do,' Margaret said gently. 'We all do. Everyone copes with grief in a different way. But remember, because you have his children, you still have part of Billy.'

As they returned to Blackdown House later that afternoon, Johnny told Charlotte about his ride on Barney.

'Gramp says I rode really well today,' he said. 'Daddy'll be pleased, won't he?'

Blinking back her tears Charlotte said, 'He'd be very proud of you, Johnny.'

'I told Gramp my daddy was dead and wasn't coming back.'

'Did you?' Charlotte was startled. 'What did he say?'

'He said he knew. Is dead for a long time, Mummy?'

'Yes, my darling, I'm afraid it is.'

Johnny nodded. 'Yes,' he said. 'That's what Gramp said.'

Chapter 26

Charlotte felt the next few weeks were the hardest in her life. While coping with her own grief, which at times threatened to overwhelm her, she had to try and keep life on an even keel for the children. Edie was easy. All Charlotte had to do was maintain the routine by which she already lived. Johnny was more difficult, and he became more and more demanding as the days went by. Billy had been a true family man and Charlotte hadn't realised how often he'd taken the load from her shoulders by taking his son out with him, playing with him, helping to bath him.

'Daddy'd let me,' became Johnny's regular reply to any refusal or prohibition from her. 'Daddy says I can.' It almost broke Charlotte's heart, because on occasion she knew that Johnny was right. She was saying 'no' to things simply because she couldn't be in two places at once... and if Billy had been there...

From a purely practical point of view she missed all the help he'd given her with their children; from an emotional one, she knew a deep and bitter chill in her life as each night she climbed into the empty bed and tried to sleep.

One morning, several weeks later, Charlotte went to see Mr Thompson, the solicitor in Cheddar who had managed her trust while she was still a minor. She had seen him at Billy's funeral, but there had been nothing more than a handshake between them as the solicitor offered his condolences. It was David Swanson who suggested that she should go and see him now.

'It would be a good idea to make sure how you stand financially, Charlotte,' he said one afternoon when she'd brought the children to tea at the vicarage. 'Although your trust was wound up some time ago, I know Mr Thompson is still advising you. And remember, I was a trustee, too, so I'm here if you want to discuss anything with me, now or in the future.'

Charlotte smiled at him gratefully. 'I know,' she said, 'and I will go and see Mr Thompson soon and have a chat with him.'

'Did Billy make a will?' David asked.

'I don't know,' admitted Charlotte. 'I doubt it. I certainly haven't.'

'Well, perhaps that's something you should consider,' David suggested. 'If anything should happen to you…'

Charlotte paled. 'If anything happened to me?'

'Well,' David said gently, 'you might want to name guardians for the children.'

They didn't discuss the matter further, but it had given Charlotte food for thought, and she continued to think about it when the children were in bed that night.

She hadn't given it any consideration until now, but she was almost certain that Billy had made no will. It had never been mentioned. What had he to leave? He made his living farming with his father. He received wages for his work on the farm and, as the son of the house, there was sometimes a bonus at the end of the year, but he had no property of his own. Neither of them had considered the necessity of making a will. Why should they? The world was at peace; they were young and had the future ahead of them. Together they would watch their children grow, guiding them along the way, seeing them reach maturity.

With Billy's death, Charlotte must now look at the future from a different perspective. If something happened to her, the children would be adrift, as she had been adrift when she lost her own parents in the war. But whom could she name as their guardians? John and Margaret were the obvious answer, but Charlotte hesitated. She was sure they would agree if she asked them, but she felt they were the wrong generation. She knew that though Margaret wouldn't have admitted it, she already found Johnny tiring, and starting again with a baby like Edie wouldn't be easy either. Of course the children would grow older, but so would John and Margaret.

She thought of Jane. She was their aunt, but she wasn't married and would have to cope alone. She was a single woman with her living to earn, her own life to lead. It wouldn't be fair to burden her with two small children.

This was how Charlotte rationalised her dismissal of her sister-in-law as a possible guardian, but if she were honest, she knew it was because she disliked Jane; disliked her and didn't want her children to come under her domination.

She thought of Naomi and Dan, but they were the other side of the country, far away from anything familiar to the children. If something should, God forbid, happen to her, Charlotte didn't want the children uprooted and moved away from the only places and people they knew. Briefly she considered Clare and Malcolm, but not for more than a moment. They already had enough on their plates. Malcolm was taking over the lease of Havering Farm on Lady Day and they would be moving out of the village.

'We shall have to work all the hours God sends,' Clare had said when she told Charlotte about the move, 'but it will be for ourselves. Malcolm is up and down about the whole thing. One minute he's thrilled to bits to have our own farm to run and the next he's panicking that he won't make a go of it and everything will go wrong.'

'But it's such an exciting chance,' Charlotte said. 'And Malcolm knows what he's doing.'

'It is, and he does,' Clare agreed, 'but it's going to be very hard. I shall do all I can, too, of course, but the house is old and needs a lot of work. Mr Flower hasn't done anything to it for years. Oh, the building's sound enough, the estate looks after that, but the inside is unbelievable.'

'And you've got Agnes.'

'And I've got Agnes,' Clare agreed, 'but I expect she'll get easier as she gets older.'

Thinking of her own children, Charlotte was not at all sure about that, but she didn't say so.

No, she thought now, there was no way she could ask Clare and Malcolm to take on the responsibility of two more children. Which brought her to the people who had always been waiting at the back of her mind. Caroline and Henry Masters. Though Henry was older than Caroline, they were still young enough to cope with two children if necessary. Charlotte loved Caroline dearly, knew that Johnny did too and Edie surely would as she grew to know her. Caroline was sensible and knew exactly how to handle children, treating them with loving firmness; understanding and dealing with their problems, as she'd understood Charlotte's fear of enclosed places and helped her cope with air-raid shelters. Caroline was the only person Charlotte could think of with whom she felt confident entrusting her children. She could only hope that Caroline and Henry would be prepared to care for Johnny and Edie should the worst happen and the need arose.

Caroline had suggested that she bring the children to lunch one day and Charlotte took her up on this, giving herself the chance to broach the subject of guardians. At first Caroline was astonished at her request.

'You want us, Henry and me, to become the children's legal guardians if anything should happen to you?'

'Yes,' said Charlotte. 'That's it exactly. I know it's a lot to ask of anyone...'

'But surely, it should be someone in the family,' Caroline said. 'Mr and Mrs Shepherd, or Jane?'

Charlotte explained her reasons for not asking them, and Caroline had to admit she understood them.

'You don't have to make a decision now,' Charlotte said. 'But perhaps you could talk it over with Henry; see what he thinks?'

After much discussion, Caroline and Henry agreed that they could be named as guardians provided that Charlotte talked to her in-laws first and explained her decision. So, before she went to see Mr Thompson, Charlotte walked over to Charing Farm to see her parents-in-law.

She asked if they knew whether Billy had made a will, but they didn't.

'I never heard him mention one,' Margaret said with a shake of her head.

'Surely he'd have discussed it with you if he had,' John pointed out.

'I don't think he did,' Charlotte said, 'but it was worth asking you. The thing is, the vicar has suggested it's something I ought to do, so I'm going to see Mr Thompson and get things sorted out.' She went on to explain about the children's guardianship. 'I know you'd do your very best for them if you had to, but...' She paused awkwardly, not quite sure how to go on now that it came to the point.

'But we're too old,' supplied John, and he gave her an understanding smile.

'But we'd cope,' insisted Margaret. 'They're our grand-children, we'd give them a home, wouldn't we, John?'

'Of course,' John agreed, 'but let's hear Charlotte out. I'm sure any decision she's made hasn't been taken lightly.'

Charlotte continued to explain what she intended. When she mentioned Jane she could see that her parents-in-law understood why she wasn't suggesting she become the children's guardian.

'Of course, whoever is their guardian, you'd all be just as important in their lives as you are now, but it didn't seem fair to ask Jane to give up her nursing and perhaps the chance of a family of her own.'

'But she might never have to,' Margaret said.

'God forbid that she would,' John put in. 'God forbid that anyone will.'

By the time she went home again, Charlotte felt that John at least had accepted her reasons for asking Caroline and Henry ahead of them. He walked with her to the farm gate.

'Don't worry about Margaret,' he said. 'She understands really, and of course we both respect your decision. It's a provision you're right to make, even though it'll probably never take effect.' He took her hand and gave it a squeeze. 'You're a good mother, Charlotte. We know our grandchildren are safe with you, whatever you decide.' With these words echoing in her head, Charlotte made her appointment with Mr Thompson.

Mr Thompson was a man in his fifties, balding with a fringe of grey hair round the back of his head. He looked with clear grey eyes through pince-nez glasses that gripped his nose. Charlotte had always felt at ease with him, ever since she'd first met him seven years earlier. He was waiting for her as she came up the stairs and he greeted her with a handshake and a warm smile as he led her into his office, asking his secretary, Miss Duke, to bring them some tea.

'Mrs Shepherd, Charlotte, if I still may call you that? I'm so sorry for your loss,' he said when he'd settled her into a chair.

Charlotte managed a smile. 'Thank you, Mr Thompson.' She was grateful he said no more, that much she could cope with.

Mr Thompson had always had a lot of time for Charlotte. Over the years he'd been her trustee they had met on several occasions and he'd come to admire her strength and common sense. 'An old head on young shoulders,' he'd once said to his wife.

He looked at her now, sitting opposite him, pale-faced but determined, and smiled. 'Well,' he said, 'what can I do for you today?'

'Two main things,' Charlotte replied, happy to get onto the safe ground of business. 'First, I need to know how my finances stand. Obviously we shan't have Billy's money coming in, so I need to know how much money I have to live on. The second is that I want to make a will.'

'Ah,' said Mr Thompson as he removed his pince-nez and rubbed his eyes before replacing them. 'That's a very sensible move.'

Miss Duke brought in the tea tray, poured them each a cup of tea and then disappeared again. As they drank their tea Mr Thompson explained how much income she could expect from Miss Edie's legacy.

'Well, as you know,' he said, 'the interest from the shares and bonds Miss Everard left you have been providing you with an income. Up until now, you've only been taking a portion of this and the rest we've been reinvesting for you. You have a fair amount of cash in the bank, available to use straight away, but if the interest from these investments has become your sole source of income, and you're relying on it for the maintenance of your family, you'll have to keep a careful watch on your expenditure. Of course you already own your house, so there is no rent to pay, but there will be other outgoings which you'll have to budget for.'

They discussed the amount of money she could reasonably expect to live on and Charlotte realised that she did, indeed, need to watch her outgoings if she were not to touch her capital.

They spent the next half-hour discussing her will, which, Mr Thompson said, would not be complicated to draw up as she wanted it. He made several suggestions for her to consider and when she finally left his office and went to catch the afternoon bus back to Wynsdown, Charlotte felt that she was beginning to get a grip on things. She was dealing with the practicalities of life, and they left her little time to indulge her grief.

Back in Wynsdown she went to collect the children from Caroline.

'Hallo, you two,' she said, 'have you been good for Auntie Caro?'

'Good as gold,' Caroline said as she led her into the sitting room.

Edie was sitting up on the floor, surrounded by cushions in case she forgot what she was doing, and when she saw Charlotte, she held out her arms to her. Charlotte bent down and scooped her up for a hug before settling her on her hip and turning to see what Johnny was doing. He was sitting up at the table, the soldiers he'd brought with him lined up in battle order in front of him.

He glanced across at her. 'The reds are the baddies today,' he told her. 'The blue men are winning.'

'That makes a change,' laughed Charlotte, and with Edie still in her arms she flopped down into an armchair, gratefully accepting Caroline's offer of tea. She felt exhausted.

'You look tired,' Caroline said as she poured and handed Charlotte a cup.

'I feel it,' confessed Charlotte, sipping the hot tea.

'Not sleeping?' asked Caroline.

'Not very well,' she admitted. 'And even when I do, I seem to wake up tired.'

'Why not ask Henry to give you something to help you sleep properly?' suggested Caroline, adding, 'I thought he had, actually.'

'He did give me some tablets,' replied Charlotte, 'but I haven't been taking them. I don't want to be woozy if I have to get up to Edie in the night.'

'I thought she was sleeping through?'

'She was, she is, but just occasionally she stirs and I have to get up to her.'

'Well, even so, I think you should come and see Henry. Perhaps you're anaemic or something and need a tonic. I'm sure he could give you something to perk you up... make you feel less tired.'

'Maybe,' Charlotte agreed wearily. 'I'll think about it. Right now I need to get these two home and ready for bed.' She set her teacup aside and struggled to her feet. 'Come on, Johnny, time to go home.'

'I don't want to,' Johnny protested. 'I want to stay here, with Auntie Caro.'

'Well, you can't,' Charlotte said firmly. 'It's time to go. Let's find your coat and boots and then we'll go home for tea.'

'We could have tea here,' Johnny said truculently.

'No, we couldn't,' Charlotte snapped. 'Auntie Caro's got things to do. You've had a lovely time with her, but now we've got to go home.'

Johnny's lip trembled. 'I want Daddy,' he said.

Before Charlotte could collect herself to reply, Caroline said, 'Of course you do, darling. We all miss him.' She gathered the little boy to her and held him close for a moment and then said, 'Tell you what, why don't I put my coat and boots on, too, and walk home with you?' She set him down and led him out of the room to find their outdoor clothes. Charlotte remained where she was for several moments, clinging to Edie, fighting the tears that threatened to overwhelm her.

When they finally reached Blackdown House, Caroline came indoors with them and stayed while the children had their tea and then helped put them to bed. She was seriously concerned about Charlotte. She knew she was stretched to breaking point; wraith-thin with a pale face and haunted eyes, it was clear she was exhausted. She waited in the kitchen, washing up the tea things until Charlotte came downstairs from reading Johnny his bedtime story. She was determined to say something.

'Charlotte,' she said when Charlotte sank onto a chair at the kitchen table, 'what are you going to eat yourself?'

Charlotte shrugged. 'I don't know, I'll find something later on.'

'That's not good enough, Charlotte,' Caroline said, her voice echoing the tones she'd used on recalcitrant children at Livingston Road. 'You have to eat properly to keep your strength up. What's going to happen to the children if you become ill?'

'I'm fine,' Charlotte said. 'Really, Caroline, you don't have to worry about me. It's just been a long day, that's all. I'll have an early night.'

'I *am* worried about you,' Caroline said more gently. 'I really think you may be anaemic. I wish you'd come and see Henry.'

'All right.' Charlotte was too tired to argue. 'I'll see if Margaret can have the children one morning and then come in to the surgery.'

'Come tomorrow morning,' suggested Caroline, anxious to strike while the iron was hot. 'I'll look after the children while you see Henry.'

'Tomorrow morning,' Charlotte agreed wearily, and with that Caroline gave her a hug and went back home.

Chapter 27

It was a dull, damp Monday morning. Daphne was the post office buying and sending off her postal order when a woman she half recognised came in. Daphne knew she'd seen her before but couldn't place her. She stood just inside the door, brushing the rain from her coat, and was greeted with a cry of delight from behind the counter by Nancy Bright.

'Jane!' she cried. 'Jane Shepherd, is that you? Lovely to see you, my dear. Home for a few days, are you? Your poor parents! They will be pleased to see you.'

'Just for a couple of days, I'm afraid,' answered Jane when she could get a word in edgeways. 'Have to go back to Bristol before the end of the week.'

'Well, they'll love having you even if it is for such a short time.' Hardly pausing for breath she went on, 'I don't s'pose you've met Mrs Felix yet, have you? Just moved into the manor, she has.'

'Well, not just,' Daphne corrected her. 'We moved in just before Christmas.' An eternity ago, she added silently.

'Well, Mrs Felix, this is Jane Shepherd, you know about her poor brother Billy, of course—'

'I just wanted some stamps,' said Jane abruptly cutting off the flow of Nancy's gossip.

'Yes, yes, of course,' Nancy said, and pulled open the counter drawer before turning to Daphne and saying, 'Of course it was your husband what found him, wasn't it, Mrs Felix? Dreadful, dreadful thing it were.'

'Thank you, Miss Bright,' Jane said frostily as she almost snatched the stamps before handing Nancy the money, and with that she turned on her heel and left the shop, allowing the door to slam shut behind her.

Daphne had by now slipped the postal order into its prepared envelope and she passed it across the counter, saying 'For the post bag, please, Miss Bright,' before she, too, hurried out of the door. Nancy looked with interest at the address before she put the envelope in the bag. She'd seen letters going there before and wondered who Mrs Higgins was.

Daphne found Jane standing outside, sheltering under an umbrella. 'I'm sorry,' Jane said, 'I didn't mean to be rude to you, but I can't stand the woman and I certainly don't want to talk to her about Billy. She's a dreadful gossip, as I expect you've already discovered. Hope you haven't got any secrets, because if Nancy Bright finds out, you may as well tell the whole village yourself!'

'No, none,' Daphne laughed and holding out her hand, said, 'Daphne Bellinger. Pleased to meet you. Isn't it a miserable day… again?'

'It is,' agreed Jane, and then she smiled and on impulse said, 'I say, shall we go for a cup of tea at Sally Prynne's?'

Daphne had not yet been to Ye Olde Tea Shoppe. She'd seen the sign but had thought it wasn't the sort of place where the lady of the manor should be seen. However, she liked the look of Jane Shepherd, and she thought, well, if she wants to go there, why not?

'All right,' she said and they began to cross the green, but as they did so, they saw Caroline Masters going in with

Charlotte and her children, and Jane turned away. 'Perhaps not,' she said. 'It'll be noisy with the children in there.'

'Come home with me then,' suggested Daphne. 'Felix is out somewhere, so we'll have the place to ourselves. We can light the fire and have tea and toast in front of it.'

'Sounds heavenly,' Jane said, and with their umbrellas bobbing above them, they hurried up the lane towards the welcoming warmth of the manor.

'Felix!' Daphne called as they came into the hall and shed their raincoats. But there was no reply. She'd been pretty sure he was out somewhere on the farm, but wanted to be certain before they settled down in front of the fire. It was ready laid and Daphne put a match to it before going out into the kitchen to put the kettle on. Jane followed her, eager to see the inside of the house. She had been there before, to a meeting with her mother, but only into the drawing room; she'd never penetrated the nether regions. As they waited for the kettle to boil, she looked round the kitchen, taking in the dresser fuller of crockery, the large scrubbed table, the shining copper pans hanging along a shelf and the range on which the kettle was beginning to whistle. There were a few breakfast dishes stacked up on the draining board of a deep Belfast sink, obviously awaiting attention.

Daphne caught her eyeing them and said, 'I'll do those later. I'm certainly not going to waste time with them now.' She opened a bread crock and pulled out a loaf. 'Here,' she said. 'I'm hopeless at cutting bread, you do it. Cut us a couple of slices each, we'll toast them by the fire.'

As Jane did as she was asked, Daphne found the butter and some jam. She made the tea and then they put everything on a tray and carried it through to the drawing room, where the fire had taken hold nicely and was snapping and crackling, its flames leaping up the chimney. Daphne set the tray down on a table and picked up the toasting fork that stood at the fireside.

'Here,' she said, 'you start toasting while I pour the tea.'

They sat companionably by the fire, drinking their tea and taking it in turns with the toasting fork.

'I'm very sorry about your brother,' Daphne ventured. 'I saw you at the funeral, of course, but didn't like to introduce myself there.'

'Thank you,' Jane said. 'It was awful.'

'Very difficult for your sister-in-law, being left with two small kids.'

'Yes, but she's not the only one. People seem to think of her and forget about my poor parents... and me.'

Jane was not quite sure why she'd opened up to Daphne, she'd only known her for half an hour, but somehow she wanted her to know. Felt that she could trust her.

'Poor you,' Daphne sympathised. For a moment companionable silence fell round them, each comfortable in the company of the other.

'Are you quite settled in here?' asked Jane as she spread her piece of toast with butter and jam.

'Sort of,' replied Daphne, 'but I do miss living in London. Apart from during the war when I was posted to all different RAF bases, I've always lived there and I find the country too quiet by half... specially in this dreadful weather.'

Jane laughed. 'This is only rain, Daphne. Wait till you've been here when it's snowed! The whole village gets cut off!'

Daphne pulled a face. 'Let's hope it doesn't snow then,' she said, 'or I'll go mad, cut off from civilisation!'

'Well, you can always come and visit me,' Jane suggested. 'I could show you round Bristol, what's left of it after the air raids.'

'Was it badly bombed?' asked Daphne, with interest.

'Some of it was,' Jane says. 'I work at the BRI, and some of it was very close.'

'BRI? What's that?'

'Bristol Royal Infirmary.'

'Bristol Royal Infirmary,' echoed Daphne. 'Wasn't that where they took...' She hesitated, realising that she was on delicate ground.

'Billy,' supplied Jane. 'Yes, they brought him in and that's where he died. Only,' she added bitterly, 'my sister-in-law didn't bother to let me know he was there, in the hospital where I work, until it was too late.'

'But that's dreadful!' sympathised Daphne.

'Typical of her,' shrugged Jane. 'Thinks she's the only one who loved him. Still,' she said, changing the subject back to her earlier idea, 'why don't you come and visit me in Bristol one day when I'm off duty? I could show you round and we could do a bit of shopping.'

'I'd love to,' enthused Daphne. Anything to get out of this godforsaken village... though she didn't put that particular thought into words; after all it was where Jane had been brought up, and Daphne was learning to think before she spoke. And anyway, she did like the idea of going to Bristol and having a look round the shops. Nothing like London, she thought, but there must be some worth visiting. 'I'll get the car and drive in one day. Felix won't mind.' She didn't actually care if Felix minded or not, but she still liked to maintain the appearance of being a good wife.

It was about ten days later when Jane rang and said she'd got a day off the next day. 'I know it's short notice,' she said to Daphne, 'but if you've nothing else planned, we could go out for lunch somewhere... have a look round the shops?'

'I'll be there,' Daphne said, and the next morning saw her setting off in the Standard.

They both enjoyed their day out. Jane took them to a small café in Whiteladies Road where they ate fish pie for lunch and then they wandered through the shops at the top of Park Street. Daphne had no money to spend and she looked longingly at the new fashions that were finding their way into the shops now that you no longer needed coupons for clothes, but she'd enjoyed Jane's company and when she finally drove home again, she felt somehow invigorated by her breath of Bristol air.

It was the start of a new and unexpected friendship, but one Daphne was pleased to have made. Jane lived outside the tight community of Wynsdown, but she knew all about it, knew the people with their failings and their foibles, and she seemed happy enough to share these with Daphne. It was soon clear that she had little time for Charlotte. She had never liked her sister-in-law and had made no real effort to get to know her. She had resented the place Charlotte had taken in Billy's heart, and felt shut out from his affections by their obvious devotion to each other.

'And now he's dead, it's my parents who are having to step in and fill the breach,' Jane said bitterly. 'Charlotte this, Charlotte that. Babysitting the children so she can have some time to herself.'

That actually seemed quite reasonable to Daphne, she would expect the same if not more if she were in Charlotte's situation, but it didn't seem the moment to say so.

Jane, now qualified as a staff nurse, no longer lived in the nurses' home. She had moved out to a tiny flat not far from the hospital, and it was there Jane and Daphne got to know each other properly, smoking and chatting over cups of tea and the occasional glass of wine from bottles that Daphne brought from Major Bellinger's cellar. There were occasions, usually over a glass of the stolen wine, when she was tempted to tell Jane all about herself, about why she'd married Felix, about Janet and about her mother's blackmail, but in the months she'd lived in Wynsdown, Daphne had been learning to keep her own counsel. So far she hadn't given in to the temptation, but there were times when she felt such frustration living with Felix that she found herself biting back the words. Discretion, however, prevailed. She'd heard Jane dishing the dirt about others in Wynsdown and Daphne decided it was better not to divulge anything to her new friend yet... after all, you never knew, did you?

However, it was a friendship that was to grow and prosper over the coming months, and for different reasons was valued by each of them.

Jane had never felt anything for anyone as she felt for Daphne. From their first meeting she had felt a frisson of excitement. Daphne was so beautiful, Jane wanted to touch her, to touch her hand, her cheek, to stroke her hair. At first she'd felt a fool. She remembered the embarrassing crushes she'd had on one or two of the older girls at school, but then so had most of her classmates at some time or other. Being 'cracked' on someone was the usual expression used when discussing this.

'Who're you cracked on, Jane?'

'Mary Broadbent, who're you?'

'Elspeth Rance, she's just gorgeous!'

'Elspeth Rance? Well, she is good at hockey, I suppose.'

'Good?! She's just brilliant... though Mary's quite good as well.'

'Who's your crack, Annie?'

'Beth Woods, I'd die for her!'

Conversations like these had been almost daily affairs

when they were twelve and thirteen, but how, Jane wondered, could she feel the same about Daphne Bellinger at twenty-eight as she had about Mary Broadbent when she was twelve? It was ludicrous, but she did. Daphne had become her *raison d'être*. She had never had more than the odd casual boyfriend since she'd left school and had not enjoyed any of the intimacy to which such relationships led. She didn't like being kissed or touched and now, suddenly, she ached for it. Daphne was the centre of Jane's world and Jane longed for her love, because love it certainly was, to be reciprocated.

For her part, Daphne was fascinated by Jane. She was a strange mixture. She had an important job and clearly she was very good at it. She didn't talk about the hospital much but you couldn't be a staff nurse in a big hospital like the BRI, Daphne reasoned, if you didn't know what you were doing. In other ways she seemed so forthright, so direct in her comments about her family and particularly about Charlotte, but all this, Daphne sensed, was a cover, a cover for something else, and she was intrigued.

As their friendship had deepened Jane had found herself fantasising about Daphne, wishing she could see her naked, run her hands over her body, wishing that Daphne would, in turn, touch her; touch her as she'd always disliked when it was a man who put his hand on her arm, let alone her knee, or worse, her breast. Now, the thought of Daphne's hands on her breasts made them tingle in aching expectation. She longed to lie on a bed with Daphne, both of them naked, skin to skin; legs entwined, lips locked, hands roaming. She wanted Daphne to herself. She hated Felix for being married to her. Daphne obviously didn't love him. It was clear to Jane from the odd comment that Daphne didn't enjoy the physical side of their marriage, and Jane longed to put that right.

She had never had a full physical relationship with anyone, man or woman, but she knew in her heart that if only Daphne would let her, she could bring her to life in her arms. She could stir her to the very core, as Jane was stirred simply thinking about it. When they were together Jane was as happy as she'd ever been in her life, when Daphne went home to Felix, Jane was left with an aching emptiness, with only her own fumblings to bring her relief.

As the time passed, Daphne could see that Jane wanted a deeper relationship than their original, simple friendship, but she held back. She was no novice to such ideas. During the war in the WAAFs, she had seen girls move on from friendship to love and sex. She tried it herself on occasion, but without any serious intent. She realised that some women found her desirable, but she hadn't encouraged them; she'd been out to catch a rich husband. She'd set out to dazzle the men and she wanted no suspicion that she was anything but strictly heterosexual.

Now, however, she had caught her husband and found his attentions more and more distasteful. She didn't want children, and their lovemaking became less and less frequent. She had no idea if Felix chose to take himself elsewhere for sex, she thought not, but she didn't care one way or the other. What she wouldn't do was release him from a sterile marriage. She didn't want him, but she did want what came with him: a comfortable life, position and money. They were rubbing along well enough. With the aid of Mavis Gurney she ran the house and made sure Felix couldn't complain about his everyday needs.

Daphne's friendship with Jane gave her an escape from the confines of her marriage and from the village. An evening at the cinema or a shopping trip with Jane were a welcome return to what had once been reality, and their friendship flourished.

Chapter 28

Henry Masters showed Charlotte into his surgery and sat her down opposite him. He didn't speak for a moment or two, just looked at her. She held his gaze for a few moments and then dropped her eyes.

'Tell me, Charlotte,' he said gently.

'Nothing to tell,' she answered. 'I'm just so tired, that's all.'

'Sleeping?'

'So-so.'

'Eating?'

Charlotte shrugged. 'I just don't feel hungry,' she said.

'Sick or just off your food?'

'Bit of both, I suppose.'

'Hmm. Any aches or pains? Headaches, stomach ache, anything like that?'

'No, not really. Headaches, I suppose, specially at the end of the day.'

The doctor nodded. 'Well,' he said, 'let's have a look at you.'

Dr Masters was very thorough, listening to her chest, checking her lower eyelids for the paleness which would suggest anaemia, feeling for swollen glands, testing her reflexes. When he'd finished he smiled at her and said, 'Any trouble with your periods?'

Charlotte shrugged. 'Well, they haven't been very regular since Edie was born.'

'And how old is she now?'

'Eight months.'

'When was your last one? Can you remember?'

Charlotte thought back. 'I don't really know,' she said uncertainly. 'Some time in November?'

'Don't worry about it,' Dr Masters said. 'It's not that important. You have to realise that you've been under enormous pressure in the last couple of months, emotionally and physically, and stress like that can play havoc with your body clock and your health in general. I'm going to take a little blood and send it away to check whether you are indeed anaemic; in the meantime I'll give you a tonic to help give you a bit more energy. I'll have it ready for you later this afternoon. Take it as directed and then come back and see me again in a couple of weeks and we'll see how you're feeling then.' He gave her an encouraging smile. 'Try to eat a little more regularly, Charlotte. If you're not eating properly you will feel tired and, I know it's difficult, but if you can get a little rest during the day, so much the better.'

Charlotte did as he told her, taking two teaspoons of the sour-tasting mixture he'd given her, three times a day.

'It tastes revolting,' she said to Caroline, who laughed and said, 'They say the worse it tastes, the better it is for you!' Charlotte pulled a face, but she continued to take the medicine and she did seem to feel less tired. Two weeks later she returned to the surgery, ready to tell Henry Masters that she didn't think she needed any more of the tonic, that she felt fine.

'I'm pleased to hear it,' Henry said, 'but I'll just give you the once-over to be sure.'

To be sure of what? wondered Charlotte as he examined her again, listening to her chest, gently feeling her abdomen.

When he'd finished he smiled at her and said, 'That's fine. Come and sit down.'

Charlotte readjusted her clothes and then took a seat on the chair opposite to him.

'Well,' he began, 'I'm glad to see you're looking less peaky than when I last saw you. You've got a bit of colour in your cheeks. Have you been sleeping better?'

Charlotte said she had and he nodded.

'That's good,' he said, 'because I think you're going to need all your energy.' He paused and Charlotte looked at him expectantly. 'I have to tell you, Charlotte, my dear, I think you're in the family way.'

The colour drained from her cheeks and she said faintly, 'What? How?'

Henry smiled. 'In the usual way, I assume. From what I can feel now, I'd say you were probably about three months. From November, say?'

Charlotte thought back to that night in November when she had finally convinced Billy that he had nothing to fear from her friendship with Harry, a night they had spent locked in each other's arms. They had made love many times after that night, but that night was especially precious in her memory, and perhaps this baby was conceived then. Another child who wouldn't know his father, but another tiny piece of Billy left to her.

Henry Masters watched the thoughts flying across Charlotte's face and waited for her to meet his eyes again before he added the *coup de grâce*. 'And,' he said, 'I think it could be twins.'

'Twins!' Charlotte gasped.

'Difficult to be sure this early,' he admitted, 'but from what I can feel at the moment, I would think it a strong possibility.

I could do an internal examination, but I don't think that's necessary at present.'

Charlotte sat for a long time saying nothing. Henry did nothing to hurry her. He knew that what he'd suspected from her first visit, and of which he was now almost certain, would be an enormous shock to her. Charlotte had given no thought to the rhythm of her body clock; since Billy's death she had been struggling with life, one day at a time, with no thought beyond tomorrow.

'Two babies,' whispered Charlotte. 'However will I manage?'

'With the love and support of those around you,' he replied gently. 'And you can be sure you have plenty of that.'

Charlotte's mind was in a whirl. 'I don't want anyone to know, not yet.'

'Well, I won't be telling anyone anything,' he promised.

'Not even Caroline, not yet!'

'No one,' Henry assured her. 'You know anything we discuss in here is completely confidential, never goes out of this room.'

Charlotte left the surgery in a daze and before she went through to Caroline to collect the children, she left the house and crossed the green to the church. Still bemused by what Henry had told her, she needed some time to herself and, without thinking, she headed to the corner of the churchyard which had become her solace. The last days of February were still chilly, but snowdrops had pushed their way up through the grass in the shelter of the hedgerow, touched by the warmth of a feeble sun. There was birdsong and more than a hint of spring in the air, new life emerging from the barren ground. New life. New life within her, too.

Charlotte stood looking down at the two headstones; Miss Edie's gently weathered by the years, Billy's, stark and new, its lettering clear-cut, carved deep.

'I'm expecting again, Billy,' Charlotte told him. 'You're going to be a father again,' her voice broke on a sob, 'and now you'll have three children who never knew you!'

For several minutes she allowed the tears to stream down her cheeks, further relief for her pent-up grief, before she began to check them, drawing deep shuddering breaths in her attempt to bring them under control. She knelt down on the hard ground between the two graves and placed a hand on each, as if to draw strength from them before she finally got to her feet again and turned away, to return to Caroline and fetch her children. As she stood up and moved away, her eyes still blurred with tears, she almost bumped into Felix Bellinger, who was placing flowers on his father's grave.

He put out a hand to steady her, and with one look at her tear-streaked face, said, 'Charlotte? Oh, my dear girl, are you all right?' Adding immediately, 'Stupid question, of course you're not.'

'I am,' Charlotte gulped, 'really. It's just…'

'It's just that when you come to their graves, it brings it all back to you,' Felix said, still holding her hand. 'Hits you again.'

'It's not just that,' Charlotte said. 'I come and see Billy and Miss Edie a lot, but today…'

'Today?' Felix prompted gently.

'Today I had to tell them.' The tears slid once more down her cheeks.

Felix waited. He didn't want to pry, he simply held her chilly hand in his and then, as she regained her self-control, proffered a handkerchief. Charlotte took it gratefully, wiping her eyes and blowing her nose.

'Sorry,' she said as she pushed the damp hankie into her pocket. 'The thing is, Dr Masters has just told me that I'm expecting again. Billy's baby. I'm going to have his baby and he's not here.'

Felix had absolutely no idea what to say to this, so very wisely he said nothing. He simply put his arm round Charlotte's shoulder and held her against him as, yet again, she struggled to overcome her tears.

At last she pulled away and looked up at him. 'I wasn't going to tell anyone but Billy and Miss Edie,' she said, 'not yet.'

'Well, I shan't be telling anyone,' Felix assured her. 'I shall be just as amazed as everyone else when you do tell.'

'I think you will be amazed,' Charlotte told him. 'Doc Masters thinks it might be twins!'

Felix watched her as she made her way back through the churchyard, her tears dried, her head erect, walking towards a difficult future.

She has tremendous courage, he thought in admiration. Not many women could cope as she has these past months.

He turned his steps slowly towards home and Daphne. Daphne, still unhappy with the move to Somerset, unwilling, or unable, to become part of village society, and he sighed. Charlotte was having an unexpected baby, possibly two. He wished he and Daphne were having a baby; a child that would cement them in their marriage, but so far there had been no sign of one.

As he crossed to the lych gate he paused at the single lichen-covered stone that stood at the head of a grave, tucked under the churchyard wall, its carving barely legible after years of neglect.

HERE LIE THREE GERMAN AIRMEN
KNOWN ONLY TO GOD
DIED 28TH JUNE 1942
REST IN PEACE

When he'd heard about the shooting down of the German bomber and learned that three of the crew were buried at the church, Felix had come looking for the grave. Despite the fact that they'd been on opposite sides, he couldn't help feeling a kindred spirit. He could have been lying in just such a grave somewhere in Germany had he been shot down over enemy territory. Now, on his occasional visits to the graveyard, he would pause to remember them lying at peace beneath that stone, and think, There but for the grace of God... No one knew their names, all identification had been destroyed in the firestorm that had consumed them and their plane when it hit the ground and exploded. What was left of their remains had been extricated from the plane and David Swanson had insisted they be given a Christian burial and laid to rest in the village churchyard. It was not a universally popular idea.

'Bloody Jerries,' muttered Bert Gurney. 'Don't deserve a Christian burial!'

'Jerries indeed,' the vicar had replied cheerfully, 'but still God's children.'

'Rest in peace,' Felix murmured now, before somewhat reluctantly he turned for home.

That evening, in the privacy of her own house, Charlotte went to the piano stool and took out Harry's letter. She read it through again and then picked up her pen and began to write.

Chapter 29

Harry was on his way back to Sydney, summoned there by a telegram from Dora.

DENNY DYING. FLY NOW. BRING ALL WITH YOU.

Harry would much rather have travelled by ship, but the summons said fly, so fly he must. It would take the best part of a week, but still much faster than travelling by sea and time was of the essence. He had never flown before and when he first boarded the plane at London Airport, he'd been extremely nervous. The air hostess had come past to ensure that he had fastened his seat belt and to offer him a sweet to suck during take-off, and though she'd smiled reassuringly, Harry felt anything but reassured; but he was glad to be going and as the aircraft lifted off the tarmac he knew a profound relief. He'd made it. He was leaving London with Denny's money and his own skin both intact.

Harry had been collecting Denny's share of the dues over the four months since Dora and Bella had left, converting it into precious stones. The money from the sale of Dora's house had been saved the same way, so that when the summons came, as now it had, Harry was able to carry Denny's wealth, and his own, in one small leather pouch, which he wore strapped to his chest.

During those months, despite the 'agreement' which had been reached, the uneasy truce he and Dora had negotiated with the two gangland bosses, it had not been easy to keep Bull Shadbolt and Grey Maxton, particularly, at bay. Harry knew he was lucky to be on his way out of London before everything exploded. He knew that they would carve up Denny's territory the moment they realised he had gone; Bull had already made inroads, and Harry guessed that Stan and the Shaws had been on his payroll for some time, keeping their eyes on him to make sure he was sticking to the deal they'd thrashed out between them until Bull was ready to move. Harry didn't mind that, better to know who the spies were. He was less sure who was already working for Grey Maxton and once the cable had come, been opened, read and immediately burned, he had been extremely careful to follow his usual pattern in the twenty-four hours before he was able to leave. He trusted neither Maxton nor Shadbolt and he wanted no hint of his imminent departure to reach their ears. He intended to be in the air and on his way to Sydney long before either of them realised he'd left. That way there could be no ambush to relieve him of the accumulated money. Denny and Dora would get their due and Harry would become a very wealthy man. He was well aware that the Hound might once more be on his tail so he'd been vigilant, but had seen no sign. Harry had slipped through their fingers.

As he hopped his way around the world over the next few days, he became more accustomed to flying, but each time he landed it was with great relief that he felt his feet on solid ground. Now the plane was finally circling above Sydney, Harry looked down through thin wisps of cloud to the city spread out below him. He felt his spirits lift a little as he saw the wide waters of the harbour glinting in the early sunlight, and the arching bridge that spanned its narrow neck. Sydney had been his home for nearly four years. He'd enjoyed its vibrant pace of life, its go-ahead outlook, and he was happy to return after the months he'd spent in the drab, post-war city London had become. He was coming home.

When he walked out of the airport an hour or so later it was to find Bella waiting for him. She ran to him, flinging her arms around him, and the undisguised delight on her face brought an unexpected grin to his own.

'How's your dad?' he asked, when he'd returned her kiss and was able to pull free.

'Hanging on,' she said. 'But he's not at home any more. I've come to take you to the hospital. He wants to see you.' She had a car waiting and they were soon speeding in towards the city centre. As she drove, confidently easing her way through the busy streets, Bella told him about their life here in Sydney.

'We like it here,' she told him. 'I shan't mind staying, not going back to London if we can't when Dad dies.'

'Well, you certainly can't do that!' said Harry firmly. And nor, he acknowledged privately to himself, could he.

When they reached the hospital, Bella led him through miles of corridors to a room in a private wing. She opened the door and then stood aside for Harry to go in. He stepped past her and found himself in a private room that smelled of disinfectant and sickness, where Denny lay in bed, Dora at his side. Harry was shaken at the sight of his erstwhile boss and mentor. He lay, grey-faced, little more than skin and bone, hooked up to a drip suspended on a stand beside the bed. The only part of him Harry would have recognised were the fierce dark eyes that still blazed above hollowed cheeks. As Harry came into the room, they were turned his way and Denny's face cracked into a rictus smile.

'Harry boy,' he croaked. 'You made it. Good to see you.' His voice was the rasp of sandpaper. 'Got my money, have you?'

Harry had, and handing over the leather bag from which he'd removed only a few choice stones, he was rewarded with a nod.

'Good,' wheezed Denny. 'I ain't got long, Harry, so it's up to you to look after my girls. All right?' He glanced at his wife sitting silently by his bed and went on, 'Dora don't want no more funny business, so you got to help her set something up, legit, know what I mean? Something legal to give her an income. You gonna do that, Harry?'

'Yeah, Denny, I'll do that,' said Harry.

'Good,' sighed Denny and closed his eyes. 'Tired,' he murmured. 'So tired.'

Bella, at a nod from her mother, laid a finger to her lips and taking Harry by the hand, led him from the room. As he reached the door he took one look back. Denny was asleep, his breath rasping in his throat, while Dora sat at his bedside, holding his hand.

Harry never saw him again. Within two weeks, Denny was dead and buried.

'He only hung on to be sure you got here with our money,' Dora said when she broke the news. She gave a faint smile. 'I'm not stupid, Harry, I know you'll have kept some of it for yourself.' She held up a hand to stem his protest. 'That's all right, only to be expected in the circumstances, but from now on everything's going to be legit, just like Denny said. OK?'

'Of course it is,' Harry assured her. 'Clean sheet. Nothing to take any of us back to England now, is there?'

'I'm talking about out here, Harry,' Dora said. 'Denny's had business out here, but I don't know what it was and I don't want no more to do with it. We got enough cash to set us up and we ain't going to be involved in any of that no more. Bella's not going to live as I have, looking over her shoulder, always waiting for that knock on the door.' She fixed him with an eagle eye. 'I know she's fallen for you... *you* know she's fallen for you, but I warn you now, Harry Black, you involve her in any dodgy business, and I promise you, you'll live to regret it.'

Finding Bella waiting at the airport, greeting him in the way she had, had indeed told Harry that she'd fallen for him. He had felt a jolt of pleasure as she kissed him, and since then he had taken every opportunity to be with her. He knew Dora didn't approve, but if Harry kept his word to Denny and 'looked after' his girls with everything above board and legitimate, what could Dora complain of?

Even so, it was Bella who made the running and when Harry finally took her as his own after the death of her father, he'd been surprised at the depth of feeling she aroused in him. Not just good in bed, though she had certainly proved to be that, but the way she smiled at him, the sight of her slim figure coming towards him, made his heart beat a little faster. When they stood at Denny's graveside, Harry had been holding her hand, but at the sight of her tears he slipped an arm round her, wanting to comfort her, feeling suddenly protective. It was an entirely alien feeling, but one that was strong and powerful. He had never felt like this, even with Lisa, whom he'd protected, on and off, since she was a child. Now Lisa was beyond his reach, twelve thousand miles away, she'd retreated to the back of his mind as she had before, only surfacing on the odd occasion as a gentle spectre, no longer in the forefront of his life. He'd received her letter in reply to his, saying goodbye, and he'd come to accept that she would never be part of his future. She was happily married to Billy and she had two children. She would never desert any of them. His future was now at the other end of the world with a beautiful woman who thought the light of day shone from him. To his own surprise Harry was beginning to feel the same and he didn't want to lose her. Dora watched the relationship grow and blossom and realised that she could do nothing about it, but she was determined that her daughter's life should be entirely different from her own. She'd loved Denny, had wanted to marry him, but the lost years when they were apart haunted her. If she could protect Bella from that, then perhaps those years would not have been in vain.

On the day they buried Denny Dunc in the cemetery in Sydney, Charlotte's letter, addressed to Harry Black, arrived at the Jolly Sailor in Shoemaker Lane. It was passed to Stan Busby who glanced at the postmark before ripping it open and reading the contents. When he'd read it he tore it across and tossed it into the bin.

'What's that all about, boss?' asked Alf Shaw.

'Some floozy of Harry's, writing to tell him she's up the spout,' said Stan. 'Like he gives a damn!'

'Not much he can do about her anyway,' Alf said. 'He's hardly gonna come rushing back from Oz, or wherever he's gone, is he?'

'Not if he values his life,' said Stan, getting to his feet. 'Come on, I got a meet with Bull. Maxton's fast becoming a nuisance what's got to be sorted.'

Charlotte's pregnancy came as a shock to everyone. Apart from Felix, that day in the churchyard, she had told nobody until the doctor was able to confirm, some weeks later, that she was indeed carrying twins. Her parents-in-law were amazed and delighted. Margaret, very emotional at the thought that Billy would live on in two more children, fussed round her, offering to look after Johnny and Edie more often, insisting she must put her feet up.

'You'll need plenty of rest,' she said, 'and we'll be there to help whenever you need us.'

Jane could hardly believe it when she heard. Trust Charlotte to make herself the centre of attention in the Shepherd family again. Still, once she'd got over the shock, she, too, was pleased to think Billy had left a little more of himself behind and she looked forward to the babies being born.

Once the news was out, it was round the village in a flash. Felix, good as his word, seemed as surprised as anyone when Daphne told him what she'd heard from Nancy Bright in the post office.

'Imagine having four children under five!' she said with a shudder. 'Three of them not yet two.'

'Yes,' agreed Felix, 'she'll have her work cut out, but,' he took Daphne's hand and gave it a squeeze saying, 'but it would be nice to have one baby, don't you think?'

Daphne didn't. She had been taking all the precautions she knew to ensure she didn't fall pregnant, but there was no way she was going to admit that to Felix. She had no intention of tying herself to a child, but she smiled and said, 'Don't worry, Felix, I'm sure it'll happen in time.'

Ever since she'd come to Wynsdown, Daphne had kept up the payments her mother had demanded, but as the months passed she came to resent more and more the five-pound postal orders she had to buy. She needed that money for herself. When it came to the June payment she decided to risk missing a month. She could always plead poverty and say she'd make it up another time if her mother wrote and complained.

It was a mistake. One evening, the week after Ethel should have received the postal order, the phone rang. Felix was in his office and picked up the receiver before Daphne had a chance to get to the phone in the hall.

'Wynsdown 318?' It was the tinny voice of the operator. 'Hold the line, please, I have a call for you.' There was a click and a clunk and then a woman's voice said, 'Is that Mr Bellinger?'

'Speaking.'

'This is Ethel Higgins, Daphne's mother.'

'Mrs Higgins,' cried Felix in surprise. 'Let me call Daphne.'

'No, don't do that, I only got three minutes. Just give her a message for me.'

'Of course, but she's here, now if you'd rather—'

Ethel Higgins cut him off. 'No, a message'll do fine. Tell her, if she misses again I'll keep my promise. And if she don't make up the difference the same thing'll happen. You got that?'

'Yes, I think so,' replied Felix. 'If she misses again you'll keep your promise and if she doesn't make up the difference the same thing will happen.'

'That's right,' Ethel said firmly. 'You tell her. She'll know.'

'Are you sure you don't want to speak to her yourself? She's just—' But even as he spoke the pips interrupted and the call was cut off.

Felix went to find Daphne at once. 'That was your mother on the phone,' he said.

'Mum?' Anxiety flashed across her face. 'What did she want?'

'Don't worry,' Felix reassured her. 'There's nothing wrong. She only had three minutes, so she just gave me a message for you.'

'Oh?' Daphne was wary. 'And what was that then?'

Felix repeated the message. 'She said you'd know what it was all about.'

Daphne forced herself to smile. 'Yes, yes. That's all right.'

'Well if you understand it, that's fine. Sounded pretty odd to me.'

'It's a little surprise we've been planning for Dad,' Daphne improvised quickly. 'It's fine, really.'

Felix shrugged. 'Good. Well as long as you've got the message.' And with that he went back into the office.

I've got the message all right, Daphne thought, cursing her mother's persistence. But she also knew that she'd been thrown a lifeline. Mum wasn't going to tell Felix this time, at least not if she sent the June money straight away. But she'd better not miss again. The trouble was she'd already spent half of June's allowance on a new summer frock.

Next morning, when Felix had ridden out on Archie to the further end of the farm, Daphne went into the office and opened the drawer to his desk. Inside was the petty cash tin. There was a handful of coins, a couple of ten-bob notes and three-pound notes. She dared not take any of the pounds, he'd certainly notice if one of those went missing, but she removed some of the silver and one of the ten-shilling notes and slipped them into her pocket. If he made any remark about missing money she'd ask him, innocently, if he kept the drawer locked. When he admitted he didn't, she'd say it was very trusting of him not to, when they had people like Mavis Gurney having the run of the house.

She took the money, one pound five shillings and sixpence in all, and scraping the rest from the housekeeping, bought her postal order and sent it off.

Felix never mentioned that he'd found money was missing from his petty cash and Daphne kept that in her mind for another time. If he was stupid enough to leave both desk drawer and cash box unlocked, it was his fault that occasionally money disappeared. Simply asking for trouble.

Charlotte's twins were born, nearly three weeks early, on the morning of Friday 7 July. She had gone into labour the evening before and Johnny and Edie had been sent to stay with their grandparents. Charlotte had hoped to have the babies in her own home, but Henry Masters had insisted that she go to the hospital in Weston-super-Mare.

'I'm not expecting any,' he said, 'but if there should be complications because it's twins, you're far better off in the maternity ward.'

John and Margaret agreed with him, as did Caroline and so, bowing to their combined pressure, Charlotte had allowed Caroline to drive her into Weston when it was clear that the babies were about to put in an appearance.

Margaret and John had helped prepare a nursery for the new arrivals. Edie was still sleeping in the cot but it had been moved in to share a room with Johnny.

Charlotte had arrived at the hospital on Thursday evening and the first baby had been born at five o'clock the next morning, a boy. A red-faced baby with a tuft of dark hair standing up on his head who screamed his disapproval of the world into which he'd just been expelled. His twin followed soon after, also red-faced and dark-haired, but somehow less angry about his arrival than his brother. Before Charlotte dropped into an exhausted sleep, she held her two sons together in her arms, resting her cheeks against their soft baby hair. They were small, but they were perfect. Tears filled her eyes as she held them close, knowing they would have to grow up without their father and that she must try to be both mother and father to them. The ache for Billy was still acute, but with his babies in her arms, she found she could face the future with resolution.

'Hallo, my darlings,' she whispered. 'Your daddy would be so proud of you!'

When Margaret and John came to visit her later in the day, they stared in awe at the two sleeping bundles in their cots.

'What are you going to call them?' Margaret asked. Despite probing by Jane, Charlotte had refused to discuss names and Margaret had been wondering if one of the babies were a boy, whether Charlotte would name him for his father. Now there were two boys, so which should carry his name?

'David William,' Charlotte said, leaning over to touch the face of her sleeping son, 'We'll call him Davy.' She turned to the other side of the bed, to the other crib, 'And Daniel William, we'll call him Danny.'

'Davy and Danny, that's perfect,' murmured Margaret.

Charlotte and the babies stayed in the maternity ward for two weeks, allowing time for Charlotte to recover from the birth and for the twins to put on weight before they came home. Margaret brought Johnny and Edie in to see their new brothers. Charlotte hugged them to her. She'd missed them dreadfully and she wanted them to know that two new brothers didn't mean they would be pushed aside.

'They're very little,' Johnny pointed out, peering into first one crib and then the other.

'You were, too, when you were first born,' Charlotte told him with a smile, 'but they'll grow.'

'And then they can play football with me.'

'When they're big enough I'm sure they'll love that.'

Johnny looked back at them again. 'Why did you have two?' he asked.

'They were both growing in my tummy,' Charlotte replied.

'Hmm.' Johnny gave this answer some thought and then asked, 'Do we have to have both of them?'

On the day Charlotte and the twins were discharged she found Naomi waiting for her at Blackdown House. She had promised to come, but even so Charlotte felt the tears spring into her eyes as she saw her foster mother standing at the front door.

'How will Uncle Dan and Nicky get on without you?' asked Charlotte as she hugged her tight.

'Oh, they're big enough and ugly enough to look after each other for a week or so,' laughed Naomi. 'Do them good to fend for themselves for a bit.'

In the days that followed Charlotte wondered how on earth she would have managed without Naomi and Billy's parents. The babies were being bottle fed, which meant that anyone could take on that job, but the days and nights blurred into one long round of feeding and changing and looking after their elder brother and sister. In the end Naomi stayed for nearly a month and by the time she left, Charlotte had managed to develop a routine that enabled her, with the help of her parents-in-law and Caroline, to manage on her own. Every night she dropped into bed exhausted, but each morning she awoke with new determination.

Though fiercely independent, she finally allowed John and Margaret to pay Mrs Darby's daughter, Molly, who had just left school, to come in each morning and deal with the laundry. With three children in nappies, that was a daily chore.

'Listen, Charlotte,' Margaret said. 'John and I have talked this through. You really have to have some help, and this is something we're able to do, and would like to.'

But it was John's words which finally allowed Charlotte to accept their help. 'Charlotte, my dear,' he said, 'please let us do this. Billy would want us to help in any way we can.'

So Molly came each day and before long Charlotte couldn't think how she'd coped without her. Molly grew very fond of the children and not only did she deal with the never-ending laundry, she often stayed on in the afternoons to take Johnny and Edie out for a walk, allowing Charlotte to catch up on an hour's sleep while the twins slept after their two o'clock feed.

When she'd first got home, Charlotte'd had a stream of visitors from the village, all anxious to admire the twins. Daphne dutifully walked over to Blackdown House with two little romper suits she'd bought on one of her visits to Jane in Bristol. She wasn't particularly interested in the new arrivals, but she knew that as Felix's wife, she'd be expected to visit and take a gift.

She looked down at the two babies, sleeping top to tail in the big pram. They looked identical.

'How do you tell them apart?' she wondered.

'Oh, quite easily now,' said Charlotte with a laugh. 'When they were in the hospital they had name bands on their wrists, but actually as you get to know them they aren't all that alike.'

Daphne didn't stay very long. She didn't want the babies to wake up while she was there. She was afraid she might be offered one to hold.

When she got home again and Felix asked how the visit had gone she said, 'They're lovely babies, but they were both asleep while I was there.'

As the weeks passed, Felix spoke again about starting a family and Daphne decided to deal with the matter once and for all.

'I've made an appointment to see a consultant in Bristol,' she told him. 'I just want to get myself checked over by a gynaecologist.'

'Couldn't Henry do that?' Felix asked.

'He could,' Daphne said, 'but I'd rather go to someone I didn't know. I don't like the idea of Henry examining me... well, you-know-where,' she placed her hand to her thighs as she raised expressive eyes to Felix, 'and then meeting him somewhere... you know?' and Felix at once agreed it would be better to go to someone else.

'Shouldn't I be coming with you?' he suggested. 'It might be my fault... you know... that we can't...'

Daphne treated him to her brightest smile. 'No, darling. Don't be silly. Let's just start with me.'

Felix looked relieved.

She made several visits to Bristol, ostensibly to see the consultant, though, in fact, she went nowhere near the hospital, and then one evening came home serious-faced. She took Felix by the hand and led him into the drawing room. 'Sit down, darling,' she said. 'We need to talk.'

Felix looked worried. 'What's the matter? Are you all right?'

'Well, I am and I'm not.'

'What do you mean?'

'I saw the consultant again today and he… well he told me some bad news. He says I've got some sort of abnormality… inside, you know?'

'Abnormality?' Felix paled. 'Are you…'

'I'm fine,' Daphne assured him. 'I'm perfectly healthy, but there's something not quite right with my insides and he's told me I shall never be able to conceive a child.' She gave Felix a tremulous smile. 'I'm sorry, darling, I know you want children, but I can't give them to you. You'll have to make do with just me.'

Felix pulled her into his arms and said, 'It doesn't matter, darling, really it doesn't, just as long as you're all right.'

Daphne held him close with an inward sigh of relief. She'd banked on the fact that he'd be uncomfortable discussing 'women's problems', wouldn't query in detail what she told him.

'And you won't say anything to anyone… to your mother, or to Henry?'

'Oh, my dearest girl, of course I shan't. What do you take me for?'

She hugged him once more, knowing they would never discuss the matter again.

She was right, they didn't. Felix tried to show his understanding, treated her with gentleness as if she had been ill and was now recovering but even so, to her disgust, he still wanted to make love.

It was one summer morning, some weeks later, that the matter came to a head. Felix turned over in bed and, reaching for her, slipped his hands round her shoulders, stroking her skin and cupping her breasts.

'Oh, Felix, don't,' she'd groaned, pulling away from him. 'Leave me alone.'

Felix had let her go, said nothing, simply got out of bed and disappeared into the bathroom. He was gone before she came downstairs and she didn't see him for the rest of the day.

Determined that she wouldn't be sitting waiting for him like a good little wife when he came home in the evening, Daphne simply took the car and drove to Bristol.

Jane had just got back from the hospital and was surprised and delighted when Daphne turned up unexpectedly at her front door.

'Daphne! Come in. What a lovely surprise. You should have rung, I'd have got something in.'

'I had to get away from Felix for a while,' Daphne said. 'I brought this.' She handed Jane the bottle of wine she'd taken from Peter Bellinger's cellar. 'Drown my sorrows. Let him cook his own bloody supper.'

'So where does he think you are now?' Jane asked, as she opened the bottle and poured a large glass for each of them.

'Don't know and don't care!'

'Here,' said Jane, handing her a glass. 'Cheers!'

'Actually,' Daphne said as she took a long pull at her wine, 'I think he might be over at your sister-in-law's. He's supposed to be mending a gutter or something.'

'For Charlotte?' Jane sounded surprised.

'Yeah, a laugh, isn't it? I'd think he was having it off with her if she wasn't so damned prissy!' She grinned across at her friend. 'This wine's good,' she said, 'I should have brought two bottles!' She held out her glass for a refill and Jane reached over to top up both glasses. As they drank their way down the bottle, Jane could see Daphne visibly relaxing, the alcohol having its effect; but it was having the opposite effect on her, making her more excited than relaxed. The evening sun was streaming in through the window, a mellow sunlight, striking flashes of gold among the soft curls of Daphne's blonde hair as she leaned her head against the back of the sofa, her huge blue eyes closed, allowing the alcohol to seep soothingly into her. Gazing at her caught in the sunlight, Jane could see the tiny pulse beating at Daphne's throat, her skin, disappearing, smooth and golden, into the open neck of her blouse to her unseen breasts below. Jane ached to touch it, to run her fingers from the curve of Daphne's cheek, tracing a line down her throat, pausing at the pulse to feel it quicken and then… Her own breathing quickened at the thought and she had to concentrate on what Daphne, eyes open now and demanding her attention, was saying.

'It's so stupid. He wants children and he knows I can't have any.' She had not admitted her deception to anyone, not even Jane. 'So we don't have to keep on "trying". I don't mind the occasional sex with him if I have to, but there's nothing in it for me.'

Jane, her heart pounding, decided it was now or never, she had to take the risk. If it turned out badly, well at least she would have tried and wouldn't spend her whole life wondering what might have been. The bottle was almost empty now and she leaned over to pour the last of it into their glasses; gulping hers down, she moved to sit beside Daphne on the sofa.

Daphne had been leaning back, sipping her wine, and was suddenly aware of Jane slipping an arm round her, pulling her close, nuzzling her neck.

'Forget Felix,' Jane whispered, taking Daphne's glass from her hand and setting it on the floor. 'You don't need him. Let *me* show you how it can be.' She undid the top button of Daphne's blouse and slipped her fingers inside, sliding one gently under the edge of Daphne's bra. Daphne froze for a moment and then, as she felt the tingle of her nipples tightening as they seldom did with Felix, she relaxed and allowed Jane to continue stroking her with one hand while pulling her clothes loose with the other. Jane worked entirely by instinct, building the intensity of her caresses as she removed Daphne's blouse and undid her bra, freeing her breasts. Daphne remained outwardly unresponsive, letting Jane do what she wanted, but Jane felt her initial tension seeping away and teasing Daphne's now erect nipples with her tongue, elicited a faint moan.

'Come into the bedroom,' Jane said huskily and Daphne allowed herself to be led by the hand into the next room.

Jane sat on the edge of the bed, pulling Daphne down beside her. She pushed her back against the pillows and still Daphne made no move to stop her, simply lay back and watched her. Jane stripped off her own clothes, and lying down on the bed beside her, brushed her breasts against the smoothness of Daphne's skin. It felt as she'd always known it would and tense with excitement Jane slid her hand up under Daphne's skirt and slipped her exploring fingers inside the leg of her panties. Daphne gave a slight gasp and began to wriggle. From then on neither of them could stop. For the rest of the evening they lay, just as Jane had imagined so often, naked in each other's arms, skin to skin, taking exquisite delight in giving and receiving the sort of pleasure that neither had experienced before.

'Don't go home,' Jane begged when at length Daphne sat up and reached for her clothes.

'I have to, but don't worry, Janie mine, I'll be back.' She leaned down and kissed Jane firmly on the mouth. 'Back for more... and more... and more.'

It was a promise that filled them both with delicious anticipation and one, they both knew, she would keep.

Chapter 31

When Felix got home that evening and saw that the car was not in its garage, he guessed Daphne had gone to Bristol to see Jane. She hadn't told him she was going, but after her rejection of him that morning he wasn't particularly surprised and knew a guilty relief himself at not having to face her again over supper. He looked to see if she'd left him anything, but there was nothing. No note, no food, no hint of when she'd be home. He shrugged, they'd had spats like this before… well, ever since they were married, really. He supposed it was normal for married couples to have their ups and downs, though he didn't remember his parents arguing, certainly not in front of him, but perhaps they had but had kept them for the bedroom.

He looked in the pantry and found himself some bread, some cheese, some home-grown tomatoes and made himself a sandwich. He'd promised to go over to Blackdown House sometime to try and clear out a blocked gutter that was causing a problem. It wasn't the first time Charlotte had turned to him for such help and he was happy to provide it.

'I hope you don't mind me asking,' she said. 'It's just that I don't like to ask my father-in-law. I'd worry about him at the top of a ladder.'

'But not me?' Felix had enquired with a grin.

'You're not as old as he is,' Charlotte retorted.

'Charlotte, of course I don't mind. I'll come over and do it one evening this week. OK?'

As Daphne wasn't at home and couldn't complain about him going out again, he might as well go this evening.

It was a lovely sunny evening and though autumn was drawing nearer, there was still warmth in the sun on his face as he walked through the village and up the lane to Blackdown House. Bessie, Charlotte's dog, barked as he opened the gate and Charlotte greeted him at the door.

He looked at her, standing barefoot at the door, wearing dungarees and a striped shirt, her hair loose about her head, and he thought, not for the first time, what a beautiful girl she was.

'Felix!' she exclaimed, her face lighting up with a smile. 'I didn't know you were coming.'

'Come to clear that gutter,' he said, returning her smile. 'Now a good time?'

'Fine. The children are all in bed, Molly's just gone home and I was just going to sit down with a cup of tea. D'you want one?'

'Better do the gutter first,' he replied, 'before the light goes. Where's your ladder?'

'In the shed. Hold on and I'll put my shoes on and come and hold it steady for you.'

By the time she'd found her shoes and put them on, Felix had fetched the ladder and was setting it up against the side of the house.

'Certainly needs doing,' he said as she came out to join him. 'Looks completely clogged up. Look, you can see there are actually weeds growing in it! That's what's causing the damp patch on the wall underneath.'

He climbed the ladder and Charlotte stood on the bottom rung to hold it firm. He reached his hand over the edge of the gutter and began pulling the damp mass of leaves which filled and overflowed from it.

'You're going to get covered in muck standing underneath,' Felix warned her.

'Hang on a minute,' she called and ducking into the back porch, returned a moment later with a large black umbrella. She took her place back on the bottom of the ladder again, holding the umbrella over her head, protected as the detritus from the gutter rained down about her.

It took over half an hour to clear that particular section of guttering, and the sun had dipped behind the hills, dusk creeping across the garden.

'It's getting too dark, Felix,' Charlotte called. 'Come down, it's too dangerous. You've done the worst part.'

When Felix finally came down the ladder he was splattered with muck, his face and his hair had an overlay of mulch and his hands were black.

Charlotte burst out laughing when she saw him. 'You're filthy,' she cried. 'I doubt Daphne'll want you back looking like that. Come in and clean up and I'll make us that tea. If you've got time for it, that is?'

'Certainly have,' Felix assured her, wondering as he followed her indoors if Daphne'd want him back at all.

When he had removed the worst of the dirt, he came back into the kitchen to find Charlotte pouring tea into two mugs.

'Sorry I can't offer you anything stronger,' she said, 'but I haven't got anything.'

'Tea's fine,' Felix said and pulling out a chair sat down at the kitchen table.

'I'm glad you've come, actually,' Charlotte said as she sat down opposite and stirred her tea. 'Not just for the gutter, but thanks for doing that. I wanted to ask you something.'

'Fire away.'

'Well, the vicar was asking me about having the twins christened.'

'Are you going to?'

'Yes, of course. The other two have been and the Shepherds would be most upset if Davy and Danny weren't. Anyway, the vicar suggested that I gave some thought to godparents and I wondered,' she hesitated and looked across at him, 'Felix, I wondered whether you'd consider being godfather?'

'Me?'

Charlotte had given careful thought to the question of godparents. She wanted Felix to be godfather to both the boys. He had been there when Billy had had his accident, he'd done everything possible to help save him. He'd been the first person she'd told about the twins. He was a man she felt she could rely on.

'Don't sound so surprised.'

'Well, I am a bit. Godfather to which?'

'Both.'

'Both! Are you sure?' Felix sounded incredulous. 'I mean, I'd be honoured, but aren't there other people who ought to be asked? Dr Masters, perhaps?'

Charlotte smiled. 'Yes,' she agreed, 'but they need two godfathers each and he's already said yes.'

'Well,' Felix's cheeks coloured with pleasure, 'if you're really sure, I'd be delighted.'

'Mrs Vicar's going to be their godmother. With the three of you I know they'll be well looked after.'

Felix walked home through the gloaming with a spring in his step. He had no children of his own, he never would have, but he now had two little boys who would be as special to him as he could make them. Today had started off badly, but it was finishing on a high note, a note of exhilaration.

When he got home, Daphne was still out, but Felix didn't care. He hugged the secret to himself and didn't even mention it to her when she finally got home. She was in cheerful mood when she walked through the door, the antagonism of the morning seemed forgotten, as Felix locked up behind her and they went up to bed

'I don't know why she asked *you*,' Daphne said over the breakfast table next morning when Felix told her of Charlotte's request. 'Just wanted the babies to have the squire as their godfather, I suppose. Thinks you'll leave them loads of money in your will.'

Felix, startled by such a remark, stared at her. 'Actually,' he said, coolly, 'I think it was because I was there to help after Billy's accident.'

Daphne shrugged. 'I suppose...' she conceded, 'maybe.'

The christening was a quiet affair, just the family and the godparents in a simple service. They gathered round the font, everyone aware of the space beside Charlotte where Billy should have stood. Charlotte felt the ever-present ache in her heart as the boys received their names, but she held herself rigid, determined not to break down again. Her grief, though still acute, was something she indulged only when she was alone.

Molly had become a fixture. She arrived every morning and stayed until the children were all in bed in the evening. She'd had no idea what she wanted to do now she'd left school, but in helping Charlotte she'd discovered that she was completely happy, working with babies and young children.

Charlotte began giving music lessons. Pupils came to her house, and with Molly there to look after the children, she could take them into the sitting room and open up Miss Edie's piano. She was a good teacher and before long she had several regulars. Though she wasn't actually short of money, it was another source of income which, having discussed it with her parents-in-law, allowed her to employ Molly properly. Molly was thinking of applying to train as a nursery nurse, but in the meantime she was gaining ample first-hand experience, helping with four children under six.

Charlotte's life settled into a routine. Johnny started school and Edie went to nursery two mornings a week. Life was not easy but at least it became manageable. Charlotte had always been a survivor and with the help of her family and friends, she was beginning to survive Billy's death.

Part Two
Coronation Day, 2 June 1953

The day of the coronation dawned misty and overcast, but at least it wasn't raining, not in Wynsdown anyway. David and Avril Swanson hurried over to the village hall where the previous day the man from Radio Rentals had installed the television. It was the vicar who'd had the bright idea of hiring a television to be set up in the hall, so that anyone who wanted to could watch the ceremony. It was only a small set with a fourteen-inch screen, but it was standing on a table on the stage so that as many people as possible could squeeze into the hall to watch. Few, if any, in Wynsdown owned a television, and it would be the first time many from the village had ever seen one, let alone watched a broadcast.

The Wynsdown Coronation Committee had had its last meeting the previous evening, just to go over everything once more, determined that every eventuality should be covered.

'I've asked Bert and Frank to come early tomorrow and set out the chairs,' Felix told them. 'But I'm not sure we'll get everyone in. I think it'll be standing room only.'

'I think it'll only be the adults who really want to look in,' replied David. 'The children won't want to sit indoors on a day's holiday to watch the coronation. They'll all be outside in the sunshine.'

'If there is any sunshine,' remarked Marjorie Bellinger. 'The weather's been so miserable these last couple of days and the forecast I heard on the wireless today didn't sound much better.'

'Well, even so, we'll set up tables for the party,' said Avril Swanson, who was in charge of the food for the celebrations. 'I doubt if a bit of rain is going to dampen the children's enthusiasm for party tea. If it's really wet we'll have to move them into the hall when the programme has finished.'

It's like VE Day again, thought Avril as she oversaw the setting up of tables on the village green next morning. All around her people were preparing for the great day. Streams of bunting were being festooned between the trees and there was a huge bonfire, built up over the previous few weeks, standing ready at one corner. Party tea, children's races, a bonfire, and a dance in the hall, followed by fireworks at midnight were the ways that Wynsdown had decided to celebrate, and the committee tasked with organising the day had press-ganged a great many of the locals into helping set everything up.

Caroline Masters was helping Avril with the food, and all the sandwiches, cakes, jelly and blancmange were ready in their respective houses on the edge of the green, to be carried out to the long tables laid up for the children's tea. The parish council had forked out the money to give every child in the village a coronation mug and these were to be presented at the tea party. A wind of excited expectation was blowing through the village.

Well before eleven o'clock the hall was filling up as people wanted to see the Queen driving through the streets in her famous coronation coach. Several of the children were sitting cross-legged on the floor at the very front of the hall, craning their necks to see all the soldiers marching through London, a place they'd only heard of, never seen. Now here it was, London in their own village hall.

The appearance of the Queen, smiling and waving as the carriage emerged from the forecourt of Buckingham Palace, made its way round the Victoria Memorial and turned in to The Mall, was greeted by cheers not only from the roadside crowds, but from the increasing numbers of people cramming themselves into the village hall. As they watched the gold state coach, preceded by guards, escorted by cavalry, drive slowly down The Mall, lined with wildly cheering crowds, most of whom had spent twenty-four hours or more in the open air to secure their places, many of those watching the television found themselves waving and cheering as if the Queen could see and hear them, too.

'It really is amazing,' Avril said to David as they stood at the back. 'Being able to see it all happening... as it happens!'

Felix and Daphne joined them by the door, Daphne squinting short-sightedly at the screen. Accompanied by Molly who had a tight grip on the toddling twins, Charlotte had brought her children down to the green. Johnny had squirmed his way to the front of the hall and was gazing up in admiration at all the soldiers marching in ranks in front of the coach. Johnny had a model of the coach, gleaming gold with its eight grey horses, but seeing the real thing was entirely different, beyond anything he'd imagined. He watched avidly as it processed at walking pace under the decorated double arches that spanned The Mall, listening to the cheers of the crowd, the sound of martial music and the clamour of bells and made his decision; one day he'd be one of those men who rode the beautiful grey horses that drew the coach. Postilions, they were called, Felix had told him. One day, he vowed, he'd be a postilion.

Charlotte remained at the back of the hall. Felix had caught Edie up and she was now sitting proudly on his shoulders with an uninterrupted view of the television. Since becoming godfather to the twins, Felix had become increasingly involved with Charlotte's family. Daphne held herself more aloof. She had got to know Charlotte over the years, but influenced by Jane, she had made no effort to develop a friendship. There were times when she resented Felix's interest in the family, but at least it gave him some children to dote on and his disappointment at having none of his own was somewhat assuaged. He had been devastated when she told him she was unable to bear children, but realising that she would think he was blaming her for something that she couldn't help, he tried to hide his disappointment. He had gradually come to terms with the knowledge that he'd never be a father, but was taking his role as godfather seriously, and all the Shepherd children had grown to love him. They had no father, but with mother, grandparents, Auntie Caro, Uncle Henry and Uncle Felix, they were growing up within a secure and loving framework. Only Johnny had any recollection of his father, reinforced by the photo of him, head thrown back, tousle-haired and laughing, which stood on the piano in the sitting room, and the wedding picture beside his mother's bed.

Before very long Edie was bored with watching endless marching soldiers and cheering crowds and wriggled her way down off Felix's shoulders and went outside to find Molly and the boys.

The children's races, organised by Mr Hampton, the head-master of the village school, took place on the green under grey afternoon skies, but the tea party that followed was warmed by the sun breaking through, giving a hint of what the temperature ought to be on a day in early June. Just before the party began, David Swanson called for quiet.

'Just one more announcement to make before we let you loose on this amazing-looking tea,' he said, smiling round at the eager faces. 'It was announced this morning that Edmund Hillary and a Nepalese Sherpa, called Tenzing, have reached the top of Mount Everest! They've conquered the highest mountain in the world!'

Everyone cheered. It was the icing on the coronation cake. The village children then ranged themselves along the outdoor tables and began tucking into the sandwiches, cakes, jellies and blancmange that were laid out before them. Few of them had seen such an array of food, even though almost all rationing was now over, and they devoured everything that was set before them.

'Are you staying for the bonfire?' Felix asked Charlotte as she stood, mug of tea in hand, watching the children demolish the food.

'No.' She shook her head. 'It'll be too late for mine. Johnny might last out, but the others never will. Anyway, Molly wants to be there this evening. I think she's got a young man in tow, and I...' she hesitated, 'I don't particularly want to go.' She didn't enjoy the village bonfire parties. They brought back memories of the last one she'd been to with Billy, when Harry had turned up out of the blue. Of course, she always took Johnny and Edie to the Guy Fawkes Night in November, they'd have been desperate if they hadn't been allowed to go, but she still felt the loss of her Billy at occasions like that.

'If Johnny wants to stay for the bonfire, I'll look after him,' Felix offered. 'You know Daphne's going to light it.'

'Of course she is! I'd forgotten,' smiled Charlotte. 'I was going to let Johnny watch from my bedroom window.'

'Not the same as being there, though?' Felix said gently.

'No,' Charlotte agreed. She gave Felix a grateful smile. 'Ask him then, I'm sure he'll be thrilled to bits.'

With Felix and Johnny at her side, Daphne, the squire's lady, edged forward and to cheers and some shouts of 'God Save the Queen', she tossed the flaming torch she'd been handed into the prepared bonfire. Doused with petrol, it roared into flame, crackling and shooting sparks high into the evening sky.

Felix and Johnny stayed for a while, watching the leaping flames, but Daphne hurried back to the manor to prepare for the dance.

Daphne hadn't been sure about attending the dance in the village hall. She enjoyed dancing all right, but not in the company of the likes of Mavis and Bert Gurney and other such. Felix knew they should put in an appearance and had persuaded her by suggesting she buy something new to wear. 'A coronation dress,' he said, 'for the squire's lady.' Their finances were on a firmer footing since he had taken out a loan and built three small houses at the end of the paddock, and occasionally he was able to give Daphne a little extra to spend.

Daphne hadn't needed to hear the suggestion twice. The next day she'd driven into Bristol and with Jane's help, chosen a new dress for the occasion. After much searching they had found just the thing, a glamorous sheath in clear blue shantung with a matching stole, both embroidered with an intricate pattern of tiny flowers. It was far too expensive, but as soon as she'd tried it on, Daphne knew she had to have it.

'Of course you must buy it,' Jane said. 'You look stunning, Daphne.'

'It's way over my budget,' Daphne said. 'I can't afford it.' It was the beginning of June and she hadn't bought the postal order for her mother yet. Dare she not send one this month? What the hell. She doubted if Mum would venture down to Wynsdown for just one month's ransom.

'It's an awful lot to pay for a dress I'll probably wear just once,' she said, still hesitating.

Jane leaned towards her, her voice soft so that the hovering salesgirl wouldn't overhear, and murmured, 'You can always wear it for me. Just imagine me sliding it down over your shoulders, the feel of the silk brushing your skin.'

The two women exchanged complicit smiles and Daphne turned to the waiting shop girl. 'Wrap it up for me,' she said. 'I'll take it.'

She wrote the cheque on the housekeeping account and hoped Felix wouldn't discover how much she'd spent on her coronation dress until he'd seen her wearing it.

'Now all you need are shoes and a bag,' grinned Jane. 'Come on, no good spoiling the ship!'

Daphne allowed herself to be led in and out of shops until her outfit was complete.

'Now, don't you let Felix have all the fun, will you?' Jane said as they kissed goodbye in her flat. 'I'll see you at the dance, Lady of the Manor.'

When she got home with her purchase she decided not to show Felix what she'd bought until she was dressed for the dance. He would know she'd overspent by a fair amount, but she hoped that when he saw her wearing the dress he'd understand why she'd just had to have it.

Felix dropped Johnny back to Blackdown House, but he hadn't stopped to chat to Charlotte. Tempted as he was, he turned down her invitation to come in, and hurried back to the manor.

When he'd changed and come downstairs, he'd found Daphne waiting in the drawing room. Seeing her there, dressed in the blue sheath that clung to every curve of her body, the colour picking up the luminous blue of her eyes, his breath caught in his throat. She was so beautiful and, he realised, it was a long time since he'd been hit afresh by that beauty; a long time since he'd felt even an echo of the love which had overwhelmed him a few short years ago.

'You look stunning, Daphne,' he said, unaware that his words exactly echoed Jane's when Daphne had walked out of the changing cubicle in the shop. Felix could see that the dress, the stole, the new high heels with the peep-toes and the matching clutch-bag had far outstripped the money he'd reckoned on paying, but for the moment he didn't care. She was beautiful and she was his. He held out an arm and together they walked along the lane to the village hall. When they got there the dance was already under way, but they paused to greet Caroline and Henry outside and they walked into the hall just as the music stopped. Their entrance was all that Daphne could have wished for. The envious eyes of the women, the lustful eyes of the men; she was a peacock among chickens and everyone knew it.

Jane was there with her parents, but didn't seem to be escorted by a partner. Daphne went across for a few words with John and Margaret Shepherd and she and Jane exchanged conspiratorial smiles; the dress was a triumph in every way.

That night, Daphne, boosted by the clear admiration she'd seen in some eyes and the envy she'd seen in others, and cruising on a gentle wave of alcohol, submitted to Felix's love-making. She undressed quickly, removing the dress herself. She felt his hands move, exploring her body, felt the heat of him as he entered her, the weight of him as he slumped on top of her, but throughout, her mind was somewhere else, somewhere else entirely.

Chapter 33

Dieter Karhausen took a taxi from London Airport into the centre of town. Here he was in the city he'd last seen from the air over eleven years ago. It was still *en-fête* from the recent coronation of the Queen Elizabeth, but it also still showed the scars of the aerial bombardment it had suffered during the war, a bombardment in which Dieter had played a part. He had survived several sorties over London, only to be shot down on an abortive raid on an aircraft factory somewhere in the west of England.

He remembered very little of what had happened to him after the German bomber in which he'd been the rear gunner had received the hit. He had vague recollections of bailing out of the spiralling plane and then being rescued from a tree in which his parachute had become entangled. The pain in his legs had been excruciating and he had passed out while he was being carried to a nearby farm for treatment. He spoke minimal English and he'd been unable to make himself understood to the men who had rescued him; enemy men, and he thought he was going to die. That he'd survived was in part due to the doctor who'd been summoned to his aid. He did remember waking up on a sofa and feeling warm for the first time in what seemed like hours. A large man with gentle hands had given him an injection, and from then he'd drifted in and out of consciousness. There'd been a girl, a girl who spoke to him in German. At first, when she told him her name, Lieselotte, he thought he must be back in Germany, but she then explained where he was, what had happened and what was likely to happen to him now. When he was taken away from the farm as a prisoner, he was again unconscious, knocked out by the painkilling drugs the doctor had administered. He had forgotten about the girl, he'd forgotten that she'd promised to try and reach his parents through the Red Cross to tell them what had happened to him. The next time he'd woken up he'd been in a prison hospital, a prisoner of war.

Charlotte, however, had not forgotten her promise. She had written down the name and address the young German airman had given her before he drifted back into unconsciousness and had prevailed upon Major Bellinger, commander of the local Home Guard, to pass on those details to the Red Cross.

It was several weeks later, through the good offices of the Red Cross, that Dieter's parents learned that he had not been killed in the plane that had gone missing during the raid over the west of England as they'd been told. Their joy was only slightly marred by hearing how badly he'd been wounded: one leg amputated, the other saved but needing several more operations. He was still in hospital, but he was alive.

'Only a leg, only a leg,' his mother Klara cried again and again as she hugged her husband tightly to her. 'Only a leg, Hans! Dieter's alive!'

They were able to write to him via the Red Cross and thus learned what had happened to him. He'd been shot down near a place called Wynsdown and a German girl called Lieselotte had spoken to him and then managed to have the information sent to the Red Cross. The gaps were gradually filled in as they worked to have him sent home.

It was abundantly clear to all that Dieter was now non-combatant and some months before the war ended, again with the help of the Red Cross, he was repatriated to his parents' home outside Cologne. His family were devastated by the condition in which he arrived back and it was difficult to get him further treatment; hospital places seemed to be reserved for those who might be 'repaired' and returned to service. Dieter had lost one leg just below the knee, and the other was stiff and straight, the muscles wasted; but he was home and he would not have to go back into the air force. Secretly and unpatriotically, Hans and Klara rejoiced.

Years of treatment followed, but gradually, with determination, Dieter had overcome his injuries. At one time he'd thought he'd never walk again, let alone fly, but now he'd done both. After several long and painful operations, he was now fitted with a prosthetic leg that, though it still made his stump ache after prolonged wearing, he could manage very well. Only a strange and rolling gait demonstrated that his legs were not as they once had been.

Following in his father's footsteps, Dieter had trained as a teacher and now taught maths in the Gymnasium where he had himself been educated. The school had closed for the summer holidays, and Dieter decided that it was time to carry out a plan that had been brewing in his mind for some months. He would go to England and find the people who had saved his life all those years ago. Eleven years. Was it really eleven years since he'd been shot down? It was time he went back to the place where he'd so nearly lost his life.

'I want to thank the doctor who looked after me,' he explained to his parents. 'I want to meet that girl, Lieselotte, who contacted the Red Cross. She kept her promise and the message got through to you. And,' he said, 'I want to stand where my comrades died, and salute them.'

His parents were less than encouraging. They understood that he wanted to meet again the people who'd been responsible for saving his life, but they also felt he might meet with rejection.

'You should think long and hard about this,' his father told him. 'You may not be welcome in that place. We are very grateful to those people who cared for you after the crash, but they may not be there any more. The wounds of the war are gradually healing, but is it wise to go back to reopen such a wound? You were bombing their homes. You were their enemy then, you may find they still think you are.'

'I have thought of that,' Dieter assured him. 'But it's a risk I have to take. They saved my life and I should thank them. Now I am fully recovered. I'm able to travel, I have the time and some money, it is something I ought to do; indeed it is something I know I have to do.'

So here he was in London, determined to find his way to the Somerset village of Wynsdown. He booked in to a small hotel near Paddington station, from where he would catch the train in the morning. The woman on the hotel reception desk looked at him fiercely as she saw his German passport and made a note of his name. She remained icily polite as she handed him a key and said, 'Room eight, second floor.'

'Thank you,' Dieter replied. He had used much of his convalescent time learning to speak English and with the help of another of the teachers who worked at the same school as his father, he could now converse fluently enough, but his accent was strong and guttural and there was no hiding the fact that he was a German.

'Will you be wanting breakfast and dinner?' asked the woman.

'Breakfast only,' he replied, 'thank you.'

'We don't do dinner,' she said with a smirk, and it was clear she'd hoped that he would ask for dinner so she could turn him down. As he moved away she called after him, 'Breakfast is served down here in the dining room,' she pointed to a closed door, 'seven thirty to nine a.m.'

Dieter thanked her again and headed up the stairs to find his room. He wasn't really surprised at his cool reception. Even though the woman had no idea he'd been in the Luftwaffe, as a Londoner she'd probably seen enough of the Germans to last her a lifetime.

He arrived in Wynsdown the following afternoon. The taxi from the station dropped him on the village green. He asked the driver to wait while he went into the Magpie to see if they had a room. Mabel assured him that they had and she watched him with interest as he walked outside again to pay off the cab.

'Though,' as she said to Jack later on, 'he doesn't really walk at all, he sort of rolls from side to side.'

'Come far, have you?' she asked casually when Dieter came back into the bar. Clearly the man was a foreigner, he spoke with such a funny accent, and occasionally they did get foreigners in Wynsdown, people who wanted to explore the area but didn't want to pay Cheddar prices.

'From London,' replied Dieter. He was not asked for his passport here, nor any form of identification, which surprised him. He simply had to sign his name in the register before she took him up a flight of stairs to a room that looked out over the village green.

'Here we are,' she said as she stood aside to let him in. 'The bathroom's just along the passage.' She smiled at him. He was a good-looking man, of middle height, in his early thirties with smooth fair hair, a strand of which fell across his forehead. His pale blue eyes were set wide apart, giving him an open, honest expression, and a mobile mouth smiled above a strong and determined chin. Yes, thought Mabel appreciatively, a very attractive man.

'Anything else you need?' she asked, pausing by the door.

'Yes,' Dieter smiled, 'I wonder if you can help me. I am looking for a doctor.'

'A doctor?' Mabel's surprise showed. She was about to ask if he were ill, but then thought better of it. The poor man obviously had difficulty walking. Perhaps that was why he'd come to Wynsdown. To find a doctor? Dr Masters?

'Dr Masters lives just across the green,' she replied. 'He's the only doctor in the village. Would he do?'

'I'm sure, yes,' nodded Dieter, though he had no recollection of the doctor's name.

'Look, you can see his house from here,' Mabel said, pointing out of the window. 'There, that red-brick house. He has his surgery from five in the evening.'

Dieter thanked her and she left him to it. Back downstairs she found Jack, coming up from the cellar from changing a barrel.

'We've got a visitor,' she said. 'And he's foreign.'

'What sort of foreign's that then?'

'I don't know, do I? He just talks with a funny accent.' She swung round the register and squinted down at the pointed writing. 'Can't really make it out,' she said, 'but looks like a very odd name.'

Jack peered at the register. 'Looks German to me,' he said.

'German?' Mabel sounded horrified. 'Why would a German come here?'

'How should I know?' Jack walked back behind the bar. 'I 'spect we'll find out soon enough.'

'He's a cripple,' Mabel said. 'He walks very funny.'

'Probably can't do much harm then,' Jack said and began to run the fresh beer through the pipes.

Mabel returned to the kitchen, but her mind was working overtime. A German! Come to Wynsdown! She wondered what people would make of that when she told them. She knew a moment of satisfaction as she realised that she knew more than the other gossips. Nancy Bright in the post office could listen to *her* for a change.

Dieter had decided that the person he could most easily find was the doctor. He knew the girl's Christian name but not her surname and he thought he'd like to talk to the doctor first. Dr Masters, the woman had said. Would he be the man who'd cared for him eleven years ago? Only one way to find out.

When he came downstairs again he could hear Mabel in the kitchen talking to someone. He didn't want to have to answer any more of her questions and so slipped quietly out of the door. He walked across the green to the house she'd pointed out and rang the bell. It was not yet five and he hoped to catch the doctor before he started surgery.

An attractive woman opened the door and looked at him enquiringly.

'Good day,' Dieter said. 'I wish to see the doctor.'

'I'm sorry, but surgery doesn't start till five,' replied the woman. 'I can show you the waiting room.'

'No,' Dieter said. 'I am not ill. I wish to speak with the doctor about a private thing.'

'Oh.' The woman looked surprised. 'I see. Well, the doctor's not back from his rounds yet. Can I be of help? I'm his wife.'

Dieter was disappointed. He gave a regretful smile. 'I am sorry, but it is to the doctor I must speak.'

'I will tell him you called,' said Caroline. 'If you can give me your name…'

At that moment a car pulled into the drive and Henry Masters got out. Seeing his wife and a strange man on the front doorstep he crossed the lawn quickly to see who had called. 'This gentleman has come to see you,' Caroline said, her relief at Henry's arrival clear in her voice.

'You are the doctor Masters?' asked the stranger.

'Yes?' Henry answered. 'Who are you?'

'I am Dieter Karhausen,' said Dieter, and added as he saw his name meant nothing, 'I was shot down here. I think you saved my life.'

'You're the German airman!' Henry said with incredulity as recognition dawned. 'It was you they cut down from the tree!' His eyes flicked down to Dieter's legs, and Dieter seeing the look nodded and said, 'Yes. And I have my legs… or most of them.'

'Look, we shouldn't be standing here on the doorstep. You'd better come in.' Henry led the way into the house and Caroline shut the door behind them.

Realising the two men needed a little time together, she said, 'I'll make some tea,' and disappeared into the kitchen.

Henry led Dieter into the sitting room and waved him to an armchair. The afternoon sun was streaming in through the open windows, and from somewhere outside they could hear the push-pull drawl of a lawnmower, the humming of bees in the honeysuckle that clung to the back of the house. The sounds of summer; almost eleven years to the day since Dieter had made his first unscheduled arrival in Wynsdown. Henry sat down and the two men considered each

392

other across the low, oak coffee table that stood between them.

'Well,' it was Henry who finally broke the silence, 'you've come back. Why?'

'The war is over,' Dieter said. 'We were on opposite sides, but even so, you saved my life... did your best to save my legs. Afterwards, I hear that you tell them that I must be put in the hospital and not the prisoner camp. If I had gone there I would have losed both my legs and not just one half.' He cocked his head and looked over at Henry. 'For this reason I come back; come back to say you, thank you.'

'I did what any doctor would have done,' Henry said. He dashed his hand awkwardly across his face. 'It was all a long time ago.' There was another silence and then he said, 'But I am glad you're well and I appreciate your coming. Thank you. However, the person you should be thanking is Charlotte.'

'Charlotte?' For a moment Dieter looked confused.

'The girl who came and spoke to you at the farm. She wrote down your name and address so the Red Cross could inform your parents you were alive.'

'Lieselotte?'

'That was her name, yes,' agreed Henry, 'but when she came to live here she couldn't remember it and was given the name Charlotte.'

'And she is still here? This Charlotte?' asked Dieter.

'Yes, she's still here.'

'I remember waking, she standing beside me, speaking in German, and I thought I was dreaming. Perhaps hallucinating.'

'Well, you could have been,' said Henry, 'the amount of morphine I'd pumped into you.' He looked down again at Dieter's legs, enclosed in grey flannel trousers, stretched out in front of him. 'And they managed to save your other leg?'

'It's not perfect,' said Dieter, 'but I am able to walk.'

At that moment Caroline appeared with a tea tray and set it down on the table between them.

'Caroline, my love, this is Dieter… I'm sorry I didn't take in your surname.'

'Karhausen,' supplied Dieter.

'Dieter Karhausen. He escaped from a blazing plane during the war.'

'How do you do, Herr Karhausen?' Caroline said politely.

'Please, Dieter.'

'Dieter. I wasn't here at the time, but of course I've heard about you.'

'Dieter wants to meet Charlotte, to thank her.'

'And the men who cut me from the tree,' added Dieter.

'Ah, well, that's more difficult,' Henry said. 'John Shepherd still lives here, but Major Bellinger and young Billy Shepherd I'm afraid are dead.'

'Killed in the war?' asked Dieter, softly.

'No. Major Bellinger had a stroke about three years ago, and Billy was killed in a hunting accident after the war.'

'Then I'm too late,' said Dieter sadly. 'But I would like to meet this Charlotte. Is this possible?'

'I expect so,' Henry said. 'She still lives here. She's Billy Shepherd's widow.'

'We can ask her if she would like to meet you,' Caroline said, joining in the conversation for the first time, 'but it will have to be her decision. She was a refugee from Germany, and may not want to…' She searched for the right words.

'Want to meet me,' Dieter finished for her. 'Please, if you know her, please will you ask her. My debt to her is much.'

'We'll certainly ask her,' Henry said, looking at his watch

and getting to his feet. 'I must leave you. It's time for my surgery. Do please finish your tea.'

Dieter also rose, tentatively holding out his hand and was pleased when Henry reached across and shook it. 'Thank you, Dr Masters. For then and for now.' He turned back to Caroline. 'Thank you for the tea, Mrs Masters. When you have spoken to Charlotte, please tell what she says. I have a room at the public house.'

Caroline and Henry saw Dieter to the front door and watched him crossing the green back to the pub, his ungainly walk marking him out as an injured man.

'Fancy him coming back here,' said Caroline as she shut the front door. 'It's taken him long enough.'

'It probably took a long time to get him back on his feet,' pointed out Henry. 'And I doubt if he'd've been very welcome here much sooner. I doubt he'll be welcome in some quarters as it is.'

'Understandably,' said Caroline. 'Too many people lost too much during the war to be able to forgive and forget that quickly.' She gave her husband a little push. 'Go on, Henry,' she said, 'you'll be late. The waiting room's half full already. I'll go over and have a word with Charlotte.'

Henry disappeared into his surgery and once she'd checked that the outside door to the waiting room was on the latch for any further patients, she locked the front door and set off up the road to Blackdown House.

Charlotte was in the process of giving the children their tea. They all cried out with delight when Auntie Caro put her head round the door and called, 'Hallo. Can I come in?'

'This is a lovely surprise,' Charlotte said when the children had finished eating and gone out to play in the garden for half an hour before bedtime.

'Will they be all right out there?' asked Caroline anxiously.

'We'll drink our tea outside,' said Charlotte. 'We can watch them from the terrace.'

They settled themselves on two of the deckchairs Charlotte had put out on the little paved area overlooking the garden.

'This is nice,' said Charlotte, relaxing back into her chair. 'Lovely surprise, haven't seen you all week.'

'No,' agreed Caroline. 'I don't know where the time's gone. Anyway, I'm here now and with some news.'

'News?' Charlotte's eyes lit up. 'What sort of news?' She'd been desperately hoping to hear that Caroline was expecting. After all, she was only in her late thirties, and many a man much older than Henry had fathered a child.

Caroline gave a rueful sigh. 'No, Charlotte, not that!'

'What then?' demanded Charlotte. 'Come on, Caro, do tell!'

'We've had a visitor,' began Caroline carefully. 'Someone from years ago...'

'Harry?' breathed Charlotte.

'No,' replied Caroline firmly, aware of the flare of hope in Charlotte's eyes. 'Someone else.'

'Well, don't keep me in suspense, who?'

'Dieter Karhausen.'

'Dieter Karhausen?' For a moment Charlotte couldn't place the name and then she remembered and her eyes widened. 'You mean the German airman?'

'The very one.'

'And he's here, in the village?'

'He's taken a room at the Magpie. He came to see Henry, to thank him for his help when he was shot down.' She looked across at Charlotte, now sitting upright in her chair. 'He wants to see you for the same reason. We told him that was up to you.'

That evening, Charlotte gave a lot of thought to the idea of meeting with Dieter Karhausen. At the time she'd come to his aid, he'd been young, hardly more than a boy, in desperate pain and about to be taken off to prison. Now, eleven years on, he was a grown man who'd fought for the country that had rejected her when she was only a child. She thought of Harry. What would he say if he was asked to meet up with someone, like Dieter Karhausen, turning up after years and expecting to be welcomed? She could only guess and knew it wouldn't be polite. But then, perhaps Dieter wasn't expecting to be welcomed, perhaps he'd come in trepidation, not knowing how, even after all these years, he'd be received. What would Billy have said? But Billy wasn't there to ask, and though she loved him every bit as much as she always had, he had slipped into the recesses of her mind, always there, but no longer the almost physical presence she had felt him immediately after his death.

Now she wondered what Felix would think. She had been using Felix as a sounding board quite a lot recently. He'd become very fond of the children, and not having any of his own to spoil, sometimes dropped by to see them, to give them small treats, even suggesting an occasional trip out, like the day they'd been for a picnic on the beach at Weston and he'd bought ice creams. All the children loved him and Charlotte had grown to love him, too. Not in a romantic way, of course, but as a friend. He was married to Daphne and Daphne had nothing to fear from Charlotte. There could never be anything more than friendship between them, but the friendship that had developed since Billy had died was deep and abiding. Charlotte knew she could trust Felix implicitly, that he would be there for her and her family as he had been from the moment of finding Billy, lying broken on the ground. She remembered the day she'd encountered him in the churchyard, how, wretchedly and in tears, she'd blurted out the news of her pregnancy and the way he'd simply put an arm round her, steadying her; the way he'd received, and always honoured, this confidence. She had trusted him and he'd never betrayed that trust.

I'll ask Felix, she thought now. See what he thinks.

In the morning, when Molly had taken the children out to the playground, Charlotte picked up the phone and rang the manor, hoping it would be Felix rather than Daphne who answered. It was.

'Charlotte,' a smile in his voice as he recognised hers, 'what can I do for you?'

'I wondered if you could come over sometime today? I need your advice.'

'Of course. What about?'

'Tell you when you get here.'

Felix looked at the pile of paperwork in front of him and pushing his chair back from the table, said, 'I can come now if you like.'

'Really? That'd be perfect. I'll put the kettle on.'

Felix arrived ten minutes later. 'I saw the children in the playground as I passed,' he said. 'They seemed to be having a high old time. There were several other kids there. Johnny was playing with some of the older ones.'

Charlotte smiled. 'I know. He's very conscious of moving up a class in September.' She made a pot of tea and saying, 'Shall we sit outside?' carried it out into the garden.

'Well,' said Felix when they were settled. 'What's up?'

Charlotte explained about Dieter having come back to the village and wanting to see her. 'The thing is, it was all so long ago, I don't know if I want to see him.'

'Then don't,' Felix said promptly, adding as she said no more and the silence lengthened between them, 'Why wouldn't you, though? You did a great deal for him.'

'I only took his name and address. It was your father who passed them on to the Red Cross.'

'Because you asked him to,' Felix reminded her. 'Mother once told me you were quite forthright and told him it was his duty.'

'Did I?' Charlotte gave a surprised laugh. 'I'm sure he'd have done it anyway.'

'Maybe,' conceded Felix, 'but it was you who asked him to.'

'It wasn't much really,' shrugged Charlotte.

'I don't think you realise what that meant to his family... and to him,' said Felix. 'I know my parents would have been eternally grateful to anyone who'd done the same if I'd been shot down and wounded.'

'Yes, I suppose they would,' Charlotte agreed.

'And now he's come to find you himself. You said Caroline says that he still has difficulty walking. It must have taken some effort to get here.'

'So, you think I should see him?' Charlotte still sounded doubtful.

'Can't see why not,' answered Felix.

'Caro said that I could meet him there, at their house if I wanted to.'

'That sounds like a good idea,' Felix said, before suggesting tentatively, 'Would you like me to be there, too?'

Charlotte's eyes brightened. 'Oh, Felix, would you? Would you mind?'

'No, not at all. I'd quite like to meet him, actually.'

When Caroline heard what Charlotte was asking she agreed at once and suggested they should ask Dieter to come after lunch, before Henry started on his afternoon rounds.

She was a little wary of the fact that Charlotte wanted Felix there, too. She had seen their friendship growing over the last few years and her heart had sunk. Surely they must realise that there was no future for them together; it could only lead to misery for both of them. Felix was married and though these days divorce wasn't unheard of, Caroline was pretty sure that Daphne wouldn't entertain the idea of divorcing Felix, even if he was prepared to suggest it. She knew Charlotte wasn't the sort of woman to settle for half measures, to have an affair with a married man, certainly not within the tight-knit community that was Wynsdown. As it was, Caroline was afraid it wouldn't be long before there'd be gossip about them in the village. She remembered the way stories had spread when Harry had turned up unexpectedly looking for Charlotte. They would soon be resurrected if people thought Charlotte was now becoming involved with the squire. She could almost hear Nancy Bright saying, 'Well, of course she was always a flighty one. Don't you remember that bloke she was seen kissing while her Billy was still alive?'

The thing that amazed Caroline was that neither Felix nor Charlotte appeared to be aware of the depth of their affections. To Caroline it was clear as day that they were falling in love and she'd said as much to Henry.

'Are they, my dear?' He looked up from his paper. 'I hadn't noticed. That could prove difficult.'

Caroline had to smile. Of course Henry hadn't noticed. Henry hadn't noticed he'd fallen in love himself until Caroline had finally pointed it out to him! Still, she worried about Felix and Charlotte. She knew them both well, particularly Charlotte, but she couldn't help feeling it would soon be as apparent to everyone else as it was to her. And now, here was the German airman turning up asking for Charlotte; reminding them all once again that she was German. What, she wondered, would the village gossips make of that?

Charlotte and Felix were sitting with Henry in the drawing room when Dieter arrived. Charlotte stood up as Caroline brought him into the room. She had only the vaguest recollection of what the young German airman had looked like and when she saw him, she knew she would never have recognised him. He crossed the room towards her, his ungainly walk reminding her of the damage done to his legs, smiling tentatively as he extended his hand. Addressing her in German, he said, 'I have come to thank you, Frau Shepherd, for all your kindness to me when I was so badly injured. My parents send you their deepest gratitude but I can assure you it is nothing, compared with mine.'

Charlotte accepted his hand, giving it a brief shake, but answering him in English she said, 'Please, Herr Karhausen, I know from my friends,' she nodded towards Caroline and Henry, 'that you speak good English, so please, we'll only speak English while you're here.'

For a moment no one seemed to know quite what to say

next, but then Felix came to the rescue by asking, 'How long are you hoping to stay in Wynsdown, Herr Karhausen?'

'Please, I am Dieter.'

'Dieter,' Charlotte said, 'this is Felix Bellinger. It was his father who commanded the local Home Guard who took you prisoner. It was his father who passed on your details to the Red Cross.'

'I come also to thank him.' He looked uncertainly at Henry Masters as if for confirmation and then looking back at Felix, said, 'But I think your father has died since the war.'

'He has,' said Felix, 'but I appreciate you coming to thank him for what he did.'

'I wish also to meet the men who cut me down from the tree.' Dieter looked anxiously at Charlotte and added, speaking German again, 'I believe one was your husband and that he was killed in an accident. I offer you my condolences for his loss.'

Charlotte nodded, but didn't reply and Dieter, returning to English, answered Felix's earlier question. 'I will stay for some days. Not many. There are other things I wish to do.'

'Such as?' Felix realised his question sounded very abrupt and softened it a little by adding, 'What else are you hoping to do?'

'I know my comrades did not survive the crash,' Dieter replied, 'but I wish to stand where they died and salute them, for myself and for their families.'

'They are buried in the churchyard,' Felix told him. 'I'll take you there if you like.'

Dieter looked surprised. 'Buried in your churchyard? Their families do not know this.'

'Their bodies were brought down from the burnt-out plane,' Felix said, 'and given a Christian burial.'

Tears sprang unbidden to Dieter's eyes, and it was with some embarrassment that he dashed them away. 'Yes, please,' he said, 'I would like to see the burial place.'

Later that afternoon, when Charlotte had gone home again, Felix took Dieter across to the churchyard and showed him the grave with its stone marker.

He stared down at it for a long time before raising his eyes and looking across at Felix. 'It is sad,' he said, 'that they have no names on their stone.'

'Well, no one knew their names,' Felix reminded him, a little put out.

'No, but I know them. I can tell them and maybe we can carve their names here at last.'

'I suppose so,' Felix said. 'I think you'd have to talk to the vicar about that.'

'Vicar?' Dieter was at a loss. 'What is vicar, please?'

'The priest, the minister.' Felix waved a vague hand towards the church.

'Ah! The pastor.'

'Yes. If you want to meet him, I'll take you over to the vicarage, but then I'll have to get back to work.'

Felix led Dieter slowly across the village green to the vicarage. He watched the way the German walked and felt a sudden admiration for his courage; for his courage and determination to learn to walk again; for his courage to come back to the place where he'd been an enemy, to offer his thanks for his life.

As they walked he said, 'If you'd like to see where the plane crashed we could walk up there sometime. Perhaps on Sunday afternoon?'

'Yes, please,' answered Dieter. 'I would like very much to see this place.'

'It is a bit of a walk,' Felix said hesitantly.

'This is no problem,' Dieter assured him, 'I can walk.'

'Well, if you're sure…'

'I am sure, Felix. Thank you.'

'I'm having lunch with my mother on Sunday, but I'll come and find you at the Magpie afterwards.'

Felix delivered him to the front door of the vicarage and having introduced him to Avril Swanson, left him in her care and turned his steps homeward. When he reached the manor he decided he couldn't face the rest of the day in the farm office, and going out to the stables, he tacked up Archie and set off round the farm in a tour of inspection. When he reached the top of the hill, he reined in and looked back at the manor house lying in a fold of the ground; an old stone house drowsing in the afternoon sun surrounded by its kitchen garden, stable yard, cowsheds and paddock. Standing at the far end of the paddock were three cottages, brash and new against the gentle green of their surroundings, the newly constructed driveway a dark slash across to the lane. All three houses were now occupied, two by people who worked in Cheddar and one by a lawyer from Bristol. The 'dormitory houses', as the village had named them, had not been a popular idea, but they were within the village fence and permission had been given readily enough with certain provisos. Felix had financed them with a loan and the profit he got from the sales which he'd immediately reinvested in the estate had been both welcome and much needed. John Shepherd had not taken up the idea of buying his own farm outright. When Billy had been killed he had lost the heart for it, it no longer seemed worthwhile.

'I'll buy the house,' he said, 'if you'll sell it separately from the land, and I'll continue to farm the land while I can, paying you rent in the usual way.' He'd sighed and added, 'Who knows, maybe young Johnny or one of the twins'll take it on in the future.'

Felix had agreed the deal and the Shepherds now owned Charing Farmhouse, but not the surrounding land.

Looking down at his home and the land his family had worked for generations, he knew a sudden weary sadness at the thought that he'd have no son to inherit and work the land, no daughter growing up within the warmth of its comforting walls. Was all his worry and hard work really worth it? Maybe Daphne was right. Maybe they should just sell up and move away.

'Not while Mother's still alive,' he'd insisted, and despite Daphne's urging, he steadfastly refused to reconsider.

Chapter 35

Avril took the young German into the sitting room, tapping on David's study door as she passed to say they had a visitor. David emerged, happy enough to be interrupted from the task of sorting out the agenda for the next PCC meeting. When he walked into the sitting room he found Avril and a young man standing by the window looking out over the garden. He had no idea who the man was, but he crossed the room to welcome him with an outstretched hand.

'How d'you do? I'm David Swanson.'

Dieter shook his hand and said, 'I am Dieter Karhausen. I am the airman shot down here in the war.'

David looked startled. 'Are you indeed? Well...'

'Felix just brought Dieter over,' Avril explained. 'He's been with Henry and Caroline, thanking Henry for his help when he was wounded; and Charlotte, of course.'

'I come to thank all the people who saved me then. As you see I am now well.'

'Why don't you two sit down and have a chat,' suggested Avril, as always the vicar's wife, 'and I'll make us some tea.'

'Good idea,' David said. 'I could murder a cup of tea.'

He looked enquiringly across at Dieter, who smiled and said, 'Tea would be very pleasant, thank you, Mrs Swanson.'

Tea, again, he thought wryly. Always tea with the English. But it was hospitality. These people hadn't turned away from him as his father had suggested they might, and he was pleased it was offered and he happily accepted. Avril disappeared into the kitchen and David waved Dieter to an armchair, sitting down opposite him.

'Now,' he said, 'tell me why you've come to see us.'

'Your wife is right. I come to Wynsdown to thank people who saved my life. Dr Masters has said me that two have died after the war, but there are others I would like to thank, the men who cut me from the tree. Mr Shepherd and others. Mrs Shepherd who tended me at her farm.' Dieter looked across at the vicar, his gaze steady, and went on, 'I also come to salute my comrades who died in the crash. Felix took me to the church to see their grave. I believe you are the one who had my comrades given proper burial.'

David inclined his head but said nothing, waiting for Dieter to continue.

'I understand you did not know the names. But "Known only to God" is sad. I say to Felix perhaps we can put their names on the stone. He said I must ask you.'

'You want their names added to the memorial?'

'They died because of the war. Life cut short, but each was a man, loved by his family. It would mean much to them... and to me, if the names can be put on the stone. I can pay for this. And...' he paused before adding, 'if you will say prayers for them again.'

'I can't see a problem with this,' said David, though he could envisage some reaction from one or two members of the community, 'and if you arrange for the stone to be updated, naming those who died, I'll be happy to rededicate it to their memory.'

Just then Avril arrived back carrying the tea tray and David told her what Dieter was asking for.

'That sounds very fitting,' she said as she poured the tea. 'Why don't you discuss it with Felix, David?'

'It was Felix who sent Dieter here,' her husband replied. 'And I think it would be a good idea for *him* to employ the stonemason, ' he went on, turning back to Dieter. 'There's a very good man in Cheddar and I'm sure Felix will help you organise it all.'

Dieter, who had felt a surprising affinity with Felix, agreed, said he would go and see him and asked for directions to the manor.

As they watched him walk down the path, David said to Avril, 'I do think it's a nice idea to add the names to the stone, but I'm not sure what sort of welcome it'll receive from some of our locals. Better to have Felix involved, and that way perhaps we can keep any antagonism to a minimum.'

'Will there be any?' wondered Avril. 'Antagonism, I mean? After all, it's eight years since the end of the war.'

'Who knows?' David shrugged. 'But people have long memories.'

'But he's no threat to anyone, now. Look at him, he's struggling to walk.'

'It's what he *was*, not what he is now, that people will think about,' replied her husband.

Had he but known it, the rumours about Dieter were already flying round the village. In the post office, Mabel had mentioned, in passing, that they had a German visitor staying at the pub.

'What's he here for?' demanded Nancy.

'I don't know,' replied Mabel, adding with a touch of self-righteousness, 'and I wouldn't dream of asking him.'

'How long's he staying?' asked Doreen Marston who'd come in during this conversation.

Mabel shrugged. 'Didn't say, but,' she decided that it was time to slip in another little nugget of information, 'he did ask me where the doctor lived.'

'The doctor?' echoed Nancy. 'What's he want a doctor for?'

'I don't know and I didn't ask,' answered Mabel, 'but he does have a limp, so maybe he's got a bad leg and's come to get it seen to.'

'Why on earth would a German come all the way to Wynsdown to see our doctor?' demanded Nancy. 'Don't they have doctors in Germany?'

At that moment Sally Prynne came in and was immediately told all about the strange German who'd come to the village and was visiting the doctor about his legs.

'Is he the bloke who was in the churchyard with the squire earlier?' wondered Doreen. 'I saw Squire with someone there, standing by that German grave, they was.'

'Surely Felix Bellinger wouldn't have any truck with a German come looking at graves,' said Nancy. 'He was a fighter pilot!'

'What did he look like?' asked Mabel.

Doreen shrugged. 'Just a bloke. Not bad-looking. Got fair hair.'

Mabel nodded. 'Sounds like him.'

'What's his name?' asked Sally.

'Not sure. His writing in our register was hard to read. Couldn't make it out.'

'You mean he wrote it like that so's you wouldn't know he was German?'

'That's silly, Dor,' said Sally. 'If he didn't want you to know he was German he'd have used an English name. Stands to reason. Anyway, what was he doing in the churchyard?'

'I told you,' snapped Doreen. 'He was looking at that gravestone for them airmen what crashed.'

'Who was?' The door had opened and Mavis Gurney came in. 'Who was in the churchyard looking at gravestones?'

'A German with bad legs who's come to see Dr Masters,' said Nancy. 'He's staying at the Magpie, but Mabel isn't going to ask him why he's come.'

'Of course not,' Mabel agreed. 'None of my business.'

This remark was greeted by a gale of laughter. 'Since when has that ever stopped you nosing?' cried Sally Prynne.

'I can't stand here nattering all afternoon,' sniffed Mabel, gathering up her shopping basket from the floor. 'I got a pub to open.' With that she swept out of the post office, leaving the others still chuckling. She needed to get back and try and find out more about her mysterious German visitor before anyone else did. She had run out of insider information.

That evening she wasn't really surprised to see Bert Gurney, Charlie Marston and Arthur Prynne walk in. Charlie and Arthur walked up to the bar and ordered three pints of scrumpy, but Bert paused at the door, looking round the bar as if expecting to see someone he knew. There was no one and he joined the others, picking up his pint and looking across at Jack to say, 'Not many in tonight, Jack.'

'Early yet.'

'Yeah. Well, heard you had someone staying. Thought we'd like to meet him,' his eyes darted round the room yet again, 'make him welcome to the village, like.'

Jack sighed. 'Oh yeah?' Clearly word of the German had got about and the women had sent their menfolk to find out more. 'Well, he's not here.'

'We can wait, can't we, lads?' Bert downed his pint in one long swallow and banged the empty glass on the bar for a refill. With some misgiving Jack complied. He could see what sort of mood Bert was in and knowing what he could be like when he was tanked up, he didn't want him causing trouble.

At that moment the door opened and Dieter walked in. It was clear to everyone that he was the man they'd come to see, an unknown man with fair hair who walked like a drunken sailor. Not immediately aware that he was a cause of any interest, Dieter came across to the bar and asked Jack for his key.

Bert moved to block his way and Dieter paused, a question in his eyes.

Bert, never one to pussyfoot around, looked him up and down. 'You're German, ain't you? What you come here for?'

Dieter stiffened. He could see the belligerence in Bert's eyes, but he didn't think there'd be any real trouble standing at the bar of a village pub.

'My name is Dieter Karhausen and I come from Cologne.'

'That's in Germany,' confirmed Charlie helpfully.

'Ah, but what you come *for*?' demanded Bert.

'I come to thank those who saved my life in the war.'

Bert looked at him narrowly. 'Oh, yeah? And who are they then?'

'The doctor and of course the men who helped cut me down from the tree.'

That really shocked Bert and his eyes widened as he turned to his mates. 'You hear that, Charlie? This is the bugger from that Jerry bomber, the one what was dangling in the tree. Old man Shepherd made us cut him down.'

'And for this I thank you,' Dieter said.

'Don't thank me,' sneered Bert. 'If I'd had my way you'd still be up there... dangling.'

'I know I was the enemy,' Dieter said carefully, 'but it saved my life... and my legs... that you cut me down and I thank you.'

'So, you come back and expect us to be pleased to see you, do you?'

'Bert,' Jack spoke sharply from the other side of the bar, 'that's enough.'

'Enough, is it? He turns up here, stays in *our* local and expects us to forget that not so long ago he was trying to bomb the hell out of us.'

Trying not to be provoked, Dieter said simply, 'It was war.'

'Yeah, it bloody was, and you were on the wrong fucking side, mate. So you can take yourself home again. We don't want your thanks. We didn't *want* to save your bleedin' life, did we?' He looked round his pals for confirmation. 'I'd have shot you and been done. Now you've had your say you can bugger off back to Col... Col... whatever place you come from. You ain't welcome here.'

'I see,' said Dieter, and reaching round him took the key that Jack was holding out to him. Without a backward glance he crossed the room and went up the stairs.

'Satisfied?' asked Jack wearily.

'Surprised at you, Jack, giving him a room.'

'His money's as good as anyone else's.'

'Well, all I can say is that I hope you're charging him double. We don't want no Krauts round here.'

There had been a hush in the bar during Bert's exchange with Dieter, but now the buzz of conversation had returned. Bert looked round at his two mates and said, 'Pity Frank ain't out tonight, he was there when we cut the bugger down.'

The three men spent another hour drinking, but Dieter didn't reappear and at last they went home. As he strode out of the pub, Bert was smirking.

'I told him,' he said for at least the fourth time. But though he had indeed 'told him', he knew somehow that he'd come off worst in the encounter, and in public, and it made him determined to get his own back. No crippled Jerry airman was going to get the better of him.

Upstairs, Dieter lay on his bed. His father had been right after all. Not everyone appreciated the effort he'd made to come back and give his thanks. He'd seen the doctor and he'd seen Charlotte. He wondered if he should leave it now and go home, but the thought left him almost at once. He hadn't just come in gratitude for his life, he'd come to pay his respects to his fallen comrades and that's what he would do. Felix had agreed to take him down to Cheddar to see the stonemason in the morning, and he would go. Their names would be carved onto the stone whether the man in the bar liked it or not, and be damned to him!

Chapter 36

When Felix reminded Daphne he was going to take Dieter down to Cheddar the next morning she said, 'What on earth for?'

There had been an uneasy half-hour the previous day when Dieter had turned up at the house to talk to Felix about the gravestone. Felix had led him into the drawing room and Daphne had followed, wanting to know who the strange man with the waddling walk was and what he wanted with Felix.

It turned out he was German, *the* German from the crashed plane Marjorie had told them about. Daphne disliked him at once and was at no pains to hide the fact. She didn't shake his hand when Felix introduced him, simply gave him an icy 'How d'you do?' before turning away to seat herself in a chair by the window. She sat in stony silence, listening as the German explained what the vicar had suggested, and Felix had at once agreed to drive him down to Cheddar to see the stonemason.

Daphne couldn't believe it and trying to put a stop to it she said, 'I need the car tomorrow, Felix. It's Jane's afternoon off and I'm going into Bristol to meet her.'

'That's no problem,' Felix had responded easily. 'We'll go in the morning and you can have the car as soon as we get back.'

'You know why,' Felix said now. 'To see the stonemason. You heard me arrange it with him yesterday.'

'But I can't think why you did. He's a German, for God's sake. We were at war!'

'We were,' Felix agreed wearily, 'but we aren't now. Daphne, he's made a great effort to come back here to thank those who saved his life and pay his respects to the rest of his crew. I wonder if I'd have bothered to do the same if our positions had been reversed.'

'Suit yourself,' Daphne shrugged, 'but I'd better warn you, Mavis Gurney's just been telling me that it nearly came to blows in the Magpie last night when her Bert discovered who this German was. She says it was Bert that helped cut him down on the say-so of John Shepherd. She says Bert wasn't happy about it then and he isn't happy to see him turning up here again now.'

'Bert Gurney and his cronies are an ignorant bunch,' Felix said. 'And you shouldn't be spreading their gossip.'

'I'm not spreading it,' snapped Daphne. 'I'm simply telling you what Mavis said when she arrived this morning. I thought you'd want to know.'

'Fair enough,' sighed Felix and then added, 'Did you tell her he'd been here?'

'I may have mentioned it.'

'And why I'm taking him to Cheddar this morning?'

'Probably.' Daphne was tired of the conversation. 'Does it really matter?'

'It's my business,' he said tightly, 'and I'd prefer you didn't pass it round the village.'

'Sorry,' said Daphne who clearly wasn't. 'I didn't know it was a secret!'

Felix closed his eyes and drawing a deep breath, said, 'I'm going now. I'll see you later.'

He was exasperated by Daphne's casual spread of his

private doings. It was no one's business but his own if he chose to befriend a German airman who was visiting the village, but now Mavis Gurney knew about the names being added to the gravestone, it was only a matter of time before that, too, would be the talk of the village.

'Don't forget I'll need the car when you get back,' Daphne reminded him. 'Jane and I'll probably go to the pictures, so I may not be back until late.'

Felix had got used to Daphne's visits to Jane in Bristol. He almost looked forward to them, having the house to himself; and she always seemed in a better mood when she came home again. 'Don't worry,' he said, 'I'll be back well before lunch.'

Daphne watched him drive out of the gate and smiled. At least she'd have the car for the rest of the day and Felix wasn't expecting her home early. There were occasions when Felix needed the car himself and said she couldn't have it. Then she had to ring Jane and say she couldn't come, disappointing them both. Occasionally she took the bus, but it wound its way through all the villages before it finally reached the city, taking for ever, and the last bus home left at ten to six.

She went into the farm office to get an envelope. It was time to send her mother this month's money for Janet. Although the deal she had made with Mum had been agreed four years ago, Daphne had risked missing only the one payment. She'd received her mother's warning then and now she was even more determined there was no chance that Felix should discover who Janet really was, not after her carefully constructed explanation of why she couldn't have children. She had even considered putting the money up by a pound to help keep Mum quiet. Things were a little more flexible financially now, but in the end she decided to wait until her mother asked for more. After all, why pay more if she didn't have to? It meant she could squirrel away a little bit more for herself.

She addressed the envelope and set out for the post office to buy her postal order. She didn't often buy one in the village, she didn't want Nancy Bright to note the regularity of the purchase and draw conclusions of her own. Those might, eventually, get back to Felix, but today she wanted to catch up on the gossip about the German airman, and the post office was the place to do that. Mavis was still working in the house, so the latest news about the grave wouldn't yet be common knowledge, but Daphne was interested in hearing more about the previous night in the pub. As she reached the village green she saw Felix setting off for Cheddar, the airman sitting beside him in the car. She wasn't the only one who'd seen them and it was already a topic of conversation in the post office when she walked in.

'How kind of your husband to give that poor crippled man a lift, Mrs Felix,' Nancy said when she saw who'd come in. 'Is he taking him somewhere special, or just for a lovely ride around the countryside?'

'I really couldn't say, Miss Bright,' replied Daphne lightly.

'I saw your husband showing him the grave in the church-yard yesterday,' remarked Doreen Marston.

'Did you? How interesting.'

'Didn't you know?'

'He may have mentioned it, I don't remember.' She crossed to the counter and said, 'I'd like a five-pound postal order, please.'

'He's German, you know, the cripple,' Nancy said as she dealt with the postal order.

'Yes, I heard.'

'He was the one that crashed during the war, he told Bert Gurney so in the pub last night, bold as brass.'

'I know, Mavis told me.'

'Mavis? Yes I s'pose she would,' Nancy said as she handed over the postal order. 'She's a bit of a gossip.'

'All right for some, buying five-pound postal orders,' remarked Doreen when Daphne had left the shop. She watched through the window as Daphne slid the postal order into its envelope, sealed it and dropped it into the post box.

'She does that sometimes,' Nancy said. 'Sends it to her ageing mother in London.'

'How d'you know that?' asked Doreen.

'Well, she certainly sends it somewhere,' Nancy said. 'Stands to reason it's to her mother. Certainly goes to London, cos I saw it on the envelope once.'

Felix and Dieter had a very satisfactory morning in Cheddar and with encouragement from Felix, Ben Turvey agreed to come up to Wynsdown in the next few days and add the three names to the headstone.

'You are very good to come with me to make the arrangements,' Dieter said. 'It would have been more difficult without you, I think. People do not like that I am German.'

Neither of them had mentioned the confrontation in the Magpie the previous evening, but now Felix said, 'I heard some of the local men were difficult in the bar last night. I'm sorry.'

Dieter shrugged. 'It was nothing, just some bad words. No fight.'

'No, well, I'm very glad to hear that.'

When they arrived back in the village they found the Magpie had just opened its doors for its lunchtime session.

'Come on,' Felix said. 'Let's have a drink. You'll have a beer with me, won't you?'

Dieter smiled. 'Thank you, Felix, I should like very much to drink beer with you.'

Together they walked into the bar where Mabel was polishing glasses.

'Ah, Mabel,' Felix said cheerfully, 'two halves of bitter, please.' He turned to Dieter. 'Have to make it only a half at a midweek lunchtime, I'm afraid.' He paid Mabel, who had pulled the beer in silence, and then said, 'Shall we sit outside? It's such a lovely day.' He picked up their glasses and led the way to the tables set out on the green. Dieter followed him, well aware of what he was doing and grateful for his support.

They sat down in the sun and drank their beer in full view of anyone who was interested; the ex-pilot squire and the German airman. A man came round the corner and seeing him, Felix waved and beckoned him over.

'John,' he said. 'Meet Dieter Karhausen. Dieter, this is John Shepherd, he's the man to thank for rescuing you from the tree.'

Dieter got to his feet and extended his hand. 'I have to thank you for my life,' he said.

John grasped the outstretched hand. 'I'm glad to see you fit and well,' he said. 'You didn't look as if you'd survive the last time I saw you.'

'Will you have a beer, John?' Felix asked.

John glanced at his watch. 'Why not?' he said. 'I've come to fetch the grandchildren and take them back to the farm for the afternoon. Gives Charlotte a break, but there's time for a swift half!' He glanced round and said, 'She's bringing them down here to meet me anyway.'

Felix went inside for the beer and John and Dieter sat down again. 'Are you quite recovered?' John asked.

'As good as I'll ever be,' Dieter assured him. 'I wanted

to thank you and your family for your help.' He paused, wondering if he should say more and then added, 'I have seen Charlotte and heard your son had an accident. I am very sorry.'

'Thank you,' John said. 'We all miss him.' He gave a faint smile which suddenly widened as he saw Charlotte and the four children emerging from the lane onto the green. He half-stood and waved to them, and the next moment he was engulfed as the children rushed across the grass to greet him, the twins clambering up onto his knee, Edie and Johnny coming to stand beside him, eyeing Dieter with interest. Charlotte followed slowly, pushing an empty pushchair and seeing Dieter, smiled.

'Hallo,' she said.

Felix reappeared with John's beer, and putting it on the table pulled up a chair for Charlotte. Thanking him with a smile, she turned down his offer of a drink.

'No thanks, Felix, once Gramp has got this lot in tow, I'm going back to the house. I've a load of things to do and a piano lesson to give at the end of the afternoon.'

John finished his beer quickly and then gathered his grand-children together. 'Come on, you lot,' he said. 'Davy, Danny, into the pushchair or we'll late for our lunch and Gr'ma will be very cross with me.'

'I want to walk,' announced Davy.

'I want to walk.' Danny echoed his brother.

'You can walk when we get to the footpath,' John said firmly. 'On the road you're in the chair.'

He turned to Dieter. 'I know my wife would like to see you,' he said. 'So do call out to the farm any time.'

'Thank you, Mr Shepherd, I would like to come. Felix will tell me the way, perhaps.'

'Sunday afternoon all right?' Felix asked. 'I'll bring him.'

'Fine, we'll see you then,' said John as he took Edie by the hand. 'Now then, Edie, you can help me push.'

They set off across the green, Danny and Davy crammed into the pushchair, Johnny striding on ahead and Edie helping her grandfather to push the twins. Turning back, Dieter caught a smile pass between Charlotte and Felix. It was nothing, and yet, he felt, it was something; the slightest softening of expression, a gentleness about the eyes, an unconscious affection. He turned away so that they should not see him notice. He realised he was not surprised. He had met Daphne the afternoon before. He'd found her cold and distant and had wondered at Felix's choice of wife. Clearly there was no warmth between them.

But Charlotte? Charlotte was beautiful. She had a serenity about her, despite having four young children to bring up on her own. She bore little resemblance to his memory of the pale-faced girl who'd stood over him as he struggled with his pain all those years ago. There were lines on her face etched by the sorrow she'd had to bear, but they added depth to her countenance and when she smiled her whole being seemed illuminated from within. She smiled at Dieter now and he felt his heart flip, but he had no illusions. He was not the sort of man girls fell in love with, certainly not girls as beautiful as Charlotte.

When John and the children were out of sight, Charlotte got reluctantly to her feet. 'Better go,' she said. 'Nice to see you again, Dieter. How much longer are you staying?'

Dieter smiled. 'I do not know. A few days more.'

As they were saying their goodbyes, Mabel came out from the bar to collect the dirty glasses.

'Of course,' Mabel said to Jack later, 'that Charlotte Shepherd's German. No wonder she was hobnobbing with him. But I'm surprised Felix Bellinger has anything to do with him, him being in the RAF.'

'War was a long time ago, Mabel,' Jack reminded her wearily.

'I know,' she said. 'Still, it just goes to show…'

Chapter 37

E thel Higgins was peeling the potatoes for tea when the pain attacked her, a stabbing pain in her abdomen. She dropped the knife into the sink and doubled up, trying to ease it away as she had for the last few days, but this time it did not ease, if anything it became sharper, making her moan with its intensity, and she slumped down onto a chair. At that moment Norman came up from the garage and found her, grey-faced and gasping.

'Ethel? What's the matter? What's the matter?'

'Nothing.' Ethel struggled to speak. 'Nothing, just—' The pain hit again and she cried out at its suddenness.

'What d'you mean, nothing?' cried Norman in alarm.

'Had some stomach ache,' Ethel gasped, 'over the past couple of days. Nothing much. Worse now.'

'You got to go to the 'ospital,' Norman said. 'Come on.' He reached forward to help her to her feet, but Ethel couldn't stand. She gripped the arms of the chair as she looked up at him, her face the colour of putty, sweat breaking out on her forehead. 'I can't,' she whispered. 'I can't move.'

'Stay still, then,' Norman instructed, heading for the door. 'I'm going to ring for an ambulance.' As he rushed down the alley to the street and the phone box on the corner, he almost crashed into Janet, running towards him on her way home.

'Hey, Dad—'

'Jan, your mum's been took ill,' he said. 'You go and sit with her, I'm going to call the ambulance.' He gave a her a little push. 'Go on, duck, I'll be back in a minute.'

Looking scared, Janet ran into the kitchen where she found her mother sitting on a chair, rocking with pain.

'Mum!' she cried. 'Mum?'

Ethel drew a deep breath and said, 'Don't worry, love. I'll be all right again directly.'

Not knowing what to do, Janet said, 'Shall I make you some tea?'

Ethel managed a smile and though she had no thought of tea, said, 'Yes. Good idea. Put the kettle on.'

Janet did as she was told and it was with great relief that she heard her father coming back up the path to the door.

'Hold on, Eth, girl,' he said. 'They're on their way.'

The kettle began to whistle, but nobody wanted tea and Norman turned off the gas. The ten minutes it took for the ambulance to arrive seemed an eternity. He paced the floor, completely at a loss, not knowing what to do, useless. Janet, whey-faced and scared, was on the verge of tears.

At last they heard the distant clang of the ambulance bell. 'You go to the end of the lane and show them where to come,' he said to Janet. 'I'll stay with Mum.'

Janet dashed off down the alley to the street, relieved to have something to do.

'Looks like it could be a burst appendix,' said one of the ambulance men as they carried Ethel out to the ambulance. 'You want to come with us?'

Norman glanced at Janet's frightened face and shook his head. He couldn't just leave her by herself.

'No,' he said. 'I'll get things sorted here and then I'll be over as quick as I can.'

'Right-ho,' said the man and with the slam of the door, the ambulance set off up the road, its bell clanging to clear its way through the traffic.

Norman went back into the kitchen and Janet ran into his arms. 'Is she going to be all right, Dad?'

'I'm sure she will,' Norman said, though he was very far from sure. 'Once they get her in the 'ospital the doctors'll know what to do.' He hugged Janet tightly. 'She may have to have an operation,' he said, 'and be in there for a while. But we can go and see her, can't we? And in the meantime, we'll have to look after each other. Now,' he looked round the kitchen, 'let's just make sure everything's OK here and then we'll head over to the 'ospital.' He checked that the gas was off and the windows closed before locking the back door and moments later they were hurrying down to the street to catch the bus.

When they reached Casualty Norman spoke to the nurse on the desk and was told that Ethel had been taken straight up to theatre.

'They needed to operate at once,' she said.

'Is she going to be all right?' asked Norman fearfully.

'I'm sorry, Mr Higgins, I can't say. The doctor will come and find you as soon as there's any news. I'll let them know you're here.'

They waited in a dingy waiting room for more than two hours. The walls, painted the colour of mud and criss-crossed with cracks, played host to a raft of yellowing posters. Norman read them all and read them all again. They could hear faint hospital noises from outside the room, the sound of voices, the squeak of a trolley, a cry of pain, but no one came to find them and the minutes dragged by.

'I'm hungry, Dad.' Janet tugged at his arm. 'Can we get something to eat?'

Norman realised he should have given her something at home, even if it were only some bread and cheese, but he'd been in such a hurry to get to the hospital, he hadn't even thought about it.

'In a little while, duck,' he said. 'We'll get fish and chips on the way home.'

Half an hour later a doctor came down to find them. He was a tall man with grey hair, clear grey eyes and a serious expression. He shook hands with Norman, introducing himself as Dr Faulkner.

'It was peritonitis,' he said. 'We had to operate at once. Your wife was lucky she came in when she did, or it might have been too late.'

'Is she going to be all right?' Norman hardly dared ask the question.

'It was touch and go,' replied the doctor. 'She'll have to stay here in hospital for a while, so that we can make sure there are no complications, but if things are straightforward from now, she should be fine and back to normal in a month or so.'

'Thank God,' breathed Norman. 'Can we see her?'

'Not today. She's only just coming round from the anaesthetic. Come in at visiting time tomorrow and she should be up to seeing you then.'

As promised, Norman bought them fish and chips on the way home, and was surprised to find that now he knew Ethel was going to recover, he was as hungry as Janet. They took the food back to the house and unwrapping the newspaper, sat down at the kitchen table to eat.

'Hadn't we better tell Daphne that Mum's been took into the 'ospital?' Janet asked through a mouthful of chips.

Norman nodded. 'Yes,' he said, 'I was just thinking the same. Trouble is, I don't know where she is... her address,

I mean. I think that Felix give it to Mum when he come here that time, just in case we ever needed it, he said.'

'Mum had it,' Janet said. 'I 'spect she put it somewhere safe.'

'Probably in the papers' box,' said her father. 'Why don't you have a look-see while I go out and lock the garage gates. With the rush to the 'ospital, I left them open, and all the world an' his wife could've been in, nicking stuff.' He screwed up the greasy newspaper and pushing it into the rubbish bin, hurried off down the alley to secure his yard.

Janet ate the last of her chips and then went to the cupboard where she knew her mother kept the old cash box. Known as the papers' box, it was where Ethel kept all the important family papers. Janet climbed onto a chair and lifted the box down from the top shelf, setting it on the table. It was locked but she guessed where the key would be. Sure enough, when she felt behind the kitchen clock her fingers found it, a small key on a piece of string.

Janet unlocked the box and as she'd expected, there were various papers her mother put there for safe keeping. There was an envelope with two five-pound notes in it, her mother's emergency money, and lying on the top was a folded paper with 'Daphne' written on the outside. Opening this up she saw a scribbled address and phone number.

Good, thought Janet. An address *and* phone number. We can ring her up and tell her what's happened.

She was about to close the box again but her curiosity was stirred by some other documents lying inside. She lifted them out and unfolded them. Birth certificates, four of them. Janet had never seen a birth certificate before and she peered at the top one. It was Daphne's.

Daphne, it informed her, had been born on 12 October 1922 in Barrack Street, Hackney. Named Daphne Ann. Father:

Norman Higgins, mechanic. Mother: Ethel Jean Higgins, formerly Brown.

Janet set the certificate aside and picked up the next one, her father's.

Norman was born on 15 March 1898 in King's Cross. His parents were named as Alfred James Higgins, a railway porter, and Mary Jane Higgins, formerly Davies.

Janet looked at this with interest. She had a vague recollection of Nan, her father's mother, but none at all of her grandfather, Alfred the railway porter.

Her mother's birth certificate named her as Ethel Jean, born 19 November 1899 in St Pancras. Her father had been John Brown, another railway porter. Was that how her parents had met, wondered Janet. Their dads working together? Her mother was named as Eliza Brown, formerly Rush.

Janet knew neither of her mother's parents, both had died in the Spanish flu outbreak after the first war. She reached for the final document, her own birth certificate, and was about to put it back with the others in the box when she noticed something. She peered at the certificate in amazement.

It gave her date of birth, 3 December 1938, and her name, *Janet*. She didn't have a second name like Daphne, but that wasn't what grabbed her attention. Her name and birthday were right, but all the rest of it was wrong. In the box for 'Father' was not her father's name, but the word 'Unknown'. In the box for 'Mother' was the name Daphne Ann Higgins.

Janet stared at the certificate. 'Daphne isn't my mother,' she said aloud. 'That's all wrong. The birth certificate people have got it wrong.' She couldn't understand it. Written there, in beautiful copperplate handwriting, were the details of her birth, but they'd got Daphne muddled with Mum and hadn't put Dad's name in the 'Father' box.

Janet heard her father's steps in the lane outside so she stuffed the birth certificate back into the cash box and quickly closed it again. What she'd seen needed thinking about and she didn't want to ask Dad about it. She'd ask Mum when they went to see her at the hospital.

When her father came back into the kitchen, he saw the cash box on the table and asked, 'Did you find Daph's address?'

Janet didn't answer, but handed him the scrap of paper.

'Oh good,' he said as he glanced down at it, 'look, there's a phone number, too. Tell you what, I'll just pop down the phone box and try and get through to her.' He pulled a handful of coins from his pocket but there weren't enough for a trunk call, so he raided the gas money in the jar on the shelf.

'Why don't you get ready for bed while I'm phoning?' he suggested. 'I won't be very long, but I think we should let Daph know that her mum's been took ill. She might want to come up and visit.' His face brightened at the thought. He loved his daughter and had been very sorry when she'd decided not to keep in touch. Perhaps, as her mother was ill, he could persuade her to come for another visit.

As soon as he'd gone out again, Janet opened the cash box and removed her birth certificate. Then she closed and locked it again and put it back on its shelf in the cupboard. The certificate she took straight upstairs and hid it under the mattress on her bed. When her father got back from making his phone call she was in bed, ready to settle down.

'Did you talk to Daphne?' she asked when he put his head round her bedroom door.

'Yes,' he replied.

'An' is she coming up?' Janet sounded excited. As a little girl she'd been fond of her sister and was sorry they hardly saw her any more.

'No, afraid not,' Norman responded sadly. 'Not for a bit, anyway. Maybe when your mum's feeling a bit better.'

Janet eyed him seriously. 'She is going to get better, i'n't she, Dad?'

'Of course she is,' he said encouragingly. 'That Dr Faulkner said it was just a matter of time. They'll look after her in the 'ospital until she's feeling well enough to come home. Now then,' he added, knowing this was a question Ethel always asked before Janet went to bed, 'you got everything ready for school in the morning?'

'Yes, of course, Dad,' Janet said and reached up for his goodnight kiss. 'There's only a week to go before the holidays.'

Janet made use of that week. She visited her mother, but when she saw her looking so pale and worn out, lying in the hospital bed, she didn't mention having found the birth certificate with the mistakes in it. No, she decided, when school finished at the end of the week she was going to find Daphne in this Wynsdown place and tell her about it. Daphne'll know what to do, she thought.

At the back of her mind there was growing unease. Several girls in her class at school didn't have fathers; girls like Rhoda whose dad had been killed in the war, and Elsie whose dad had gone to live with someone else, after. But one girl, Marion, had never had a dad. She used to say she was really a princess who'd been stolen from the hospital at birth and been given to her mother to look after. When they were younger, her friends had half believed her, but when Rhoda told her gran, her gran had laughed and said that was a load of rubbish; that Marion's mum was a fool who'd got caught. Everyone knew that Marion's dad was some soldier home on leave. 'Had his fun,' said Rhoda's gran, 'and was never seen again. Silly cow didn't even know his name.' Marion and her mum only had each other.

Could something like that have happened to Daphne? Janet wondered, before dismissing the idea as too ridiculous to be given serious consideration. No, certainly not. She, Janet, had both a mum and a dad. But the idea niggled and she needed Daphne to tell her it was all wrong.

The question of the train fare had exercised her mind, until she remembered the emergency money in the papers' box. Once her plans were laid, she faced her father with them, ready with answers to get her own way.

'We break up tomorrow, Dad,' she told him when they were eating their tea on the last evening of term. 'I'm going to go and visit Daphne then.'

'To visit Daph? When?'

'On Saturday. I'm taking the train.'

'Has she asked you?' demanded Norman in amazement.

'Sort of,' Janet lied. 'I rang her from the call box again, just to tell her how Mum was doing, and I said I wanted to come and stay for a bit. And she said OK. She's going to meet me at the station.'

'She ain't coming up here to see yer mum, then?' Norman sounded disappointed. He hadn't phoned Daphne again in the hope that if she had no news of how her mother was doing, she might decide to come up to London to find out for herself.

'Not just yet,' Janet answered, improvising quickly. 'She said we'd come back together in a week or so.'

Norman scratched his chin and thought about this. In some ways Janet going to stay with Daphne would make life a lot easier for him. He wouldn't have to worry about her once school was closed and her at a loose end. Would she be all right, going down there to Somerset on the train by herself? He said this and Janet laughed out loud.

'Oh, Dad,' she cried, 'I'm not a kid any more, I'll be fifteen at Christmas and leaving school. Of *course* I'll be all right.'

So, Norman reluctantly agreed and though Janet had already removed the emergency ten pounds from the papers' box and hidden it with the birth certificate, she accepted the pound note he gave her for her fare. That night she packed her case, putting both the birth certificate and the cash in at the bottom and piling her few clothes on top of them.

On Saturday morning Norman had been going to shut the garage and go with her to Paddington, but as he was closing up the night before, a last-minute rushed job came in, the car to be ready again by Saturday lunchtime. Norman couldn't afford to turn away business and so, reluctantly, he'd seen Janet off to catch the bus by herself. As she gave him a final hug, she said, 'I didn't tell Mum I was going. I didn't want her to worry. If you tell her, she'll be fine about it, won't she?'

Would she? Norman wasn't at all sure about that, but it was too late to consult Ethel now, and after all, Daphne was expecting Janet and was going to meet the train. Yes, he convinced himself, Janet'd be fine. It'd do her good to get out of London and spend a few days in the country, breathing fresh country air. Yes, she'd be all right.

When Janet reached Paddington station she bought herself a single ticket to Cheddar, wherever that was. She had been to the local station and made enquiries about how to get there and the man had looked it up for her. The nearest station for Wynsdown was Cheddar and she knew she had to change twice on the way. What she was going to do when she got to Cheddar she wasn't sure, perhaps there'd be a bus... yes, surely there'd be a bus. Janet was used to living in a city where buses passed every few minutes, but if there wasn't one for some reason, she had Daphne's telephone number in her pocket and she could ring up and ask to be fetched. As she boarded the train at Paddington, she felt a shiver of anticipation, a mixture of nervousness and determination. Daphne certainly wasn't expecting her, but she could hardly turn her out when she'd come all the way from London and had nowhere else to go. She gripped her suitcase tightly and set it by her feet when she'd found a window seat in a third-class carriage. The journey was long and Janet was pleased that she'd thought to bring a doorstep sandwich made with the last of the cheese ration to eat on the way. With that and an apple she'd have to make do until she got to Daphne's.

When at last she had managed the two changes required, she got out at Cheddar station. As she gave up her ticket she looked about her. The porter saw her standing alone and asked if he could help.

'You look a bit lost, miss,' he said. 'Someone meant to be coming to meet you, are they?'

Bucked up at being addressed as 'miss' as if she was a grown-up, Janet said, 'I was hoping there was a bus to Wynsdown.'

'There is,' the man told her, 'but it's Saturday. Last bus in half an hour.' He directed her to the bus stop in the main street. She saw a telephone box. Should she ring Daphne and ask her to come and fetch her? No, she decided, I'll wait and see if the bus comes. Time enough to ring Daphne if it doesn't.

Not wanting to risk missing the bus she went straight to the stop. As she waited she rehearsed what she would say when Daphne, or perhaps her husband Felix, opened the front door and found her on the doorstep; what they might say to her was a different thing altogether. When the bus arrived she clambered aboard, paid her fare and asked the driver to tell

433

her when they got there. Then as the bus lumbered out of the village and up the hill, Janet stared out of the window at the alien countryside; open fields, no streets and hardly a house in sight.

The bus rumbled into a village and stopped outside a pub on the village green.

'Wynsdown,' the driver told her and she gathered up her suitcase and, along with several other passengers, got off. Here there were houses all round, but which one was Daphne's? The address just said The Manor House, Wynsdown. Which house was The Manor House? Somehow she'd thought it would be obvious. Who could she ask? There were a few people about, but none of them was taking any notice of her. She glanced back at the pub. Better go and ask in there, she supposed. She was about to do so when she saw a figure walking across the green towards her. She thought she recognised him but stared at him for a moment or two just to be sure before stepping hesitantly forward.

Felix had been to see his mother. Just recently she seemed much more frail, and he liked to look in on her every couple of days. They'd had a cup of tea and a chat and then he'd said he had to get back.

'There's a stack of paperwork waiting for me,' he said. 'Daphne's gone in to Bristol, to see Jane, so I'll have a chance to get on with it before she gets back. We'll see you tomorrow for lunch.'

As he was approaching the village green the Cheddar bus arrived, disgorging its passengers outside the pub. The sky was grey with dark clouds threatening rain and most of the people scurried away, hoping to be home before the heavens opened. One lone traveller stood, a suitcase at her feet, watching the bus disappear. She was young, about fourteen or fifteen.

Even as he looked at her he thought she seemed vaguely familiar, but he couldn't place her. She came towards him, clearly
wanting to speak to him. Was she lost? he wondered.

'Felix?' She stopped in front of him and looked up into his
bewildered face. 'Felix? It is you, isn't it?' Now they were so
close she felt suddenly uncertain. 'Felix?'

Felix nodded, saying, 'Yes, I'm Felix Bellinger, and you
are...?' He let the question hang in the air.

'You don't recognise me, me do you? I'm not surprised
really, you haven't seen me for ages. I'm Janet. Daph's sister.'

Felix stared at her, she'd only been a child when he'd last
seen her. 'Janet?' he said incredulously. 'What are you doing
here?'

'I've come to stay. Mum's not well and Dad's sent me to
Daphne.' She shifted awkwardly on her feet, uncomfortable
with the lie, but compounding it said, 'He wrote. Didn't you
get the letter? Didn't you know I was coming?'

'No,' Felix replied, 'no we didn't, but that doesn't matter
now you're here. It's lovely to see you. Come on, let's go
home. Have you had anything to eat?'

'I had a sandwich on the train.'

'And you came all this way by yourself? On the train by
yourself?'

'Of course,' cried Janet scornfully, 'I'm not a baby. I'm
nearly fifteen! And Dad said Daphne would be there to meet
me at Cheddar, but when she wasn't, there was a porter who
told me which bus to catch... and here I am.'

'Well,' said Felix, 'I'm glad you're here safe and sound.
Come on, let's get home before it rains. I think Daphne's
visiting a friend in Bristol, but she'll be back soon.'

*

Daphne was indeed visiting Jane. She hadn't seen her for two weeks and she'd driven up to Bristol to spend the whole day with her. Since the day Jane had actually seduced her, and they'd passed from being friends to being lovers, Daphne had lived a double life. She had to be careful, but she found that she could cope better as Felix's wife now that she had the security of Jane in the background. She never encouraged intimacy with him, but on the rare occasions he did take her in his arms, though she still found it distasteful, she found herself able to submit, lying passively until he'd finished and rolled away.

With Jane it was quite different. Jane usually took the lead as she had that first day, but Daphne never held back, was never submissive unless required to be, and then it was submission with an animal edge. When she did take control it left them gasping, exhausted and yet aching for more.

Now they were indeed soulmates, they could talk about anything and everything. Daphne had finally told Jane how she had lied to Felix about being unable to conceive. 'I still have to be very careful, just in case.'

'Well,' Jane had giggled, 'you're quite safe with me. I promise not to get you pregnant.'

Today, Jane was waiting for her, her face flushed with anticipatory excitement.

'Did you bring it?' she cried as Daphne let herself in to the flat.

'Da-dah!' Daphne held up the carrier bag and Jane beamed at her. 'Can we do it today?'

'What I brought it for,' grinned Daphne.

'And you didn't let Felix…?' Jane let the question hang.

'Course not, silly,' said Daphne. 'It was your idea!'

'Go and put it on then. I promise not to look.'

She waited in eager anticipation for Daphne to reappear,

and when she did, dressed in her blue coronation dress, Jane found she had difficulty in breathing.

They spent the whole day in bed, getting out only to open one of Peter Bellinger's bottles of wine and bring the brimming glasses back to bed.

'Felix'll be wondering why his wine cellar is nearly empty,' Jane said as she drained the last of the wine into their glasses. They lay, completely relaxed amid the tumbled sheets, the bedroom windows open to summer air that cooled their heated bodies.

'I don't think he goes down there much, but anyway, there are still loads of bottles, all in racks and I always take from the back.'

This weekend Jane had both days off, and Daphne had originally suggested that she stay the night as she sometimes did, telling Felix that they were going to the pictures, or meeting some of Jane's other friends.

'Sorry,' Jane said, 'no can do. I've said I'll go home this evening and visit the parents.'

Daphne pulled a face. 'That means I shan't see you till Friday!'

'Well,' Jane said, absent-mindedly stroking Daphne's thigh, 'I'm staying home till after lunch tomorrow. Why don't we meet up at the quarry after that?' She flicked her tongue across her lips. 'Know what I mean?'

Daphne did know and smiled. They had met several times in the old quarry, sheltered beneath an overhang of rock and hidden from view by the brambles that had long since colonised the area. It was a private place, their private place, perfect for illicit love.

'Do my best,' she said. 'Probably have to have lunch with the mother-in-law, but I'll see you there, later on.'

Daphne gently removed Jane's fingers from her thigh and leant over to kiss her.

'I'd better get going,' she said as she slid off the bed. She hated to leave Jane lying back on the bed, her long legs still spread, but she gave her one final kiss and then another before getting up and putting her clothes on.

Jane watched her as she dressed. 'Where does Felix think you are today?' she asked idly.

'With you,' Daphne replied. 'He knows I'm with you, but he doesn't know what we're doing.' She rolled her eyes. 'I make that bit up.'

'I suppose I'd better get up, too,' said Jane, without moving. 'I'm expected in time for dinner. But I'll see you tomorrow.'

'Promise.' And with that Daphne closed the bedroom door firmly on the sight of Jane naked on the bed, and left the flat.

Outside, she walked through the freshness of the evening to where she'd parked the car. Her whole body seemed to be vibrating with life as she sat in the car and drove home. She was amazed that Felix hadn't noticed the change in her when she came home from visiting Jane in Bristol. Perhaps he had. Perhaps he thought she had a lover there, that she was having an affair. Well, she thought as she drove up over the hills towards Wynsdown, she was, but not the sort he would imagine.

She pulled into the manor driveway and parked the car. As she got out, the front door opened and she saw someone standing on the step. For a moment she didn't recognise her daughter, but when she did it was as if the whole world were tilting.

'Janet?'

'Hi, Daphne,' cried the girl. 'Surprise, surprise!'

'Janet, what the hell are you doing here?' Daphne stared at her daughter in horror. 'What's happened, are Mum and Dad here too?'

'Course not.' Janet shook her head. 'You know Mum's in the hospital having her appendix out, and Dad's got the garage.'

Daphne glanced into the hall to see if Felix was near enough to overhear. She hadn't told him that her mother was ill, she knew he would have nagged her to go and visit and she had no intention of doing so.

'When did you get here? How did you come?'

'On the train, of course.' Janet fixed her sister with a stare as she repeated the lie she'd told Felix earlier. 'Didn't you get Dad's letter, saying I was coming? Telling you to meet me at the station?'

'No, I didn't. Why've you come?'

At that moment Felix appeared at the front door. 'Aren't you girls coming in? You're getting wet!'

'Of course,' said Daphne, gathering her wits. 'I was just so surprised to see our Janet here, and all so grown up.' She reached out and took her daughter's hand. 'Let's go inside, and you can tell me all about it.'

Determined to keep the conversation light and general until she could get Janet alone to discover the situation back in Hackney, Daphne chatted carelessly as she rustled up a scratch meal of scrambled eggs and bacon. As Daphne placed the plate in front of her, Janet stared at the food. How did Daphne get hold of enough eggs and bacon to fill three plates?

'You didn't tell me your mother was in hospital,' Felix said to Daphne when he joined them at the table. 'Janet's been telling me how she was rushed in with a burst appendix.'

'I didn't know,' asserted Daphne, the warning in her eyes silencing Janet before she could say anything to the contrary.

'Janet said your father rang when it happened.'

'He can't have got through,' Daphne said, 'unless of course Mavis took a message and forgot to pass it on. It would be just like her.'

Felix let the matter drop. He knew that Daphne must be lying, but decided not to have it out with her in front of her sister.

'So, tell me how poor Mum is doing,' Daphne said, turning back to Janet.

'She's getting better, but she'll be in the hospital for a while yet,' Janet replied, adding with wide eyes, 'She nearly died, you know. The doctor who talked to Dad said that she only just got there in time.'

Hearing this, Daphne was surprised to feel a twinge of anxiety. Her mother had been so near to death and she hadn't known. How might she have felt if Mum had died and she hadn't seen her again? Relief, tinged with guilt... or guilt tinged with relief?

'But she's on the mend now, isn't she?'

Janet, her mouth full of scrambled egg, nodded.

'Well, that's good then,' Daphne said.

At the end of the meal Felix said he had work to do and

disappeared into the farm office. Daphne gathered up the dirty plates and put them in the sink.

'Better get these sorted, I suppose,' she said, turning on the tap. 'Then I'll show you where you'll sleep.'

'Oh, I've been up there already,' Janet told her. 'Felix showed me.'

They had hurried home as it began to drizzle, Felix leading the way down the lane and in through the manor gates. When she saw the house Janet stood stock-still, staring.

'Is this your house?' she whispered. 'Does Daphne live here?'

'Yes, this is where we live. Come on, Janet, let's get in out of the rain.' He opened the front door and Janet followed him inside, her eyes round at the sight of her sister's home.

Felix had been rather at a loss as to what to do next. 'Tell you what,' he said. 'Why don't I show you where you'll be sleeping and you can unpack while I make us both a cup of tea and perhaps find some cake.' He picked up her bag and led the way upstairs, opening the door of the blue spare room.

'This is your room,' he said, exactly as if he'd been expecting her and the room had been prepared. He stood aside to let her in.

Janet was entranced by the room with its blue curtains and blue bedcovers. There was a fireplace with an embroidered screen covering it, a chest of drawers with a china ballerina dancing across the top and a wardrobe built into one corner. She went to the window and kneeling up on its window seat, looked out over the driveway and the front garden. Fancy Daphne living in a house like this. No wonder she didn't want to come back to visit them in Hackney.

'I'll leave you to it,' Felix said. 'Bathroom's just opposite. Come down when you're ready.'

Janet had listened to his steps going down the stairs and then crept back out onto the landing. She used the toilet and then went quickly and quietly along the landing opening doors and peering into the rooms beyond. It was clear which was Daphne and Felix's, furnished with a large bed, a heavy old wardrobe and a dressing table untidy with bottles and jars. Some of Daphne's clothes were heaped on a chair, but apart from some slippers under the bed and a shirt thrown over another chair, there seemed to be little of Felix in the room. She peeped into the other rooms, one of which had obviously been Felix's childhood bedroom, with a well-filled bookcase and a shelf displaying model aeroplanes, but the rest looked Spartan and unused. She closed the doors on those and went back into her own room. She didn't unpack her clothes, simply removed the birth certificate and put it under her pillow, ready to show it to Daphne when the moment arose. It had been as she closed the case again that she'd heard the car turn into the drive and ran down the stairs to greet her sister.

'Well,' said Daphne when the kitchen was clear, 'let's go and sit down and you can tell me why you really came.' She saw the light showing under the door to Felix's office and knowing he was safely out of the way, led Janet into the sitting room, shutting the door firmly behind her. 'Now,' she said, 'what are you doing here?'

'We broke up for the holidays and with Mum in the hospital for some time yet, Dad thought it'd be a good idea if I came to you for a while.'

'What did Mum say?'

Janet shrugged. 'She doesn't know, or she didn't. 'Spect Dad's told her by now.'

'I can't believe it was Dad's idea to send you off down

here.' Daphne fixed her daughter with a gimlet eye. 'In fact, I don't believe it. It was your idea, wasn't it?'

'He wrote to you.'

'No, he didn't,' said Daphne firmly. 'You're lying. You lied to Felix and now you're lying to me. I'm not stupid, Janet.'

Janet shifted awkwardly under Daphne's gaze. 'I wanted to see you.'

'Did you?' Daphne's voice was laden with sarcasm. 'Or did you just want to come and sponge off us for a few weeks?'

'I wanted to ask you something,' Janet said defensively. She hadn't been sure how welcome she was going to be, but had been more worried about Felix's reaction to her unannounced arrival than Daphne's. She'd got it wrong. Felix had been welcoming, but Daphne was decidedly hostile.

'Oh,' said Daphne cautiously, 'and what was that?'

Janet decided to grab the bull by the horns and said, 'Are you my mother?'

'What?' Daphne, startled by the question, but pretty sure her mother would not have told Janet about her parentage, managed to inject laughing incredulity into her voice. 'What on earth gave you that crazy idea?'

'Well, are you?' demanded Janet, her eyes never leaving Daphne's face.

'No, of course not! Where did you get that from?'

Janet evaded the question. 'I was going to ask Mum, but with her being so ill, I thought it was better to come and talk to you.'

'Well, I'm glad you didn't suggest such a thing to Mum,' Daphne said. 'She'd have been devastated. And,' she went on, 'I hope you didn't say anything to Dad, either. What*ever* made you think such a thing?'

Daphne's fierce protestations were beginning to convince

Janet that the fears she'd tried to set aside had been justified after all. Birth certificates couldn't be wrong, she'd known that really; so, she was indeed like Marion and her father was unknown. Why did Daphne keep denying it? Janet wanted to know more and decided not to mention the birth certificate yet.

'Well,' she said, 'it was something someone said at school.'

'Who said? What?'

'Rhoda's gran told Rhoda.'

'Told her what?'

'Told her I was your daughter, not Mum's.'

'Well, I don't know who Rhoda's gran is,' growled Daphne, 'but she's lying, lying in her teeth.' She reached out and took Janet's hand. 'Don't think about it any more,' she said. 'It's all a pack of lies. I'm glad you came to me and didn't worry Mum and Dad with any of this.'

Janet looked her firmly in the face and said, 'Does Felix know?'

At that moment the sitting-room door opened and Felix came in. Overhearing this last remark, he said, 'Does Felix know what?'

'That Daphne ain't my sister. She's my mum!'

Daphne fought to control the impulse to slap Janet hard across the mouth as Felix, startled, said, 'What? What did you say?'

'Janet's got some bee in her bonnet,' said Daphne quickly. 'Something about being my daughter. Some girl at school's been spreading lies and of course she's upset.' She forced a smile to her lips and said, 'I'm just thankful that she came to me and didn't worry our parents with such rubbish.'

'Janet, Daphne's right,' Felix said gently. 'We haven't been able to have children... because Daphne can't. She has

444

something wrong inside and can't have a baby. So, you see, it's just an unkind rumour someone is spreading about you.'

'You're wrong,' said Janet. 'She can have a baby, she had me!' Red-faced, she was almost in tears. She flung herself out of the room and up the stairs, returning moments later with the birth certificate in her hand. She thrust it at Felix. 'There,' she said. 'This was in Mum's papers' box. I found it when I was looking for your address.'

Daphne jumped to her feet and made a grab for the document, but Felix twisted away and unfolded it. He scanned its details and then read it again, his face paling beneath its summer tan. Without a word he handed it back to Janet and walked out of the room.

Daphne snatched it from her, crumpling it into a ball and throwing it across the room. 'You stupid little cow!' she snarled. 'You've ruined everything!'

'No,' cried Janet. 'You ruined everything. Why didn't you tell me?'

'It was Mum's idea. There was no reason for anyone to know. It was to protect you, you silly little bitch. So that you wouldn't be a bastard!'

'Nothing to do with you, then?' snapped Janet. She was not stupid or silly and she had a great deal of both her mother and her grandmother in her. 'Not your fault that you got pregnant sleeping around with soldiers.'

'He was a sailor, actually,' snapped Daphne, 'and it only happened once.'

'So all my life has been a lie, right from the moment I was born.' In that moment, Janet shrugged off her childhood and looked at her mother with adult eyes. 'If you'd admitted it when I asked you just now, treated me like a grown-up, you could have explained and Felix need never have known.'

She walked across the room and retrieved the crumpled birth certificate, smoothing it between her fingers, folding it carefully and putting it in her pocket. She stalked to the door before turning to Daphne and saying, 'You say *I* ruined everything? No. It ain't my fault "*Mummy*", it's yours!'

Daphne heard her stamping up the stairs and then the slam of her bedroom door. Stupid child! Stupid, stupid child! She paced the room, her mind working furiously. How was she going to placate Felix now? He would know she had lied to him from the start, that she hadn't been a virgin on their wedding night. He would probably guess that she had actively been avoiding conceiving a child, even though she knew it was his dearest wish. What was he going to say? What was he going to do? She needed to get away. She needed Jane. She'd go to Jane. But Jane wasn't at the flat, she was staying with her parents. Daphne went out into the hall. The house was silent. She crept up the stairs and saw lines of light showing beneath the doors of both the blue spare room and Felix's old room. The door to their bedroom, Felix's and hers, stood open and the room was in darkness. She walked quietly along the landing, went in, shut the door and locked it behind her.

Janet lay in bed in the blue room. She had been unprepared for the extreme reaction her revelations had provoked. She was sorry for Felix. He'd been kind to her and she liked him. He'd been so chillingly angry when he'd looked at the birth certificate, it was clear that Daphne had never told him that she'd had a child. And Daphne? Daphne was raging! What on earth was going to happen in the morning?

Exhausted, Janet closed her eyes. It had been a long day and despite the turmoil of her emotions, she finally drifted into an uneasy sleep.

Felix did not sleep. He too lay on his bed, his mind

churning with what he'd learned that evening and the wider implications. Janet was Daphne's daughter, that much was clear, and it meant that the whole of his life with Daphne was founded on a lie. She had pretended to be a virgin, refusing to sleep with him until they were married. A lie, the first lie. When he'd met her, he wouldn't have been surprised to discover she'd had some sexual experience; the way some girls behaved had altered during the war. He wouldn't have blamed her for it. Maybe he could have come to accept that she already had a child if she had told him, if she'd been honest and perhaps explained the circumstances. But she'd lied, she had lied because she wanted him to marry her. Not for love, he could see that now, but for what marriage to him would bring. He'd loved her, but she'd used him. She had lied about not being able to have children. He had believed her, but Janet was the living proof of that lie.

Felix's anger was cold. The hot flashes of anger that had erupted occasionally during their marriage were nothing to the ice-cold anger that gripped him now. Their whole marriage was founded on lies.

Daphne spent the night gathering her things together. She would pack her bags and go with Jane when she returned to Bristol in the evening; leave Felix to stew in his own juice, and as for that stupid girl, Janet, well, she could take herself back to London and good riddance.

'I'm leaving,' she told Felix next morning. 'I'll go and stay with Jane for a while. She'll put me up until I decide what I'm going to do. I'll go with her when she goes back to Bristol this evening.'

'Suit yourself,' replied Felix. 'What about Janet?'

'What about her? Send her back to London, I should.'

Daphne had tried to ring Jane at Charing Farmhouse, but

there was no reply and she realised that the Shepherds must have gone to church. She glanced at her watch and seeing that the service would soon be over, she decided to walk up the lane in the hope of being able to snatch a quick word with Jane; put her in the picture. When she reached the church, she found the congregation already spilling out onto the village green. Jane was standing with her parents as they chatted with the Masterses. Edging forward, Daphne heard them talking about the German airman who'd turned up in the village. She caught Jane's eye, but Jane merely smiled and with the faintest shake of her head indicated that she couldn't talk just now. Daphne, who certainly didn't want to explain what had happened last night to anyone else, nodded and having mouthed 'the quarry', she moved away again. She would meet Jane as planned in the afternoon and tell her what had happened then.

She didn't go back to the manor until she saw Felix and Janet leaving the house and heading towards Eden Lodge. Was he really taking Janet there for lunch? She'd give anything to see old Ma Bellinger's face when they were introduced. She'd lay money on the fact that Felix would introduce her as Daphne's sister, and how would snobby Marjorie deal with Felix's cockney teenage sister-in-law?

She brought the cases she'd packed down to the front hall and left them ready to put into Jane's car when she collected her later. She put some buttered bread, a hard-boiled egg and an apple into a basket for her lunch, picked up the picnic rug and set off to meet Jane. She'd be early, but she didn't mind that and she was determined to be away from the manor when Felix got home again.

Chapter 39

Felix didn't send Janet straight back to London, as Daphne had suggested. He took her round to Eden Lodge for lunch, and having introduced her to his mother as his sister-in-law, he half-explained the situation.

'Janet came down here to stay with us because their mother's in hospital,' he said, 'but unfortunately Daphne isn't here just now so I wondered if Janet could come to you for the night. It wouldn't be right for her to stay with me, alone in the house.'

'Where is Daphne?' asked Marjorie. 'Has she gone to London to visit her mother?'

'No,' Felix replied abruptly. 'She's left.'

'Left? As in left for good?'

'I assume so.'

'I see,' said Marjorie, even though she didn't. She wasn't really surprised that their marriage was in trouble, what did surprise her was the fact that Daphne had apparently walked out leaving everything, everything she'd schemed and planned for, behind. Marjorie bit her tongue and asked for no further explanation. Felix would tell her in time if he wanted to and it certainly wasn't the time for saying 'I told you so!' In the meantime, she agreed that it wouldn't be proper for Janet to stay at the manor with only Felix living there and she'd make up a bed for her at Eden Lodge.

'I would prefer you didn't discuss what happened last night with my mother,' Felix had said to Janet before they set out. 'I'm going to introduce you as Daphne's sister. Please let's stick with that for now.'

Janet, shaken by the passions her revelation had unleashed, had been happy to agree. She'd woken this morning wishing she'd never come, and lying in bed, wondered how quickly she could get back to the safe familiarity of the home; back to Mum and Dad. She wished she'd never found the birth certificate. Mum was her mum, and Dad was her dad, whatever that piece of paper said. She didn't want to see Daphne, she didn't want to see Felix, but she couldn't stay in her bedroom for ever, so, eventually, she plucked up courage and came cautiously downstairs. She found Felix in the kitchen, drinking a cup of coffee, but, thankfully, there was no sign of Daphne. She paused on the threshold and he looked up.

'I'm sorry,' she began and then stopped. She had no idea what else to say.

Felix gave a bleak smile. 'Don't be,' he said, 'it would all have come out at some time. It's not your fault.'

'Where's Daph?'

'She's gone out. I think she's going to stay with a friend for a few days, until things blow over. Come and have some breakfast.'

'I want to go home,' said Janet, a quiver in her voice.

Felix looked at her pale and anxious face and smiled at her. 'Of course you do,' he said gently, 'but I don't think you can today. Tomorrow I'll take you in to Bristol and put you on the train.' When he'd suggested that she might like to stay the night with his mother she leaped at the idea. She didn't want to spend a moment longer under Daphne's roof; she never wanted to see her again.

Janet was almost as impressed with Eden Lodge as she had been with the manor: big rooms with comfortable furniture, lovely curtains and pictures on the walls. When they sat down in the dining room to a lunch of roast chicken with potatoes and vegetables she couldn't help saying, 'Where do you get all this food? We never have food like this.'

'It's because we live in the country,' Marjorie said. 'Most people keep hens so there are plenty of eggs and nearly everyone grows some vegetables. We're spoiled today because one of our hens had stopped laying and so she's providing us with meat rather than eggs.'

Janet put down her knife and fork and looked at the meat on her plate. Chicken? Could she really eat that? She'd never eaten chicken. But the aroma arising from her plate was so appetising, she picked up her cutlery again and cut off a tiny piece of the meat to taste. It was delicious and before long her plate was empty.

'My dad's got an allotment and Mum cooks what he grows.' She hesitated as she thought of Mum in their small kitchen, but then went on, 'But we don't get nothing like this.'

After lunch Felix left Janet with Marjorie and set off to collect Dieter from the Magpie. On the way up the hill, Dieter spoke of the vicar and the dedication of the updated stone. 'He is a very good man, I think,' he said, puffing a little as the path got steeper. Felix paused for a moment, ostensibly to show Dieter the view but in fact to allow him time to catch his breath. They stood for a moment on a ridge and Felix pointed out the various places visible.

'I love the view from up here,' he said. 'You can see for miles.' He pointed across to the sea shimmering in the distance. 'That's the Bristol Channel and beyond that you can see the coast of Wales.' He turned and pointed to the clump of trees further over, standing out against the clear blue of the summer sky. 'That's Charing Coppice, over there,' he said. 'That's where you fetched up in your tree.'

Dieter followed the line of his finger, but shook his head. 'I don't remember,' he said.

'Probably a good thing,' Felix said. 'I wouldn't want to remember if it was me.'

He'd already told Dieter that he'd been a fighter pilot, and Dieter had said, 'They were all very brave, your pilots. We couldn't beat them down.'

'Shit scared much of the time,' Felix said.

'That's what makes them brave,' said Dieter, 'fighting on when shit scared.'

'I suppose it was the same for your lot,' said Felix.

'Yes, too many dead... on both sides.'

Now, they walked on in companionable silence and reaching the top of the hill, dropped down into a shallow valley on the other side.

'Nearly there.' Felix could see Dieter was struggling, but it was clear that he wasn't going to give up.

'Good!' Dieter grinned at him, but his face was covered with a sheen of sweat.

Further on, the path joined an overgrown track that led towards a rocky outcrop, stark fingers of rock pointing upward, and below them the open crater of the worked-out quarry. They followed the track until it reached the edge of the rocks, where it dipped down into the hollow below. Long years of extracting stone by hand had left a semicircular gash in the hillside, now gradually being reclaimed by nature.

Felix paused again and said, 'There's the quarry, the plane hit the ground just by those rocks. My father was one of the first there, but it was a fireball, nothing they could do.'

The two men stood together, looking down. 'I'll wait here,' Felix said, 'if you'd like to go down on your own.'

'No,' said Dieter after a slight hesitation, 'no, we go together, as friends now.'

They walked into the quarry, its rocky walls and floor now half-covered with scrub and brambles. Dieter went ahead to where it was still possible to see the blackened stone where the aircraft had burned so fiercely. The summer sun warmed his face as he stood and remembered Leutnant Franz Herschel, Oberfähnrich Alex Braun, Oberfeldwebel Joseph Adler. He guessed there had been very few remains to be carried down to the churchyard and buried, but he knew their names, had flown with them as a team, and now those names would be carved on their headstone. If little else, their names would remain. Dieter closed his eyes.

Felix stood in silence beside him, wondering if he were praying, or fighting tears, or simply remembering his comrades. A rustling in the bushes as a bird swooped out and into the air made Felix look round. His eyes rested on a jutting piece of rock and a memory, long forgotten, returned to him and made him smile. It had been under that rock, in the hidden hollow below it, that he'd first kissed a girl. What was her name? Angela, yes, that was it, Angela someone who'd come to stay at the manor with his cousins, Clive and Chris, one summer. She'd been older than he and knew what she was doing and it had been most exciting. How old had he been? About fifteen, probably; an eternity ago.

Dieter was walking slowly round the rocky floor and when he reached a convenient chunk of stone, he sat down, pleased to give his aching legs a rest before the walk back to the village.

'You all right?' Felix asked, concerned.

'Of course,' Dieter replied. 'I just rest a little and think of my friends.' He turned his face to the sun and again closed his eyes. Felix wandered across to the jutting rocks and scrambled up the side until he came to the overhang. He grinned at the thought of his fifteen-year-old self, clasped in the arms of Angela, learning that when you kissed someone it was better if you opened your mouth. He leaned over the top and peered down into the hollow and found to his horror that the space was occupied. Two people, both naked, stared up at him, the horror in their eyes matching his own. As if turned to stone, neither of them moved, their pale bodies curled together as elegant and erotic as a classical sculpture. The few seconds he stared down lasted an eternity, before he jerked himself back, away from the edge of the overhang and slithering noisily down the scree, landed awkwardly beside Dieter.

Dieter looked up at his pale face and said, 'Are you OK, Felix?'

Felix managed a shaky smile and said, 'Yes, of course, I slipped coming down. It's very overgrown.' He took a deep breath, looking round the little quarry, and then said, in a voice as steady as he could make it, 'Ready to go, then?'

'Yes, yes, I am fine. Thank you for bringing me.' Dieter got slowly to his feet and together they walked back to the track and began the climb up the hill. Both of them were lost in thought, but those thoughts couldn't have been further apart. Dieter was enjoying the summer warmth and the beautiful sweep of the countryside, his mind at rest now that he'd paid his respects to his dead comrades. Felix, who'd thought things couldn't get any worse in his marriage, had just discovered that they could.

Dieter was saying something and Felix suddenly realised that he hadn't heard a word.

'Sorry, Dieter, miles away. What did you say?'

'I was saying that when Mr Shepherd asked me to visit his farm you said you would take me to it.'

So he had. At the time, before his world turned upside down, Felix had been happy enough to suggest it. But now? The Shepherds? Could he face John and Margaret after what he'd just seen? Could he face anyone?

'Is it far?' Dieter was asking, already assuming they were on their way.

'No,' Felix replied, 'no, it's not far.'

He led the way across the hill, following the path through the fields to Charing Farm. No, it wasn't far. Not far enough. Nowhere was far enough from what Felix had just seen. They walked in silence, Dieter becoming aware of a change in Felix, but having no clue as to what had caused it. Was it something he'd said or done? He hoped not; he could think of nothing.

And then they were there, heralded as usual by the farm dogs. As they entered the farmyard they found John Shepherd lifting Edie down from a pony. He raised a hand in salute and set the child down.

'Uncle Felix!' cried Edie in delight and rushed over to hug him. 'Gramp let me ride Muffin. He's new!'

'Lucky you, Edie!' Felix swung her up onto his shoulders and she gripped his head with her fingers.

John greeted Dieter with a handshake and then led them round the house to the garden where they found Margaret weeding a flowerbed and Charlotte sitting in the sun, shelling peas. Johnny was kicking a football about with Danny and Davy, who were running happily round in circles. For a moment Felix paused, taking in the scene of normality, a family enjoying the summer sun on a Sunday afternoon, before Edie urged him on with her heels, calling, 'Mummy, Uncle Felix is here!'

Charlotte looked up, her face breaking into a smile when she saw him. She set aside the basket of peas and said, 'Felix, how lovely. Edie, you really are too big to ride on Uncle Felix's shoulders now.'

'She's fine,' Felix said as he swung her back down to the ground. 'I've brought Dieter over.'

Dieter had seen Charlotte's joy at seeing Felix. I was right, he thought, but what will happen about that shrew of a wife?

John stepped forward and introduced Dieter to Margaret. She'd been expecting him and greeted him warmly.

'I'm pleased to see you looking so well, Dieter. May I call you Dieter?'

'Please. Here among friends I am Dieter to everyone.'

Margaret made tea and they all sat in the sun, while the children played round them.

'You're very quiet, Felix,' Charlotte said softly. 'Have you found Dieter difficult?'

'No, on the contrary,' Felix answered. 'We've been to the quarry. He wanted to see where his comrades died.'

'Was there much to see?'

A vision of the two naked bodies in the hollow flashed, unbidden, into Felix's mind.

'No,' he said, his voice gruff. He cleared his throat. 'No, very little.'

Charlotte looked at him with concern. 'Felix, are you all right?'

He forced a smile and said, 'Fine. Never better.' And turning away gave his attention to what Margaret was saying to Dieter.

'I'm sorry my daughter isn't here to meet you. She's gone for a walk, but perhaps she'll be back before you go.'

Faced with the thought of Jane arriving home at any

moment, Felix got to his feet. 'I'm afraid I have get back,' he said. 'I said I'd look in again on my mother later this afternoon.'

Dieter stood up at once, but Felix said, 'You don't have to come, Dieter. You can easily find your way back from here.'

'You can walk back with us,' Charlotte offered, and, saying, 'If you are sure?' Dieter sat down again. He was surprised at Felix leaving so soon, but he himself was happy enough to spend more time with Charlotte.

Felix took his farewell with a wave of his hand and set off down the path towards the village. The thought of seeing either Jane or Daphne again made him shudder.

For a long moment after Felix's face had vanished from above them, Daphne and Jane remained immobile. They had heard Dieter and Felix arrive in the quarry, though they hadn't realised at first who it was. Then Daphne had recognised Felix's voice and she'd given a little gasp.

'Felix!' she mouthed to Jane.

Jane's eyes widened. Daphne put a finger to her lips, and grinned. Fancy Felix being so close while they were in each other's arms; Daphne quivered with the deliciousness of it. As they heard the two men talking outside, only feet away from them, she pulled Jane closer, her excitement heightened by Felix's proximity. And then, suddenly, there he was, staring down at them, his eyes blank with disbelief. They heard him slithering down the quarry wall, heard Dieter's voice and Felix answering, the sound of boots on stone and then silence.

It was Jane who finally pulled away and said, 'What are we going to do now?'

Daphne shrugged. 'Nothing.'

'What do you mean, nothing?' Jane's voice squeaked with apprehension.

'I mean nothing... nothing we hadn't already planned. We'll do what we'd agreed, except that I won't wait for you to pick me up. You go back home and leave in the usual way. I'll go back, collect my stuff and drive myself to Bristol. I'll meet you at the flat.' She reached over and kissed Jane on the lips. 'This changes nothing!'

'It changes everything,' Jane told her. 'He won't have you back now.'

'No, he won't,' Daphne agreed, 'but I don't want to go back.'

'What will he tell everyone?' Jane shuddered to think of their affair becoming common knowledge. 'What's he going to say?'

'He'll say that we've decided to separate, and that I've moved in to share a flat with my friend Jane. Lots of women share flats. Come on, Jane,' Daphne said, her tone rallying, 'it means we can be together. No more going home to Felix; no more putting up with *him* when I can have *you*!'

They dressed quickly and with a brief kiss they set off in different directions: Jane to Charing Farm, trying to appear to her parents as if nothing had happened; Daphne hurrying back to the manor to collect her stuff and leave. She didn't know if Felix would be there, but she'd deal with that if necessary. She thought he'd probably steer clear of the house for a while. She could almost feel sorry for him as she remembered the look of stupefaction on his face.

She approached the house with caution, but there was no sign of anyone there. Letting herself in, she went into Felix's study and opened his desk. There was the cash box in the drawer that he used for petty cash. She opened it and stuffed the contents into her handbag. Only a few pounds, but it would all help. She wondered if he'd stop paying her allowance into her account; probably, but not, she hoped, immediately. Then she picked up her cases and carried them out to the car. She was just in time. As she pulled out of the drive and turned into the lane towards the village, she saw Felix rounding the corner from the other direction. She didn't stop.

Felix saw her drive away with a sigh of relief. He was in no mood for confrontation. That was for another day. Daphne had gone, and at present he never wanted to see her again. He turned in at the gate and went indoors in search of the whisky bottle.

Chapter 40

Charlotte got the children bathed and into bed. They were all tired after the excitement of the day. Both Johnny and Edie had had a ride on the new pony, Muffin, and the twins were already tugging at Gramp's trousers, asking to be put up on Barney. There had been a game of hide and seek, the boys had played football of a sort, and then Felix had turned up with Dieter in tow. To Charlotte's disappointment, Felix hadn't stayed long, but Dieter had waited and walked home with her.

Before they'd left Jane had come back from her walk, even more snappish than usual. She was introduced to Dieter, but she had hardly a civil word for him before she stumped off upstairs, collected her overnight bag and slung it into the boot of her car.

'I've got to get back,' she told her parents.

'It's been lovely having you home for the night,' said Margaret as she kissed her cheek. 'Come out again soon.'

'Of course, Mum,' Jane promised, wondering as she did so if she'd ever be able to come back to Wynsdown if her affair with Daphne became public knowledge.

'You look, tired, darling,' Margaret said. 'You're working too hard. Time you had a proper holiday.'

'It's not easy, Mum.'

'I know, but you should still think about it... find yourself a nice doctor and settle down.'

'For goodness' sake, Mum, don't start!'

Margaret gave a rueful smile. 'I'm not. Dad and I just want to see you happy and settled.'

'I know,' Jane sighed. 'I know.'

When Jane had gone, Charlotte packed up the children's things and with the twins sitting squashed into the pushchair and the other two cavorting along beside them, she and Dieter set off back to the village.

Edie watched Dieter's rather unsteady progress and after a while she said, 'Why do you walk funny like that?'

'Because I had an accident and I hurt my legs.'

'Don't they work any more?'

'They do, but not well like they used to.'

'You should go to the doctor's,' Edie advised. 'Our doctor's called Uncle Henry.'

Dieter smiled. 'That's good advice. I'm going home tomorrow, but perhaps I will visit my doctor when I get there.'

'I didn't know you were leaving so soon.' Charlotte, over-hearing this conversation, fell in beside him.

'Yes, I have finished all I came to do here. Perhaps I will return when the names of my comrades have been added to the stone in the churchyard. Mr Swanson will...' he hesitated, looking for the word, 'say prayers for them again. He will write to me when that will be.' He turned and looked at Charlotte. 'If I cannot come, will you go there... stand with them for me? They were not bad men. It is war that is bad.'

Charlotte looked at his earnest face and took his hand. 'Yes, of course,' she said. 'I promise.'

Dieter smiled at her. He knew she was a girl who kept her promises.

They had parted at the village green, Charlotte and her children trailing up the last couple of hundred yards to

Blackdown House. Dieter watched her and her family until they turned the corner and were out of sight and with a sigh walked back to the Magpie. He knew he would never come back to Wynsdown, there was nothing for him here. He had met Charlotte, and having done so, knew there would never be anyone else, but he also knew she wasn't for him. If Felix ever managed to free himself from his cold bitch of a wife, then, Dieter knew, he would find happiness with Charlotte, and it was a happiness he didn't begrudge either of them.

Back at the Magpie he told Jack and Mabel he would be leaving the next day and asked them to arrange for Fred Jones to collect him in his taxi the following morning. It was time to go home.

Charlotte was playing the piano when she heard it: a knock at the front door. She rested her hands on the keys, cocking her head to listen. It came again. She looked at her watch and wondering who it could be at nearly nine o'clock on a Sunday evening, she went to the door.

'Felix!'

'Can I come in?' He was standing propped up against the door jamb, as if for support.

'Of course.' Charlotte stood aside to let him pass and he stumbled into the house. 'Are you all right?'

'Yes, of course I am,' replied Felix, his words slightly slurred.

'You've been drinking.'

'A bit.'

'A lot,' remarked Charlotte, but with a smile to soften her words. He staggered into the sitting room and slumped down onto the sofa. Charlotte went and knelt beside him, reaching for his hands.

Goodness knows how much he's had, she thought as he looked up at her with red-rimmed eyes and she was treated to a blast of alcoholic breath.

'Felix, what on earth has happened? What's the matter?'

'Everything,' Felix answered.

'Tell me.'

'I can't,' he groaned. He'd come to Charlotte for comfort, but now he was here he knew he couldn't tell her everything.

'Felix, I'm here. You can tell me anything. Is it Daphne? Has something happened to her?'

'Is it Daphne?' Felix gave a mirthless laugh. 'Oh, it's Daphne, all right.'

'What's happened to her? Is she ill?'

'No. She's gone.'

'Gone?'

'Walked out.'

'Oh, Felix.' Her grip on his fingers tightened. 'Dear Felix, I'm so sorry.'

'Are you? Well, I'm not.'

'You're not?' Charlotte was confused.

'No, she's gone and I'm glad.'

Why, then, she wanted to ask, have you hit the bottle? What she actually said was, 'Are you? D'you want to tell me about it?'

'No... yes... I don't know.' He closed his eyes and for a moment Charlotte thought he'd fallen asleep. Silence settled round them and she let go of his hands, wriggling to make herself more comfortable on the floor. At her movement Felix's eyes opened again, and for a moment he looked about as if he didn't know where he was. Then seeing Charlotte sitting on the floor beside the sofa, he rubbed his eyes.

Encouraged by this, Charlotte took his hand again and

said, 'I'm not trying to pry, Felix, you don't have to tell me anything that you don't want to. I just hate seeing you so miserable.'

'Angry,' Felix said. 'Angry, not miserable. I should have realised ages ago.'

'Realised what?'

'That it's all been a lie,' Felix said bitterly. 'It's been lies from the very beginning.'

'Lies?'

'From the very beginning, my marriage to Daphne was founded on lies.'

Charlotte waited, still holding his hand, her thumb gently caressing his; simply waited for him to speak. At last, his voice soft and low, he told her everything that had happened over the weekend. Well, almost everything. He did not mention going to the quarry with Dieter and what he'd discovered there. He couldn't bring himself to confide that to her or anyone.

As she listened, Charlotte longed to reach out and take him in her arms, hold him close as she would one of the children to comfort him.

'Oh, my dearest Felix, I'm so sorry,' she murmured when he'd finally finished and silence slipped round them again. Felix raised their joined hands to his lips and said, softly, 'Don't be. Don't be sorry, Charlotte, it's left me free. Free to love you.'

'Me?' Charlotte looked up in amazement.

'You.'

'But...'

'Up until now I felt bound to Daphne. I knew I didn't love her any more, but I was married to her.'

'You still are,' pointed out Charlotte. 'Married to her.'

'Yes, but not bound to her. She's been having an affair for months, maybe years.'

'An affair? Who with?'

'That doesn't matter,' Felix said. 'Someone in Bristol, but as far as I'm concerned her infidelity releases me. I'm free to love someone else.'

'And that's me?'

'It has been since that day in the churchyard when you told me about the twins.' He looked down at her, anxiety in his eyes. 'From that day it sort of crept up on me and then suddenly I realised that I loved you. I wanted to look after you, protect you, become part of your life. I do love you, Charlotte. Do you mind?'

'Mind?' Tears sprang to Charlotte's eyes. 'Mind? Why should I mind, Felix?'

'Because of Billy. Because it's too soon?'

'Is it? Is it too soon? I don't know.' She closed her eyes for a moment, thinking of the void Billy had left behind, her sorrow at his loss, her anger at fate leaving her abandoned and her aching loneliness without him. Felix, not daring to speak, remained silent as he watched the emotions pass across her face.

'I loved Billy with all my heart,' Charlotte said softly. 'I still love him, but he's not here to love *me*. He's a part of me, he always will be, he's a part of my children. Maybe it is too soon, I don't know yet. The idea that you love me is too new. I've got to get used to it. To believe it.'

'Believe it,' Felix said. 'Take all the time you need. I'm not going anywhere, but my darling girl, please believe it.' He stroked her cheek. 'I know you still love Billy but I'm hanging on to the hope that maybe, one day, you'll have room in your heart for me, too.'

'Oh, Felix, you're there already. I don't know when or how, but you're there. I love you and now, unbelievably, here you are, loving me.'

'Charlotte,' Felix's voice was husky as he repeated her name, 'Charlotte.' He drew her into his arms, crushing her against him as she raised her face for his kiss. 'My darling girl.'

When they finally broke apart Charlotte gave a choking laugh and said, 'You taste of whisky!'

'I know, I'm sorry. Drowning my sorrows.'

'The whisky doesn't matter,' Charlotte said, 'but,' her voice became more serious, 'you're still married to Daphne.'

'I won't be.' Felix looked down into her eyes. 'I promise you I won't be for long.' Adding anxiously, 'Will you mind being married to someone who's divorced?'

Charlotte peeped up at him. 'Married? Are you asking me?'

'Of course I'm asking you. What do you take me for?'

Charlotte reached up and stroked his face. 'Then the answer's no, I don't mind, not if it's to you.'

'It'll take time and there's sure to be gossip,' Felix said with a sigh.

'I know,' Charlotte agreed. 'There always is in this village, whether there's foundation for it or not.'

'Still, I think with Daphne gone, we should be very careful not to give them any ammunition,' Felix said. 'I don't want them gossiping about you and the children.'

'Nor do I,' Charlotte agreed, 'but if they do, we'll survive.'

It wasn't long before the news that Daphne had left Felix was round the village. She'd packed her bags and gone; she'd driven off in the car, leaving him with no transport; she'd left the house in turmoil. It was Mavis Gurney who was the fount of information. She'd arrived on Monday morning to find Felix alone in the house.

'Mrs Bellinger away, is she?' she asked, standing at the office door and peering in at Felix.

'Gone to visit a friend, Mrs Gurney,' he said without looking up.

'So, what d'you want doing, then?'

'Just your usual Monday morning, please, Mrs Gurney.' He glanced up and smiled at her. 'Thank you.'

Mavis went out into the kitchen and looked round. It was surprisingly tidy. An empty whisky bottle and a dirty glass stood on the table, but there was no other washing up waiting for her in the sink. She went upstairs to change the bed. When she reached the landing, she saw that two extra bedrooms had been used. The bed in the blue spare room was tumbled and unmade; the bed in Mr Felix's old bedroom the same, and when she got to the master bedroom, it looked as if a tornado had swept through. The wardrobe door stood open, showing that only Mr Felix's clothes were still hanging there. Some of the drawers in the chest were pulled out and completely empty; the dressing table bare of its usual clutter. This bed was also unmade, the sheets tossed aside, the pillows lying on the floor.

Mavis stared round her. It didn't take a genius to see that Mrs Felix was going to be away for more than a few days. And who'd slept in the blue room? Some floozy of Mr Felix? Or perhaps they'd slept in here. Was that why Mrs Felix had gone? Clearly all was not well in the manor house and Mavis couldn't wait to discuss what it meant with her friends.

'Of course,' she said piously to Sally Prynne whom she met in the post office on her way home, 'I don't know why she went, but I can tell you for nothing that she ain't going to be back any time soon.'

'Well,' Nancy Bright said, as usual joining in her customers' conversation, 'I never liked her much. Always thought herself too good for the likes of us.'

'Oh, she weren't so bad,' declared Mavis, proud of her inside knowledge, 'once you got to know her, like. Worked for her for near on four years, I have. She weren't so bad. Couldn't cook and clean properly, but I suppose she did her best.' She lowered her voice conspiratorially. 'We all know they was a bit strapped for cash, don't we?'

Nancy nodded. 'Perhaps that's why she's gone.'

'More like she's got a fella, don't you think?'

'One with more money?'

'Maybe.'

'Never seen her with one.'

'No, well you wouldn't, would you? She'd have to be ever so careful.'

'More likely to be him,' suggested Sally Prynne, 'Mr Felix, I mean. Maybe he's got a bit on the side and she's copped on.'

'Well, whatever it is,' Mavis said, 'she's gone and everything she owns has gone with her. She's even took the car!'

Felix had left Mavis washing sheets and gone to see his mother. 'I'm afraid Daphne's taken the car and disappeared,' he said, 'so I can't take Janet to Bristol today, Mother. She could go on the bus and train, I suppose.'

'Why not let her stay with me for a couple more days?' Marjorie suggested. 'I'm enjoying her company. She's a breath of fresh air, and from what she says, her mother will be in hospital for a week or so yet.'

'Are you sure? That would one less thing for me to worry about.'

'Absolutely.'

They put the idea to Janet and she was thrilled. 'Really? Can I stay here with you for a bit? I don't want to go back and tell Mum about Daph running off. It was my fault.'

'You can stay as long as you like,' Marjorie assured her. 'You can write your mum a letter and tell her where you are and say that you'll come straight home when she's better. How's that?'

'And I don't have to tell her about Daphne going off?'

'Not if you don't want to.' Felix had explained to Marjorie about Janet's revelation and now Marjorie reached forward and took the girl's hand. 'And remember, my dear, none of it's your fault.'

'And,' Janet said with the optimism of youth, 'she might have come back by then.'

Felix was pretty sure she wouldn't be back and this became a certainty when the post arrived the following day. Recognising Daphne's writing, Felix took it into the office and opened the envelope with some reluctance.

DEAR FELIX,

Just in case you wondered, I'm not coming back. I was going to leave you anyway after Janet telling her tales. There were too many lies between us for us to go on as we were. And the largest one of all, which you only discovered by the greatest bad luck, was Jane. Well, not a lie exactly, but something between us that can never be resolved. So, I'm not coming back. If you want to marry again (maybe that little creep Charlotte, I always had my doubts about her), you'll have to get a divorce. I don't think you can divorce me for going off with another woman, so either you'll have to provide me with evidence of your adultery, perhaps with Charlotte? so I can divorce you, or you'll have to wait for however many years it is and say I deserted you. Well, I suppose that's fair enough, I have.

You can of course cause a stink by suggesting Jane and I are lovers, but we shall hotly deny that and no one can prove it. Few people will believe it and it will only antagonise Jane's family and with one thing and another they've been through enough and you're too decent to do that. Too decent altogether really, such a bore to live with.

Of course some money would be nice, but I shan't need as much as before. The one good thing about Janet turning up is that I can stop paying my mother the blackmail money every month to keep her mouth shut. Now you know everything, she's nothing to blackmail me about. I'll get a job somewhere round here. In a garage maybe. It's funny, but I shan't mind working if it's for me and Jane.

Anyway this is the last time you'll hear from me unless you decide to let me divorce you, in which case we can arrange it all.

You shouldn't have married me. I never loved you then and I don't hate you now, I have no feelings for you at all.

Your wife... because I am still your wife,
DAPHNE
P.S. I'll keep the car for now.

Felix read the letter through several times and then reached for the telephone and rang Mr Thompson's secretary to make an appointment.

Mr Thompson read the letter twice and then looked at Felix over his spectacles. 'You say she's having a lesbian relationship with this Jane.'

'Yes.'

'I see.'

'Do I have to go on paying her an allowance?' Felix asked.

'Not if she's left the marital home of her own accord. If she's chosen to live somewhere else when you're providing her with a perfectly adequate home, I would say not. But, Felix, I'm not a lawyer who's had much to do with divorce. If you're planning to sue for divorce you need a specialist and there are an increasing number of those.'

'No, I understand that,' replied Felix, 'but I just wanted some general thoughts.'

'Fair enough, and one of them is, don't destroy this letter. It states her intent to leave you for good, and that constitutes desertion. I can't encourage you to follow the "adultery" route, though many people do, because it is illegal.' He cocked his head questioningly. 'May I ask you, if it's not presumptuous, do you wish to remarry?'

'Very probably,' Felix replied carefully.

'Charlotte?'

Felix didn't answer and Mr Thompson nodded. 'Fair enough,' he said again. 'But I wouldn't want her embroiled in a messy divorce. I have no legal standing with her any more, of course, but over the years I've grown very fond of her.'

Not as fond of her as I have, Felix thought as he left the solicitor's office and rode home. He stabled Archie and then walked over to Blackdown House. Caroline was there having tea with the children. Charlotte felt the colour flood her face when Felix appeared at the back door.

'Caro,' she said, 'could you keep an eye on the children for a minute or two? I just need a word with Felix.'

Caroline smiled. 'Of course, take your time.' Like the rest of the village she knew Daphne had gone, and she'd been wondering what the future now held, if anything, for Charlotte and Felix.

Charlotte and Felix went out into the garden. As soon as they were out of sight Felix gathered Charlotte into his arms, kissing her and holding her close. Her response thrilled him, the way she gave herself up to his embrace, returning his kisses with a hunger that made him want to laugh and weep at the same time. When they finally broke apart, she looked up into his eyes and said, 'Hallo.' So he kissed her again.

Felix had already told Charlotte about Daphne's letter, but had not allowed her to read it. He was determined to keep her ignorant of the part her sister-in-law had played. He knew Charlotte didn't particularly like Jane, but he didn't want to make it impossible for them to meet with at least a degree of cordiality when their paths crossed, which they undoubtedly would, at Charing Farm. 'I've an appointment with Mr Thompson,' he'd said. 'I want to see what he advises.'

'Well?' Charlotte said now. 'Tell me. What did Mr Thompson say?'

'He read the letter and he said he thinks that in time I'll be able to sue for divorce for desertion. He's not a divorce lawyer as such and he suggests that when the time comes I should instruct a specialist... and in the meantime I have to behave myself. No breath of scandal must attach itself to me.' He drew her to him again. 'Charlotte, sweetheart, it may take some time, but will you wait for me to disentangle myself?'

Charlotte, reaching up to kiss him, murmured, 'Felix, I'll wait as long as it takes.'

Have you read the first part of Charlotte's story?

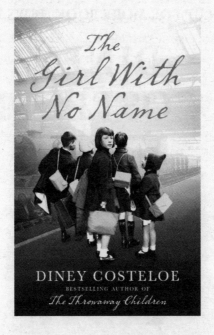

~ London, August 1939 ~

Thirteen-year-old Lisa has escaped from Nazi Germany on the Kindertransport. She arrives in London unable to speak a word of English, her few belongings crammed into a small suitcase. Among them is one precious photograph of the family she has left behind.

Lonely and homesick, Lisa is adopted by a childless couple. But when the Blitz blows her new home apart, she wakes up in hospital with no memory of who she is, or where she came from. The authorities give her a new name and despatch her to a children's home.

With the war raging around her, what will become of Lisa now?